Praise for the novels of Brenda Novak

"*The Perfect Couple* was fast-paced
and extremely engaging from the very first page....
Once I started, I couldn't stop! Definitely, most definitely
add *The Perfect Couple* to your reading list."
—*True Crime Book Reviews*

"Novak delivers another expertly crafted work
of suspenseful intrigue heightened by white-knuckle danger
and realistically complicated romance."
—*Booklist* on *The Perfect Couple*

"I guarantee *The Perfect Couple*
will keep readers on the edge of their seats...
The story line sizzles."
—*Romance Reviews Today*

"Realistic and gritty, this story grabs the reader by the throat
on the first page and never lets go."
—*RT Book Reviews* on *Watch Me*

"Gripping, frightening and intense...
a compelling romance as well as a riveting and
suspenseful mystery...Novak delivers another winner."
—*Library Journal* on *The Perfect Liar*

"[A] chilling, sensual tale that features a host of skillfully
developed characters and intricate, multilayered plotting.
Sacramento-based Novak (*The Perfect Liar*)
writes gripping romantic thrillers."
—*Library Journal* on *The Perfect Murder*

"As always, Novak's plotting is flawless,
and her characterizations are rich and multilayered.
What sets this story apart from the rest is the intensity
of the romance...A keeper." (4.5 stars, Top Pick)
—*RT Book Reviews* on *The Perfect Murder*

BRENDA NOVAK

KILLER HEAT

MIRA®

Recycling programs
for this product may
not exist in your area.

ISBN-13: 978-0-7783-2831-5

KILLER HEAT

Copyright © 2010 by Brenda Novak, Inc.

For questions and comments about the quality of this book please contact us at
Customer_eCare@Harlequin.ca.

www.MIRABooks.com

Printed in U.S.A.

To Gail, one of my new B.F.F.s. You're a generous soul. May all your good karma come back to you....

Dear Reader,

Not long ago I was invited to speak in front of a writers' group in Prescott, Arizona. Because I love Arizona, I accepted. I also agreed to stay with one of the group's members so they wouldn't have to put me up in a motel.

Once I arrived, I learned that this member didn't actually live in Prescott, where I'd be speaking. She lived in a place called Skull Valley. I didn't recognize the name so I had no idea it would be remote. I was driven into the desert and sheltered in this wonderful woman's guesthouse, but she was a stranger to me at that time and I arrived in the middle of the night, already disoriented as to where, exactly, I was. The main house, which I visited briefly, didn't feel very close to the guesthouse (which they had to drive me to). If you've read any of my suspense books, you know I can have a rather dark imagination. That night the wind blew constantly, rattling the door on the screened porch. It sounded just like someone trying to break in. I lay awake listening and feeling very vulnerable because there was no phone service, internet—or even cellular coverage. I was completely cut off in a strange and lonely place. What would I do if something terrible were to happen to me? I didn't even know which direction to run should I need help—I could easily have ended up wandering lost in the desert.

Needless to say, that proved to be a very long night, especially when I began spinning a story in my head about the bones of several murdered women being found not far from where I was staying. I tried not to allow such ideas to flow, but the setting was just too perfect. A serial killer began to take shape in my mind...the serial killer in this book. So as you read, think of me huddled alone beneath the covers of a stranger's bed on a cold night in January, somewhere in the middle of the desert, without so much as a cell phone....

I'd like to extend a special thank-you to Vincent J. Abbatiello and his wife, Jill (Jillsy to her friends) Abbatiello, a lovely couple who live on the gold coast of Long Island and winter in Palm Beach and St. Thomas. Vince is a periodontist and implant surgeon who graduated from Harvard Dental School. Jillsy is an active fundraiser for various charities who loves her show horses and two Maltese, Maxie and Suzzie. You'll see Jill and Vince's names pop up in this novel as characters, a privilege they purchased to help me raise money to fight diabetes.

I love to hear from my readers. Please snail mail me at P.O. Box 3781, Citrus Heights, CA, 95611 or visit me on the web at www.brendanovak.com, where you can read about my other books, enter various drawings, sign up for my newsletter, download a free 3-D screensaver (that moves), or check out the results of my latest online auction for diabetes research (something I hold every May on my website). To date, my donors, shoppers and I have raised more than $1 million!

Here's to love and to life!

Brenda

"Resentment is like drinking poison and waiting for the other person to die."

—Carrie Fisher, American writer and actress

1

Francesca Moretti thought she couldn't be seeing what she was seeing. So much junk cluttered the salvage yard that it could be any number of things, right? She wasn't *that* close. And it was wrapped in a painter's tarp and partially hidden behind some wood pallets, sawhorses and stacks of roofing material. But the longer she examined the size and dimensions of that shape, the more convinced she became. It *was* a human body.

Filled with revulsion, she shrank back into the shade of the closest outbuilding. The blazing July sun, bouncing off the sea of car carcasses, bent bicycle frames, even obsolete farm equipment, made her feel as if she was trapped in an oven instead of running down a lead on the outskirts of Prescott, Arizona. But it was panic and not heat that threatened to suffocate her.

Could this really be happening? *Again?* In her last big case, she'd located what was left of the missing wife and mother she'd been hired to find. The discovery had made national headlines; Janice Grey's murder probably would've gone unsolved without Francesca. She'd provided the missing piece of the puzzle that confirmed a murder had taken place, which allowed investigators to go ahead and prosecute their prime suspect. But that type of thing didn't happen very often and certainly not to the same private investigator. Francesca had pretty much decided it would never happen again. Not to her, anyway. And then…this.

Trying to ignore the Doberman who'd started barking like crazy the moment she set foot in the yard—fortunately, the dog was chained to the back of the house—she stared at what appeared to be a shock of brown hair spilling out from under that paint-speckled tarp. She wanted to identify the body, make sure it was her client's sister, as she suspected.

But that could wait. She thought she smelled decomposition. And, judging by the stiffness of the corpse, apparent from the odd angles underneath the tarp, the body was in full rigor. There was no reason to look any more closely; the memory would only keep her up at night. Better to let the county homicide investigator handle the situation from here on.

Yes, get help. That was what she needed to do. Immediately. She didn't want to ruin any forensic evidence linking April Bonner to the man who'd killed her.

Hands shaking, she fumbled in the purse slung across her body, searching for her iPhone. She was breathing shallowly. Try as she might she couldn't override her body's automatic response.

Calm down. You're okay. Everything will be fine. You wanted to add missing persons to your list of services, remember?

She'd wanted to solve some difficult cases.

But that was just it. Locating people who'd gone missing wasn't supposed to be this easy. And the goal was to find them *alive*.

Finally, her fingers encountered the phone. She was scrolling through her address book for Investigator

Finch's phone number when she heard footsteps—the purposeful stride of a man wearing boots from the sound of it—and brought her head up fast. She wasn't alone? There'd been no answer when she knocked at the old wood-frame house facing the road, and she hadn't heard a vehicle. But that didn't mean anything. This was a big property, ten acres.

So weak she doubted she could run even if she had to, she peered around the corner of the building. She couldn't see whoever was approaching.

Sweat, rolling from her hairline, dripped into her eyes. She blinked to clear her vision and prayed for a burst of adrenaline to stop her knees from turning to jelly. What was wrong with her? In her line of work, the threat of physical injury—or death—came with the territory. She'd known that from the beginning. But she'd always imagined herself as so much tougher, so much calmer in the face of danger. She hadn't reacted like this when she was a cop, or when she'd found Janice's remains scattered in that gully, had she?

No. But she'd worked property crimes when she was with Phoenix P.D. and, after that, the Maricopa County Sheriff's Office. And the day she found Janice, she'd been with a group of search-and-rescue guys she'd hired to scour land the police had decided was too far out. They'd stumbled across *bones,* which distanced her from the violence that had taken Janice's life.

This was different. Francesca had just discovered a recent kill. She was alone in a relatively remote location. And no one else had any idea where she was. She hadn't even notified Heather, her assistant, other than to say she'd be out most of the day running down leads. She'd driven from her home in Chandler two hours to the south and didn't know anyone in the area.

"Who's there? And what do you want?"

It was a man, all right, and he didn't sound pleased to have a visitor. His harsh voice set the dog barking at a far more feverish pitch.

Unwilling to answer, and afraid to poke her head around the shed again for fear he'd see her, she pressed her back against the rough wood of the building. The bartender at the Pour House had told her he'd spotted a woman resembling April getting into a truck driven by the guy who owned this salvage yard: Butch Vaughn. She'd come out here hoping to speak to Vaughn. But after finding the figure beneath the tarp, she knew it wasn't the time or the place to confront a possible killer. Especially a killer with a Doberman that could easily be released. The police could deal with it.

"I know you're there," he said. "Demon's making damn sure of it."

Demon had to be the dog. What an appropriate name...

"What are you doing trespassing on my property?" His footsteps had grown less decisive. He wasn't quite sure where she was. "Don't you have any manners?"

Her actions said more about her nerve than her manners. Pushing, even when others didn't want to be pushed, and looking, even when they didn't want certain things to be seen, was part of her job. Although she hadn't always been so assertive, her desire to succeed had forced her to overcome her natural reluctance to pry. Timid private investigators weren't going to help anyone. If the owner of this property hadn't been seen with April, who'd been missing for three days, Francesca would never have considered intruding on his privacy.

Glancing behind her, she wondered if she should make

a break for her car. Could she get around the house and all the way to the road before he caught her?

If her heart wasn't already racing, she thought she might have a chance. Five years ago, she'd taken up running as a way to relieve stress and stay in shape. She prided herself on her athletic ability. But a quarter mile had never seemed as far as it did at this moment. And she had no illusion that she could outsprint a man who was in top physical condition. She'd seen this guy's profile on the dating Web site where April had first come across him. If Harry Statham was really Butch Vaughn, as she now believed, and the muscular picture he'd posted was anywhere close to accurate, he was definitely fit....

"What's the matter?" he called out. "Cat got your tongue?"

Her other option was pepper spray. Just after she'd been accepted into the police academy, her father had accidentally been shot by his own partner during a drug bust and been confined to a wheelchair ever since. Seeing him struggle with the loss of his mobility day after day, year after year, left an impression she wasn't likely to forget. As soon as she quit the force to open her own investigative agency, she'd stopped carrying a gun. She no longer even owned one. But she needed *some* protection.

"I want to know why you're snooping around," he called out.

Was this Butch? It had to be. He'd said "my property." Did he realize what she'd found? He had to at least suspect, didn't he?

Doubting she'd be able to outrun him, she thrust a hand into her purse. He was coming up on the other side of the building; he must have guessed where she was hiding. The crunch of his soles striking the rocky desert soil ratcheted up her tension as if he had an external crank that stretched every nerve taut and tightened every muscle.

Where was her pepper spray? Had she lost it? She'd never really had to use it. She kept it with her as a precaution...

Shit! It wasn't there.

She still had her phone in her hand. She dialed 911 but dared not speak into the receiver. He'd be on her before she could say two words. Whatever was going to happen would be over by the time the dispatcher could send a squad car. She had to run.

As she pivoted, her hand finally touched the cool metal of the canister. It'd been lost in the jumble of her belongings.

Thank God. Preparing for the confrontation to come, she withdrew her pepper spray and held it ready. But he didn't walk around the corner as she expected.

She couldn't hear his steps anymore. Was it possible that he didn't know where she was, after all?

Swallowing hard, she held her breath and listened carefully. Where was he? What was he doing?

She didn't have to wonder for long. Thanks to the dirty window at her elbow, she caught a brief glimpse of movement inside the building and realized it was actually an office and he was coming *through* it. There was an exit right next to her!

Whipping around, she jumped out of range of the door he flung open and sprayed him. At least, she *tried* to spray him. Nothing came out. Why, she had no idea. Her actions made him flinch and throw up his arms to protect his face and that was it. But seeing him up close confirmed her suspicions—Harry Statham was indeed Butch Vaughn. The man pictured on that dating profile looked identical to the owner of this salvage yard—the last person, as far as she could determine, who'd seen April alive.

Throwing the can, she heard it hit him but didn't pause to see where. She was too intent on running. But no matter how hard her arms and legs pumped, she could hear him gaining on her.

The dog barked and yelped and growled as it pulled at its chain. She tried to ignore it. As dangerous as that animal sounded, it couldn't hurt her. For now…

A second later, the dog became her last concern as Butch grabbed her purse, which was flapping behind her, and used it to jerk her to a stop. Yanking back, she fell when the strap broke. Then she dropped her phone, which bounced out of reach, and because of the sudden release of tension, he fell, too.

"Who are you? What the hell are you doing here?" Gripping her by the ankle, he dragged her toward him.

The hot dirt burned her bare arms and legs. A sleeveless blouse and skirt were probably the worst things she could've worn. He was dressed in blue jeans and a muscle shirt, which protected him, to some degree.

"Answer me!" he grated as they rolled around—she wrestling for her freedom, he trying to subdue her—but she was breathing too hard to respond. All she could think about was escape. She had to keep fighting regardless of the scrapes, the bruises and the burning ground.

It wasn't long before he managed to pin her down. He had her left wrist, but before he could grab her right, she sank her nails into his cheek, gouging him deeply. She knew she'd gotten him good when he cursed and drew back.

His sudden recoil made it possible for her to scramble

out from under him. She got hold of her purse but he obviously realized she was about to escape and caught it, too. She had to let go. It fell away, spilling, as she found her feet and darted around the house.

Although her BMW waited on the road ahead of her, her car keys were either in her purse or on the ground with her cell. She couldn't drive anywhere, but she ran for her car, anyway.

Her sandals slapped her heels, and the smooth hard soles made her skid here and there, so it was a miracle she reached the front yard. Once she did, she hoped to flag down a car, but the road was empty. And Butch didn't have any neighbors. Her one advantage was the fact that she'd done more damage with her nails than she'd expected. When she glanced over her shoulder, she could see Butch coming after her, but he wasn't moving too fast. He staggered, wiping at the blood that dripped from his left eye and cheek.

She'd hurt him, which scared her even more. Fury rolled off him in waves.

Her breath rattled in her throat as she fought to make her shaky limbs follow her brain's commands. If he caught her, she was dead. She could see a steely resolve set in as he shook off the pain and started to jog.

Thank heaven she'd left her car unlocked. It was a bad habit but she could only be grateful in this particular moment. Wrenching open the passenger door, which was closest, she got in and slammed it just as he stretched out his hand to stop her. He had to yank it away to avoid having his fingers crushed. Then he went for the door handle.

Lock! Lock! Lock! Frantically, Francesca swiped at the console and the upholstery, searching for the button that would secure the doors. In her panic, she couldn't remember where the damn thing was—but she managed to hit it before he could open the door. She'd never heard a sound more comforting than the *thunk* of the locks snapping into place or the ineffective catch of the lever as he pulled it to no avail.

Closing her eyes, she gulped for air and would've been relieved, except that he was more enraged than ever. Glaring down at her, he banged on the window. "Hey!"

Frozen with terror, she stared up at him. If he got in, it would be over in minutes. She didn't even have her iPhone.

Had emergency services received any indication that she'd tried to call? Were they sending help? Or had they assumed her call had been a misdial or a crank?

"What the hell's wrong with you, lady?" he yelled. "I just want to talk. I want to know why you're here."

He knew she'd found the body. She could see it in his eyes. He was trying to convince her that she hadn't really seen what she'd seen, that it was safe to trust in the trappings that surrounded them—the swing set in the front yard, the kiddie pool off to the side, the hand-painted welcome sign on the door. But she wasn't that easily fooled. As much as the domesticity of the scene might tempt her to think she'd leaped to the wrong conclusion, especially when she saw the wounds she'd inflicted on his cheek, she knew killers often looked like the most mundane husbands and dads. She'd studied them in her work; rarely was it obvious that they were monsters.

Rocking forward, she covered her head. He was *so* close. All he had to do was break the glass. There was no one else around, no one to hear the window shatter or her cry for help.

"Go away!" she sobbed.

Suddenly, he stopped banging.

She sat up to see him using the bottom of his shirt to clean the sweat and blood from his face. Then he checked behind him, apparently searching for something, and stalked off toward the only tree in the yard. A bat leaned against the trunk, next to a ball and glove. Hefting it, he came toward her as if he intended to break the window. Before he could take a swing, however, the sound of a car engine drew their attention to the road. An old Impala chugged up.

Determined to get the driver to help her, Francesca crawled into the other seat and laid on the horn, but the effort proved to be unnecessary. The woman behind the wheel slowed, then turned in and parked as if she owned the place. She'd planned to stop here all along.

Clearly torn, Butch glanced between Francesca and the driver of that car. A little boy also sat in the Impala. Window down, round face sweaty, he waved and yelled from his car seat, excited enough that even Francesca could hear him. "Daddy! Daddy! We're home!"

Butch's expression changed instantly. Dropping the bat, he strode over to the Impala.

Now! Francesca let herself out on the side facing the road. She couldn't expect the Impala's driver to come to her assistance, as she'd originally hoped. Not if this was Butch's wife. Francesca had to assume she was still on her own, because chances were she really was.

Locating her spare key beneath the back bumper, she tore it free. At the same time, the child got himself out of his car seat and demanded Butch pull him through the window.

The woman rushed around to join father and son. As Francesca darted back to the driver's seat, she heard, "What's going on? *What happened to your face?*"

Butch's reply was too low for Francesca to make out, but the woman's next question carried easily on air already saturated with heat and threat and panic. *"What? But why? Who is she?"*

This had to be Butch's wife, as she'd guessed. The timing of her return home had most likely saved Francesca's life. But Francesca wasn't planning to stick around long enough to thank her or tell her about the body stashed amid the junk in the salvage yard. She was getting out of here while she could.

Climbing behind the wheel, she tossed the magnetic container that had held her spare into the passenger seat, started her engine and punched the gas pedal.

2

"Holy shit." Jonah Young came to a stop so abrupt Investigator Finch, with the Yavapai County Sheriff's Office, slammed into the back of him.

"What the hell?" he muttered, but Jonah didn't move. The woman Finch was taking him to meet sat in a chair just inside the entrance to the investigator's cubicle. Cradling a cup of coffee, she had a blanket wrapped around her shoulders as if it was the middle of winter instead of the height of summer. But he knew she was fighting off more than the chill of the building's aggressive air conditioner. She'd just been through a harrowing ordeal. When he called, Finch had told him that a P.I. from Chandler had been attacked. Finch's partner, Hugh Hunsacker, had taken some deputies and gone directly to the salvage yard, where the incident had occurred, but Finch had stayed behind and asked Jonah to come down and have a talk with the victim. He hadn't mentioned any names.

"I know her," he said.

With his bald head, goatee and various tattoos, Finch resembled a biker more than a cop. "You do?"

"We attended the academy together."

Jonah had been careful to keep from being overheard

but Finch hadn't. Francesca Moretti glanced at them over the rim of her coffee cup. Then she lowered it and any question that he could be mistaken about her identity disappeared. Even with her long dark hair mussed, her mascara smeared and her top lip swollen to almost twice its normal size, there was no mistaking the amber-colored eyes that riveted on his—or the contempt that instantly settled over her classic Italian features when she recognized him.

"Oh, boy. Doesn't look as if she likes you," Finch said, and skirted past him.

Jonah reluctantly followed. Francesca *didn't* like him. And he'd given her good reason. But that was ten years ago. Surely they could put the past behind them now. She seemed to have gotten over him fairly easily, had never returned his calls when he'd attempted to apologize. And from what Finch said, there could be some connection between the missing teacher she'd been searching for and the murders they were hoping to solve. Figuring out who'd killed the women dug up in Dead Mule Canyon mattered more than his personal discomfort. Jonah had never been involved in a case so disturbing.

The investigator gestured toward him. "Ms. Moretti, you might remember—"

"Jonah Young," she finished, never taking her gaze off him.

Finch hurried on. "Yes. I'm not aware of how familiar you two are with each other since the academy, but these days Jonah works for Department 6, a private security firm out of Los Angeles. They contract with individuals, companies, even different police entities, to consult on or assist with various hard-to-solve cases. I've asked him to—"

Her focus still on Jonah, she interrupted again. "I

knew you weren't with Phoenix P.D. anymore, or we would've run into each other. I thought maybe you'd been kicked off the force."

Sure, he'd screwed up all his personal relationships during the short period during which they'd known each other, but he'd never even come close to losing his job. Ever since he was a little boy, he'd wanted to be a detective, and heading up investigations via the private sector was a better deal all around. With Department 6, he faced similar challenges, but he had more freedom and a much bigger paycheck—the best of both worlds.

"Sorry to disappoint you. They promoted me to detective within a year after you left. It was *my* choice to move on," he said, but as he made his point, he wished he didn't sound so damned defensive.

"Yeah, well, I'd accuse you of sleeping your way to the top, but the people above you were all men, and I know very well how much you like the ladies."

Obviously uncomfortable with the way the meeting was deteriorating, Finch cleared his throat. "Look, I realize there's some bad blood here. I don't know what it's all about, but I don't need to know. I called Jonah in because I think the case he's working on might be related to the man who just attacked you. Seeing as we have a big problem, more than one, and very few leads, it's certainly worth investigating. Maybe this'll be the break we need."

At last, she pulled her attention from Jonah. "What are you talking about? Tell me he's not searching for April Bonner. She lives in Maricopa County. That's out of your jurisdiction."

"We haven't hired him to look for your missing person," Finch said. "He's on a much bigger case."

Lines appeared on her otherwise smooth forehead. "Than *murder?* I told you, I just found April's body!"

"And Investigator Hunsacker is out there checking into it."

"Why aren't *we* with him?" she asked. "Her body's not easy to find, but I can show you where it is."

"You were shaken up when you got here. I didn't want to put you through it. Besides, Hunsacker will manage or he'll call us, and I can drive you out there. This is important." With his broad back to the opening of his cubicle, Finch began to whisper. "I've asked Jonah to speak with you regarding a burial site discovered by a hiker and his dog two weeks ago."

"A burial site," she echoed.

The investigator frowned. "It contains the remains of seven women. There may be even more. We're still looking."

Francesca's jaw dropped and, at least for the moment, Jonah got the impression she'd forgotten her resentment toward him. "I heard about that on the news, but it was reported as some ancient Indian burial ground. It's in Dead Mule Canyon, near that small town—Skull Valley."

"That's right. We haven't corrected that report because...well, because we don't want to throw the community into a panic until we know what we're dealing with and can offer some information."

And they preferred to escape the overwhelming pressure that would go with a public outcry. Jonah guessed that was as close to the truth as anything. No police department announced that they had a serial killer on their hands if they could help it. Many did everything they could to hide the fact, hoping the perpetrator would eventually move out of their jurisdiction. But there was no need to explain this. Francesca had worked in law enforcement long enough to understand the dynamics.

"And when the site was discovered, there *was* some question as to the age of those bones," Finch added.

"What's changed?" she asked.

"It's since been determined that they're—" he lowered his voice even further "—recent."

For the first time, her implacable facade cracked, revealing a hint of vulnerability. "How recent?"

"A couple are as old as five years," Jonah replied. "The other women have only been dead for a few months."

Leaning forward, she set her coffee cup on Investigator Finch's desk. "Are you telling me you think the man who just attacked me might've already murdered *seven* women?"

Jonah wasn't absolutely convinced of that. What were the odds she'd be able to escape a violent psychopath when she'd encountered him on his own turf? What this guy had done to his victims proved he was utterly ruthless. But if there was one thing police work had taught him, it was to keep an open mind. "It's a possibility," he conceded. "Somebody murdered them."

"Oh, God." She jumped to her feet, turned to Finch. "And you're not letting the public know to be cautious? To avoid strangers? Not to take risks?"

Jonah stood in the opening behind Finch while the shorter, stockier man tried to quiet her. "Keep your voice down! We don't want to disseminate the information prematurely. We could tell pretty quickly that it wasn't an old Indian burial ground, but we weren't sure exactly what it was until we got a forensic anthropologist in here. We've set her up in the old community center and given Jonah an office there, too, but that kind of work doesn't go fast, not with such an extensive site."

"But—"

"We just got her initial report last night," he went on, refusing to be interrupted. "We were planning to release a statement this afternoon, but then you arrived. Now I figure we might as well wait and see what Hunsacker finds at the salvage yard. Maybe this guy who attacked you, this Butch Vaughn, is our man."

Having a suspect would certainly go far toward mollifying the public. But Jonah didn't point that out, either.

Francesca smoothed her skirt. Dirty and wrinkled, it hit her just above the knees, showing calves as tanned and toned as they'd been when he knew her before. The only difference was the abrasions on her knees.

"That would explain why April was still in the yard," she said. "Maybe, since the discovery of those bodies, Vaughn's been forced to find a new place to dispose of his victims and hasn't come up with a location he's comfortable with."

Jonah shoved away from the divider, nudging Finch aside. "Or he simply hasn't had an opportunity to dispose of her in a more permanent fashion."

The way Francesca suddenly refused to look at him told Jonah she was still having trouble including him in the discussion. Although she'd lowered her defenses for a moment, she'd already raised them again.

"Like I told you," she said to Finch. "I think he's married, which would limit his movements. I saw his wife or significant other and his kid. If it wasn't for them, I wouldn't be here. He was just getting ready to bash in my window when they drove up."

"Other people live at the property?" Jonah asked.

She didn't like talking to him; he could tell by her unwillingness to elaborate too much on any one thing.

"It looked that way. So why he's trolling for women on matchmaking sites designed for singles, I don't know."

"Plenty of married men do that," Finch said. "They can troll from the comfort of their own homes while their wife and kids are asleep."

"Did he use his real name on that profile?" Jonah asked.

She dug at her cuticles while she talked. "No, a pseudonym. Harry Statham."

"I guess a little insurance never hurt anybody—" Finch started to say but Jonah spoke at the same time.

"How did you connect Harry Statham to Butch Vaughn?"

"Before she left Saturday night, April told her sister, who's my client, that she was going to meet her new love interest at a bar called the Pour House here in Prescott. Since that was the last time any of her friends or family heard from her, and she didn't report to work on Monday, I went to the Pour House to see if she ever showed up. The bartender told me that while he was outside having a smoke he saw a woman fitting April's description getting into a truck with Butch. He knew him as a regular and confirmed that he looked exactly like the guy in the picture I showed him from the dating profile. He said he couldn't have gotten it wrong—the truck had a Prescott Salvage logo on the door."

Jonah tried to piece it all together. "Why would he use his own truck?"

"Maybe he wasn't planning on killing her when he picked her up. At the very least, he wasn't planning on getting caught, right? A lot of murderers use their own vehicles."

"But if Butch is married, he wouldn't kill April and

leave her in the salvage yard, where his wife could stumble across her."

"Actually, if you saw the place, you wouldn't find that idea so far-fetched," she said. "The yard is ten acres. And it's a maze. You could hide a dinosaur in there. I'm not even sure how I spotted the body with all the junk piled around it. He probably still plans on transporting it somewhere else."

"With ten acres, he wouldn't necessarily have to transport it off the property," Finch said.

"True," Jonah agreed but turned back to her. "So what happened when you first got to the yard?"

She scowled. "I've already been through it all with Investigator Finch. If you want to know, just have him debrief you."

Finch loosened his tie and sat on the edge of his desk, straining the seams of his chinos, which were a little tight on the thighs to begin with, due to the bodybuilding regime he so often talked about. "I realize we've been through some of this. But Jonah has a lot of experience with these types of cases. Two months ago he helped Texas authorities bring down a hospice worker responsible for the deaths of six elderly men and women. That's why we brought him in. I'd like him to hear the details from your own lips, if you don't mind."

Her displeasure didn't ease, but she returned to her seat, crossed her legs and began to explain what he'd missed before he arrived.

The phone rang; Finch answered it while they talked.

"Did you see under the tarp?" Jonah asked when he understood that she'd gone onto the property and started looking around after no one answered her knock. "Were you able to make a positive ID?"

She didn't seem completely comfortable with her response. Shifting in her chair, she admitted that she'd chosen not to go that far.

The urgency in the investigator's voice interrupted them. "Son of a bitch. You've got to be kidding me!"

"What is it?" Jonah asked.

Finch held up a hand; he wasn't finished with the call. "No, I'm bringing her and Jonah out there now. Don't let anyone go anywhere until then."

Feeling the same alarm he saw in Francesca's face, Jonah waited for the investigator to slam down the phone. "Well?"

"Vaughn wants us to file charges against Ms. Moretti."

"For what?"

The gold chain Finch wore around his neck disappeared as he buttoned his collar and tightened his tie. "Assault."

Francesca came to her feet. "What about the body?"

He grabbed his sports jacket from the back of his chair and herded them out of his cubicle. "Hunsacker can't find a body."

3

At Butch's place, four police cars and an ambulance cluttered the sides of the road. As Investigator Finch slowed to a stop, Francesca caught sight of a young paramedic treating Butch's injuries right there in the front yard. Already sporting a bandage over his left eye, presumably where she'd hit him with the pepper spray canister, he allowed the medic to dab some antiseptic on his cheek. But Francesca got the distinct impression that he was trying to make her look bad.

Somehow, in the short span of time since she'd driven off, he'd hidden April's body. Now he was playing up his injuries as if Francesca had attacked him for no reason.

His wife, another man far slighter in build who looked just like his wife, and an older couple stood beside him while his four- or five-year-old son played in the yard. Francesca wasn't sure if the older people and the smaller man were friends, family or neighbors, but the way they rallied around him made her think they were close, probably family. All the adults glared at her as Finch wedged his sedan into a spot not far from where she'd parked her BMW less than two hours ago. But it was the hatred in Butch's eyes that unnerved her.

"He's a murderer," she muttered.

Finch shoved the gearshift into Park. "Yeah, well, we need proof. So let's find it."

Jonah made no comment but, even as upset, distracted and worried as she'd been, Francesca hadn't been able to forget that he was the man who sat behind her in Finch's car. She hadn't seen him in ten years and yet her reaction to him hadn't changed. It was as if she had some sort of internal radar that pinged at regular intervals when he was within range. Obviously, basic attraction couldn't be trusted. He wasn't the type of man she ever wanted to be with. After what he'd done, there was no question about that. So why did her heart skip a beat every time she looked at him?

Refusing to acknowledge the emotions Jonah made her feel, she got out of the car. One situation at a time. She was going to lead Finch to April Bonner's body, then get the hell out of here. She'd go home, strip off her dirty clothes and sink her scraped and bruised body into a nice hot bath, where she'd soak until she was as wrinkled as a prune before diving into bed. Tomorrow would be another day—hopefully, a day she could spend at her newly remodeled office with the assistance of Heather, her receptionist, as she delved into her work. A day with no dead bodies or homicidal maniacs.

Investigator Hunsacker approached them first, wearing a tan-colored lightweight suit with distinct rings of sweat at the armpits. Although it was nearly five o'clock, the temperature hadn't dropped more than a degree or two from the high of one hundred and eight; Hunsacker's weight obviously made it difficult for him to tolerate the heat. Only five foot seven, no taller than Francesca, he had to weigh three hundred pounds. Sporting long Elvis-style sideburns to go with his slicked-back hair, he wasn't much to look at. He didn't move well, either. He'd worn the sides of his mahogany-colored wing tips so far down on the outside edges that his feet appeared deformed.

"There's no proof of Mr. Vaughn having done anything illegal," he told Finch as soon as he was close enough to speak. "Certainly no proof of murder."

"But I saw the body!" Francesca insisted.

Hunsacker's eyes matched his black hair. They moved in Francesca's direction, then darted back to Finch. "You didn't tell her?"

"Not yet." Finch frowned. "I want to make sure we're talking about the same figure and the same tarp."

"Should we take care of that now?"

Finch cast a glance at Butch. At least six feet six inches tall, he towered over everybody else like a giant lumberjack or the wood carving of Daniel Boone Francesca had once seen at a campground. "In a minute. Let me talk to Mr. Vaughn."

Hunsacker waved them past. "Be my guest."

"What didn't you tell me?" Francesca whispered as they circumvented Hunsacker.

"You'll see."

There was no opportunity to press him for an answer. She had to deal with Butch, whose animosity stabbed her like a million invisible darts.

Refusing to be intimidated, she held her head high, but found it difficult to remain calm, especially with everyone else studying her, too. The police and paramedics watched her with open curiosity; those who weren't with the police watched her with hostility. The people clustered around Butch *had* to be his family.

"Why'd you attack my husband?" Because the paramedic stood between them, Butch's wife came forward before Butch could, but Jonah intercepted her.

After what she'd already been through, Francesca couldn't help being grateful for the shield he provided. But she was determined not to show it. A few minutes ago, *he* was the enemy.

"I was only defending myself," she replied coolly. "I came here to speak with Mr. Vaughn regarding—"

"You were *what?*" Butch had overheard. "Did *I* sneak onto *your* property? Was *I* going through *your* stuff? No. You had no business here." Stepping past the paramedic, he shifted his attention to Finch and adopted a far more plaintive tone. "I didn't mean to make her think I was dangerous. I was only trying to figure out if she was stealing from me. Or if she'd come around hoping to sell me something." He grimaced as he raised a hand to his cheek. "Maybe I surprised her, but there was no call for violence."

"She gouged him good," the paramedic volunteered.

Francesca nearly asked the medic to butt out but chose to ignore him instead. "What about the woman you murdered and stashed under that tarp?" she demanded, speaking to Butch. "Have you told your wife about *that?*"

A pained expression, one that said she must be nuts for even suggesting it, settled over features as big and bold as the rest of him. He looked like a prizefighter, bulky but powerful. His dark hair needed a good trim—the front hung down practically to his eyes, and he had a wide nose that was slightly crooked, as if it'd been broken once or twice in the past. He wouldn't have been attractive, except that his chin was strong enough to carry off such an intensely masculine face. "There is no body."

Francesca had no intention of backing down. "I saw it with my own eyes."

The old lady Francesca had noticed before pulled away from the man who'd been consoling her. "You don't know what you saw. My son-in-law is a wonderful person. He'd never hurt a soul."

Only the slight man with a fair complexion and pale blue eyes standing beside Butch's wife seemed to look on without agitation. What was his take on this? Francesca wondered.

Butch drew the woman back. "Elaine, stay out of it. This lady is crazy. Who else would come onto a man's land and nearly claw his eyes out?"

Francesca had seen what she'd done to his eye and cheek. The pepper spray can she'd thrown had split his eyebrow and she'd scratched his face. But she hadn't blinded him, hadn't even come close. He was exaggerating his injuries, hoping for pity. "*You* came after *me*," she said.

"Give me a break! Do you really think I'd look like this and you'd look as good as you do if I'd wanted to hurt you?"

"How dare you claim *I'm* the one who's at fault here!" she cried, but then she felt Jonah's hand at the small of her back.

"Take it easy."

Take it easy? She was shaking, from rage and the memory of Butch wielding that bat. He'd intended to smash in her window; he'd been that determined to reach her. What reason could he have for going to such lengths *except* to hurt her? If he was truly concerned that she might've stolen from him, he could've jotted down her license plate number and called the cops. He knew she wasn't getting away with anything. She'd even left her purse behind.

The old lady wrung her hands. "This is so wrong! I

don't understand what's going on. Everyone knows Butch wouldn't hurt a soul."

"Calm down, Elaine," the elderly man, presumably her husband, said. "All this upset isn't good for you."

It wasn't good for anyone. Struggling to control her emotions, Francesca filtered out everyone and everything except Butch, who was spinning the tale of the afternoon's events to his own benefit. "What have you done with it?"

His pained expression didn't change. "With *what?*"

"With the body. I saw it there. If it's gone, you must've moved it. Where?"

"I didn't move anything! It was a mannequin. That's what you saw. This is a junkyard, lady. You never know what you're gonna find."

A *mannequin?* Could that be true? There was nothing else remotely similar to a mannequin in the yard. For the most part, Butch collected metal. A mannequin would've been an unusual item, even here. But that had to be what he'd shown Hunsacker. Otherwise, Finch's partner wouldn't have reacted so oddly when she arrived. *You didn't tell her?*

A hard knot formed in the pit of Francesca's stomach. "No," she said, shaking her head. She'd smelled death, hadn't she? Yes. Maybe. Had she imagined it?

Spreading his arms wide, Butch appealed to the cops as if to say, See? She's irrational.

"Stop it!" she snapped. "You know what happened here as well as I do."

"And I've told the truth. But if you won't believe me, come on. Let's go take a look."

He was too eager to prove himself. The knot in Francesca's stomach grew bigger.

Investigator Finch caught Butch's arm as he started off. "Why don't we let Ms. Moretti do the showing?"

Butch didn't appreciate being touched. His gaze lowered pointedly to Finch's hand and a muscle flexed in his cheek. But as soon as Finch released him, he laughed and shrugged. "Fine by me. She likes to make herself comfortable on other people's property."

"Spare us the unnecessary commentary," Jonah growled.

Butch seemed to notice him for the first time. Until that moment, he'd been looking only at Francesca—at least, when he wasn't pandering to the cops. "Who are *you?*" he asked with apparent disdain.

Jonah coolly assessed Butch, as he might look at a man with whom he was about to step into the boxing ring. "Jonah Young."

Butch's eyes swept over Jonah as if taking note of his smaller but more defined body, assessing him in return. "A cop?"

"A consultant."

"They bring in consultants for assault cases, do they?"

Jonah's lips curved into a thin-lipped smile. "I'm not sure this *is* an assault case."

That shut Butch up, told him that there might be at least one person present who wasn't buying his act. When his nostrils flared, Francesca decided he didn't like having a skeptic, any more than he liked being touched or having to suffer this influx of policemen. Still, he adjusted his expression and, if anything, broadened his insolent grin. "Well, you can always ask Investigator Hunsacker. I've given him and the rest of these boys access to the whole yard. They've poked through it all. If there was a body here, they would've found it."

Hunsacker joined them just in time to confirm it. "That's true."

Francesca could feel Hunsacker's support of Butch. Finch's partner regretted being here. But she refused to let that shake her. She couldn't imagine how Butch had sidestepped what should be coming to him, but… something wasn't right.

"We appreciate your cooperation," Finch said. Then he sent her a pleading look and straightened his tie. He was beginning to sweat, too. Small beads gathered on his forehead. She got the impression the weather wasn't exclusively to blame. She felt a little dizzy, a little nauseous, herself. The only person in her corner seemed to be Jonah, and she guessed he was sticking by her out of guilt, or some crazy notion that doing so might redeem him for his actions of ten years ago.

Would she embarrass herself? Maybe. A mannequin, especially if it was covered and seen from such a distance, could easily be mistaken for a human. Plastic or wooden limbs would even explain the "rigor" she'd noted. But what about the stench? Hadn't she smelled rotting flesh?

She couldn't say for sure. She only knew she couldn't have been wrong about the level of danger she'd sensed when Butch came after her. Just the memory of how he'd looked at her when she managed to lock him out of the car made her skin crawl. He'd wanted vengeance, pure and simple. And she believed he would've taken it.

The walk around the house and into the salvage yard seemed to drag on forever. With every step, tension hummed through her like the electricity passing through the high-voltage wires overhead. Butch's wife carried their son. He and his family trailed behind her, along with Jonah, Finch, Hunsacker, the paramedic and his partner and the deputies. They formed quite a group and would provide quite an audience.

Butch's confidence and swagger told her this wouldn't end well, but she was stubborn enough to have to see for herself.

The dog was secured to his usual spot. As soon as they came into view, he barked and strained against the chain that held him as if he'd like to devour one of them, but Butch snapped a command for him to "shut his trap" and he did. He whined and danced instead of acting aggressive, but he watched with razor-sharp interest as they crossed in front of him.

The office where Francesca had hidden earlier wasn't difficult to locate. Neither was the spot where she'd seen the body—because the body was still there. The sawhorses and pallets had been shoved to one side, making a path, but the tarp-covered figure remained.

Once again, she felt hesitant to approach. It looked so real. But this time she didn't stop until she stood barely a foot away.

No scent of decay filled her nostrils, only the astringent smell of desert scrub, which grew between the wrecked car bodies and other odds and ends. She told herself this might mean April Bonner was still alive. But she didn't really believe it.

Stepping forward, Butch pulled back the tarp, showing her exactly what he'd told her she'd see. A mannequin. "I keep it covered to protect it from the sun," he explained.

Francesca had to squint against the glare of that sun, but now there was no mistaking what she was looking at. She'd jumped to the wrong conclusion earlier. Finding Janice Grey's remains a year ago had set her up, made her think she'd solved April's case the same way. But, obviously, this was very different....

Finch fondled his goatee, then dropped his hand. "I'm terribly sorry for the trouble we've caused you and your family," he told Butch. "We'll get out of here and let you return to whatever you'd be doing if you weren't entertaining us. Ms. Moretti, shall we go?"

"I told you he was innocent!" Butch's mother-in-law cried.

"And look what you did to his face!" his wife added. The dog braved a bark and, surrounded by so much animosity, Butch's son began to cry. But, once again, the slight blond man seemed oddly detached from the whole scene. Did he know something he wasn't saying? Possibly, but not necessarily. He attracted her attention simply because he was so...placid.

"He attacked *me*," she repeated, not taking a single step. Was she imagining it or was the color of the mannequin's hair a little different from what she'd seen earlier?

Squeezing her eyes closed, she quickly corralled that thought. The hair color *couldn't* be different. What were the chances that Butch had been able to trade out the real body so fast? *Very* small. She was grasping for any way to avoid the chagrin and embarrassment of having dragged the police out here with such a wild accusation; that was all. She'd never been in a situation like this, where the integrity of her work was called into question, didn't even know how to react to it.

"Ms. Moretti?" Finch again.

"Just a minute." *I know you're there.... What are you doing trespassing on my property? Don't you have any manners...? Who are you...? What the hell's wrong with you, lady? I just want to talk....* Butch hadn't actually threatened her with violence, hadn't said anything that suggested he might kill her. And yet she'd known she was in serious trouble. Or did her panic all stem from having mistaken this mannequin for a corpse?

Jonah came up beside her. Knowing that he'd had a front-row seat to what had to be her most embarrassing moment *ever* made her humiliation complete. She'd often dreamed of running into him again, but those fantasies had always included an element of satisfaction, of finding some proof that he'd lived to regret cheating on her. After what he'd witnessed here, he had to be glad they hadn't ended up together. "You okay?"

Lifting her eyes, she found Butch waiting for her reaction, a victorious smile on his lips. There was something twisted in his expression. Was she the only one who could see it? Dared she trust her own instincts after *this?*

"I won't press charges if you'll give me an apology," he said.

Part of her agreed she should be big enough to admit her mistake and say she was sorry so they could move on. But another part rebelled at the thought of making *any* concession. He was dangerous. She should know. She was the one who'd been alone with him. She'd seen what he'd been like, the sudden change that'd come over him when his wife and son returned. Maybe he hadn't *stated* his intent, but she'd felt it down to the marrow of her bones.

"You're still the last person to see April Bonner alive," she said.

He blinked in surprise. "Excuse me?"

"What did you do to her?"

"I don't believe this shit!" The veins stood out in his neck as he appealed to Finch. "I've been as cooperative

as I could possibly be. I've let your men parade around
my property for almost two hours, treating me like I'm
some kind of killer. I've proven that *all* her accusations
are false—and you allow her to say *this?* Get off my
property! Now! Every one of you! And don't ever come
back!"

Finch took hold of Francesca's elbow. "Let's go."

She refused to budge. "I'll leave as soon as he returns
my purse."

Butch's gaze locked with hers. He hadn't answered
her question about April Bonner. Instead, he'd diverted
attention away from the real issue by getting angry and
playing the martyr. Why? She thought she knew, but
he'd already won this round. There was no chance the
police would believe her or act on her suspicions after
this debacle.

He finally deigned to break the silence. "I don't know
what you're talking about."

"My *purse.*" She spoke slowly, as if he didn't possess
the IQ to understand regular speech. "You grabbed it
when you were chasing me and broke the strap. It fell on
the ground and spilled—right over there." She pointed
to a bare patch of dirt closer to the back of the house.
"What did you do with it?"

"I didn't do anything with it. You must've lost it
somewhere else, or had it stolen from your car, because
you didn't leave it here." He appealed to the uniformed
policemen who were waiting to see what would happen
next. "Did anyone see a purse lying around?"

Muttering and shaking their heads, they came to a
consensus. No one had seen it. Francesca suspected
Butch had collected her stuff before the police arrived.
He'd hidden it, and now he was punishing her for defy-
ing him.

She turned to his wife. "You came home before he had a chance to gather it all up. You must've seen it. My iPhone was on the ground, too."

Butch's wife had her lips pressed so tightly together she could barely speak. "I didn't see anything."

The old lady—Elaine—chimed in, too. "Why are you doing this to us?"

They had no idea that the man they were trying so hard to protect had very likely killed a woman. They didn't want to believe he was capable of it.

"There will come a day when you'll be sorry you protected him," she said.

"Now she's threatening my family!" Butch complained, and this time when Finch took hold of her arm, she could feel his fingers digging into her flesh.

"We're leaving. *Now*."

Again, she resisted his tug. "Not without my purse, my car keys and my phone."

"You're *sure* you don't have her things?" It was Jonah who stepped in. "Because that could cause you some real problems down the road. And I, for one, would hate to see that happen. You being such a nice guy and all."

Butch offered him a taunting smile. "The consultant speaks. How much are they paying you for this visit, anyway?"

"That's none of your business," Jonah replied. "Just answer the question."

"I don't have her purse or anything else that belongs to her."

Francesca jerked away from Finch. "He's lying!"

Obviously deliberating, Jonah stared Butch down. But Francesca didn't like the decision he reached. "Forget it. For now," he added, but she couldn't. She was afraid she'd never get that stuff back. And the thought of Butch

having her address book, her wallet and her credit cards
sent chills down her spine.

"No! It was here. He's got it. I won't leave without my
purse and phone."

"He said he doesn't have it." Grabbing her again, Finch
began dragging her away and, when she fought him,
Jonah took her other arm.

"You're a crazy bitch, you know that?" Butch yelled
after her.

Fighting tears of frustration, Francesca twisted to get
in one parting shot. "And you're a monster!" she yelled
over the barking of the dog, which was suddenly frantic.
"What happened to April Bonner? What did you do with
her, huh? And if you're married, why were you submit-
ting a profile to a dating service?"

"It was a joke," he said. "My wife knows about it.
And, last I heard, that wasn't illegal."

"Damn it, Francesca, don't make things worse."
Jonah's mouth moved close to her ear so only she could
hear. "Live to fight another day," he breathed. Then he
and Finch shoved her into the car and slammed the door
so she couldn't say anything else.

4

Butch stood at the corner of his property, watching as the police drove away. He was in big trouble now, and he knew it. Maybe this time there'd be no way out.

Paris came up beside him. Fortunately, Elaine and Warren had taken their son inside. Although he lived with his in-laws, they usually minded their own business. It was Paris's freak of a brother, Dean, who got on his nerves. Dean hovered on the porch behind them, hoping to overhear what they had to say, but for his own safety he didn't venture any closer. Butch was almost sad about that. Angry as he was, he could've used a target.

"Did you go on a dating site?" Paris asked. "Did you submit a profile?"

There was no point in attempting to deceive her. If she wanted the truth, all she had to do was search dating sites. Or go to that Moretti woman, who probably had a copy of his profile. Why give Paris a reason to do that? They had to stick together at all costs.

When he didn't answer, Paris lowered her head. "That's what I thought."

"I didn't kill her," he insisted.

She shaded her face, apparently eyeing the little puffs

of dust that'd been kicked up by the police cars. "It says quite a bit about you that I'm relieved to hear it."

The sarcasm bit deep, made him bristle. "It's not as if you're perfect, Paris."

"At least I can be faithful."

"I can't help it. Sex is all I think about."

"And now you were the last person to see a woman who went missing. Don't you realize what that means? What if she's dead? What if they find her body and it has your DNA on it? They'll put you behind bars!"

"I *wasn't* the last one to see April Bonner alive. There's no way. Unless she killed herself, someone else had to be involved."

When his wife didn't respond, he looked over and found her watching him carefully. "You believe me, don't you?" he said.

Sighing, she shook her head. "I don't know what to believe anymore. All I know is if this Moretti woman keeps digging, our son could lose his father."

"Don't talk like that. Moretti's done here." He could only hope that was true, that this wouldn't go in the direction Paris feared. When he was a boy, his stepfather used to punish him by locking him in a box the size of a coffin out in a metal shed. During the summer, he'd nearly suffocate. Small, confined spaces still terrified him. He already knew he could never bear living in a jail cell.

"How do you know she's done?" she asked.

"Because I'll make sure of it."

"Who was she?"

He could tell by the change in her tone that she wasn't referring to the investigator. "Who are you talking about? April Bonner?"

"Who else?" She sounded weary, as if this incident

might get the best of her despite how hard she'd fought to keep their family together.

He could easily recall April's kind brown eyes, her timid but eager smile, her round cheeks, her body, soft from lack of exercise. They'd exchanged some intriguing e-mails, but she hadn't turned out to be his type at all. "No one. She was just a…a means to an end. You know that. That's all it ever is."

"What happened with her that was so different from all the others?"

"Nothing. The night didn't end well, I'll admit that. You know how I get sometimes. But I didn't kill her."

Paris shoved her hands in her pockets. "It has to stop, Butch."

He slipped his arm through hers and was gratified when she leaned into him. He hadn't lost her yet. And he never would. "It will. I promise. Don't give up on me. We've come so far. We can get through this, too."

Francesca had canceled her credit cards and cell service. She'd also left a message with a locksmith, asking him to contact her first thing in the morning. Now that she was finished with everything, at least everything she could do after hours, she was lying in bed, pretty sure she'd never had a more miserable afternoon. She'd been involved in some tragic cases—peripherally when she was with Phoenix P.D. and then the Maricopa County Sheriff's Office, and more directly after she'd started her own agency—but never had she experienced anything more enraging than having Butch Vaughn flat out lie to her. It was one thing to have him claim he hadn't meant to frighten her; she'd expected that. But she'd never dreamed he'd try to keep her purse, or that he'd take so much joy in making her feel powerless. Now he had her iPhone, her car keys—and her house keys because they were on the same ring—her wallet and her ID, all of which he'd basically stolen from her right beneath the noses of ten police officers.

He thought he was clever. But she wasn't about to let him get away with what he'd done to her or to April Bonner. If he'd killed April, she'd find the proof she needed to put him away. The poor woman had to be somewhere. And what about those other bodies, the ones in the mass grave Finch had told her about? Was Butch responsible for those murders, as well?

It held the remains of seven women....

She believed Butch to be capable of extreme violence. She'd never met an individual who scared her as much.

This was what some of the people she took on as clients went through, she realized. Now she'd become a victim, too. She tried telling herself it was good experience to have, that in future she'd be better able to relate to their feelings of helplessness and frustration. But trying to find something positive in what she'd gone through didn't make these late-night hours tick by any faster.

Agitated and restless, she stared at the ceiling. Although she tried to avoid it, she kept picturing Butch sitting at his kitchen table going through her purse while the rest of his family slept. Was he holding her driver's license right now, memorizing her address? Had he checked MapQuest to determine the best route to take to her house?

Surely he wouldn't be *that* obvious. Besides, she lived two hours away, which meant he'd need a wide margin in which to be gone. But just knowing how easy tracking her down would be made every creak and rustle— normal noises on any other night—sound like someone was attempting to break in. She was so wound up she could feel her pulse beating in her fingertips.

Would morning *never* come?

Why hadn't she listened to Jonah? He'd asked her not to go back home tonight. He'd encouraged her to stay with a friend for a few days, give Butch time to cool down. But Butch wasn't the type to cool down. The way his muscles had contracted when she'd continued to challenge him for her purse made her believe she'd never be completely safe, not as long as he was free. And hiding wouldn't solve the problem, not when Butch could simply use one of her business cards, a stack of which could be found in her purse, to come up with her office address. He could attack her midday as easily as at night. Crimes took place at all hours. If he really wanted to hurt her, he'd find a way.

"Butch can go to hell as far as I'm concerned," she muttered. And if he broke in and attacked her, maybe she'd send him there. She'd brought a large carving knife to bed with her. She also had a new can of pepper spray in the top drawer of her nightstand. She'd squirted a little on the sidewalk to make sure it worked—something she'd taken for granted with the old one that she wasn't willing to do again.

Were those precautions enough? Maybe not. She couldn't imagine actually having to stab someone. A gun would be a much more practical form of defense.

Maybe she *should* get one.… She'd never been tempted before, but she'd never been so rattled, either.

Her hand was growing sweaty on the handle of the knife. She couldn't go on like this.

Forcing her fingers to unclench the weapon, she put it on the nightstand. If she did fall asleep, she didn't want to roll over on top of it. But there was little chance of nodding off. She'd have to relax for that to happen. And she couldn't relax. When she wasn't thinking about Butch, she was thinking about Jonah. How ironic that he'd pop up on a day when she was so ill-equipped to deal with his reappearance in her life.

Talk about rotten luck and terrible timing....

Running a finger over each eyebrow as if she could smooth away the anxiety, she replayed the argument that had ensued after Finch had pulled away from the salvage yard.

Jonah: "What the hell's wrong with you, Francesca? Are you trying to get yourself killed?"

Francesca: "Weren't you listening? I was trying to get my purse. He has the keys to my house, my cell phone, my wallet, everything!"

Jonah: "I understand that. But you had no proof, no basis for accusing him. It was your word against his. Why provoke him?"

Francesca: "You think I should've let it all go without a fight?"

Jonah: "I think you don't take on a man like that unless you know in advance that you've got him by the balls. He'd already allowed Hunsacker and his men to search the whole place. It wasn't as if we could force him to let us look again. That would require a warrant."

Finch: "And, in case you're wondering, there's no way we could get a warrant. You were the one who was trespassing. You're also the only one who inflicted bodily harm."

Francesca: "He tackled me! These abrasions and burns don't mean anything?"

Finch: "They don't constitute an attack as obvious as the scratches you left on his face."

Jonah: "He could easily make up an excuse for that,

say you flew into a panic when you thought that mannequin was a body and fell while you were running away. How would you prove otherwise?"

Finch: "I'm telling you, any judge I approach would act to protect Vaughn's rights, to stop a possible lawsuit if for no other reason."

Francesca: "A lawsuit?"

Finch: "He could sue the city for 'misconduct.'"

Francesca: "Since when is following up on a lead considered misconduct?"

At that point, the investigator had turned to face her for the first time since they'd left the salvage yard. "We descended on him like flies on shit because you're an investigator. I believed you when you told me there was a body in that junkyard." Here, he'd smacked the steering wheel. "Damn it, you hadn't even looked at it!"

Francesca: "I made a mistake, okay? That doesn't mean he's not responsible for April's disappearance."

Finch: "No, it doesn't. But we need proof before we go barging in there again. Solid proof. More than just your word."

Francesca: "Fine. I'll get the proof!"

Finch had shot her a sullen look. "You do that."

Jonah: "Considering what's happened, the smartest response is to cut your losses and stay out of it. Your life is worth far more than whatever you had in that purse. Let us take it from here."

This comment had caused her to twist around in her seat. "So you *do* think he's dangerous."

Jonah: "I plan to find out. That much I can promise."

Francesca: "Well, for the record, I'm not worried about my perfume and my lipstick, okay? I'm worried about him having my personal information."

Finch: "Cancel your credit cards and change your locks."

Jonah: "And until you can do that, don't go home. Rekey your house and your car, put in a security system at your office, if you don't already have one, and stay with your parents."

That wasn't an option. These days, her parents spent their summers in Montana, building their dream house near her brother, Samuel, who was older by six years and had a wife and three children.

Francesca: "In other words, leave my home unprotected."

Jonah: "Your safety is more important than your house."

Francesca: "But I can't leave the house to him. Who knows what he'd do? He could install video cameras in my attic, sabotage the window locks, drill peepholes."

Jonah: "You can have it inspected before you go back."

Or she could defend her turf, refuse to let him disrupt her life.

Francesca: "Thanks for the advice, but it never pays to run from a bully. That would only endanger whoever I chose to stay with. All he'd have to do is follow me from the office."

Finch: "There's strength in numbers. It certainly beats staying alone."

Francesca: "Giving him the upper hand won't make me any safer. I'm not going to run and hide."

Jonah: "You haven't changed a bit. You had too much pride for your own good ten years ago, and you've got too much now. Don't you have a boyfriend you can stay with for a few weeks?"

Roland Perenski, her last love interest, had appeared

in her mind in that moment, but she hadn't been with him in two years. She hadn't even heard from him. She was pretty sure he'd married the woman he'd dated after her.

Francesca: "Just stop. I don't want to talk to you anymore, especially about my love life."

Jonah hadn't spoken again, even to say goodbye when she got out of the car. She'd slammed the door, climbed into her BMW and headed directly home, but she was still thinking about him. Why, she couldn't say. So what if he looked better than ever? With that thick dark hair falling across his forehead, the slight cleft in his chin and the perennial five-o'clock shadow that was such a marked contrast to his light green eyes and wide sexy smile, he'd always turned heads.

No, it was never his looks she'd had a problem with.

A noise outside her window sent her heart pounding, so she threw off the covers and sat up. Forget trying to sleep; this was torture.

Grabbing the cordless phone from her nightstand, she called her best friend, Adriana Covington, and refused to feel the slightest bit guilty for disturbing her. If anyone deserved to be awakened in the middle of the night as a result of Jonah's reappearance, it was Adriana.

"Hello?" her friend mumbled.

Grateful that Adriana's husband hadn't answered, Francesca toyed with the locket she wore around her neck. "You sleeping?"

"Isn't that what most people do at three in the morning?" There was no irritation in her voice, only curiosity. "Where are you?"

"Home."

"What's going on? I thought maybe you were in trouble."

Francesca led a very stable life. She wasn't currently in a relationship so there was no romantic angst. She worked too much to date very often and rarely hung out at bars or other singles' gatherings unless it was to stop by for a few minutes after work with Heather, her twenty-two-year-old receptionist. That gave Heather a break from the constraints of her single-parent life. Francesca didn't consider herself a success in the "popular girl" category, but she'd established quite a glowing reputation in the investigative industry, especially after finding Janice Grey's remains. That investigation hadn't ended the way anyone would hope, but she'd been able to give Janice's family resolution and justice. Sometimes that was all a client could ask.

Anyway, it wasn't as if late-night calls were usual for her. "I ran into Jonah today."

A long silence ensued. Finally, Adriana muttered, "Hang on. I'm going into the other room."

Francesca probed her sore lip with her tongue while she waited. When Adriana came back on the line, she noticed that her friend sounded far less sleepy. Funny how the mention of Jonah could do that.

"Where did you see him?"

Even with all the other guys who'd come afterward, for both of them, Adriana hadn't needed a last name. There'd been only one Jonah. And neither one of them would ever forget him. "In Prescott."

"He lives there?"

"No, I think he lives in California. He works for a private security contractor based in L.A."

"What's Prescott got to do with anything, then?"

"He's consulting on a case in Yavapai County, which is where my own case took me today."

"Is he married?"

"I don't think so. He's not wearing a ring."

"Okay. So…what happened? What'd he say?"

"Nothing, really. Our paths sort of…collided, that's all." She'd humiliated herself in front of him, but explaining that would only repeat the humiliation.

"I don't understand. You don't have anything to say about it?"

She had plenty to say. She just didn't know how to get it out. "I guess not."

"Are you telling me this to make me feel terrible again, Fran? To punish me? You think what I did isn't hard enough to live with?"

Francesca covered her face. Calling Adriana had been a mistake. She'd forgiven her, hadn't she? She'd told her she had; they'd patched up their friendship and moved on. "No. I'm telling you because…I needed to tell someone. And that's what best friends are for."

"What you're saying is…you still have feelings for him."

"No! I… It was a shock, that's all."

"A shock."

"Yes."

"And now you want someone to tell you that whatever you felt was normal."

She'd felt as if she had an anvil crushing her chest. Could she really expect anyone to tell her that was normal? "Maybe that's it. I mean, how much could he have meant to me? We were all so young, only what… twenty-three?"

"But you've never gotten over him, never fell in love so deeply again."

"Of course I've gotten over him." As for love, love was overrated.

"I know better." Adriana blew out a sigh. "God, I made a mess of things, didn't I?"

Francesca had never felt so torn between wanting to punish and wanting to console. It was true that Adriana had made a terrible mistake. She'd destroyed Francesca's relationship with Jonah. And she'd nearly destroyed their friendship, too, a friendship that had lasted since pre-school. But Jonah deserved his share of the blame. It wasn't as if Francesca could hold Adriana entirely responsible for the affair. As a matter of fact, during the past several years, she'd found it easier and easier to pin most of the blame on Jonah. That had enabled her and Adriana to go on as though there'd never been a betrayal.

"It's over," she said. "It's behind us. I just..." What? Wanted the pain to go away for good? Couldn't imagine why seeing Jonah had been so earth-shattering? What was she hoping to accomplish by dragging Adriana back into that vortex of hurt and recrimination?

"I wish I could undo what I did," Adriana said. "Not a day goes by that I don't regret hurting you. But...it's too late, Fran. There's no way I can change what I did. All I can do is tell you how sorry—"

"Don't. You've apologized enough." Why torture her? She'd had to give up her baby, hadn't she? That must've been hard. The pregnancy had been hard, too. She'd been sick for five of the eight months it'd lasted and bedridden for the final three.

"I still think about her, you know," she said.

"Of course you do." These days Adriana had two little boys with Stan. There had to be moments when she looked at them and couldn't help remembering the little girl she'd borne before they came into her life. "Do you ever regret your decision to give her up?"

"No. I wasn't ready to take on a child. I wasn't even through with school. I had no resources. And it wasn't as if Jonah and I were planning to be together. We both knew what happened that night was…out of line, nothing we'd ever repeat. He cared too much about you to—"

Francesca jumped to her feet. "Don't even say that."

"It's true. I don't know why he came on to me. It was…like he was purposely chasing you away, *daring* you to love him. You know how easily spooked he was. But I could tell he cared by how broken up he was afterward."

Despite the lump suddenly clogging her throat, Francesca fought to keep her voice level. "We were just stupid kids. We didn't know what love was, neither of us."

The tenor of Adriana's voice changed. "He didn't want me to give her up. Did I ever tell you that? He offered to raise her. But I wouldn't agree to it. He wasn't any more ready to be a parent than I was.… It took a bit of convincing, but he'd finally agreed we should contact a good agency and let them do their thing. They found a great couple who was dying to have a baby and couldn't. The Williamses."

"Have you heard from Jonah since he came to the hospital that day?" Francesca already knew Adriana had never communicated with the Williamses. It'd been a closed adoption. But she'd often wondered if Adriana and Jonah had kept in touch, if only occasionally. In her determination to forget, to move on and allow Adriana the same opportunity, she'd never asked.

"No. Not once."

"I hadn't heard from him, either." Not since they'd muddled through the next few months of working for the same police force, avoiding each other. By Christmas, she'd moved from Tempe to Chandler and secured a position with the Maricopa County Sheriff's Office. "Not until he walked into the sheriff's station today."

"How'd he treat you?"

She wasn't sure how to describe the meeting. There'd been a surfeit of negative emotion but, considering their history, that wasn't unexpected or unusual. "Fine." She hadn't waited to see what he'd do; she'd gone on the offensive. *I know very well how much you like the ladies....*

There was another long pause. "Are you okay, Frannie?"

For the first time since she'd picked up the phone, Francesca thought of Butch Vaughn and her gaze shifted to the knife on her nightstand. The blade gleamed in the light streaming in from the hall. She usually didn't sleep with lights on, but tonight she'd left almost all of them blazing.

It'd be easier to talk about Butch than Jonah, but why scare Adriana? Then neither of them would be able to sleep.

"Of course. I shouldn't have called." She didn't really understand why she had, not after so long. For a brief moment she'd been angry again and had wanted to lash out, that was all. The memories had crowded too close. "I'll let you go. We can talk tomorrow."

Adriana hesitated. "Will we have to talk about Jonah?"

"Damned if I know." She hung up, but the pain she'd heard in her friend's voice wouldn't let her leave it at that. *Will we have to talk about Jonah?* Although what had happened ten years ago still hurt, especially after seeing Jonah today, Francesca didn't want Adriana to suffer any more than she already had. What was the point?

Aware that she was the only person who could release

her, Francesca picked up the phone. But when she pushed the talk button, she couldn't get a dial tone. Assuming the phone hadn't had a chance to reset after she'd disconnected, she waited a few seconds and tried again.

Nothing.

"What the heck," she complained. It was such a bother not having her iPhone.

Then it dawned on her. She didn't have her iPhone because Butch had kept it; he'd made her dependent on her home phone. And now...

"No," she breathed, but in her heart she knew. He'd cut the line.

5

Someone was out late.

Smiling at the fact that he'd caught Butch yet again, Dean stood at the back of the house, scuffing his shoe against the hard patch of dirt where his brother-in-law usually parked his big red truck under a metal carport. He could still smell the exhaust of the diesel fuel, could make out a dark spot on the ground where the engine had leaked oil. In the moonlight, it looked like blood....

So where was Butch this time? The way he'd pawed through Francesca Moretti's purse after Paris went to bed made it all too easy to guess. He was going to pay the private investigator a visit. Paris had to know he was going, too, but she was turning a blind eye. Again.

The fact that she refused to see what Butch really was drove Dean crazy. Well, crazier than he already was, he thought, and chuckled at his own joke.

"You're a bad boy, Butch," he whispered into the darkness. "Such a bad, bad boy." But Butch definitely made life interesting. Dean had to give him that.

Feeling safer than when his brother-in-law was stalking around the place acting like the king of all he surveyed—his sister's husband was such a Neanderthal—Dean walked around the front of the house to the gate, took the key from his pocket and let himself into the salvage yard. Ever since he was a child and his parents took him to see a magic act where the magician could escape anything, no matter the lock, he'd been fascinated by the concept and spent hours on the Internet, learning to pick locks himself. But it was trial and error that had made him good. He could've picked this lock instead of using a key. He did it all the time, just to keep his skills well-honed. But he wasn't in the mood for a challenge. It was tougher than any house lock he'd ever encountered.

Demon barked, but only to say hello. The noise wasn't anything that would rouse the fam. He barked worse than that at a squirrel or a lizard.

"Hey, boy. How are you tonight?" Dean stopped long enough to give the dog a scratch. As friendly as Demon was to him, the sheer power in his body reminded Dean too much of Butch. He didn't want to think about the damage either of them could cause if they really wanted.

Inhaling the warm night air, he closed his eyes to savor the unique scent of the yard—desert, metal, animals, residual cigarette smoke, motor oil. He liked all those smells. This was where he felt the best. These acres were more exciting to him than Disneyland to a kid, especially when it was late and Butch was gone. Then Dean had the run of the place.

Mentally skimming through the list of the various hidey-holes he'd created over the years, he tried to decide where he wanted to spend his time tonight. But he immediately chose the same thing he'd been doing every night, at least lately—searching for Butch's cache of women's underwear. There had to be one here somewhere. He'd seen several pairs under the seat of Butch's truck or hidden in his office, where Paris was less likely to come across them. If Dean had his guess, they were trophies and went into some sort of collection. And he was dying to see how many there actually were.

So where should he start? The old boxcar? The cellarlike space he'd dug beneath the shed? The cavity he'd tunneled out of the junk heap along the back fence? That pile of oil barrels had been there since Dean was three or four years old….

The yard had so many titillating secrets, didn't it? And, like the underwear cache he hoped to find, the best of those secrets were thanks to Butch.

Take the body in that old freezer. Julia. The young runaway who'd lived with them for a few months. Dean hated that she was dead. He'd liked her when she was alive. But there was some comfort in knowing she'd never leave him.

He figured he'd keep her company while he waited for Butch to return. The exact time of his brother-in-law's arrival might be of interest.

Francesca held the knife and the pepper spray in one hand while she closed and locked her bedroom door. Such a flimsy barrier might not stop an intruder, especially an intruder who looked as powerful as Butch. But if he tried to reach her through the hall, he'd have to deal with that locked door and she'd definitely know he was coming.

Every bit as jittery as she'd been in the salvage yard, she drew a steadying breath. She'd been on edge since her last encounter with Mr. Vaughn, which made it all too easy to fly into a panic now. But panicking wouldn't help. She had to be able to think clearly.

What next? What more could she do?

Setting her weapons aside, she shoved the dresser

across the hardwood floor toward the door she'd just locked. Maybe her actions would be pointless—maybe he'd break the slider leading from the porch overlooking her pool. But she had to seal off as many points of entry as possible so she could monitor those that were left. Doing something was better than doing nothing.

After wrestling the dresser over to the door, she crouched against the wall where she could keep an eye on the windows as well as the slider. Now that she'd blocked out the light that had been filtering in from the hall, the darkness felt thick and palpable. She would've liked to throw the switch in her bedroom, but she didn't want to make it any easier for Butch to see in. As counterintuitive as it seemed, darkness was safer.

What a bastard, she thought. Did he really believe he could get away with coming after her?

Apparently, he did. And maybe it was true. As long as he didn't leave any evidence behind, he could do whatever he wanted without fear of punishment. Clever killers often escaped the consequences of their crimes, didn't they? Of course they did. But whether or not she came out of this alive, Francesca was determined to make sure he left *some* proof of his identity.

His blood would work nicely.

A thump outside her window made her heart seize. Was that him?

Trying to differentiate one shadow from another, she studied the murky shapes beyond the glass until they began to blur. She was straining too hard. Blinking to give her eyes a rest, she peered out again.

This time she thought she spotted a man....

No. It was the tree that provided shade for the deck. Fear was causing her imagination to play tricks on her.

Breathe. Briefly letting go of the pepper spray, she

wiped her damp palm on her bare leg, then did the same with the other hand, the one holding the knife. She wore a T-shirt and panties, nothing in which she felt comfortable confronting anyone who might try to overpower her.

She considered dressing so she'd feel less exposed, less vulnerable. But then she'd have to set her weapons aside for longer than a millisecond, and she was afraid he'd strike as soon as she did. It felt as if he was watching her already, waiting for the perfect opportunity….

Was he looking in while she was trying to look out? The idea that he could be so close raised the hair on the back of her neck. Had he brought his bat? Would he come crashing through the slider? Or would he bide his time—until the unrelenting tension took its toll on her nerves—and use her key?

As the minutes stretched out and nothing happened, she crept to the closest window and raised her head above the pane. The yard appeared empty. The gardener had been by earlier today. She could smell the fresh-mown grass, see the meticulously trimmed plants in the side yard.

The gate stood open. She remembered closing it when she'd locked up for the night, but the latch didn't always hold….

She needed to see more.

Through the next window, she could make out the area around the deck and pool. Moonlight glimmered off the water and bathed the lounge chairs in pearly white. But she saw nothing that might—

Wait! At the shallow end. A dark shape sat in one of the chairs. No, he was *lying down*. She was sure of it. His hands were propped behind his head and he was staring up at her room as if he didn't have a care in the world.

She jerked her head back. Had he seen her? What was he doing just…lying there?

Heart thumping erratically, she crawled to the slider, which afforded her the best view of all. Sure enough, she had a visitor—a visitor who was doing very little to hide his presence. She got the impression Butch *wanted* to be seen. While she watched, he leaned over to pick up a small rock and threw it at her window. It missed the glass but hit the side of the house with a *crack*.

He wasn't sneaking around, as she'd expected. Clearly he wanted to frighten her.

And he did. Far bolder than she'd thought he'd be, he seemed completely unafraid of the consequences. He was flaunting that lack of fear, letting her know he enjoyed the game he was playing.

What should she do?

She didn't get the chance to decide. Before she could respond in any way, he rose into a sitting position and cocked his head as if he'd heard a noise that put him on alert.

What was he reacting to? Possibly nothing. He didn't seem *overly* concerned. He came to his feet and stood there, gazing at her room from beyond the patio. Then he offered her a mocking salute, as though he knew she could see him, and strode calmly to the fence, which he jumped.

A few seconds later she heard what must've chased him off—the crackling of a police radio—and rushed to the front of the house. A cruiser sat at the curb.

Suddenly far less concerned about her state of undress, she unlocked the door and charged through it, down the driveway and right up to the officer's lowered window.

"How did you know to come?" she asked the cop who sat behind the wheel, writing a report.

He put aside his clipboard. "Professional courtesy. Gentleman by the name of Jonah Young called in, said you were being harassed and asked if we could drive by every once in a while. I've been by twice already. Why? Somethin' wrong?" He glanced around.

Heedless of the tears streaking down her cheeks, she sank onto the blacktop. It was over. For tonight.

But what about the next time? Butch would be back. His brazen behavior made it a certainty.

So? Are you going to answer? Will you do it?

Jonah rubbed his tired eyes, then reread Lori's text message for probably the fifteenth time in three days. He needed to respond to her at some point. Ex-wife or no, he should be civil. But he wasn't ready to address the issues her request dredged up. The clock on the wall showed three in the morning. He'd been up for nearly twenty-four hours and was in no frame of mind to formulate an answer that sounded halfway polite. Considering how things had gone down when they were briefly married, which seemed like another life since it was before he'd ever become a cop, he didn't feel he owed her any special consideration.

On the other hand, he couldn't see a lot of reason to deny her what she was asking for. It wasn't that big a sacrifice. And he'd made his own share of mistakes in life. Francesca was proof. Besides, he was over Lori. He believed she'd be a good mother. So why not write the letter? Why not support her attempt to adopt a baby?

Resentment had to be the answer. It'd been more than a decade since he'd learned the truth, yet he still cringed whenever he pictured her sleeping with the partner she'd left him for. All those days and nights when Lori had said she needed some "girl time" he'd thought she and

Miranda were seeing a movie or shopping. He'd never dreamed they might be romantically intimate—because he'd been operating under the mistaken belief that he and Lori were, on the whole, happily married. That they had a normal sex life and would someday start a family. Lori had always seemed eager enough to make love. There'd even been times, plenty of them, when she'd initiated it.

But that was before she decided he never had and never would be able to fulfill her needs. It wasn't until she asked him to move out that she claimed she'd never been turned on by him, that all the moaning and writhing had been for *his* benefit.

Just the memory of those words made him wince. During that final argument he'd realized she'd been involved with Miranda before she ever met him. If she'd been confused about her sexuality it would've been so much easier to forgive her. But, according to her, she'd known since she was a girl. Which meant their whole relationship had been a front, a lie. She hadn't told him the truth because her family was absolutely opposed to same-sex relationships. She knew they'd never accept her lifestyle or respect her choice, and she was afraid she'd lose her position in the family business as well as her inheritance if they found out. She'd also wanted to have her own children and knew only a man could give her that.

Apparently, she'd seen him as some kind of sperm donor. But that was before she'd learned she couldn't have children. Jonah was sure that news had made it a whole lot easier to toss him aside.

"Hey, what are you doing here? I thought you were going to your motel."

Startled, he glanced up to see Dr. Leslie Price, the

forensic anthropologist he'd been working with since he'd signed on to help with the Dead Mule Canyon murders. Diminutive and soft-spoken, the doctor was in her early sixties. Her white hair reminded him of his mother. So did her confidence and dedication to her craft. But the similarities ended there. As a successful corporate attorney, Rita Young dressed in bold colors with designer labels and took no time to nurture anyone or anything. She could be combative, even with him, and threw her support behind one worthy cause after another. Dr. Price, on the other hand, settled for plain white lab coats and nurses' shoes and refused to argue with anyone. She also limited her devotion to *one* cause—making the dead speak through the evidence left in their bones.

"I could ask the same of you," he said. "You told me you were going to lie down in the back."

She offered him a sheepish grin. "I did. For a while. That couch isn't the most comfortable."

Lack of comfort wasn't the real problem. Jonah was willing to bet she was so exhausted she could sleep in a closet standing up. The fine lines age had etched around her eyes and mouth were growing more prominent as the week wore on. She couldn't rest because she knew they had work to do. The bones lying on the tables that'd been set up for her in this makeshift lab weren't just bones to her—or to him. They represented victims, victims who deserved justice for what they'd suffered.

Jonah had spent a lot of hours here, trying to help. Without the information only she could provide, he didn't even have a good place to start the investigation. But that should be changing very soon. Now that they'd arrived at an approximate victim count, which hadn't been easy due to the number of bones that'd been scattered or broken in two or more pieces, they were busy establishing the biological characteristics, the time since death and the cause and manner of death for each set of remains. The more quickly they learned what these bones could tell them, the more information he'd have with which to direct the investigation.

"I hope you're letting your girlfriend know that the woman you've been spending your nights with is old enough to be your mother." She nodded toward the phone in his hand. "Handsome guy like you…she's got to be wondering."

He grinned. "Fortunately, I don't have a girlfriend."

"Fortunately?" She settled at the next table, where she'd been piecing together pelvic bones most of the evening.

"My job can be tough on close personal relationships. The travel. The hours. You know." He shoved his phone into his pocket and went back to measuring those femurs and tibias that weren't broken. Dr. Price would use his allometry measurements to determine the general height of each victim. She'd also examine the thickness of the bones to suggest a body type.

There was a great deal of work to be done yet, and soon she'd be doing it exclusively with the help of the trained assistants who came in during the day. His strength lay on the investigative end, using the information she provided. That information just hadn't been coming quickly enough, so she'd trained him to do some of the simpler measuring.

"Close personal relationships are what will keep you sane in all this." She ran her finger over the sciatic notch of a pelvic bone. A broader notch indicated a woman; a narrower notch indicated a man. But some didn't seem particularly wide *or* narrow. She'd told him these final few were the tricky ones. That was why she'd taken a short nap. She'd hoped to come back refreshed.

Going by her frown, he wasn't sure the nap had improved her ability to decide.

"That depends on the relationship," he said. "The people closest to you can also drive you crazy."

"My best guess is female."

"If you're talking about the person driving me crazy, you'd be right," he teased, purposely misunderstanding.

She laughed. "I was talking about this victim." After making a notation, she set the pelvic bone aside. "Anyway, it's not like that for me. My family is the reason I do what I do. I want to make the world a better place... for them."

He wondered how eager she'd be to fall into another man's arms if her husband unexpectedly announced that he'd been in love with his golfing buddy all along. Jonah's experience with Lori had altered his outlook on relationships, made it difficult for him to trust. Not long after the divorce, he became good at spotting at least one fatal flaw in every woman he dated. That flaw insured his emotional safety, kept him from making any commitments.

He felt his lips twist into a humorless smile as he recalled the argument he'd once had with his mother. She'd told him he needed to stop trying to prove his desirability to every available woman he met, that he should quit thinking with his cock. Offended by her blunt assessment of his behavior and her language—she was his mother, after all—he'd snapped at her to stay out of his business, told her she didn't know what she was talking about.

But now he could see that she'd been right all along. She usually was. Unfortunately, that didn't make her any easier to put up with. No one could get on his nerves faster than she could, probably because they were too much alike. Although he wasn't nearly as high-strung or brutally frank, he was stubborn to a fault and determined to live life on his own terms. That meant he was going to take a few hits, and he had.

"Do you think you'll ever get married?" Dr. Price asked.

"Maybe someday." He didn't mention that he'd already been married. He never told anyone, hadn't even told Francesca. Tying the knot when he was so young, and for such a short period of time, to a woman who claimed she'd never been attracted to him seemed better forgotten. Only his mother and sister knew he'd been married, and the friends who'd attended the wedding, of course. But even they had no idea of the real reason for the divorce. Terrified that word would leak back to her family, Lori had begged him to keep silent about her homosexuality. How her parents could continue to believe Miranda was her "roommate" he'd never understand. Except…he hadn't seen it, either, had he? Lori just didn't fit the stereotype.

"Marriage isn't easy," she said. "But if both people go into it with the proper attitude, with real dedication and loyalty, it can work."

It hadn't worked for his parents, but as dynamic and talented as his mother was, Jonah didn't blame his father for bailing. He couldn't imagine how Wesley had remained in the relationship as long as he had. He'd stayed until Connie, Jonah's older sister, was in college and Jonah had nearly graduated from high school. That was admirable, considering it was difficult to put up with his mother for a weekend, let alone twenty years. "I'll take your word for it."

She'd started to say something else when his phone rang. Covering a yawn, he muttered, "Just a sec," and dug it out of his pocket. "Hello?"

"Mr. Young?"

"Yes?"

"Sergeant Lowe here, from the Chandler Police Department."

Immediately conjuring up the image of Francesca sitting in Investigator Finch's cubicle, scratched and bruised from her confrontation with Vaughn, he stiffened. "Is anything wrong?"

"No, Ms. Moretti is fine, but…I thought you should know…someone cut her phone line tonight."

Shoving his stool away from the table, Jonah got to his feet. *"Someone?"*

"I'm afraid we can't say who. Ms. Moretti definitely has her suspicions, but we canvassed the yard and there wasn't anyone lurking around. The good news is that we didn't see any evidence that whoever cut the line tried to enter the house."

There wouldn't be evidence. Butch Vaughn had a key. "How'd you find out about the phone line?"

"Officer Burcell was sitting in front of the house when Ms. Moretti came running into the street, clearly upset. He checked out her claims and she was right."

Jonah felt Dr. Price's attention but ignored it. "Can I talk to her?"

"I'm afraid you'll have to go by the house. It'll take some time for the telephone company to fix the line, and I'm calling from the station."

"What about the officer who's out there—Officer Burcell? He's got to have a phone."

"Burcell is currently responding to another call."

Jonah curled his free hand into an agitated fist. *"You're telling me she's all by herself?"*

Taking exception to his tone, the sergeant grew brisk. "We'll continue to drive by periodically, but we can't camp out there all night. There was no apparent threat—"

"No threat? Her phone line was cut!"

"That could've been a prank by some teenage boy. We have a whole community to protect, Mr. Young, not just this one woman," he said, and hung up.

As Jonah put away his phone, he gazed at all the cracked skulls and jawbones around him. Because teeth followed predictable maturation patterns, they were a fairly reliable indicator of certain biological characteristics, such as age. They could also help in identifying an unknown victim via dental records. Jonah couldn't wait for these bones to be connected with names, which could then turn into leads pointing to Vaughn—or someone else. He wanted to keep pushing forward here with Dr. Price so he'd have something to run with. He hated to pull out until the job was done.

But he wasn't about to leave Francesca vulnerable while he measured femurs. He'd seen the glitter in Vaughn's eyes when he'd been questioned about April Bonner. Maybe Francesca had screwed up and called a mannequin a body, but she claimed Vaughn was the last man to see April alive. It was entirely possible that he'd killed her.

Picking up the tibia he'd recently measured, Jonah turned it over in his hands, noting a fine-line fracture. Maybe Butch was responsible for the death of this poor woman, too.

Purposely avoiding Dr. Price's curious stare, he raised his eyes to take in the entire room full of bones. Maybe

Butch was responsible for *all* of them. And now that Francesca had drawn his attention, she might be next on his list.

"I've got to go," he said, and jogged out to the car he'd rented when he arrived in Arizona.

6

Jonah found Francesca sitting on her front porch with a butcher knife in one hand and a cup of coffee in the other. Judging by the weariness that hung on her like an oversize coat and her general dishevelment, she hadn't slept—or showered. But it was early, only five-thirty. The sun was just creeping over the horizon. None of her neighbors were up, so the windows around them remained dark, the street quiet. The one other person Jonah had spotted so far was the newspaper man.

"You look like hell," he said while he carried her paper across the lawn. That was a bit harsh as greetings went. But he had to compensate for the sudden jolt the sight of her, so skimpily dressed, gave his system. She wasn't wearing a bra beneath that baggy T-shirt. He'd clued into that at first glance. Then there were the short cutoffs that made her legs look like they went on forever….

Her eyes narrowed as he reached her. He half expected her to use that knife to chase him off her property. Lord knew he deserved nothing less. But Finch and Hunsacker were so pissed off about the way everything had gone down yesterday, he was her only ally when it came to Vaughn, and she must've realized it because she dropped the knife on the round table beside her and took a sip of coffee.

"Rough night, huh?"

She swallowed before answering. "He thinks he can get away with terrorizing me."

Sitting in the chair across from her, he examined the pepper spray on the table between them. "You're sure it was Butch?"

"Who else would it be?"

The faint purple of a bruise blossomed on her right knee, and her lip was still swollen, but even at her worst Francesca was classically beautiful. That hadn't changed. "Are you saying you did or didn't get a glimpse of him?"

"It was dark and he wasn't that close to the window. But I saw someone the same size and shape as Butch, no question. After he cut the phone line so I couldn't call for help, he sat at the pool throwing rocks at my window."

Stretching out his legs, Jonah crossed them at the ankle. "Not exactly the stealthy approach one might expect from a serial killer."

"It wasn't stealthy, but it was effective." She ran a hand through her hair, combing it with her fingers. "He scared the shit out of me."

"Ah, just the reaction he was looking for." Picking up the knife, Jonah pressed his thumb to the blade, which wasn't that sharp. "Is *this* your defense? What you use to chop tomatoes?"

"For your information, that's a carving knife. And it's the best weapon I've got, since I don't own a gun."

He knew why she was reluctant to own a firearm. Her father had gotten caught in the cross fire during a drug bust. Jonah might've urged her to buy one in spite of all that; he had no confidence that she'd be able to fight Butch off with a kitchen knife. But he didn't want her to fight; he wanted her to run. "You could've stayed someplace else, like I told you to."

She raised a hand. "Don't start. I can't hide out and hope this problem will take care of itself. If I do that, Butch will just be waiting for me when I return—if he doesn't catch up with me sooner."

"So how *do* you solve the problem?" He wanted to add *without getting killed,* but figured she was traumatized enough.

"By bringing him down, of course."

He turned over the knife in his hands. "That might be better left to others, Fran."

She blanched. "Don't call me that."

"Isn't that your name?"

"That's what my friends call me. It's Francesca to you."

"Not *Ms. Moretti?*"

"I'm feeling generous," she said with a shrug.

Setting the knife aside, he considered his options and decided to tackle the past. It was the only way she might let him help her. "Look. I know I'm not your favorite person. I don't blame you for hating me. If you want another apology, I'll—"

"I don't want anything from you," she broke in. "I don't even want to *see* you."

Although he'd expected a harsh response, the vehemence behind her words lacerated some part of him he hadn't realized was still vulnerable. "I get that, too," he said. "But let's not allow the mistakes of the past to make what's going on now that much worse. If we're both mixed up in this thing, we might as well pull together, get through it the best we can."

"And how do you suggest we 'pull together'?" She

hugged her legs to her chest. "By pretending you didn't do what you did?"

"You could forget about it."

"What?"

He folded his arms. "Unless there's some reason you can't."

He definitely had her attention now. "Like…"

"Like you've never gotten over me." Knowing she'd rise to *that* bait, he arched his eyebrows in challenge, and she laughed without mirth.

"Don't flatter yourself."

"Then why waste your time hating me? Let bygones be bygones so we can deal with the issue at hand."

"You're asking me to forgive you."

"Nothing that generous. I'm merely asking you to pretend we're work associates with no history."

Her dark eyes flashed with emotion. "That won't change who or what you are."

The regret he'd suffered for his behavior suddenly felt so fresh it seemed as if he'd betrayed her only yesterday. But there was no taking it back, and if he was going to have any chance of protecting Francesca, they had to get beyond previous hurts and old anger. If Butch and April were connected to the Dead Mule Canyon slayings, they'd have a better shot if everyone cooperated.

"I'm not asking you to fall back into bed with me," he said.

Her chin went up. "Good thing. You know how far you'd get with that."

"I do," he said softly, and the honesty in his admission seemed to defuse her anger.

Slumping in her seat, she stared down at her bare toes, the nails painted a sparkly gold. "Fine. I guess you're all I've got to work with. So we'll just—" she took a deep breath "—keep it professional until this case is solved."

"Great. Now that we've called a truce—" he indicated the house "—why not go in and get some rest? I'll keep the big bad wolf from the door while you're out of commission. And when you get up, you can show me everything you've collected on April Bonner. That's probably the best place to start. At least we know her identity and that she had a connection to Vaughn."

"You mean…you're going to *stay?*"

"That's exactly what I mean. You're about to keel over. You need sleep." He needed sleep, too, but he hoped his fatigue wasn't quite as apparent. At least he hadn't been stalked and scared half to death during the night.

She was tempted to accept the offer; he could tell by the way she nibbled at her swollen lip. "If you stay, that doesn't make us friends."

"I thought we just established that we're work associates."

"*Temporary* work associates."

"So…what do you have to lose? Want to get some sleep or not?"

Fatigue won out. "That'd be nice," she admitted. "For a few hours. But don't let me sleep too long. We've got a lot of work to do."

"Check out while you can. If this goes the way I think it might, you're going to need it," he said, and opened the newspaper.

Reluctant to see evidence of her life, everything he'd missed in the past ten years, Jonah remained on the porch. But all the little things he'd wondered about since he'd last seen her ran through his mind until he gave up and went inside, where he could study the photographs

on her walls and tables and guess at the people in those
photographs as well as their significance to her.

One showed her and her mother skiing. In another,
she stood in front of the Lincoln Memorial. She had a
guy with her, someone important judging by the way
they held each other, eyes dancing as they laughed into
the camera.

Frowning, Jonah decided the guy looked too…oily for
her. But the two of them appeared to be having a great
time. Was the mystery man a politician? A lobbyist?
What had taken them to Washington, D.C.? And was this
person still in her life? If so, why hadn't she asked *him*
to stay with her last night? For that matter, why hadn't
she gone to his place? Even more curious, where was he
this morning, when she really needed him?

Jonah's eyes flicked to the next picture, which showed
the same dude. He must've been special to Francesca.
Maybe he still was. Maybe he traveled a lot and was out
of town….

A photograph of Francesca with her brother and her
folks sat on the wet bar. They were in a little bistro that
made him think they'd gone to Italy as they'd always
wanted. There was a second picture of a younger Francesca with another guy—not the politician; *before* the
politician—posing at the Grand Canyon. All of this suggested she'd spent the past ten years dating and traveling,
not just working. She seemed to have gotten along fine
without him.

That made him feel slightly better. It also made him
feel slightly worse. But he didn't want to consider why.

He noticed some other photographs on the fireplace
mantel, turned to examine them and froze. The first one
was of Adriana. It'd been years since he could remember what she looked like. Now that he was reminded, he

realized that Summer showed a marked resemblance to her mother. She had the same dark blond hair and blue eyes, the same shape to her nose and face. But even at the age of nine, Summer was tall, and she was rail-thin, like he'd been growing up.

His throat so dry he could hardly swallow, he shifted his gaze to the other people in the picture. A man stood behind and to the right of Adriana, and there were kids— two boys. Obviously, she was married and had a family. In gold embossing along the bottom, it said, "The Covington Family, Adriana, Stan, Levi and Tyler—Merry Christmas, 2009." Stan was her husband. Only five foot eight or so, he was still quite a bit taller than she was. With a severely receding hairline, he appeared to be a few years older, too. Truth be told, he wasn't the handsomest guy in the world, but the kids were cute. Jonah hoped Adriana was happy. He hadn't meant to affect her life to the degree that he had. He'd been so busy self-destructing he hadn't worried about what the splatter might mean for those around him. And the way she'd always watched him, with those hungry eyes.... She'd thought she hid her feelings well. As far as anyone else was concerned, maybe that was true. But he could sense that she had a crush on him.

Would he have exploited her feelings if he hadn't been drunk that night? He wanted to believe he wouldn't have. But who could say? Maybe he really was that big an asshole.

Pulling his eyes away, he forced himself to stop looking at Francesca's pictures. His past weighed heavily enough on him. Every month, when he wrote a check to the Williamses, he wished he'd been a better person. Not because he begrudged his daughter the money. Paying for items Burt and Sylvia might not be able to afford had been his idea, his way of trying to shoulder the responsibility for his choices. Although Summer's adoptive parents had at first refused his help, they'd changed their minds once they realized he meant well and would keep his word not to interfere in their lives or try to contact her. So far he'd sent her to band camp, bought her a flute, covered some of her school clothes and paid the hospital bill when she broke her ankle in soccer. He guessed the Williamses pocketed the extra, because he'd sent a lot more than that, but he didn't care. Every once in a while they rewarded him for his financial support by sending him photographs, copies of her report cards or a picture she'd drawn in school. And that meant a lot to him. He knew the money didn't make up for what he'd done, but at least he was doing everything he could to compensate.

He wasted too much time mulling over his mistakes, wondering about Summer, how things might've been different with Francesca if he'd met her later in life, once he'd gotten his feet firmly underneath him again....

"I need some coffee." Helping himself to the grounds stored in a kitchen cupboard, he started a pot. He was just getting out a frying pan to cook some eggs when his phone buzzed to tell him he'd received a text message. Hoping it was Investigator Finch or Hunsacker sending word that they had a break in the Dead Mule Canyon case, he pulled it from his pocket. But this text wasn't about work. It came from Lori.

What a bastard you are! Why won't you answer me?

Beyond tired, he rubbed a hand over his face. He needed to respond so she'd leave him alone. He understood that it was often difficult for same-sex couples to adopt, which was why she was trying to do it as a single person instead. But, either way, he couldn't see how his reference would make any difference. It was just so typical of Lori to get some idea in her head she couldn't shake. Because she worked for her family, she felt her father's reference would be discounted due to bias and, since Jonah was essentially a cop, his word would make her look particularly appealing. *If your ex-husband will recommend you, that's saying something.*

How she expected to continue keeping her lesbianism a secret from her parents once she adopted a baby and that child started growing up and telling everyone he or she had two "moms," he didn't know. Lori insisted the child would call Miranda by her first name. Jonah doubted that would work, but he'd already expressed his opinion and she wouldn't listen to him.

There was no time to go into this again. A quick I'll get it to you soon would have to suffice for now. He was too busy to mess with writing a letter he wasn't convinced would have the slightest impact.

Good thing she didn't know he was in Arizona. She lived in Mesa, which he'd passed through on his way to Chandler. She'd insist on seeing him and wouldn't be happy when he refused.

The sound of a car door made him pause before he could finish typing in his reply. Someone had pulled into the driveway.

Slipping his phone in his pocket, he went to the window, where he could see the front grille of a blue van. He had his hand on the 9 mm in his shoulder holster when a woman came into view carrying two foam cups.

Not Butch. Adriana. She'd put on a little weight since that Christmas photograph had been taken, but there was no mistaking her identity.

Jonah wondered how she was going to feel about seeing

him again and couldn't imagine she'd be too pleased. But he had to intercept her or she'd wake Francesca.

"Why'd I have to come back to Arizona?" he grumbled, and met her at the door.

At first, she didn't notice him. She was preoccupied with fixing the lid on one of the drinks she carried. But when she glanced up to reach for the door handle and found it already open, with him standing there, her jaw dropped and so did the hand holding the cups in their cardboard container. The whipped mochas she'd brought would've spilled all over the stoop if he hadn't grabbed them.

"Jonah," she breathed, and stepped back as if any kind of contact might burn her.

"Adriana." He offered her a smile but his effort to be friendly did little to calm her.

She gave a shake of her head and self-consciously shoved the strands of hair that'd fallen from her messy ponytail back into place. Not only was she surprised, she didn't like that he'd caught her at her worst. He knew because that was exactly how his sister would've reacted to the same situation.

"I—I didn't realize Francesca had company. But that's okay. I can come back later," she said, and left the drinks behind as she fled to her van.

Jonah hadn't meant to scare her off. But he let her go. Francesca needed to get some sleep. And he wasn't eager to entertain Adriana on his own. He'd never expected to see her again. Francesca, either, for that matter.

Francesca could call her later, he decided. The fact that Adriana's picture was on the mantel and she could walk up to the house as casually as she had indicated the two were still friends. No thanks to him, of course. But that gave him one less thing to feel guilty about.

His phone vibrated with another text message. "Damn it, Lori. When you ask someone for a favor, you're not allowed to be so demanding."

He went inside to put down the cups so he could check his phone, but this time it wasn't Lori. It was Investigator Finch.

If you're up, call me.

Going into the laundry room, he closed the door so the sound of his voice wouldn't carry to the bedroom and dialed Finch's cell.

It rang twice before transferring to voice mail.

Jonah didn't leave a message. He was about to redial when the lingerie on a small rack above the dryer caught his eye. A see-through lacy black bra and matching thong hung inches from his face. They had to belong to Francesca. But who was she wearing underwear like that for? The man in the D.C. photograph?

The ringing of his phone dragged his attention away from the underwear. It was Finch.

"What's up?"

"We've got a body on our hands. A real one this time."

He gripped the phone tighter. "What did you say?"

"You heard me. Call came in less than five minutes ago. The owner of Skull Valley Chocolate and Handmade Gifts found a corpse slumped against her door when she arrived for work."

"No one else spotted it?"

"This isn't your usual downtown. It's basically four corners with a handful of businesses that are spread out. Not a lot of people out here."

"I see. Is the victim a man or woman?"

"Woman."

"Any chance she could've died of natural causes?"

"Wishful thinking, Mr. Young? No. It's a homicide."

"Do we have an ID?"

"Body was naked, no purse or anything. The shop owner was so hysterical it was tough to get a description. I did get the color of hair. Brown. That's not much, but it fits the gal Ms. Moretti's been searching for."

The one Francesca thought Vaughn had killed. "April Bonner."

"That's her."

"Are there any witnesses who can tell us what happened?"

"None that I've heard about. It's a ranching community, so not a highly populated area. There's a general store and a gas station, a café, an auto repair shop. That's it. But I'll be able to tell you more once I get there. Are you coming yourself?"

"I'm coming, but…I'm two hours away."

"I thought you had a motel here in Prescott."

"I'll explain when I see you."

"Hurry," he said.

Jonah punched the end button and let himself out of the laundry room. Francesca had only been sleeping for two and a half hours. But he was confident that she'd want to visit the scene. In any case, he wasn't going to leave her behind. The timing and placement of the body made him far too nervous that it was connected to the man who'd visited *her* last night.

7

Francesca rolled over to escape the hand that was shaking her shoulder, but the persistence of the person trying to wake her eventually pulled her through the dense fog of unconsciousness.

"Hmm…what?" Opening her heavy eyelids, she blinked at the blurry face above her, recognized Jonah and smiled. He was so handsome. The strength of his arms and the warmth of his body made her eager for his touch, so eager that she took his hand and pressed it to her cheek. It'd been so long….

Then she remembered what he'd done. They weren't lovers anymore. They weren't even *friends*.

Pushing his hand away, she scrambled up against the headboard, out of reach, and tried to collect her muddled thoughts. The salvage yard. Jonah striding toward her. The mannequin. Investigator Finch's anger. Butch by her pool. Those weren't easy memories to confront but they were what reality had waiting for her. Rested or not, she had to deal with the situation she'd fallen into yesterday and find a way out before it was too late.

"It's time to wake up *already?*" she mumbled to cover her lapse in judgment.

When he didn't answer right away, she checked to see

if he was gloating over that moment of weakness. But he didn't seem to be. A stark expression appeared on his face—until he realized she was watching. Then the mask of indifference he'd worn ever since she'd learned about Adriana fell into place. "We've got work to do," he said. "Do you need a shower?"

"Shower?" She yawned. "Wasn't it you who said I should sleep while I can?"

"That was before Investigator Finch called to tell me there's been another murder."

Those words dispelled her fatigue. "Do we know the victim?"

"We don't have a name yet. But, from the description, it could be April Bonner."

April's death was nothing more than Francesca had expected, and yet she didn't want to believe it. "No…"

"I'm afraid so."

"And all because she was lonely. All because she took a chance on the wrong guy."

He said nothing. In a way, Francesca had taken a chance on the wrong guy, too. *Him.*

"Was it Butch?"

"Might've been. The body was found in Skull Valley, which is only fifteen minutes from Prescott, even closer to his place. And we both know he was active last night."

"How does he do it? How does he slip out of his house without anyone noticing? He's got a wife, a family. Don't they wonder where he goes at night?"

"Maybe they're too afraid to face what he might be."

"Skull Valley's near the location of the burial site you've been working on, too, isn't it?" she said. "Don't tell me he dumped her in Dead Mule Canyon."

"Not quite. She was discovered on the sidewalk in front of a shop."

"Butch loses his favorite dumping ground and has to come up with an alternative, so he shoves her out in downtown Skull Valley?"

"That makes it sound like he acted out of desperation or had nowhere else to put her. I don't think that's the case. Skull Valley was probably convenient. It's small and remote, which lowers his chances of being seen. But he had other choices. There's always the desert, where he'd have even less chance of being seen."

Jonah was right. Butch had had plenty of choices. So why did he make that one? It wasn't as if he'd been in a hurry last night. He'd put the body in a public location on purpose.

"He's angry." She'd felt it, hadn't she? He was furious with all of them, especially her. "And he's trying to make a statement."

Jonah stood. "What kind of statement?"

"That he's not afraid of the police."

"That's the same message he was trying to send you last night."

"Exactly."

He motioned for her to get off the bed. "Come on. We've got a two-hour drive ahead of us."

She scooted past him. "Just give me five minutes to shower."

Francesca's eyes felt as if they were filled with sand even after her shower. She didn't have time for makeup, but she took a few seconds to rub some aloe vera on the backs of her arms and legs where the hot ground had scraped and burned her skin yesterday. She also put up her hair and swiped on some lip gloss. Then she dressed in brown linen capris with a turquoise blouse, got her Gucci sandals and went to the kitchen, where she could smell food.

It'd been a long time since she'd had a man in her house, let alone one who cooked. "Smells good. What've you got?"

Jonah stood at the window with his back to her. When he turned, she saw how bloodshot his eyes were and realized he was tired, too. The beard growth on his jaw was more pronounced than usual, but his exhaustion showed even more in a certain lethargy. Such sluggishness wasn't characteristic of someone who possessed as much energy and athletic grace as Jonah.

"Eggs," he said. "That's all you had, unless you count a six-pack of yogurt that expired three months ago. Don't you ever eat here?"

"I've been on the fly."

"Looks like it. You hungry?"

"Starved." He'd set her plate on the table across from where he'd obviously eaten. Tossing her shoes beside her chair, she headed to the coffeepot first. "But if I plan to get through this day, I need to start with a jolt of caffeine."

"You've actually got options," he said.

Although she tried not to pay attention, the pectoral muscles flexing beneath his T-shirt as he moved showed her that his chest hadn't really changed much. Maybe he was a little more muscular than when they'd dated, but he was still lean. And she had to admire the fit of his jeans. They rode low on his hips, molded perfectly to his butt and legs.

"What options?" she asked.

"You can take a thermos of the coffee I made, or—" he indicated the Starbucks cups on the counter "—have the mocha drink Adriana brought over. Although I'm afraid Adriana's offering might be melted at this point."

No longer tempted to admire his body, she stopped before she could reach the counter. He'd just mentioned her best friend, hadn't he? He'd tried to drop it into the conversation as smoothly as possible, but he was putting her on notice that Adriana knew he was there. "She… came by?"

"About thirty minutes ago."

"And brought us both a drink."

"I think the second one was meant to be hers, but… she changed her mind about staying."

For some reason, the image of Adriana coming face-to-face with Jonah made Francesca sick inside. No matter how many years passed, or how convinced she became that she was finally over him, she couldn't help imagining him and Adriana together, and that always evoked nausea. "What did she say when she saw you?"

"That she didn't realize you had company. Then she nearly dropped the drinks and ran away."

"That must've been disappointing."

"How so?"

She heard the caution in his tone but ignored it. "That's definitely not the reaction you got the last time you were alone with her," she said, then poured coffee into her travel mug.

He didn't try to justify his actions. Neither did he point out that he'd tried, numerous times, to apologize. He accepted the barb without complaint and turned back to the window. But Francesca knew she shouldn't keep letting her anger get the best of her. She couldn't berate him every time something struck a nerve. It wasn't as if he *had* to be here, had to put up with her insults. He was trying to stop a killer.

Let bygones be bygones. God, if only she could.

Closing her eyes, she drew a deep breath. "Sorry, I won't mention it again." She added a dash of cream to her coffee before putting on the lid. "Let's go."

He glanced at her breakfast. "You're not going to eat?"

She eyed the eggs and toast he'd made for her and tried to recover her earlier enthusiasm, but she knew she wouldn't be able to force it down. "I'm not hungry."

She'd just told him she was starving, but he didn't call her on it. Frowning, he retrieved her plate and rinsed the food into the garbage disposal before getting out his keys. "You can ride with me if you want."

But then they'd be stuck going everywhere together until he drove her home. And her home was two hours away from where he was currently working, so that didn't make sense. Being professional allies was one thing; spending every minute together was another. He brought what she most wanted to forget to the forefront, made it clear that she'd never loved anyone as much as she'd loved him. "No, thanks. I'll take my own car."

With a nod that suggested he was as relieved as she was, he gave her directions and left.

Jonah tried to reach Finch several times, but the investigator wasn't picking up. He probably had his hands full. No telling what he was dealing with at the crime scene. The details Jonah had already heard were pretty damn gruesome.

But it would've been nice to have something besides Francesca to concentrate on. He definitely didn't want to spend the whole drive thinking about the pictures he'd seen in her house or wondering about that politician fellow she'd been with. Nor did he want to keep reliving that moment when she first woke up and took his hand. That'd brought all the longing he'd felt for her right to the surface. He'd been just about to cup her cheek, to let himself touch her as he'd wanted to touch her all these years, when she'd suddenly realized what she was doing and withdrew.

Maybe she'd assumed he was her Washington, D.C., boyfriend. He'd been foolish to think her receptiveness to him had changed over the course of one nap. He hadn't believed it, not really. His reaction had been instinctive. Had he taken a second to consider it, he would've known better than to respond even if she did reach out to him. He'd never expected to avoid the consequences of what he'd done, didn't believe he deserved more than he'd earned. He had only himself to blame for losing Francesca. He just wished he could stop *wanting* her.

He'd thought he had. If someone had asked him yesterday whether seeing her again would affect him like this, he would've denied it. But every time he looked at her he felt the same pull that'd scared him a decade ago.

His phone rang. Figuring it was most likely Finch, he checked caller ID on his Bluetooth.

But it was his mother.

He was close enough to Skull Valley that he considered ducking the call. His mother wasn't really the type of diversion he'd been hoping for. But she'd only call back. So he decided to get it over with. "Hey, Mom."

"Where are you?" she asked.

"Driving."

"That doesn't tell me much."

"Still in Arizona, working that series of murders. Something wrong?"

"I got a call from Lori this morning."

Oh, shit. Now she was contacting his mother? "You didn't tell her I was in Arizona, did you?"

"Of course I did. Why wouldn't I?"

"Because it's none of her business, for one."

"She's upset, Jonah. She said she's been trying to get in touch with you but you won't respond."

Considering the personal information he kept hidden for Lori's sake, it took nerve for her to involve his mother. But she'd always had a lot of nerve.

Tempted to tell Rita everything, he wondered how she'd respond if he blurted out that Lori's roommate wasn't just a roommate. That Lori had been gay since before she'd married him.

But he didn't do it. Why bother? Lori didn't mean anything to him anymore, not even enough for revenge. It was simpler to pretend their problems had been far more mundane. "I've been busy," he said instead.

"Too busy to return her call?"

"Mom, she's my *ex*. That doesn't make her my top priority. Why should I drop everything when she contacts me?"

"Why not? It wouldn't hurt you to help her out."

Did she even understand what his ex-wife wanted? What had Lori told his mother that had motivated Rita to jump in with both feet? Lord knew it didn't take much, but she had to have been given some excuse. "What is it she needs?" he asked, just to see what his mother would say.

"You don't know?"

He caught a glimpse of Francesca's BMW in his rearview mirror and sped up. Murder case or no murder case, he could live without the confusion she inspired in him. "Not exactly."

"It's some sort of a character reference so she can adopt a child from the foster care system."

A child from foster care? Hardly. She was competing with other would-be parents for an unborn child. But he didn't correct her. Sometimes Rita went off half-cocked without knowing all the details. Life was easy for her—all black and white and full of snap judgments. This was a perfect example. "And how's my character reference going to make a difference?"

"I can't imagine. But she thinks it will. And it wouldn't take you more than a few minutes to do her this favor."

"Have a little faith, Mom. I'll get to it when I can."

"How about sooner rather than later, Jonah? Divorced couples don't have to be enemies, you know. Take me and your father, for instance."

He switched lanes. "Dad's remarried, Mom."

"And your point is?"

"He's never the one who has to deal with you. His wife runs interference."

"That's not true. Anyway, Jolynn and I get along."

Barely. Because he was close to his father and stepmother, Jonah knew that Jolynn was less than pleased about being Rita's designated contact. She was just better with people, better with Rita, than his father, so she got stuck with the job. "How does that relate to anything?"

"I'm encouraging you to make peace with Lori, to stop holding a grudge."

"Right. Got it. Thanks for the advice," he said dryly.

When she hesitated, he expected her to switch topics, but she didn't. Evidently, that call from Lori had her thinking about the fact that he was past thirty and still hadn't remarried. "Lori's such a good person, so supportive and friendly."

Yeah. Whenever she wanted something…

"You don't think the two of you could ever get back together, do you?"

"No. *Never.*"

She acted surprised by the absoluteness. "Wow, I never would've guessed you were so bitter. You seemed like such an ideal couple, and then it was over, just like that. I'm still not sure why you two broke—"

"Irreconcilable differences," he cut in. "I've got to check my GPS, Mom."

"So check it," she said.

"My phone won't let me talk at the same time. I'll call you later, okay?"

"Fine," she said with a huff. "But don't forget to contact Lori."

"I heard you the first time. Thanks again, Mom." He hung up. After that little stunt, Lori could wait until he got back to California for her damn letter. He didn't have time to pull over, whip out his laptop and do it now, anyway. According to his GPS, he'd passed Peeples Valley and was coming up on Kirkland. That meant he was only seven miles from Skull Valley, and Francesca wasn't far behind.

What would they find when they got there? he wondered. But nothing could've prepared him.

8

The smell drifted all the way to the car, triggering such revulsion Francesca almost couldn't force her legs to carry her the short distance to where she saw Finch and Hunsacker. They were with several police officers and a few other people, probably from the Yavapai County Medical Examiner's Office, judging by the van, working outside the chocolate and gift shop. Once she did get close, she regretted it. She'd hoped to identify April from the picture she had with her; she'd wanted to know for sure that her latest missing person had been found. April's sister, Jill Abbatiello and her husband, Vince, had been distraught ever since she didn't report for work on Monday. Of course, murder was the worst possible outcome, but it was at least an answer, which relieved the wondering and the waiting. However, the state of the corpse made visual identification impossible.

"You okay?" Jonah asked.

She hadn't realized that she'd crowded so close to him. Professional pride demanded she back up, tell him she was fine. But she was trying so hard not to retch that she couldn't move or speak. Fortunately, Finch whirled around and spotted them, interrupting before her inability to react became obvious.

"What's *she* doing here?" He addressed Jonah while hiking a thumb at her as though she wasn't standing within earshot.

Francesca understood that he was angry about yesterday, but holding a grudge over a little humiliation seemed pointless. How could he worry about something so petty in light of *this?* Not long ago, the blob of putrefying flesh sitting on the concrete had been a living, breathing human being….

As Jonah's eyes shifted to the victim, his nostrils flared, which told her he was struggling with what he saw, as well. Still, he kept his voice steady. "I thought she might be able to identify the deceased, but—"

"Actually, I'm glad you brought her," Finch broke in, and nudged Francesca as he motioned to the victim. "Now this is what a corpse looks like."

Despite the dizziness that nearly overwhelmed her, she somehow remained standing and managed to give him a dirty look as she found her voice. "No kidding."

Hunsacker joined them. "So? Do you recognize her?"

Too preoccupied to put him in his place, even when he laughed, Francesca answered without the stinging reprisal that would've been part of her response on any other day. "No."

The victim's head looked like a jack-o'-lantern that'd softened and caved in on one side. Her right eye was missing and her nose had been so badly pummeled it resembled putty more than human flesh. The features that were still distinguishable were swollen out of all proportion and her tongue protruded in a grotesque fashion.

Jonah's stoic expression melted into a grimace. "Looks as if she took a severe beating."

Finch sobered. "Like the others. You can bet she's got plenty of broken bones to go with that fractured skull."

Hunsacker rolled his feet to the outside in his habitual way. "So you think this might be the work of the same killer?"

"Dead Mule Canyon's only a few miles away," Jonah said. "The victims there were beaten, too."

"Shit." Hunsacker spat on the ground.

"Once word of this gets out…" Finch didn't finish.

Francesca was listening but it felt as if she stood at a distance too removed to participate. Mostly, she could hear her own heart pounding in her ears. The body wasn't easy to look at, but would've been worse if those wounds had been recent. The coagulated blood surrounding the woman's injuries appeared to have dried a day or two ago, based on the blackish color. It was the dirt that Francesca found curious. Tiny granulated rocks, the kind so characteristic of desert soil, clung to the woman's hair and her gaping wounds, suggesting she'd been buried and subsequently disinterred.

Why? Why would a man kill a woman, bury her, then dig her up and prop her in such a public place? How could anyone be so morbid?

Francesca didn't ask this question, but when she tuned in to the conversation again, she realized Finch had inadvertently answered it.

"He's proud of his work, eh?"

Jonah thrust his hands in his pockets. "He definitely wants it to be seen."

"What a monster," she murmured, but was this monster the same man who'd sat in her lawn chair last night throwing rocks at her window? Was it Butch?

The image of him wielding that bat popped into her mind. It was a frightening memory. But his audacity, his lack of fear, provoked her at the same time. He wouldn't get away with this. She'd make sure of it.

Anger provided some much-needed adrenaline, making it easier to stay on her feet, breathe, think. "A bat could've done this."

Hunsacker didn't seem impressed with her detective skills. Either that or he wasn't willing to credit her with much intelligence. "So could plenty of other things."

"How long do you think she's been dead?" she asked Finch, but it was Jonah who answered.

"At least thirty-six hours."

Francesca tried to rub away the goose bumps that'd jumped out on her arms. The temperature was quickly climbing and would likely top yesterday's high before the day was over, but somehow she felt chilled to the bone. "How do you know?" she asked. Having switched her specialty from employer-solicited background checks to missing persons only a year ago, she hadn't seen a lot of death.

Obviously warmer than she was, Finch loosened a tie that'd already been loosened once. As usual, he looked uncomfortable in his work clothes. "He knows it's been at least that long because there's no rigor. Rigor generally comes on in the first twelve hours, remains unchanged for twelve hours and dissipates in another twelve."

"From the bloating, I'd say it's actually been longer," Jonah added. "See the marbling? Takes a while for that to set in, even in this heat."

Because Francesca couldn't think of a worse indignity than being left sprawled on the ground, naked, for the whole world to see, and in such a horrific condition, she hadn't let her gaze fall any lower than the neck. Now that she had a reason to look, however, she could see that the woman's stomach had swollen to the size of a large watermelon. Her belly had also taken on a grayish-green cast, much like a bruise, and the inky weblike veins that showed on the torso seemed to be traveling up the neck, toward her face.

This corpse could've stepped right out of the movie *Zombieland,* Francesca thought sadly. No one should have to suffer the way this woman had. No one should be displayed in such a state.

"So how long would you say?" she pressed.

"We'll let the M.E. determine that," Finch said, but Jonah spoke at the same time.

"I'd say a good five days."

Five days… That took the murder back to Sunday, which was awfully close to Saturday, the night April Bonner had met Butch Vaughn at the Pour House.

Francesca sat alone at a table in the Palace Restaurant and Bar in downtown Prescott. Touted as the oldest frontier saloon in Arizona, the Palace had been in operation since 1875 or thereabouts. But, according to the story she'd read on a placard posted here in the historic district, in 1900 a drunken miner kicked over a kerosene lamp and started a fire that destroyed most of the town, including the Palace and a lot of other saloons on what was then called Whiskey Row. Even the state's first capitol building, a log cabin, had burned to the ground.

Fortunately, some of the men who were there that night were either sober enough or smart enough to drag the highly carved bar, which had come all the way from New Jersey, out of the Palace and into the street. They continued to drink and watch the fire from there, but when the saloon was rebuilt a year later, the bar took its rightful place once again. Now it stretched along the wall to Francesca's left. Memorabilia, including guns, ammunition, money and other artifacts from the 1800s, as well as bits and pieces of information about Palace regulars like Doc Holliday, the Earp Brothers and Big Nose Kate, hung on the rest of the walls. She studied these relics as she listened to a honky-tonk piano player, who was dressed in period costume, and waited for her burger.

Hungry though she was after skipping breakfast, she doubted she could eat. What she'd witnessed in Skull Valley was too new, too present in her mind. She'd spent an hour with Jonah and the investigators at the sheriff's station afterward, sharing what she knew about April, but that suddenly seemed like a thimbleful of information compared to what there should have been to adequately represent a life. April had never been married. She'd had just two romantic relationships in her life, only one that lasted a year. She'd been thrilled to finally meet someone when she began e-mailing back and forth with "Harry Statham." All the other teachers at her school, even the principal, talked about how happy the promise of their "love" had made her. And Francesca could see why. Harry had pretended to be everything a woman could want. Claiming he was a widower who'd lost his wife six months earlier, he'd flattered her with compliments on her picture and the cleverness of her responses, told her he wanted to take care of her for the rest of her life and keep her safe. He'd sent her gifts, too.

Francesca had read the e-mails she'd found on April's computer, but thinking of them hit her harder today than ever, and she wasn't ready to drive home yet. After losing her purse, her cell phone, her car and office keys, even the security she'd once enjoyed at her house, she felt she'd been cast adrift, somehow cut off from regular life. She couldn't even retreat to Adriana's, which would've been natural for her under any other circumstances. Suddenly, after more than a decade, Jonah stood between them again. No way did she want to discuss his presence at her place this morning, but she knew any conversation they had would be awkward if she didn't.

So she'd chosen to recuperate at the Palace. The old saloon wouldn't remind her of the years she'd spent in the police academy and, subsequently, as a rookie cop with Jonah, her confrontation with Butch yesterday, the body at the gift shop or the fact that this morning's find might be connected to April Bonner's disappearance as well as seven other murders. She loved history, spent at least one weekend a month visiting Arizona's many ghost towns. But the upbeat music, the chatter of the tourists who streamed through, the high ceilings and wooden floors, didn't carry her away as she'd hoped. She kept picturing the abused corpse propped outside the gift shop and thinking about the bat Butch had wielded so eagerly.

Whoever had killed that woman had done so in a brutal manner. If it was Butch, he was one sick bastard. And that sick bastard seemed to have become fixated on her. She even wondered if he'd dug April—assuming this *was* April—out of the ground and placed her in the center of Skull Valley as some sort of message. Why would he provide the police with a body, which could offer so much evidence and other information, unless he had a compelling reason?

Yesterday's events could've given him that compelling reason. She'd gone to his salvage yard to search for April and brought the police down on him. And he'd basically flipped her off by delivering what she wanted in any condition but the way she preferred.

He was the real deal. So why hadn't he tried to enter

her house when he had her in such a vulnerable position last night? Why had he settled for letting her know what he *could* have done?

Because he thought he could get to her anytime he wanted....

The waitress appeared with her meal.

Francesca managed to smile and offer a brief thanks, and then attempted to eat a French fry or two. But she couldn't taste the food and her stomach felt too queasy to force it down.

Giving up without touching her burger, she tossed fifteen bucks on the table and left the relative safety of the Palace. As much as she wanted to blend in with the shoppers outside and be anonymous for a while, she needed to get to a pay phone and call her assistant. Heather must be going crazy. She hadn't heard from Francesca all day. They usually kept in fairly close touch. But then, Francesca usually had a cell phone.

That was what she needed to solve first, she decided. She had to shake off her fatigue and her reaction to the events of the past twenty-four hours and buy a new cell. While she was waiting for her phone to be activated, she could use one of the other phones at the store to call Heather; Heather could make sure her home line was repaired and check in with the locksmith, who hadn't been able to leave a message because of her severed line.

But in order to buy a new phone, she needed to withdraw some money from the bank. And without her ATM card or her ID that wouldn't be easy.

Fortunately, she knew the manager of her local branch. She could only hope he'd believe her about her purse being stolen. She'd try to get there before closing and hit the DMV tomorrow. There wouldn't be enough time to do everything in what was left of today.

Butch had put her in a real bind.

And this might be just the beginning.

"Hey, I'm taking off."

Jonah blinked, realized where he was and lifted his head off the desk to see Dr. Price at the door. He'd gone into the back office to check his e-mail and contact a forensic profiler he'd used in the past and must've fallen asleep. Fatigue still dragged at him, but he was hoping he'd feel better in a few minutes. At least he'd had a nap. "Good. You need a break, a chance to return to regular life," he told her.

"I don't really have a choice. It's my daughter's birthday and I promised to watch the kids so she and her husband can go to dinner. You can't let work take over completely, you know? You have to draw a line somewhere."

He got the impression that pep talk was aimed more at herself than him, but she was right. She needed to be there for her kids, despite the case they were working on. "I agree."

She arched a motherly eyebrow at him. "I hope you're going to leave, too."

"Why's that?"

"Because a two-hour nap won't compensate for all the sleep you've lost in the past few days. We can't run ourselves into the ground, Jonah. We've got to be fresh in order to do our jobs."

That was true, too. But in a situation where every minute counted, taking time off felt as if he was putting lives at risk. After this morning, he was more motivated than ever to remain vigilant. "Does that mean you'll be heading home after you babysit?"

A wry smile curved her lips. "We'll see what time the lovebirds get back."

"Right." He chuckled at her evasive reply, knew that if the "lovebirds" got home early she'd wind up here until midnight or after. "Have you heard from Finch or Hunsacker?" he asked before she could go.

"No."

"Thanks. Enjoy your grandkids. And be safe."

"I will. Get some dinner, okay?" She threw those parting words over her shoulder. Then he heard the main door close as she went out and checked his phone for a list of the calls he'd missed while he was asleep.

Nothing from the investigators. Had they heard from the pathologist? Had they been able to identify the body they'd removed from Skull Valley this morning? It was a bit early to hope they had, but Finch had said the M.E. planned to do the autopsy right away. That was exactly what Jonah thought should happen. Because they were looking at such a prolific killer, the wheels of justice needed to move a lot faster than usual.

With a yawn, he scrubbed his face with one hand and continued down the list of missed calls. He hadn't heard from Francesca, either. Other than leaving a message with her assistant, which he'd already done, he had no way of getting in touch with her.

He should've brought her here after their meeting so she could see what they were working with. But she'd left the sheriff's station rather suddenly, while he was speaking to Finch and Hunsacker about the woman who found the corpse. He hadn't gone after her because he'd known that what she'd seen had upset her. He'd felt she needed some space.

Now he regretted giving her that space. He had no idea where she was or where she planned to spend the night. He hoped it wasn't at home again. Maybe Butch had only been playing with her when he showed up next to her pool last night, but a man like that could get serious very fast.

Taking a deep breath, he dialed Finch, who answered immediately.

"Investigator Finch."

"Hey, where are you?"

"At the morgue with Dr. Jernigan. We're in the middle of the autopsy."

"Anything useful?"

"Lacerations in the vaginal cavity suggest she was raped."

"Before or after death?"

"Before."

"And the cause of death?"

"Blunt-force trauma. Unless she was also poisoned, which we won't know until we get the tox screens back."

Blunt-force trauma came as no surprise. Neither did the rape. "Is there any trace evidence that might help us identify her attacker?"

"No, but now we have a better chance of identifying the victim without having to resort to dental records, although we'll probably go that route just to confirm."

"What are you talking about?"

"She has a tattoo on her inside right thigh—a butterfly emerging from a cocoon."

Jonah rubbed the razor stubble on his chin, realized he hadn't shaved or showered today and decided to head over to his motel so he could clean up. "That seems pretty distinctive," he said as he shut down the computer he'd been using. "Did April Bonner have a tattoo like that?"

"We're trying to find out. I've contacted Mesa P.D. but the detective in charge of the case is out on a family emergency and the guy who's stepping in for him hasn't even had time to look at the file. He said he'd dig it out and get back to me, but I'm guessing I won't hear from him until tomorrow."

"Francesca might know whether April had a butterfly tattoo." He took his car keys out of his pocket and turned off the lights in the office. "If she doesn't, she could always check with the sister who hired her."

"I thought of that, but I can't reach her."

"Her cell's gone and her home phone's out. I told you what happened last night."

"I know. I was hoping the home line had been fixed, but whenever I call, it rings off the hook."

Jonah's eyes skimmed over all the bones, broken and otherwise, lying on the tables in the main room as he let himself out. Two of Dr. Price's helpers were still working. They glanced up when they heard his voice and waved goodbye.

"That's probably not unusual," he told Finch. "Depending on workload, it could take the phone company a week or two to get out there." But being unable to reach Francesca made him uneasy all the same. "What about her office?"

"Tried that. Spoke to some receptionist who said she'd give her a message. Past few hours the receptionist hasn't even picked up. My call transfers directly to voice mail."

The assistant, someone named Heather, had promised to relay a message for Jonah, too, but that was it. She wouldn't share any information on whether or not her boss was in, had been in or would be in. "Shit."

"You seriously think Francesca might be next on

Butch's list?" Finch sounded skeptical. Or maybe he only wished the situation wasn't what it seemed.

Jonah's rented Volvo chirped as he pressed the unlock button on his key ring. "You don't?"

"That'd be pretty damn bold. He's got to know that if she gets hurt, he instantly becomes our number-one suspect. Would he really put himself right between our crosshairs?"

The heat of the day had blasted Jonah like a furnace the second he walked outside, but the inside of the car was even hotter. "No matter what we suspect, we'd still have the burden of proving it. And he thinks he can out-smart us."

"You really believe he's that confident?"

Jonah slipped on his sunglasses, started the engine and cranked the air conditioner to high before taking off. Fortunately, his motel wasn't far. About the time the interior of the car grew comfortable, he'd be getting out again. But it would be insufferable without *some* air coming through those vents. "He outsmarted us yesterday, didn't he? We were forced to leave with our tails between our legs while he kept Francesca's personal belongings."

"That wasn't *our* fault."

"Maybe it was. Maybe there was something in that salvage yard Hunsacker should've seen or found or suspected. He couldn't have performed a very thorough search, not in the time they were there. They had ten acres to cover. And let's face it, he was probably shown that mannequin, thought he understood what had caused the problem and decided he was wasting his time, so he searched with half an eye. Either way, Butch Vaughn won. Easily. And I'm sure that only confirmed his belief that he can get away with anything."

Silence. Then Finch said, "Hunsacker admits he

could've performed a more thorough search. I've discussed it with him. He was embarrassed when he saw the mannequin and started to backpedal in case he invited a lawsuit or some blight on his record."

"There you go."

"Stealing a purse is a far cry from murder, though."

"He was the last person to see April Bonner alive. Even if the body at the morgue isn't April, she's still missing. *Something* happened to her after she met up with Butch Saturday night."

"All right, all right," he said. "I'll put Vaughn under surveillance until we can figure out what the hell is going on."

"That should help." If Finch had a couple of uniforms keep an eye on Butch, Francesca could go home tonight. She might even be able to begin rebuilding her sense of security. Jonah felt better already. "I'll see if I can get in touch with her, tell her what's going on and find out if she knows anything about a tattoo."

"How are you gonna do that? Drive all the way out there?"

"If I have to," he said, and hung up. But he knew he had one other option. Adriana would probably be able to tell him where to find Francesca or how to reach her. Maybe Francesca was even at her house. But contacting the woman with whom he'd made the biggest mistake of his life wasn't something he wanted to do.

9

Adriana had never expected to hear from Jonah again. After that night when she'd taken him home with her, they'd spoken only a few times. He'd apologized the following morning, as soon as he saw he was in her bed, even though what'd happened was more her fault than his, and he hadn't called her after that.

No doubt it would've ended there, but then she'd found out she was pregnant and arranged to meet him. When she broke the news about the baby, he'd responded calmly, politely. Except for the sudden tightening of his jaw, he'd been careful not to reveal how upset he was. To his credit, he'd assumed full responsibility and said he'd pay for whatever she chose to do. But when he asked her what that might be, she'd had to face the truth—he was offering her money to fix his mistake. He wasn't suddenly realizing that he'd loved her all along. Sleeping with him hadn't changed anything. Being pregnant didn't change anything, either. He'd never cared about her the way he cared about Francesca, and he never would.

Adriana couldn't remember anything else in her life ever hurting quite as much as his rejection. It wasn't that she'd meant to get pregnant. She hadn't. They'd used protection. But she couldn't deny that she'd harbored some hope that the baby would bring them together. She'd wanted Jonah badly enough that she'd risked her relationship with Francesca, and would've done so again if he'd been the least bit receptive. Which made her feel like the worst person in the world. What kind of woman stabbed her best friend in the back over a guy? It didn't help to see how heartbroken and regretful *he* was because of what they'd done. She'd never forget his hollow-eyed, haggard appearance when he met her that night at Starbucks. She remembered thinking at the time that he must not have slept since they'd been together.

She still felt guilty about her role in what had occurred. Nothing would've happened if she hadn't chosen to believe his drunken advances actually meant he had feelings for her. So she was grateful when Francesca had managed to forgive her. Somehow, they'd repaired their friendship and put her actions behind them. She'd thought it was all over, at last.

And now this. Jonah was back. She'd seen him at Francesca's this morning, and he was on the phone with her right now.

"How'd you get my number?" She glanced into the living room where her two boys had been watching TV but were currently wrestling on the floor. Normally, she would've scolded them. She was afraid someone would get hurt or knock over a lamp. But today she let them go. At least they were occupied and didn't seem to notice that she was suddenly having difficulty breathing.

"You're listed under your husband's name," he said, "which I saw on a picture at Francesca's."

Had he felt a little tug when he'd seen that picture? Something had made him memorize her husband's name....

But that was exactly the type of thinking that'd gotten

her into trouble before. None of this meant what she wanted it to. "Why are you calling?"

"I'm sorry. I know this is unexpected and…awkward, at best. I wouldn't have bothered you, except…I'm looking for Francesca."

Of course. Why else would he contact her? If she hadn't been so blinded by desire ten years ago—desire and selfishness—she would've been able to see the truth even then. "She's not here."

"Have you heard from her today?"

"No." The rumble of a car engine brought her to the kitchen window. Her husband had just come home from his office downtown, where he ran his medical practice. Hoping it would take him a few minutes to greet the kids before he came looking for her, she dashed up the stairs to their bedroom and closed the door. He knew about Jonah and the baby she'd given up. She'd told him all about it when they were dating. But she was sure he assumed, as she had until this morning, that if she ever met Jonah again he'd have no effect on her.

"Can I give you my number, in case she does get in touch with you?" Jonah asked.

That was it? They'd created a child together but he had nothing more to say to her than "please give my number to Francesca"? He hadn't asked about her husband, her kids, how she'd been…

She closed her eyes. "I— Sure. Why not?" She *had* to agree, didn't she? A refusal might inform him of how she felt—reveal her pounding heart and sweating palms. She loved all she had, but Jonah reminded her of old dreams and what it was like to be young, to experience the kind of bone-melting desire that could burn out of control.

"Thanks. You ready?"

"Yeah." She jotted his number on the pad her husband

kept by the bedside for when he awoke with a thought he didn't want to forget. Then she ripped off that sheet, folded it into a tiny triangle and slipped it in her back pocket.

"What—what brought you back?" she asked before he could hang up.

She already knew about the cases in Prescott; she was really inquiring about finding him at Francesca's house, and he seemed to understand that.

"I don't know," he said. "I guess the price we paid wasn't high enough."

A click signaled that he'd disconnected just as she heard her husband coming up the stairs. "Adriana? Where are you, babe?"

"I put a clean towel on the back of the toilet, in case you get up before me and want a shower."

Shifting her attention from her laptop, which was open on the kitchen table, Francesca conjured up a smile for Heather's sake. Nearly six feet tall and bone thin, her assistant had a pale face and long dark hair with streaks of blond that came from a bottle. "Thanks. I really appreciate your help."

"No problem. *Mi casa es su casa.* Such as it is," she added with a shrug. "You need anything else?"

"No, this is great." Although she'd tried to infuse her voice with enthusiasm, Francesca considered those words a fairly transparent lie. She'd never felt so out of place, never dreamed it'd be necessary to spend the night with her twenty-two-year-old employee. For one thing, Heather lived in a small apartment and didn't have room for guests. For another, as a single mother caring for a three-year-old boy, she already had her hands full. Francesca didn't want to be an imposition.

But she couldn't face going home. Not tonight. So what if she was doing the exact opposite of what she'd told Jonah she'd do? And so what if a small part of her felt sheepish for wimping out? She was too emotionally and physically spent to deal with returning to the house. It didn't matter that Heather had met the locksmith and had the locks changed. Francesca no longer felt safe. She needed to get some sleep without having to worry that Butch might pay her another visit as soon as she closed her eyes. It wasn't as if she could go to a hotel. She'd ordered a new debit card and replacement credit cards before going to the Apple store to get another iPhone, but they were coming in the mail and wouldn't arrive for several days. Until then, she couldn't do anything that required a card.

She supposed she could've stayed with Adriana…. But she couldn't handle the complexity of their relationship right now. It was hard enough coping with the feelings Jonah had dredged up.

The unopened messages waiting in her in-box beckoned to her. Reading her e-mail brought a measure of relief because it felt normal. She could get lost in work and forget that she was sitting in an unfamiliar kitchen with cracked linoleum, secondhand furniture and a noisy dishwasher so old it hooked up to the sink. But she needed to be polite, didn't want to ignore Heather. "Sean down for the night?" she asked, making small talk.

Heather responded while gathering up her son's toys and piling them in a toy box shaped like a plastic turtle. "For the time being. Lately, he's been getting up a lot. The doctor said I shouldn't be too quick to respond when he calls out for me, so don't worry if I let him fuss a little. I'm trying to teach him to sleep through the night so I won't have to go through my days feeling like the walking dead."

"No problem. Do whatever you have to. I'm not here to get in the way." Francesca wasn't even sure she'd be able to hear Sean. Her bed was in the living room, on the lumpy sofa.

As she bent to retrieve the last toy, Heather's shirt rose up, revealing a large tattoo on her back—Alberto, the name of Sean's father. In prison for armed robbery, he still had nearly two years, but Heather was determined to wait for him. He'd promised to marry her when he got out, make them a family, and each square of the calendar on her wall showed a number—the days left in his term. Six hundred and thirty as of today, which sounded like an eternity to Francesca. She often wondered how Heather tolerated having the man she loved locked up. But Heather never complained. She'd had a rough childhood and didn't seem to expect a lot out of life.

Finished with the toys, she stretched her back. "Okay, well, I know it's early for bed, but I'm going to turn in, if you don't mind."

It was only ten after nine, but it felt much later than that. Francesca planned on following her example, just as soon as she'd downloaded all the information that'd been stored in the iPhone she'd lost. Fortunately, she had a copy of everything on her computer. God bless the iPhone and its syncing ability. "I don't mind a bit. Get some sleep while you can, huh?"

"You, too. You could use it." She headed down the hall but turned back before reaching the bedroom. "I almost forgot—we were so busy this afternoon—but you got a ton of messages today. I brought them home, just in case you weren't coming in tomorrow." Twisting her hair up and fanning her neck, she went to her purse, which was sitting on the counter, and eventually handed Francesca a stack of messages fastened with a paper clip.

"You might want to check your voice mail, too, if you haven't already," she said. "Some of the people who called wanted to be transferred. Others had me take a message."

"Will do. 'Night." Francesca listened to Heather's steps recede as she started through her messages. Jillian Abbatiello's name was at the top of the stack. No doubt she'd also left a message on voice mail. April's disappearance was so recent, they talked every day. Jill had to be wondering where Francesca had disappeared so suddenly. Francesca hadn't called her because she wasn't sure whether or not to tell Jill and Vince about the body in Skull Valley. Wouldn't it be better to wait until she knew whether or not that corpse was April?

But no word was agony, too. Which was worse for April's family?

Deciding to hold off until tomorrow morning, she set the message aside. Investigator Finch's name was on the next slip. The two after that came from Jonah. All three said the same thing. "Call ASAP."

Did they have new information? If so, it might solve the dilemma of what to tell Jill and Vince.

Disregarding the rest of her messages, she called Jonah first. Finch hadn't fully forgiven her for embarrassing him. Jonah would be more forthcoming with any details the M.E. managed to find, anyway.

"Hello?"

She felt a flutter in her stomach the moment she heard his voice—and cursed her weakness. "It's me."

"Jeez, it's about time you called. You scared the shit out of me, you know that? You can't go dropping off the face of the earth and expect me not to think the worst, Francesca."

Covering her eyes, she tried to rub away some of her fatigue—and wished she could ignore her appreciation of his voice. They used to talk for hours on the phone, whenever they couldn't be together in person. "Sorry. I've been busy putting my life back in order, as much as that's possible in one afternoon. I'm not used to anyone keeping tabs on me, so I wasn't aware I should check in."

"After this morning? Are you *nuts?*"

"I understand why you might've thought the worst. But you can relax. I'm fine."

"Where are you?"

Her eyes circled the room, taking in the old wooden cupboards, which had been repainted so many times they hardly closed, the chipped enamel sink, the 1960s table and chairs covered in lime-green vinyl upholstery, the ancient toaster. Did she really want to tell him? He might wonder why she hadn't chosen to stay with Adriana, and she'd rather he didn't realize he still had the power to tear them apart. "How do you know I'm not home?"

"Because *I'm* at your house."

She sat up straighter. "Why?"

"When I couldn't find you anywhere else, I thought maybe you'd eventually come here."

"But…it's locked. How'd you get in?"

"I didn't." His yawn came through the phone. "I fell asleep on the porch while I was waiting for you."

"You're kidding."

"No. Why?" He'd obviously noted the sharp edge to her voice.

"Because Butch doesn't like you any better than he does me," she snapped. "You're lucky he didn't decide to stop by and bash your head in while you were taking your snooze."

"I didn't fall asleep on purpose, Francesca."

Pushing out of her chair, she began to pace. "It doesn't matter. Just leave. Get out of there now. Don't you have a—a wife or a girlfriend or something who'd be unhappy about you taking such risks?"

"I have neither. And I've got my gun. I'll use it if necessary."

She imagined how easy it would've been to sneak up on him while he was unconscious. "Now that you're awake, shooting an assailant might be a possibility."

"A distinct possibility. I have nothing to worry about."

"Fine." She wiped the image from her mind. She was so rattled she perceived danger lurking around every corner. Maybe she was overreacting, assuming Butch was a threat to everyone.

And maybe it was true…

Either way, Jonah was merely a work associate responsible for his own safety. She had to remember that.

Sidling up to the window, she parted the curtains to stare out at the empty, second-story landing. "So… why'd you call me earlier? What's happening with the body?"

"The M.E. finished the autopsy two hours ago."

"And?"

"The victim was raped before she was killed."

She didn't want to acknowledge that. "Anything else?"

"She has a small tattoo on the inside of her right thigh."

Francesca experienced a surge of hope. She couldn't imagine such a straightlaced teacher getting a tattoo.

Maybe that corpse wasn't April Bonner, after all. But when she hung up so she could call Jill and ask, she didn't like the answer. Yes, April had such a tattoo.

They'd found her.

Francesca explained the situation as gently as she could. She even spoke to Vince, who got on the extension. The Abbatiellos were understandably broken-hearted; it made her feel terrible that she could offer no solace, except the promise that she'd do all she could to bring April's killer to justice.

By the time she said goodbye, she was clammy with sweat that wasn't entirely due to the minimal air-conditioning in Heather's apartment. Pressing her forehead to the glass of the picture window in the living room, she called Jonah back. "It's her. Jill just told me they each got a butterfly tattoo on April's thirtieth birthday."

"You might want to have her draw a picture of it, just to be sure," he said.

"I will—tomorrow. Let's give her and Vince tonight to deal with their grief."

"They'll check the victim's dental records, too," he said, "but it sounds pretty certain."

"That means Butch is the killer, Jonah," she said.

"We don't have any proof of that yet," he reminded her.

"In a way, we do. He was done with her. He'd already buried her. He would've left her where she was if it wasn't for me."

"How do *you* figure into this?"

"Digging her up and leaving her for the police was his way of taunting me, scaring me, making me feel powerless."

There was a long pause. "I hope you're wrong about that."

"I'm not. He's proud of his work, as Finch said earlier. And he wants to prove his superiority to the police. He's left all the other people he's murdered in the ground, hasn't he?"

"As far as I know. We're the ones who dug up the bodies in Dead Mule Canyon."

"Exactly. Are you prepared to tell me it isn't the same guy? You think we have *two* killers going around raping and beating women to death in such a sparsely populated area? No. He dug up April because of me, to show me what I have to look forward to."

"Don't even say that," he said. "Anyway, I've convinced Finch that we need to keep an eye on Butch. They'll be watching him."

"Starting when?"

"Tonight, I hope. If they're not there now they should be soon."

That news brought some relief, at least for the moment. She could go home tomorrow and enjoy a short reprieve from the anxiety that'd been pumping through her blood like oxygen. But what if one week led to the next and Butch never acted suspicious? The police couldn't sit there indefinitely. He could outwait them. What with budget constraints, it wouldn't even be hard—a few weeks, a month at most. And then…

Something jumped from the roof onto the landing, causing Francesca to rear back. She dropped her phone before realizing it was only a cat. A *black* cat…

"What's wrong? Francesca? You there?" Jonah's voice came to her as if through a tunnel when she retrieved her cell.

"Sorry. I was…startled by a cat, that's all." She

managed a laugh but, with her heart still racing, knew it only revealed how frazzled she was.

"You okay?"

"Of course," she said. But she couldn't help being a little spooked. Maybe it was her imagination, but that cat seemed like a harbinger of doom. It stared boldly up at her with its unblinking, tawny eyes. Then it twitched its tail and sauntered away.

So what if it was black? she told herself. She wasn't superstitious.

"Fine. Call me if anything comes up," Jonah said.

"You do the same." A click confirmed that he was gone.

Trying to relax despite what they'd learned, she drew a deep breath, but before she even set her phone aside, another call came in—from Unknown Sender.

10

Having lost sight of the cat, Francesca let the drapes fall into place and answered her phone on the way back to her laptop. "Hello?"

"Is this Francesca Moretti?"

She didn't recognize the voice, and it was a little late for a sales call. "Yes…"

"This is Dean Wheeler."

"Who?"

"Paris's brother."

Thinking this had to be a referral from a previous client, she sank into the seat she'd occupied earlier. "I'm afraid I don't remember a Paris."

"Paris Vaughn. Butch's wife?"

She'd been about to shut down her computer, but as she heard this, her fingers hovered in midair. Was her caller the slim young man who'd watched the events at the salvage yard with such ambivalence? It had to be. He spoke as if she should know him. "What can I do for you, Dean?"

"I wanted to tell you I've found your purse."

She closed her laptop without bothering to power it down. "What did you say?"

"The purse you lost?"

There'd been no "losing" involved. Butch had stolen it from her. But she didn't insist on the truth. She preferred to see where this was going. "You're prepared to return it to me?"

"Of course, now that I've found it."

She listened for proof that Dean wasn't alone but couldn't hear anything—no voices, no television, no car engine in the background. "I appreciate that. Where was it?"

"In the salvage yard, just like you thought. Isn't that strange? I don't know how we missed it."

Could Dean really expect her to believe it had been overlooked, when she knew exactly where she'd dropped it and under what circumstances?

What was going on here? Was Dean trying to do her a favor? Or was he somehow in league with Butch?

"Your wallet's inside and everything," he added, as if she should be inordinately pleased.

"And my phone?"

"Yep. That, too."

"How'd you get my number?"

"It's on your checks."

Of course. Her address was there, too. Her business cards provided her office information. Her telephone contained a complete list of all her friends, clients and associates, as well as a detailed calendar of upcoming appointments. Her video card gave the location where she rented her movies. Her key ring held the supersaver card for her local grocery store. Heck, anyone who got hold of her purse could even tell what kind of tampons she used.

She'd never considered just how much information her purse might reveal about her—until she'd lost it.

"Would you like to come by and pick it up?" Dean was saying.

Had he forgotten what had occurred during her last visit? This guy wasn't quite...*normal*. He acted as if she and Butch liked each other, as if there'd never been any trouble. "I don't think so, Dean. That brother-in-law of yours is a bit too dangerous for me to feel comfortable walking onto the property again."

"Oh, Butch won't care if you come. He told me I could call you."

She felt her eyebrows slide up. "He did?"

"Of course. He doesn't need a woman's purse." He laughed as though he found the words *Butch* and *purse* in the same sentence incredibly funny.

So why would Butch return her belongings? Because he already had all the information he could get and wanted to draw her back to Prescott? Or was there another reason for making it available to her?

"Are you coming?" he asked.

She'd already canceled her credit cards; it was too late to save them. But she could sell her old iPhone, and she'd spent nearly three hundred dollars on the purse itself. Then there was her driver's license. Just avoiding a trip to the DMV was worth trying to make some sort of arrangement. "Can you meet me somewhere off-site?"

She hoped that by getting Dean alone and away from the watchful eye of his brother-in-law, she might be able to talk to him. If Butch was really the person who'd killed all those people in Dead Mule Canyon, the members of his household must have noticed *something* amiss.

"I don't know about that," Dean hedged. "Butch said to have you pick it up here."

"I could ask the police to get it for me."

"No, I don't think he wants the police to come back."

Was this a personal challenge, then? Was Butch trying to determine how frightened she was? Whether or not he'd managed to cow her with his middle-of-the-night appearance and the stomach-turning proof of what he'd done to April Bonner?

If so, making her fearful had to be important to him. It was possible that he intended to strip away her sense of well-being and security, make her paranoid, before he finished her off. In that case, she probably stood a better chance of putting off a life-and-death encounter if he believed he hadn't yet attained his goal.

He hadn't, had he? Okay, so she didn't go home tonight. And maybe she spent too much time looking over her shoulder and jumping at anything that moved—like that damn cat. But she wasn't about to let him win whatever he'd started between them. "So what are you saying?"

"You can pick it up here if you want it."

Her mind ran through various scenarios. She supposed she could go in with a wire, have the police waiting in the wings in case of trouble. Maybe Butch would threaten her or do something that would make it possible for Finch and Hunsacker to arrest him. Getting him off the street would certainly be worth the risk, especially if they could hold him until they gathered enough evidence to prosecute him for April's murder.

"Fine," she said. "When?"

"Tomorrow?"

"What time?"

"First thing in the morning."

"Ten is the earliest I can make it. As Butch knows,

from having driven to my house yesterday, I live two hours away."

"Are you hoping I'll confirm that he was gone?"

"And if I am?" Dean was odd. Different. Would his testimony even help?

"I was sound asleep last night," he said.

"And the other nights? He's left before. I'm sure of it."

"I don't want to talk about Butch. There are too many other interesting subjects."

"Like…"

"Your friends."

"What about them?"

"They're *really* nice. And they think so highly of you. You should be proud."

Francesca brought a hand to her chest. "What are you talking about?"

"Adriana and Josephine and Heather. I like them all."

Josephine was her aging neighbor. After having both knees replaced two weeks ago, she could barely get around. No way could she defend herself against someone like Butch. "How would you know my friends?" she breathed.

"I called them earlier, when I was trying to get hold of you. I went through your address book. I like the way you categorize. You make it easy to tell friends from clients. I even left a message at your office with that nice Heather person who said she's your assistant."

What the heck? Bracing the phone with her shoulder, Francesca shuffled through the messages she'd set aside. Sure enough, there was one from Dean Wheeler. Because it didn't mention her purse—just his name and number—it wouldn't have meant a thing to her even if she'd seen it.

"I'm glad you kept the same cell number," he said. "You never pick up at home."

Could he be as oblivious as he was making it sound? Or was he laughing at her? "The line's been cut."

"Really?"

Had he already known? She couldn't quite tell.... "Really."

"How long will it take to get that fixed?"

She ignored the concern in his voice, wasn't sure she could trust him. "The telephone company will get to it as soon as they can." Due to recent layoffs, they had a backlog of work orders and couldn't send someone out right away. But she didn't add that.

"That must be a relief. Well, just so you know, Adriana's been trying to reach you. You should give her a call. She's worried about you getting your purse back. She even offered to drive over here and pick it up."

So why had Dean refused? Francesca was curious about that, but didn't ask. She didn't want to make Adriana a focal point. The last thing she needed was for the people closest to her to come to the attention of someone like Butch or his odd brother-in-law. "No reason to drag my friends into this. We've got it covered, right?"

"Now we do. I'll let you go. But please tell Heather I hope her son sleeps through the night."

He knew where she was staying! She got the feeling he'd been following her, but it was more likely that he'd spoken to Heather just before she'd left the office to pack Francesca's overnight bag while Francesca was at the Apple store. Regardless, like Butch—maybe because of Butch—he was trying to frighten her.

"Quit it," she said flatly.

"Quit what?"

"Mentioning my friends. They have nothing to do with you or Butch or whatever's going on here, so just leave them out of it."

"What do you mean 'going on'? I was only trying to be nice."

If that was true, why did she have alarm bells going off in her head? "It's Butch I'm worried about," she said.

"He's not what you think he is, Francesca. Really."

The way he used her first name, as if they knew each other, grated on her, too. "Tell April Bonner that."

"Who?"

"The woman your brother-in-law met last Saturday at the Pour House. Her body turned up this morning outside the Skull Valley Chocolate and Handmade Gifts shop, less than fifteen minutes from your house."

Another voice came on the line, this one louder and blatantly taunting. "You sure it wasn't a mannequin?"

Francesca recognized Butch's laugh. "You think it's funny?"

"I think *you're* funny," he said, still laughing.

"Why'd you move her, Butch? Don't tell me you went to all that trouble just for me."

The laughter suddenly stopped. "*Nothing's* too much trouble for you."

Swallowing hard, she gripped the phone more tightly. "Good. Because the forensic evidence you provided will come in handy when the investigation moves into the prosecution phase."

She hadn't said *if;* she'd said *when.* And she'd been bluffing. She couldn't say for sure that the police or the M.E. had been able to glean *any* forensic evidence. They'd taken samples. Now they had to wait for the lab results. But she wasn't all that hopeful. It wouldn't be easy to get foreign DNA from a body that'd been buried, disinterred and dumped elsewhere, especially a body that was in such an advanced stage of decomposition.

Still, she'd succeeded in turning the tables on him. Tension came across the line as palpably as if he'd started swearing at her.

"You don't scare me," he ground out.

"You don't scare me, either," she lied. "See you in the morning."

As soon as she disconnected, Francesca dropped her phone on the table and laid her head on her arms. As much as she wanted the whole situation to go away, it was far from over.

Francesca felt Jonah glance in her direction every few seconds while he drove. When she'd called to tell him about the conversation with Dean and Butch, he'd already left Chandler, but he'd insisted on coming back to get her. He said she'd be safer with him than staying anywhere Butch might look. But as far as Francesca was concerned, *safe* was a relative term. Being around Jonah risked things besides physical injury or death.

They needed to get to Prescott with plenty of time to prepare for tomorrow, however. She had no idea how long it would take the police to get her set up with a wire and put the proper surveillance in place.

Besides, despite an abundance of restless energy, she didn't feel like driving two hours on her own. They'd taken her car because they hadn't wanted a change to alert Butch that the police might be involved, but Jonah had the wheel. She wasn't sure she'd ever been quite so exhausted or upset, and couldn't say whether she'd been right to stand up to Butch or not. But after talking to Dean, she wasn't as worried about herself as much as her friends. Her iPhone contained *everyone's* address, everyone who was remotely important to her. That meant Butch and Dean knew where Adriana lived with her husband and two kids, where Josephine lived—alone since her husband had died three years ago—and where Heather and Sean resided in that subsistence-level apartment. He even had her parents' phone number and address, here in Arizona and where they were staying in Montana, should he care to take advantage of it.

Would he try to hurt someone she loved? Should she warn everyone immediately? Or wait and see if a threat really materialized?

She didn't want to throw her entire circle of family and friends into a panic. But by the time she knew whether the threat was real, it could be too late….

Jonah broke into her thoughts. "How's April's sister holding up?"

"Not well." Francesca would never forget the quiet sobs that'd come across the line. What had happened to April made no sense. She'd been such an unlikely victim. She hadn't been living on the fringes of society as a hooker or a crack addict. She'd been a straight-A student who'd become a third-grade teacher—Teacher of the Year, two years prior. She volunteered at the library and was kind and helpful to children at school who didn't have a nurturing family. "Jill feels guilty on top of her grief, which makes it worse," she explained.

He slung an arm over the steering wheel. He was wearing a clean pair of jeans and a T-shirt and had showered and shaved since she'd last seen him, but even with his cheeks smooth and his hair combed, he wasn't the polished type. He was a "take me as I am" kind of guy who didn't bother with tattoos, earrings, cologne. Fortunately for him, he had more than enough assets to pull off his minimalist approach.

"Why would she feel guilty?" he asked.

She pretended she hadn't been admiring him. She knew better than to get caught up in that, didn't she? She was just too tired to fight her natural inclination. It'd been so long since she'd been with Jonah. She couldn't help wondering if he kissed the same, touched the same…

Clearing her throat, she told herself it didn't matter and answered his question. "She's the one who encouraged April to try an online dating service. That's how she met her own husband, so she was high on the idea and thought it might work for her sister."

He made a clicking sound with his tongue. "That's too bad."

It was worse than "too bad," but no words were adequate and she understood that.

Suddenly, Jonah looked over and saw her studying him again. She'd been searching for subtle changes in his body. His thighs were slightly thicker. His hands had a few more nicks and scars—or maybe they had a lot more. Hard to tell in the dim glow of the instrument panel. His biceps seemed more pronounced beneath the soft cotton sleeves of his Cabo San Lucas T-shirt.

She thought maybe he'd ask her what she was looking at, but he didn't. Their eyes met and held, then his eyebrows jerked together as he returned his attention to the road. "Any chance you could get some sleep?" he asked.

Had he spoken merely to break a silence that had become too intense? She got that impression. There was no real expectation in the question. He knew how wound up she was, that it would be impossible to relax so soon.

"No. First I need to decide whether or not to contact the people Dean mentioned."

"You were staying with Heather. You didn't tell her before you left?"

"She was already asleep when he called, and I wasn't sure waking her was a good idea. She has no family in this part of the country and her boyfriend is in jail. Where would she go in the middle of the night with a three-year-old?" Refusing to let her gaze linger on him, she frowned and watched the pavement rush beneath their tires. "I wrote her a note, telling her not to divulge any information to Butch Vaughn, Paris Vaughn or Dean Wheeler, should they call, and to contact me in the morning so I could explain why I had to leave, but…maybe I should've done more."

"What about Adriana?" he asked.

She'd planned on calling Adriana, but by the time she'd finished her conversation with Jill, Jonah had arrived to take her to Prescott. "I definitely need to call her."

"What are you waiting for?"

Some privacy. She feared Adriana would pump her for information about Jonah, and she didn't want him overhearing the whole thing. But it'd be after midnight by the time they got to Prescott. If she was going to warn Adriana, she'd better do it now. Adriana's name had been in that stack of messages she'd received from Heather, too. As soon as she'd hung up with Jonah, Francesca had flipped through the rest of them, but she hadn't yet tackled her voice mail. She'd started to, then heard that it was full and hung up. Twenty messages? Too many. She couldn't deal with her regular clients in the midst of all this. Besides, quite a few of those messages were probably from Adriana. She was nothing if not persistent.

The phone rang twice before Adriana picked up.

"Where the heck have you been?"

"Dealing with a case."

"A man by the name of Dean Wheeler called here. You must've left your purse in Prescott because he was trying to return it to you. I've called and called, hoping to get you, but—"

"He got hold of me. I'm heading there now. But I wanted to let you know about something that's going on, something that has me worried."

"What?" she asked, then fell silent as Francesca explained.

"This Butch guy came to your *house?*" she said when Francesca was done. "You were afraid he might try to break in when you woke me up last night, and you didn't say a word?"

They'd been too busy talking about Jonah. "I didn't want to scare you. I figured I could handle it myself. But now...I think you need to know that he might try to hurt me by hurting people I love. He has your address as well as your phone number. Tonight his brother-in-law, Dean, mentioned you and Josephine, even Heather and her son."

"And you believe this man, this Butch, killed a woman?"

"I believe he may have killed a lot more than one."

"My God, this is surreal. Like something out of a movie."

"It's not. Take it seriously, Adriana."

"How?"

"Lock your doors and windows. Tell your husband to watch for any suspicious activity. Keep a cell phone handy in case you need to call the police."

"You're scaring the shit out of me," she said.

"That's what I'm trying to do. Then you'll be cautious, watch out for strangers, look around whenever you leave the house."

"What about you? So what if this guy has your purse? Maybe you should just let him keep it."

"I'm hoping it'll help maintain contact. If he's focused on me, he won't be out killing anyone else. I hope."

There was a brief silence, then Adriana asked, "Does Jonah know about this?"

"Yes."

"He called here earlier, too. He wanted me to give you the message that he's trying to reach you."

"Thanks for letting me know." She wasn't sure why she didn't admit that he was sitting in the car next to her. Like everything else about the three of them, it was complicated.

Glad she'd given Adriana some notice, Francesca felt the tension begin to seep from her body. "I've got to go. I'll check in tomorrow."

"Francesca?"

She hesitated. "What?"

"If things between you and Jonah are heating up again, I hope…well, I hope you won't let the past stand in the way of…of a reconciliation. If that's what you want. If that's what you *really* want."

"It's not what I want," she said. She had no intention of asking for a second helping of the kind of hurt he'd dished out a decade before. For all she knew, he'd lied about having a girlfriend.

"If you're sure."

"I'm sure."

"Maybe he's changed, Fran."

"And maybe he hasn't."

A scowl tugged at the corners of Jonah's mouth as

he shot her a glance. He could tell they were talking about him.

"Right," Adriana said. "Okay. Well, be careful."

Was it Francesca's imagination or did her friend sound relieved? "I will."

Francesca pressed the end-call button and glanced up to find Jonah watching her.

"I was never really attracted to her," he said. "I—"

Wincing, she held up a hand. "Don't. Really. That only makes it worse."

His knuckles showed white on the steering wheel. *"How?"*

"Because it means you tore my heart out and stomped on it for nothing!" Oh, God, she was going to be sick. What was wrong with her? She'd come to terms with this years ago, hadn't she?

If so, her mind had forgotten to notify her body. She felt exactly as she'd felt when she first learned the truth, as if there wasn't so much as a day separating that moment from this one.

"Stop the car," she said.

"Here? What for?" He was obviously confused, but she didn't have time to explain. Neither did she want to. It was bad enough that *she* understood the effect he had on her.

"Just pull over, please!"

He must've heard the panic in her voice because he slammed on the brakes, bringing the car to a stop only seconds before she stumbled into the tall weeds along the shoulder and lost what was left of her dinner.

11

Jonah wanted to believe it was the lack of sleep and the stress that were taking a toll on Francesca. When she got back in the car, she muttered something about eating a hamburger that must not have agreed with her. But she wasn't sick because of what she'd had for dinner. It was his fault she'd been ill. Only after she'd called Adriana and he'd tried to tell her, once again, why he'd done what he'd done had the color drained from her face.

That he had no one to blame for her pain except himself was rather ironic. If anyone else had hurt her, he would've kicked some ass. Hell, he *was* kicking ass. He'd been kicking his own for a decade. But all the self-recrimination in the world wouldn't dull the sharp edge of regret.

"You okay?" he asked once they were on the road again. She'd pushed her seat back and closed her eyes, but he knew she wasn't asleep. He wished he could take her hand and simply hold it. But he didn't dare. He didn't deserve the pleasure it would bring him.

"I'm fine," she said. "Better. I—I'll call Josephine in the morning. She goes to bed early. No need to wake her. Butch won't be going anywhere tonight. The police are watching his place, aren't they?"

She was as tough as any woman he'd ever met, and yet she suddenly seemed so fragile. How could he have hurt her the way he had? He couldn't blame it all on the alcohol. He'd known what he was doing. He'd acted consciously—to destroy what he wanted most. "That's what they said."

"She'll be okay for tonight," Francesca repeated. "Everyone will be okay for tonight."

She was trying so hard to convince herself that Jonah muttered a few words in agreement. But when he was with Francesca and he had to face what he'd done and what he'd lost because of it, he felt as if the world would never be right again.

"What's wrong, honey?"

Her husband's question came out of the dark, and it made Adriana aware that she'd been tossing and turning. "Nothing, why?"

"You've been restless ever since you went to bed. Is everything okay?"

"Of course." She fought to put some lift in her voice. "Why wouldn't it be?"

"You tell me."

"There's nothing to tell." Grimacing, she hugged her pillow closer. That wasn't a lie, was it? Nothing had happened.

"Would you like me to rub your shoulders?" he asked. "Help you relax?"

She felt too guilty to accept. Stan was a wonderful man—a talented pediatrician, a generous husband, a fabulous father. She loved him. So why did she feel the acidic burn of jealousy whenever Jonah was in Francesca's life? Even now, after so many years? And what did that make her? A disloyal wife as well as a disloyal friend?

"No, thanks," she said. "You've got to be tired."

"I'm never too tired to touch you."

Knowing he couldn't see her, she smiled with a trace of bitterness. How would he feel if he knew that, tonight, she'd pretend he was Jonah? "Thanks, but I'm not in the mood for a massage."

"So…you won't tell me what's going on?"

"I've just been thinking about the baby I had. You know, before the boys," she replied, which was true. She'd been brooding about her first child almost as much as Jonah and Francesca and all the rest of it. What would her life have been like if she'd had the chance to raise her daughter with her father? Jonah was all she'd ever wanted.

Stan rolled toward her and slipped his arm around her waist. "Are you wishing you'd kept her, honey? After all this time?"

The ceiling fan circled above them, providing some relief from the heat. Closing her eyes, Adriana concentrated on the brush of the air against her cheeks. "Maybe. I can't help wondering what she's like. Does she resemble me or Jonah? Does she have a good home? Is she happy? What if I'd decided to keep her?"

"You have to assume she's happy, Adriana. And why not? You know she went to a good family. Don't second-guess yourself. The questions you're asking will only eat at you, and the emotions they create could turn into guilt and destroy the peace and happiness we have within our own family."

When she didn't respond, he curled more closely around her. "What do you say?"

"I know you're right."

"Of course I'm right. I'm a doctor," he teased. "Leave the past where it is."

"I'm trying," she whispered. But what he didn't understand, what she wanted to tell him but couldn't for fear she'd reveal too much, was that she hadn't dug up the past. The past had come calling all on its own.

The shower was running. Francesca could hear the pipes whine. That meant Jonah had to be back. What time was it?

Squinting to see through sleep-blurred eyes, she checked the old-fashioned alarm clock on the nightstand. Nearly four. She'd been asleep for five hours.

It felt as if it'd only been five minutes.

A red light flashed on the desk, distracting her. Shoving herself onto her elbows, she realized it was Jonah's phone. There was a message waiting for him. Maybe more than one. Was Finch trying to get hold of him? What had they decided in her absence? Although she'd originally planned to join Jonah and the county investigators last evening, she hadn't made it to the sheriff's station. After being sick, she'd fallen asleep in the car and, once they reached Prescott, Jonah had insisted on bringing her to his motel room so she could continue sleeping while he met with Finch and Hunsacker.

The water went off and, as much as she tried not to, she imagined Jonah stepping out of the shower, completely naked with rivulets of water running off him. The intimate image sent a tingle through her, which dissolved the sleepiness of a moment before.

He opened the door slightly, probably to vent the steam, and she felt the hot, wet air roll out like an ocean wave. It chased away the chill of the air conditioner, which was set lower than she set her own. She supposed the coolness was one of the reasons she'd slept so soundly. She'd burrowed beneath the duvet, something she couldn't do very often in Arizona, at least in the summertime, and hadn't even heard Jonah come in. Until the racket of the shower had eventually coaxed her into wakefulness, she hadn't turned over since climbing into his extra bed.

The sound of his movements drew her eyes to the door, and memories when they'd been together ten years ago began to spill out of the vault in the back of her mind.

"There you are," Jonah breathed.

They were at her parents' house in Phoenix, had just been swimming. She'd gone in to change out of her suit and get ready for dinner when he surprised her by slipping into the bathroom.

She'd seen him in the mirror. "What are you doing here?" She'd felt so secure from accidental intrusions she hadn't even bothered to lock the door. Because of his wheelchair, her father couldn't use this particular bathroom. They'd had two specially designed and installed to accommodate him on the first floor—in the master suite and in the guest bathroom. Her mother hadn't been swimming. She'd merely sat by the pool, so she didn't need to change. And her brother no longer lived at home.

Jonah shut the door quietly behind him. "Looking for you."

She'd just untied the strings to her bikini top, but she held them in place as she turned to face him. "We made love last night."

His eyes swept over her, appreciative, hungry. "So? Do I only get one ticket a day? You've been driving me crazy in that suit."

Laughing, she jerked her head toward the door. "Get out of here. My parents are home."

"Your mother's making dinner. Your father's on the phone. We're safe."

"For how long? They'll be calling for us soon. They're too excited about getting to know you."

"They can wait five minutes."

She rolled her eyes. "*You* can wait another hour or two until we get home."

Flaunting a devilish grin, he moved closer. "And what if I can't?"

"Jonah!" She'd spoken with a hint of exasperation, as if she might refuse him, but they both knew she wanted him as badly as he wanted her. She couldn't get enough of him. After watching his long lean body cut smoothly through the water, hearing the timbre of his voice as he talked and laughed with her parents and feeling the subtle pull of his attention—an attention that never wavered from her, even when her parents thought he was fully involved in the conversation—she felt the warm, melting sensation that let her know her body was ready for him.

"You don't really want me to leave, do you?" He ran his lips up her neck and teased the strings of her top out of her hands.

"I'm not sure."

"Let me help you decide." His mouth found her breast as his hand slipped confidently and possessively inside her bathing suit bottom.

For another moment, Francesca tried to hang on to her sanity. "What if my parents—"

"They won't guess a thing. We'll be very, very quiet."

Only a second later, he made a liar of himself when he groaned, but she smothered that groan with a kiss that said everything about "take me now" and nothing about "I'm not interested." Then there was no deciding. As soon as they could get rid of their wet suits, he had her up against the wall with her legs wrapped tightly around his hips.

Francesca remembered how he'd dropped his head back as he made love to her, how his muscles had bunched, how she'd begun to quiver in response. He'd carried her so high that day, given her such complete satisfaction—

The light snapped off as the door slid open, jerking Francesca into the present. Jonah had told her he loved her in that bathroom at her parents' house. He'd said it just as they'd finished making love, while the goose bumps still stood out on her skin. She'd gotten the impression that loving her scared the hell out of him, and that admitting it was difficult, but he'd acted like it was too true to deny. That was how he'd said it, anyway.

But his love had been a lie. She needed to remember that. Maybe he could carry her to heights of pleasure she'd never experienced with anyone else. But she'd never suffered the same depth of pain with another man, either. When it came to Jonah, the pendulum swung far too wide.

Trying to ignore the way her body ached for him, she rolled over to face the wall as he came into the room. He rummaged through his luggage, then went back into the bathroom, presumably to dress.

Before he could come out again, she found herself imagining another night, the first night they'd ever made love. They'd been dating for several weeks, playing it safe. Then one night he made her a fancy dinner. He bought wine and flowers and attempted to prepare lasagna, but they became so engrossed in conversation out on his deck, so preoccupied with each other, that everything burned. They ended up ordering Chinese takeout, which they'd eaten outside so they could let the house air. After that, she'd tried to say good-night and leave, but he'd kissed her at the door and she'd lost all desire to hold back. They'd made love in the living room, the kitchen and, finally, his bedroom. From that night on, they'd been together almost constantly. It wasn't until he'd told her he loved her that he started drinking too much and acting strange. It hadn't gone on long enough that she was seriously worried about it, but...

The bed across from her creaked as he settled into it. She could smell his scent in the room—subtle but unmistakable. Now it grew stronger, making her even more aware of him.

How could she remember only a basic sketch of the other men she'd dated, even Roland, yet recall every detail of Jonah's body? The soft hair on his muscular chest. The breadth of his shoulders. The width of his hips. The firmness of his buttocks as she gripped them while he moved on top of her. The way his lips brushed hers when he was in a teasing mood, when he was in a tender mood, when he was in a sexually aggressive mood...

There must be something wrong with me, she thought.

Because she still wanted him. Even after everything he'd done.

Morning came far too soon. Jonah could hear Francesca in the bathroom, getting ready. He knew she'd already showered; the water had gone on earlier. He'd been dozing ever since. But it was nearly eight-thirty, definitely time to get out of bed. Finch and Hunsacker were expecting them by nine. They needed to get a wire on Francesca before she headed over to the salvage yard. Jonah would be listening in with both county investigators a few blocks away; two other cops would park a van out front and pretend to be with the electric company.

Sitting up, he yawned and tried to rub the sleep from his face. He really had to get onto a decent schedule. Grabbing snatches of sleep wasn't enough.

Fortunately, there was coffee. Francesca had a pot brewing; he could smell it.

"Thanks for making coffee," he called out to let her know he was up.

"If I pour you a cup, can you wait a few minutes for the bathroom?"

Dropping back onto the bed, he stared up at the ceiling. "Sure, no problem."

"One cream, two sugars?"

She remembered. "Yeah."

"Just a sec."

Soon after that she came out dressed in a pair of linen shorts, matching sandals and a burnt-orange top with fabric flowers clustered around the neck. "How do I look?" she said, handing him a cup of coffee. "Calm, cool and collected? Or can you tell I'm scared?"

As he accepted the cup, he tried to convince himself that she was no prettier than any other woman. But that was a lie he couldn't sell. "You look fine. Perfectly composed." He took a sip and sent her a grin. "How do *I* look? Ready to kick some ass?"

She arched an eyebrow at him. "Your hair's a mess and you're not wearing a shirt or shoes."

"I'm talking about the determination on my face."

"Is that what it is?"

"What did you think?"

"I think you look…sleepy," she said. "Relaxed. But

there's no need for you to be anything else. *You* won't be walking up to that door. *You* don't have to worry."

He didn't? Did she believe he wouldn't care if what he heard over that radio turned out to be the sound of a bat cracking her skull? He and Finch had devised the best plan they could to protect her. The closest they could get to the salvage yard was to have some guys wearing coveralls pose as utility workers, but he was still uneasy. If Butch decided to hurt Francesca, there was no guarantee they'd be able to stop him in time. Murder could happen in seconds. "Right. I have nothing at stake."

His BlackBerry went off before she could respond. Grateful for the distraction, he picked it up from the desk where he'd left it charging, and checked caller ID. It was Dr. Price. "Hello?"

"Jonah, it's Leslie."

Leaning against the desk, he took another sip of his coffee. "How's my favorite forensic anthropologist?"

"How many forensic anthropologists do you know?"

"At least two."

"That's what I thought. And yet I'm flattered. Go figure."

He smiled at the humor in her voice. "I don't pick favorites lightly. What's going on?"

"I'm calling because I thought you'd want to know as soon as possible."

"Want to know what?"

"The evidence techs digging at Dead Mule Canyon found something this morning, about a quarter mile from the original site."

A group from the Yavapai County Sheriff's Office worked in that canyon from dawn until dark every day, going over the area inch by inch. They were using all the men they could spare. It was a huge job and would probably take another two weeks, but in order to solve these murders, they needed every piece of evidence they could find. "Tell me it's not more human remains," he said, and set his coffee down long enough to open the drapes. Another sunny day in Arizona. No surprise there. Monsoon season wouldn't hit until August.

"No. Thank goodness. This looks like something that might've belonged to the perpetrator."

Although Jonah could sense Francesca watching him, he didn't glance over at her. She made him feel too many emotions he didn't want to feel, emotions that were better left undisturbed, especially now, when he was so determined to treat her like any other work associate. Maybe he'd been a shitty boyfriend, but he'd always been a good cop. He couldn't help hoping this case would give him the chance to right the past—as much as that was possible. No matter what, he wouldn't let her down again. "What is it?" he asked Leslie.

"A business card. It's tattered and torn, but it's legible."

"And the name?"

"The Pour House. Have you ever heard of it?"

Almost of their own volition, his eyes jerked over to Francesca. She'd mentioned that bar. April had met Butch there on Saturday. "The Pour House has also popped up in relation to that other case I was telling you about yesterday," he said to Leslie.

"The woman found murdered outside the Skull Valley gift shop? You think the two are related?"

"Sounds like it to me."

"Finding this card would be awfully coincidental otherwise," she agreed.

He scratched his bare chest. "No kidding. Thanks for letting me know."

"You bet. You coming in today?"

"Probably not. I'm planning to work the April Bonner side of the equation, see how far I can get with that."

"Makes sense. But before you go, I also wanted to tell you that we have a match on those veneers."

Getting a little anxious due to the time—they were down to a mere twenty minutes before they were to report to the sheriff's office—he skirted Francesca on his way to the bathroom. "The teeth? Why didn't Pelusi call me?"

"He tried to about an hour ago. When you didn't pick up, he called me, thinking you might be here."

Ernie Pelusi was the street cop assigned the task of going from dentist to dentist, looking for the man who'd performed the cosmetic dentistry they'd noticed on one of the victims. Jonah had taken to him immediately. Ernie reminded him of one of the guys he worked with at Department 6—Roderick Guerrero. "I had my phone off. Trying to grab a few hours' sleep."

"You mean you don't work twenty-four hours *every* day?" she teased.

Relieved to have some privacy, he closed the bathroom door and leaned against it. "Not every day. So what about the veneers?"

"A dentist by the name of Greg Johnson recognized his own work. He said the woman for whom he created those veneers was Bianca Andersen, age thirty-three."

"If she was reported missing she's not on any list I've seen."

"As far as I know, she wasn't reported."

"Why not?"

"No idea. But Ernie's got her dental file."

Which would have her name and address. "Do we have *any* idea how long she's been missing?"

"From the condition of her jaw, I'd guess over a year."

But now that he knew her name, chances were good he could learn more.

At the prospect of having even a few answers to their many questions, a surge of hope filled Jonah. He'd solve this case and head back to California, leaving Francesca better off—safer—than she would've been without him. Maybe that couldn't make up for his mistake, but at least he wouldn't be doing any more damage. "We're going to get this guy."

"We don't have any choice," she said. "This kind of killer won't quit on his own. You and I both know that."

12

After summoning her courage, Francesca followed Jonah into the sheriff's station. On the ride over, he'd told her about the Pour House card at Dead Mule Canyon, and Bianca Andersen and her veneers, which had done nothing to settle her nerves. It was bad enough thinking Butch was responsible for what she'd seen outside the gift shop in Skull Valley. Assuming he was the reason there'd been seven corpses buried in Dead Mule Canyon was simply…overwhelming, especially when Jonah kept warning her not to let Butch get her alone.

"Where the hell have you been?" Finch wanted to know as soon as he saw them striding down the corridor toward him. "I've been calling."

Francesca checked her new phone. Neither county investigator had bothered to try her, but she didn't mention it. Jonah responded. "We can still make it by ten."

"Only if we hurry." Finch waved at Francesca. "Get her wired up."

"You got everything else ready?" Jonah asked, leaning on the partition.

Finch had his hand on his phone. "I'm making sure of that this very second."

Hunsacker came out of his cubicle a few feet away,

carrying a handful of wires, which he handed Jonah, along with some duct tape. "It's harder to conceal a wire when you're not wearing a jacket," he said to her.

She glanced from him to Finch to Jonah. "You're kidding, right? I wear a jacket in the middle of the summer and I might as well announce on a blare horn—'I'm doing this to hide a wire!'"

He shrugged. "Just sayin'. I mean, you're pretty thin. Any bump is gonna stand out."

Compared to Hunsacker, everyone was thin. "Then maybe *you* should go in and wear the wire," she said.

His lazy-dog eyes narrowed. "Funny. Almost as funny as sending us to the salvage yard in search of a dummy. Little did we know we were dealing with *two* dummies."

She smiled sweetly. "And yet the woman I was looking for shows up dead on a street corner and now we're heading right back. Who's going to have the last laugh, Investigator?"

"Maybe Butch is." He lowered his voice. "If he kills you today."

"Cut it out," Jonah growled.

Hunsacker shot him a sullen look for interfering but seemed to realize he'd gone too far. "Let's get moving," he said, and walked away.

"I can't believe that guy's married," Francesca grumbled. "His wife must be blind *and* stupid."

Finch, who'd just finished dialing, was holding the phone to his ear, but jumped into the conversation, anyway. "Stop wasting time."

Jonah passed the surveillance equipment to her. "There's a bathroom around the corner."

Holding a hand over the receiver, Finch stopped her before she could go anywhere. "Whoa, wait. She won't be able to get that on by herself. We're in a hurry here. Help her out, Jonah."

Jonah raised his eyebrows as if asking Finch to take care of it, but Finch wanted it to happen right away, and he was clearly busy. "I'm trying to see where the hell our utility team is," he said. "They were supposed to be out there at seven this morning. We can't all arrive at the same time."

Slightly offended by Jonah's reluctance, Francesca walked toward the bathroom. "I'll figure it out."

Muttering something under his breath, he caught up with her and took the device from her. "It's not a big deal. Lift your shirt."

She did, and he taped the tiny recording device to the small of her back. Then his fingers trailed along her bare skin as he brought the wire around her body. He stopped every few seconds to secure it with pieces of tape she tore off for him, but he kept his head bowed and worked efficiently. Indifferently.

"You can take it from here," he said when he reached her bra. "Feed it up and under."

"Got it." Relieved that he was finished, that she didn't have to smell the fabric softener on his clothes or endure the close proximity of his body anymore, she took the mic, and he turned away so fast it was as if he'd found it repulsive to touch her.

Why does it have to be Jonah who's involved in this case? Why can't it be someone else? she thought as she situated the mic between her breasts and lowered her shirt.

They tested the equipment. When they were satisfied that it worked properly, they trooped downstairs and into the parking lot. She was to take her car and go alone; they were to follow in an unmarked police vehicle.

"You okay?" Jonah asked as he handed over her keys, which he'd pocketed after driving earlier.

She mustered a disinterested smile. "Sure. What's he gonna do? Kill me?"

Judging by his dark scowl, Jonah didn't appreciate the joke. "We'll be listening. If there's trouble, we'll be there right away."

"What I won't do to avoid a trip to the DMV," she said, but she knew—they all knew—she wasn't doing this for the articles she stood to recover. She was doing this to save lives. The sooner they could get some hard evidence on Butch, the sooner he'd go to prison. Then she wouldn't be afraid to return to her own home, and all the other women out there that might come into contact with him would be safe—including Adriana, Heather and Josephine.

All business, Jonah grabbed her arm. "Make sure you speak up, so we can hear what's going on. And, whatever you do, *don't go inside.* You go inside, no telling what might happen."

"Don't scare her too much," Hunsacker interrupted. "We're not even positive this is our guy."

Francesca glanced back in time to see Jonah silence Hunsacker with a glare. "Better safe than sorry," she heard him say, but what she was doing had very little to do with her safety. There was a reason Butch had asked his brother-in-law to invite her back to Prescott, and it sure as hell wasn't because he felt guilty for stealing her purse.

Surprisingly, everyone seemed to be home. Several vehicles, including Butch's wife's Impala, jammed up the driveway. His son, dressed in a baseball uniform, was tossing a ball out front.

Butch's brother-in-law answered the door almost before Francesca could ring the bell, as if he'd been watching for her. Although Francesca had braced herself for the worst—after seeing that body in Skull Valley, who wouldn't?—she was quickly losing her fear. Surely Butch wouldn't attack her in front of his whole family.

"You made it." Dean offered her a pleasant smile. "Come on in."

Jonah had warned her not to go inside, but Francesca was beginning to think that, once again, they'd put out a lot of effort that would prove wasted in the end. Whatever Butch had in mind when he asked Dean to call her—or gave permission for Dean to call her if that was how it'd happened—didn't seem to be nearly as diabolical as she'd believed.

Still, she made an attempt to remain on the stoop. "That's okay. I'll just get my purse and go."

"You won't come in?" He sounded confused. "I think Butch wants to talk to you."

Remembering how Butch had changed the second his family had come into view, Francesca cast a glance at his son. As long as that child remained in the vicinity, she'd be fine. She needed to push this a little further, had to walk away with *something*. For one thing, she didn't need Hunsacker and Finch making fun of her for crying wolf again. "Okay. Maybe for a few minutes."

Obviously pleased, he moved out of the way and held the door.

She imagined Jonah cringing as she stepped into a middle-class home that smelled like hot dogs and could've been decorated by her grandmother. A purple sofa sat against flocked wallpaper on violet carpet. Tables with doilies and gold lamps completed the effect.

Butch's wife was too young to have a house like this; it had to belong to the old couple she'd met before.

"Nice place."

Dean laughed. "You think so?"

"You don't?"

"I guess. I quit seeing it ages ago. It's just...home."

"How long have you lived here?"

"My whole life."

She'd already guessed as much. "Your parents owned it before Butch?"

"They still own it. The house and the salvage yard. But when they retired, they turned everything over to Paris's husband. He runs it, and they live downstairs in their own apartment. Butch said a smaller place would be easier for them to take care of so they can travel. They can head out whenever they want, but they never go anywhere."

"Why not?"

"If you ask them, they'll say they don't want to leave me. I've heard it a thousand times. My mother says she keeps me 'grounded.'"

Apparently, Francesca had been right about the house. She'd also been right about Dean. He wasn't quite normal. "I see. Well, it's nice that Butch could take over. Your parents must really like him," she said, just to see how he'd react.

He leaned close, as if he was about to confide a great secret. "It's Champ they're crazy about. It's Champ we're *all* crazy about."

The name threw Francesca. "That's a...dog?"

"No. The boy!" he said with a laugh. "The dog's name is Demon."

"Nice names on both counts." She wondered if he

could tell she was being sarcastic, but he didn't seem to notice.

"Butch chose both."

"I suppose Champ is better than Rover."

"I'd rather have a cat than a dog," Dean volunteered. "But Butch is allergic to cats. He shot the Persian I grew up with the day he moved in."

It wasn't difficult to understand why he'd be unhappy with Butch's actions. "I hope you had a say in that decision."

"Me?" He shook his head. "I don't have a say in *any* decision."

"Why not?"

He studied her. "You can't tell?"

"I wouldn't have asked if I could."

"I've got mental problems."

Strange, he didn't mind admitting that. "Meaning…"

"Sometimes I can't think straight." He tapped his head. "But it's okay because the pills keep me on track. I'm fine as long as I take my pills."

Which would explain his detached behavior when she'd seen him before. He'd been doped up.

"Anyway, Princess was getting old," he said. "It was time to put her down."

"Most people take their pets to a vet."

"Butch is his own vet. He's his own doctor, too. But you don't really care about that. What you want to find out is how I feel about what he did to my cat, because you know you'd feel like shit if you were me." He cocked his head as if seeing her from a whole new angle. "I like you. You're smart."

A voice came from the kitchen, and Francesca realized that Paris had been standing just inside the doorway, listening, the whole time. "I didn't know she was here to visit *you*," she said, entering the living room. "I thought she wanted to pick up her purse."

"We're getting to that," Dean said. "Jeez, can't you let me talk to a pretty girl now and then?"

With a grimace, Paris folded her arms. "Pick one who hasn't scratched up my husband's face. Pick one who isn't as crazy as you are."

"Excuse me?" Francesca said, but Dean interrupted.

"Isn't Champ supposed to be at his little league game about now? You know how angry Butch'll be if he's late. 'Cause if he's late, the coach won't let him play. And Butch doesn't like it when his little boy sits on the bench."

"Like you used to do?" she said. "Game after game? That won't happen to Champ. My son's a *good* athlete. He takes after his daddy. He'll play."

Dean motioned for his sister to butt out. "Ignore her," he said to Francesca in a loud whisper. "She's not happy with me for inviting you over. She doesn't like it that you're better-looking than she is."

"Get her purse, Dean, and get her out of here," Paris said.

Before Dean could respond, the back door slammed. Someone else had just come in.

A flicker of fear replaced the anger in Paris's eyes. "I'll be right back," she said, and pulled car keys out of her pocket as she hurried to the front door. "Champ, grab your bag!" Francesca heard her call as she went out.

"Seems Butch always gets his way around here," Francesca said.

Dean whistled. "Like I said, you're smart."

A shadow darkened the place where Paris had first entered the room, and Francesca glanced up to see Butch filling the entire doorway. She'd thought he looked big *outside.* Inside was a whole other story. He had to duck beneath the door frame just to pass from room to room. Of course, the doors in this old house were lower than most, but still.

"I'd like to talk to you," he said.

Francesca felt her eyebrows go up. "I'm all ears."

"Not here. Not with this retard listening in. Let's go out to my office."

Francesca wasn't feeling quite as safe as she had when she first went into the house. The people she'd considered insurance—Paris and Champ—were gone. Butch obviously had no respect for Dean, who might not have the sense to intercede if something went wrong, anyway. And she hadn't seen the old folks. Were they in their apartment? If so, there was a better chance they'd hear her scream if she stayed put.

"I'm not going anywhere with you."

He gestured at Dean. "Get her purse."

"Where is it?"

"Wherever you put it after playing with all her stuff."

Dean squirmed uncomfortably. "I didn't play with your stuff," he mumbled, his face red. "I was just... admiring it." He slanted an accusing glare at Butch. "And Paris had it last."

"Then it's probably in the bedroom. Get it, fruitcake. Now," Butch snapped, and Dean scrambled to obey.

"Is it really necessary to treat him so badly?" Francesca asked.

"Live with him for a day, then see what you have to say about how he's treated."

She refused to back down. "He's your wife's brother."

"Are you sure you want to waste your time talking

about my crazy brother-in-law? Because he's my problem, not yours. And I thought you'd be more interested in hearing about April Bonner."

At the mention of April's name, Francesca's heart skipped a beat. "What do you have to say about April?"

Footsteps indicated that Dean was already on his way back. "Not here. In my office. You coming?"

The opportunity was too good to pass up. She was wearing a wire and could get the whole conversation on tape—although she highly doubted he was about to confess. More likely he'd make up some story to cover being with April last Saturday night. But maybe in the midst of telling that story he'd slip up. Catching him in a lie could help break this case wide-open.

"Here." As Dean handed over her purse, Francesca noticed that his mood had changed drastically. Gone was the friendly Dean, the childlike Dean, even the embarrassed Dean. Now he seemed angry—brooding and angry. But, considering how he'd been treated, she found those emotions justified.

"Go take your medication," Butch said. "I can always tell when you try to skip."

Dean glared at him again, then turned on his heel and left the room.

"So what's it gonna be?" Butch asked.

Francesca didn't bother to check her purse for her phone or her wallet. What was there was there. She had bigger concerns. Slinging the strap over her shoulder, she raised her chin. "Where's your office?"

13

As she'd expected, Butch's office was the ramshackle building she'd hidden behind when she'd first spotted that mannequin and thought it was a corpse. About four hundred square feet, it had two doors, four windows, a large metal desk, a few office machines and an old air-conditioning unit, which sounded as if it was leaking water, hanging out the window closest to Butch's chair. A tiny apartment sat off to one side, an obvious addition. Francesca could see part of a bed through the open doorway, but she didn't have the impression the apartment was currently occupied.

The scent of cigar smoke clung to the cheap wooden paneling and brown shag carpet. Francesca could also smell dog, even though the Doberman was currently chained up outside. A pot of coffee sat on top of a makeshift minibar constructed of wooden planks and cinder blocks. Everything around her pronounced Butch king of the junk heap.

"Sit down." Shoving a pile of newspapers off a chair of cracked vinyl, something he'd probably pulled in from the yard, he waved her into it. Then he helped himself to a cup of coffee without offering her one, took a seat across from her and propped his feet on the desk.

"What?" she said when he scowled at her without speaking. "You wanted me here for a reason."

He gulped down some coffee. "We got off on the wrong foot the other day. But I won't apologize for that. You had no right to trespass on my property." He touched his cheek as if remembering the moment she'd gouged him. "Or scratch my face like a damn hellcat."

"Unlike what you told the police, you were chasing me!" she argued.

"I was just trying to figure out what you wanted."

She couldn't believe he'd continue to lie when, as far as he knew, they were alone. "By tackling me? Come on. You already put on a circus for the police. I was there, remember? I *know* what happened. You were feeling a lot more than curiosity."

Shifting so he could reach the desk while his feet remained on top of it, he put down his coffee cup and picked up a heavy crystal paperweight, which he tossed from hand to hand. "Maybe I was."

"So now you're admitting it?"

"I'm admitting that I was trying to hide something. But not what you think. I had no intention of murdering you when you came here. I've never killed anyone."

She watched that paperweight shift from hand to hand, thought how easy it would be for him to bash her head in before Jonah or Finch or anyone else could rescue her. "Then why did you react the way you did when you found me on your property?"

"Because I knew what you were. The last stranger who came snooping around here all dressed up was also a P.I."

"Looking for yet another missing person with a connection to you, no doubt," she said dryly.

A hint of malice passed over his face but was gone

almost as soon as it appeared. "Looking to catch me with a woman other than my wife," he corrected.

Francesca brought her purse around so she could prop it in her lap. "You think Paris is collecting proof that you're unfaithful? Considering the profile you posted on that dating Web site where you met April, that shouldn't be too hard. A quick Internet search would do it. I'd be happy to help—for free."

The animosity didn't reappear, as she'd thought it would. Instead, he laughed. "Paris would never leave me. It's not like I'm sneaking around on her, so you got nothing on me. As long as I'm discreet and my emotions don't get involved, she lets me do whatever I want. It's my girlfriend's husband who has a jealousy problem."

His girlfriend? Francesca hadn't expected him to divulge another ongoing relationship. She hadn't even expected him to have one. Or maybe that was how he worked. Maybe he kept various women on the side as girlfriends until they became too demanding, or he tired of them, or the desire to kill grew too strong to resist. "What's your girlfriend's name?"

The paperweight landed on his desk with a thud. "None of your business. I won't drag her into this. She's got her hands full dealing with that husband of hers. She doesn't need any more trouble, especially from you."

"Interesting. You seem to care about her—enough to protect her, to some extent—and yet it doesn't bother you that you're breaking up her marriage."

"Why would it?" he said. "I don't owe her husband any more than I owe you. I never forced her to sleep with me. The way I look at it, she's breaking up her own marriage. That's her choice. But it doesn't mean I'll make it easy for the people her husband hires to document us so he can take away her kids."

Francesca didn't conceal her smirk. "You're telling me that was all that had you worried when I showed up here, Butch? What your girlfriend's husband might do with proof of her infidelity?"

He spread his hands wide. "Believe it or not."

Rocking back, she folded her arms on her purse. "What about April?"

"What about her?"

"They found her body yesterday."

There was a brief hesitation. "She's dead?"

"You didn't know?"

"Was it on the news?"

"I can't say. I haven't watched the news." She'd been too focused on basic survival, Jill and Vince, her phone line. She hadn't even turned on the TV last night at Heather's apartment. "When I got to where she was dumped, there were no reporters. But you're the last person to see her alive."

He took another sip of coffee. "She was perfectly fine when I left her. If someone hurt her, it wasn't me."

Did the news of April's death upset him? Not that Francesca could tell. He seemed agitated but not particularly upset. "I just told you that a woman you've been involved with is dead. You don't care?"

He smiled. "Of course. Can't you tell? I'm broken up inside."

She hoped the sarcasm carried through to Jonah and the others. "Any chance you can prove she was alive when you went your separate ways?"

His chair creaked rhythmically as he swiveled from side to side. "No more than you can prove she wasn't."

"Do you mind telling me what you two did Saturday night?"

"Not at all. We met at the Pour House at seven o'clock.

Then we drove out to a little Mexican place called the Rio Grande about fifteen miles from here. After dinner, we were anxious to be together, if you know what I mean, so I pulled off the road and we, uh, got busy in my truck."

"You're saying you had sex with her."

The swiveling and its attendant creaking stopped. "I'm saying it was consensual."

Somehow, Francesca couldn't see a teacher like April being quite so easy. According to April's sister, and the e-mails she'd read on April's computer, this was the first time April had actually met Harry Statham, aka Butch. And everything else in her life revealed her as conservative, cautious. In Francesca's mind, Butch was only admitting he'd had intercourse with April to explain any foreign DNA they might find. He was smart, smarter than the average rapist, if that was the appropriate term. "And then?"

"After it was over, she wanted me to take her home with me. It was as if she thought fifteen minutes of sweaty sex committed us for life. I told her I couldn't do that. I was tired and had to work the next morning. I don't know how I could've made it any plainer that the date was over. But she was so insistent that I finally had to tell her I was married. That was when the shit really hit the fan. She freaked out. Started screaming and demanding I stop the truck."

"On the highway?"

"That's right, on the highway. I didn't want to let her out. I knew it was a hike to get anywhere from that point. But she wouldn't listen. She was sobbing and hitting me, and we were weaving all over the road. When she opened her door and threatened to jump, I pulled over and let her out." He steepled his fingers. "I'm not proud of how the night ended," he added, "but I had no choice other than to let her do as she wished. I've never seen a woman so worked up."

"You sound surprised that she'd be unhappy, Butch."

His smile dissolved and he dropped his hands. "I am. She was a stupid bitch. I bought her a meal and she gave me a quickie. As far as I'm concerned, it was an even trade. We both had a good time. She loved the buildup, the e-mails we exchanged, the idea that she was falling in love. I gave her that for weeks. And then she had to ruin it all by acting as if I'd cheated her. I mean, what did she expect?"

"Maybe she wanted more than fantasy. Maybe she wanted it to be real."

"Give me a break," he muttered.

"Was a little honesty too much to ask?"

"Everyone knows you can't believe half the shit you read on the Internet. She should've been more careful."

"Sometimes hope makes you believe things you otherwise wouldn't."

"Not if you're smart. How she could mistake a quick piece of ass for true love, I don't know, but once I realized, I knew I had to end it right there."

"And telling her you were married was the fastest way."

"Yeah."

Francesca hated him even more for breaking April's heart before killing her. She was tempted to let him know it, to tell him how pathetic she thought he was. But she didn't. She figured she might get more out of him if she kept her opinions to herself. "When you left her on the highway, that's the last time you saw her?"

"That's the last time I saw her."

If what he said was true, anyone could've picked her

up. Butch knew that, of course. He'd concocted his story to create doubt, to suggest that some mysterious killer might've come upon her after he'd driven off. The chance of that happening wasn't great, but it *was* a chance, and that was all he needed to create reasonable doubt. "Why are you so forthcoming with me, Butch?" she asked.

"Because I'll have to talk to the police, anyway, and you're making more out of Saturday night than it was. I'm an innocent man. I don't need you or anyone else causing me trouble. I have a family to support."

She pinched her lips as she considered him. "An innocent man doesn't try to terrorize a woman."

"I flirted with her online, took her out to dinner and had consensual sex with her. I didn't terrorize her."

"I'm talking about *me*," Francesca said.

Lines of frustration appeared on his forehead. "I already explained that. I thought you were hired by my—"

"No, at my house," she broke in. "What were you doing *at my house?*"

His frustration gave way to confusion. "You've lost me. I've never been to your place." Stretching to reach the air conditioner, he adjusted the knob to high, which started the fan spinning so loudly she was worried the police wouldn't be able to hear what was coming through her wire.

She raised her voice to compensate. "You came over and cut my phone line."

He put his feet down one at a time and leaned halfway across the desk. "Maybe *someone* cut your line, but... It. Wasn't. Me."

It was. Francesca was sure of it. Maybe she hadn't been able to make out the details of his face, but she'd seen his size and shape. And the timing couldn't be a coincidence. Besides that, the person who'd come hadn't actually attempted to break in. Why would anyone cut her telephone line for no reason—unless it was an act of revenge, a message like the one she would've expected to receive from Butch?

He was playing with her. It was almost as if he knew she was wearing a wire.

She had to get him to say something that might make the police realize he was dangerous. Otherwise, his explanation of their encounter at the salvage yard, and his claim that he hadn't been to her house, could seem plausible. If Butch managed to convince Finch that he wouldn't hurt her or anyone else, Finch wouldn't waste the man-hours necessary to continue surveillance. "Stop it. I know better."

"It *couldn't* have been me," he protested.

"Why not?"

"Because I was here all night. Ask my wife."

She gripped her purse with both hands. "I'm getting the impression your wife would say *anything* to protect you."

"We stick together. But she's not lying, and neither am I."

"What you're telling me doesn't make sense," Francesca said. "Who else could it have been?"

He slapped the top of his desk. "How the hell should I know? It could've been anyone. A Peeping Tom. A meddlesome neighbor. A jilted lover."

She shook her head. "It was you."

Some of the anger slithering beneath the surface of his control was beginning to show. "Why would I waste my time?"

"Because you weren't happy when I left here. Because

you wanted me to feel vulnerable. Because you're sick in the head. Take your pick."

He stood. "I shouldn't have tried to talk to you. You're not listening. You're too paranoid. I came after you when you were here because I'm sick of the investigators my girlfriend's husband keeps sending over. I wanted to make it clear I wouldn't put up with being spied on or harassed, especially on my own property. That's it. Nothing to do with murder."

Francesca wasn't making any progress, so she decided to take the conversation in a different direction. "Have you ever heard of Bianca Andersen?"

"Who?" he said, but he'd jerked at the name as if he'd recognized it, as if she'd surprised him.

"Bianca Andersen."

His expression darkened. "No."

"Aren't you going to ask me who she is? Or why I'm mentioning her?"

"I'd like you to leave. Now."

"Her remains were found in Dead Mule Canyon, Butch. That's not far from here, is it?"

"I wouldn't know. I've never been there."

"You're sure about that?"

He rounded the desk. "I'm done talking to you. Get out of my office."

She stood but refused to back away, even when he stepped right up to her. She had to get him to make a mistake, to give away a detail they could use, or she would've accomplished nothing by coming here. And she had a greater chance of getting him to reveal his true nature while he was upset. "Or what?"

"Or I'll call the cops. I've tried to be nice. I returned your purse—"

"After stealing it in the first place," she broke in.

"I didn't steal it! It was gone by the time I came back to look for it. I think my freak of a brother-in-law grabbed it. That's all I can figure, because he's the one who brought it to me last night."

Francesca remembered ringing the doorbell and getting no response. "Dean was home that day?"

"Of course he was. He's usually home. He can't drive because of his meds. Besides, you've seen what he's like. Who'd want to hang out with him?"

"Honestly?" she said. "He seems a lot nicer than you."

"Maybe you should get to know him better."

"Maybe I will."

He shoved a hand through his hair, making it stand up in front. "This was a mistake," he said, and stalked out, leaving her alone in his office with that air conditioner chugging for all it was worth and his coffee growing cold on his desk.

Could Butch be telling the truth? Francesca wondered. She could see him getting fed up with the actions of some jealous husband. She could even understand how her own fears might've created certainties in her mind that shouldn't have been there. She'd mistaken that mannequin for a corpse, after all....

She could've bought it—if he hadn't acted so strange when she mentioned Bianca Andersen. He knew Bianca; Francesca was sure of it.

"I'm done here," she said to the men who were listening.

She was about to let herself out when she caught sight of movement at the window and realized Dean was peering in at her. Tossing her newly recovered purse over her shoulder, she headed for the door. She thought he might scurry off, pretend he hadn't been stealing glimpses of her through those dirty panes, but he didn't. He waited. Then he fell in step beside her.

"What'd Butch have to say?" he asked.

The sun burned so bright it blinded her. Rooting through her purse, she came up with her sunglasses. "Nothing. Why?"

"You two were in there for quite a while."

Once she had her glasses on and could see him without squinting, she tried to analyze what he was feeling, without success. He held himself rigid, as if he was upset, and yet his voice was as calm as ever. "He apologized for our little misunderstanding the other day."

"Is that what you think it was? A misunderstanding?"

Stopping, she faced him. "Isn't that what *you'd* call it?"

He glanced around as if he was taking a big risk by speaking out. "He's not a nice person," he whispered. "You should know that."

It was Francesca's turn to see if she could catch a glimpse of Butch, but they seemed to be alone. "Give me some specific details, Dean."

At the gravity in her voice, he shook his head. "No. Never mind. I don't know anything. Butch is a good guy, like I said on the phone. I didn't mean it when I said he wasn't. I swear," he said and, running with an awkward gait, he took off for the house.

14

Jonah watched Francesca pull the wire out from under her shirt and place it on the conference table.

"So? What do you make of what you heard?" she asked.

Finch sat next to her, near the blackboard, Hunsacker across from her. Jonah had purposely taken the seat farthest away, near the television stored on a rolling cart in the corner. Now that he knew she was out of physical danger, at least for the moment, he couldn't think of anything except the smooth texture of the skin he'd felt when he taped that listening device to her body. And because physical gratification should've been the last thing that mattered to him, considering the gravity of the situation, he was more than a little irritated with himself. If he was going to do his job the way it needed to be done, he had to overcome his attraction to Francesca.

Why couldn't his body stop craving what his mind was telling him he could never have?

"The brother-in-law knows something," Finch said.

"That's the feeling I got," Francesca agreed. "But he's scared."

Finch tapped his pen on the wooden table. "If Butch is what we think he is, Dean has reason to be scared."

"Hang on a second." A yellow writing pad waited in front of every seat, ready for any meeting that took place. Hunsacker pushed his away. "We can't jump to conclusions. Dean seems scared, but it could be unwarranted. He already admitted he's crazy, told you flat out that he can't think straight without his daily meds." He turned to Finch. "You saw him the other day. He was on his feet but he was completely zoned out. A person like that could imagine just about anything and believe it was real. Until we have hard evidence, I'm not so sure we should focus exclusively on Butch. He could be telling the truth about dropping April at the side of the road."

"I, for one, don't believe it," Francesca said.

"Because you made up your mind that he was a killer from day one. I'm just saying we can't ignore the possibility that it could be someone else," Hunsacker reiterated.

Refusing to look at Francesca for fear his eyes would betray the conflict inside him, Jonah kept his gaze fastened on Finch. "Before we do anything, we need to talk to Dean's shrink or whoever's prescribing his medication, find out what he's diagnosed with and what he's taking."

"We also need to check with the staff at the Rio Grande and make sure Butch and April really came in that night," Finch said. "If we poke around the area enough, maybe we'll find someone who saw or heard something that'll either corroborate or refute his story."

"Butch has more to hide than what happened to April," Francesca warned.

Hunsacker scowled at her. "What are you talking about now?"

"You should've seen his face when I mentioned Bianca Andersen."

Telling himself she was no different to him than any other woman, Jonah allowed his eyes to rest where they'd been tempted to go all along. "He recognized the name?"

Obviously agitated, she rewound the tape and played it for them again. "Listen."

Have you ever heard of Bianca Andersen?

Who?

Bianca Andersen.

No.

Aren't you going to ask me who she is? Or why I'm mentioning her?

I'd like you to leave. Now.

"That isn't particularly revealing," Hunsacker said the moment she hit the stop button.

Francesca's eyebrows shot up. "Can't you hear the tightness in his voice? And what about his refusal to even talk about her? If it was true that he'd never heard of her, he would've responded with more curiosity. He would've wanted to know why I was asking about her, what connection I thought she might have to him."

"Not necessarily," Hunsacker argued. "Not everyone would react the way you would. Maybe he was afraid you were trying to drag him even deeper into a mess he knows he's better off avoiding. He sure as hell understands that you're not his friend. You've made that clear to all of us."

"I wonder how much you'd like him if he stood outside your car holding a baseball bat as if he was going to bash in your window?" she said.

Hunsacker frowned. "He already explained why he did that."

"And I'm explaining that I saw fear in his eyes when I brought up Bianca," she said. "He doesn't want to be connected with another dead woman. He knows what that'll mean."

Hunsacker persisted. "Even an innocent man wouldn't want to be connected to a dead woman. No one wants to be falsely accused. Besides, a guilty look, fear in his eyes, none of that can take the place of forensic evidence. Why do you have such a hard time understanding that we can't just act on your gut instinct?"

Hoping to derail the conversation before it could turn into another argument, Jonah jumped in. "Don't start on her. She's telling us what we couldn't see because we weren't there. She's not saying it's proof. Sometimes gut instinct is what determines the direction we should take. You know that."

"How about if you quit defending her?" Hunsacker snapped. "I can think for myself. It's not as if you're my boss. You're the hired help here."

Jonah drilled Hunsacker with a meaningful glare. "You want to go over that again?"

Hunsacker adjusted his position, putting even more strain on the buttons holding his shirt together. "You're a consultant, okay? That's all I'm saying. You're here to give advice. I'm reminding you of your role."

"My 'role' is to provide your department with the benefit of my experience and to help solve these murders in the most efficient manner possible. You got a problem with that, you need to talk to the sheriff, because if you remind me of my 'role' again, I'll see to it that one of us gets kicked off this case, and it might not be me."

When Hunsacker didn't respond, Jonah leaned forward. "In other words, forget whatever it is you're holding against Ms. Moretti. Got it?" He knew he was probably being too much of a hard-ass. It wasn't his style. But he was hoping to provoke Hunsacker. If Hunsacker told him to go to hell, he'd have a good excuse to approach the sheriff and have himself replaced with someone else from Department 6. One second, all he wanted to do was return to California and forget he'd ever seen Francesca again. The next, he was eager to prove that he wasn't as bad as she thought. Regardless of his feelings, however, he had enough to do without tolerating a belligerent investigator, especially one as mediocre as Hunsacker.

Finch nudged his partner. "Come on, Hugh. I know you're stressed. We all are. But fighting among ourselves won't help."

"We're just as important to this investigation as *he* is," he grumbled, jerking a thumb at Jonah. "Maybe we're not getting paid the big bucks, but we're local. We're the ones who know the area and the mind-set of the people living in it."

"What are you after?" Jonah asked. "An ego boost? Are you not feeling *valued?*"

Hunsacker's watery eyes lifted. "I know Butch, okay?"

Silence engulfed the room, a silence that stretched until Finch murmured, "What'd you say?"

Releasing a heavy sigh, Hunsacker rubbed his forehead. "He goes to my church."

"And you didn't think to mention it before now?" Jonah asked.

"I didn't want you to assume I was biased, that a previous...affiliation would get in the way of the investigation." He glowered at all of them. "Because it won't. I've just been trying to point out that Butch is innocent until proven guilty, and we currently have no proof that he's done anything wrong."

"We've got to start somewhere, Hugh," Finch said.

"I have a slightly different perspective on Butch." He hesitated. "I've seen his good points."

Francesca slid the wire she'd put on the table to one side. "Which are..."

"When Peggy lost her job at the supermarket last year, we went through a hard time financially, okay? It happens to the best of us." His tone challenged any one of them to disagree. "We assumed she'd have no problem getting on somewhere else so we didn't start saving soon enough. And then she didn't get a job for several months, and we began to fall behind on our mortgage. We were about to lose the house when some of the people at my church took up a collection."

"You never said a word to me about any of this," Finch said.

Hunsacker shot his partner a self-conscious glance. "You knew Peggy lost her job."

"But I didn't realize you needed help, that you weren't making ends meet."

"You have your own problems." He spoke into his chest now. "And I didn't want you to know. I guess...I guess I was embarrassed. It's not easy to talk about."

"Don't tell me Butch contributed," Jonah said.

Hunsacker's double chin wagged as he lifted his face. "He did. He lent us a thousand dollars, much more than anyone else. And you can tell he doesn't have a lot. That says something about a guy, doesn't it? That he'd help an acquaintance who was down on his luck—without asking for anything in return?"

When no one answered, he added, "Sociopaths aren't supposed to feel empathy."

"That doesn't mean they can't ever be kind," Francesca said. "Maybe he liked the ego boost of being able to help you, a cop."

"If so, he never rubbed my nose in it." Hunsacker shrugged. "He never spoke of it at all. Treated me just the same as he ever did."

"Still, we know Butch is no saint—" Francesca began, but Hunsacker cut her off.

"He might not be faithful to his wife. He might not be all that nice to his mentally impaired brother-in-law. But maybe he has reasons for what he does that we know nothing about. Maybe his wife is frigid and won't let him near her. Maybe his brother-in-law is such a pain in the ass he can't stand living with him but does it because Dean has nowhere else to go. Who can say? I can't believe he's a killer. I need proof. But so will a jury," he said, as if that justified his stance.

"We aren't going to charge him without proof," Jonah said.

"I realize that. I'm just…asking you to keep an open mind, to understand that this guy is a decent person, at least some of the time, and that maybe there's someone else out there, someone we're overlooking."

"Like Dean?" Francesca said.

"Like Dean," Hunsacker replied. "If he's somehow following Butch around, he could certainly have come across April after Butch left her."

"He can't even drive," Finch pointed out.

"Legally," Hunsacker clarified. "That doesn't mean he never gets behind the wheel. I've seen him at church and other places by himself, plenty of times. I've never wondered how he got there, but I'm telling you he seems to get around okay."

"Question is…does he have the presence of mind to hide his crimes?" Jonah asked. "Because whoever's doing the killing is pretty damn good at covering his tracks. Look how long he's been active. Some of the remains we've unearthed at Dead Mule Canyon have been in the ground for five years. Going undiscovered for such a lengthy period isn't typical of someone who kills due to hearing voices or some other mental problem. Those killers act out and move on and generally don't do a good job of cleaning up, if they even try."

"Maybe he's not good at hiding what he's been doing," Hunsacker said. "Maybe it's just that everyone already assumes he's incapable, so they look past him."

Jonah's eyes locked with Francesca's. "That's possible."

Covering her face for a second, she tried to imagine Butch as a benefactor. "Whether it's Butch or Dean doesn't make much difference to me. They both have my address." She dropped her hands. "They have the addresses of all my friends and family, too."

Standing back, well out of reach, Adriana peered through her partially opened front door. A man with a slight build and a heart-shaped face, made pointier by a patch of beard growing on the end of his chin, stood on her stoop. With large blue eyes and fine blond hair, he appeared to be no older than twenty-five, and he looked innocent, completely unthreatening. But she knew his baby face could hide more than his age. "*Who* are you again?" she asked.

"Dean. Dean Wheeler."

That was the name she'd thought he said, the one Francesca had mentioned with Butch Vaughn's on the phone last night. Knowing this man was connected to someone Francesca believed had murdered quite a few people, Adriana tightened her hand on the door handle in case she needed to slam it fast, and was glad she'd been cautious enough to leave the chain in place. Fortunately, she'd put the boys down late for their nap, so they were still sleeping, although it was close to dinnertime. Otherwise, if they were up, they'd be running around, maybe even playing in the front yard, making it very difficult for her to feel she could protect them. "Butch Vaughn's brother-in-law?" she said.

"That's right." He smiled broadly. "You know Butch?"

"Francesca told me about him."

His smile dimmed a bit. "What'd she say?"

"Not much."

"They don't get along," he explained.

She let her breath ease out. "Right. She told me that."

"Did she tell you she thinks he's a murderer?"

How should she answer this? "Is he?" she asked.

"Oh, no. My brother-in-law can seem formidable, but he's really not what Francesca thinks."

The heat was beginning to overpower her air conditioner. Adriana wanted Dean to go away so she could close and lock her door—then call her husband and ask him to come home early. "I hope you're right."

"Did she mention me, by any chance?"

This question surprised Adriana. Why would he suppose Francesca would mention him? "Um, she said you had her purse, if that's what you mean."

"I don't have it anymore. I gave it back." The satisfaction in his voice indicated he was very pleased with himself.

"That was nice of you."

"I'm always nice." Craning his neck, he tried to look into the house. "Where are your kids?"

Her heart began to beat faster. "They're not here."

"Are they with your husband?" Dean didn't seem in any hurry to go.

"Yes, yes, they are. But they should all be home soon. Any minute, actually."

He turned around, studied the yard. "What does Stan do for a living?"

Hoping to get him to leave, Adriana allowed her confusion to show. "I'm sorry, but...I'm not sure I understand why you're here, Dean. What can I do for you? And... how do you know my husband's name?"

"Oh." He laughed as if he should've explained earlier. "Now I understand why you're nervous. There's no need to be. You see, it's right here." He reached into his pocket and pulled out a stack of pictures tucked in protective plastic sheaths that Adriana recognized as belonging to Francesca. "Stan Covington." He flipped to the wallet-size of her family's Christmas picture. "Says so right there. That's you, isn't it?"

She couldn't deny it. "Yes."

"And those are your boys, Levi and Tyler?"

Swallowing hard, she nodded.

"They're cute. I wish I could meet them."

Forcing a smile, she narrowed the opening of the door by another inch. "Like I said, they're not here."

"Too bad."

Silence fell, but he didn't seem to care how strained and awkward it was. "I'm afraid I still don't understand what you want," she said at length.

His eyes widened as though it should be obvious. "I've got these." He pointed to the pictures. "They're Francesca's. I'm returning them. They must've fallen out of her purse."

Were there other things that'd "fallen" out, as well? Would he bring them all back, one by one? "I see.

That's…very sweet of you." She suddenly noticed that he was wearing two different tennis shoes. Was he not aware of it? Or was it something he'd done on purpose? "I'll tell you what. Why don't you leave the pictures with me? I'll give them back to her for you."

That wasn't the answer he'd been hoping to hear. Visibly reluctant, he hesitated but ultimately handed the pictures through the door. "I wouldn't want her to think I'm trying to keep them," he said.

"Right."

"I'd never do that."

"Of course you wouldn't. Thanks for bringing them by."

"Tell her I stopped at her house, too, but no one was home. Fortunately, you two don't live very far apart."

If he'd already been to Francesca's, why hadn't he left the pictures on her doorstep or in her mailbox? "I will. I've got to get back to what I was doing. Dinner's in the oven," Adriana said.

"Oh, sure. No problem. But, before I go, would you mind giving me a drink of water? It's really hot this afternoon, and I've got a long bus ride back to Prescott."

Adriana's pulse kicked up even more. She'd have to take the chain off the door in order to fit a glass of water through the opening. And she wasn't willing to do that. She had her boys at home. No way would she provide this odd man with the opportunity to break in on them. "I'm sorry," she said. "I—I'm afraid I can't do that."

He seemed stunned. "Why not?"

Before she could answer, Tyler's voice rose behind her. "Mommy, who's here?"

Dean's vanishing smile told her he knew she'd lied to him. She even thought she detected a hint of shrewd calculation behind that innocent face. But she couldn't focus on trying to figure out what he might be thinking or feeling. Tyler was pushing to get between her and the door so he could see, and she was doing her best to block him. "I've got to go," she said, and closed the door.

Grabbing her oldest son, Adriana whispered for him to be still and, probably because he could sense her anxiety, he listened. "Please leave…please leave," she muttered above his head. Dean wouldn't go around the house and try to get in some other way, would he? There was no reason for him to bother. They'd had such a short exchange, one that shouldn't have meant *anything*.

Then why was she so rattled?

Because he didn't seem to understand that her polite responses were merely civility and not friendship. When he'd realized she'd lied to him, he'd seemed so…betrayed, as if she somehow owed him access to her children. It gave her the creeps.

"What's wrong, Mommy?" Tyler whispered, his body now stiff with fear.

"Nothing, baby. It'll be okay. Just…just be quiet for a few minutes and come with me." She planned to lead him to the kitchen window, where she could look out and, hopefully, confirm that Dean was leaving. But she didn't stop there. A scream drew her to Levi's bedroom instead.

15

Her parents were trying to reach her. Francesca stared at her family name on caller ID and almost let the call transfer to voice mail. With everything else that was going on, she didn't have time to chat. Besides, she hadn't yet decided how much she wanted them to know about what was happening in her life these days. She saw no point in worrying them, not when they'd come straight back to Phoenix if they thought she was in any danger. But they offered emotional support and a good sounding board—and they'd worry about her safety just as much if they couldn't get hold of her.

Deciding to reassure them, and be judicious with the other details, she stepped out of the lobby of the fast-food restaurant, where Jonah was meeting a cop named Ernie, and answered.

"Hello?"

"Fran?"

"Hi, Dad."

"What's going on? Your mother says she's been trying to reach you at the house for two days. It rings but your voice mail never comes on."

Because the line had been cut. Francesca contemplated telling the truth, but resolved not to. "Something's wrong with my service. They're working on it. Why didn't she just call my cell?"

"She did. More than once."

There were all those voice mails she'd received yesterday, the ones she hadn't taken the time to go through. And this morning she'd turned off her cell so she wouldn't be interrupted. She hadn't turned it back on until a few minutes ago. "I'm sorry. I wasn't even aware that you guys were trying to get hold of me. I haven't had a chance to listen to my messages."

"Why not? What's up?"

She smiled at the intrigue in his voice, knew his question revealed a professional interest as much as a personal one. "I've been working a new missing-persons case."

"A woman? A child?"

"A woman."

"Any luck finding her?"

Plugging one ear, she turned away from the street so she could hear. "The hunt is over. Her body was discovered yesterday."

There was a brief silence. "I can see why you've been busy. How old was she?"

"Only a year older than me."

"What a shame," he said with a reverence she appreciated. "Do you know what happened?"

Because her father was the type who'd go stir-crazy if he didn't have something important to do, and he missed his job with the force, he hadn't entirely stopped working. He took on various cold cases, pro bono. His wheelchair didn't get in the way of that. "It looks as if she was beaten with a baseball bat."

"A crime of anger."

"Anger against her specifically or anger against women in general?" she asked.

"Could be either, I suppose. Do you have any suspects?"

"Only the man who saw her last."

"He have an alibi?"

"He hasn't given the police a formal statement yet. They'll be moving on that soon. They sent me in with a wire first, hoping to get him to talk more freely. Now they want to put some time between the two conversations, give him an opportunity to think about it...."

"Did he tell you anything interesting?"

"Not really. But we've got the conversation on tape, so we'll see if he changes his story. As far as an alibi goes, his wife will most likely cover for him, which means... it'll be up to us to place him at the scene of the crime. If we can find where the murder was committed, that is. The body was transported and dumped."

"Sounds precalculated."

"There's a possibility this guy is tied to other murders, maybe seven of them."

"Holy hell."

A man honked and shouted at her, but she ignored it. "Exactly."

"Who's *us?*" her father wanted to know.

"Us?"

"You said, 'It'll be up to us.' You're working with the police?"

"I am. The Yavapai County Sheriff's Office and a consultant from California." She didn't mention Jonah by name. She knew her parents wouldn't be thrilled to hear that the man who'd broken her heart was back in her life, even if only in a professional capacity.

"A consultant, huh?"

"Apparently, he has experience with this type of case."

"Is anyone using the words *serial killer* yet?"

"Not publicly. But news is bound to get out soon."

"This will be a tough one."

"I know." It was already tough. She remembered the terror she'd felt the night before last at her house. But she had to see this through. Although Jill had said she'd pay her when Francesca promised not to abandon the investigation, Francesca didn't have the heart to charge for her services, not after what Jill and Vince had lost. Maybe that wasn't the smartest business decision she'd ever made but, at this point, it wasn't about generating income. Francesca *wanted* to bring April's killer to justice. The way things were going, the life she saved might be her own.

"Just remember, serial killers like to take their victims somewhere they feel comfortable, safe. Find that place, and you'll likely find the crime scene."

Butch would feel most comfortable at the salvage yard. But they didn't have enough evidence to get a search warrant, not after the search they'd already performed, as cursory as it'd been thanks to Hunsacker's sense of indebtedness to their primary suspect.

Still…there had to be a way to get a better look at Butch's home turf. Even with his family at the house, he'd have all the privacy he'd need in one of those sheds or among the gigantic rows of rubbish. Predators had hidden their victims in much smaller yards than his, hadn't they? Take Jaycee Dugard, for example. She'd been held hostage in a tent behind a fairly regular suburban house for twenty-four years. Or that Austrian woman who'd been kept in the basement dungeon of her own father's house for sixteen years.

Francesca wished they could somehow lure Butch

off the property and take a look around while he was gone….

"Francesca?"

"What?" She'd let her mind wander, missed something her father had said.

"I asked if you'd like me to do a background check on your suspect, see what I can learn from here."

Walt was very talented on a computer and even better at tracking down pertinent information over the phone. "That'd be great, Dad." Maybe he'd come across a detail they would've missed. "While you're at it, see if you can find a link between Butch Vaughn and another victim, a woman by the name of Bianca Andersen, okay?"

"Sure. Let me get a pen so I can take down her information."

Jonah walked out of the Jack in the Box just as her father came back on the line. "What was that name again?"

"Hang on." Francesca covered the phone. "Is that Bianca's dental file?" she asked, nodding at the cardboard folder he held.

"Yeah."

Taking it from him, she opened it and recited the patient information, including Bianca's social security number. "Keep an eye out for the name Dean Wheeler, too," she said.

"Who's Dean Wheeler?"

"Butch's brother-in-law. He's got some mental health problems. I'm trying to figure out what that means and what medication he's on."

"I'll see what I can find. What's Butch's address?"

She gave him the address of the salvage yard, explained Butch's living arrangements and provided Walt with April Bonner's name and address, too.

"Who's helping out?" Jonah wanted to know.

"My father."

A hint of wariness entered his eyes, but he managed a casual smile. "How's he doing these days?"

"Good. Fine."

"Who's that?" her father asked.

"The consultant from California."

"What, I don't have a name anymore?" Jonah said.

"Call me if you come up with anything," she said into the phone, and disconnected before responding to Jonah. "Did you really want me to tell him your name?"

Jonah watched her drop her phone into her purse. "I thought we'd decided to let bygones be bygones."

"*We* decided that. My father never agreed."

"He's still holding a grudge?"

"What do you think?"

Frowning, he hooked his thumbs in his pockets. "You had to tell 'em, huh?"

His comment made her angry. "Wait a second," she said. "Don't act as if *I* was disloyal to *you*."

His eyes were troubled when they met hers. "God, Fran, haven't you ever screwed up? Done something you regret?"

She couldn't take the torture on his face. She wanted to forgive him, knew in that minute that she *could* forgive him. But if she let go of the past, she'd only fall for him again, and she couldn't allow that. Why set herself up for more hurt and disappointment?

Scrambling to shore up her crumbling resentment, she threw back her shoulders. "Nothing that resulted in a child."

He stared at the ground for several seconds before meeting her gaze again. "Thanks for reminding me."

Pressing her palm to her forehead, she searched for

the words to explain. "Look, I told them because..." Because she'd needed them. She'd lost her boyfriend and her best friend at the same time. And once she'd chosen to hang on to her friendship with Adriana, she'd had to tolerate a pregnancy that should never have happened, had to watch Adriana give birth to the child of the man *she* loved. Her parents were the ones who'd helped her make sense of it all, who'd helped her rebuild the part of her that'd been so damaged. "Because I never thought we'd see each other again. It's not as if I ever expected... this."

He pinched the bridge of his nose. "You were right to do what you did."

She was pretty sure he was being sincere. And it was true; if he'd been faithful to her, she would've had nothing to tell. So why did it feel as if she was the one who'd wronged him?

Turning away, he hit the button that unlocked the doors of her car. "You driving or am I?"

Grateful for the change of subject, the return to business, she tried to tell herself that whatever residual emotions remained between them didn't matter. They couldn't ever be together. So what if she could forgive him? She'd never be able to trust him. The way he attracted women, who was to say the urge to cheat wouldn't prove too great someday, just like it had with Adriana? "Where are we going?"

"To talk to Bianca's family and friends, try to figure out how she ended up buried in Dead Mule Canyon and see if anyone remembers her associating with a guy named Butch Vaughn."

"What if he used an alias?"

"We'll get as far as we can with a description."

"Finch and Hunsacker won't have a problem with us following up on this lead?"

"I just cleared it with Finch. They're busy at the Rio Grande and they need the help."

"How far is Bianca's last known address from here?"

"According to my GPS, about twenty minutes." That wasn't really close to the salvage yard, but it wasn't terribly far, either.

"I'll drive," she said. Then maybe she'd be less tempted to stare at him and remember what it'd been like to feel as if her next breath depended on his.

The man who came to the apartment door had a head of curly dark hair, a full beard and an earring in one ear. From the sweat dampening his T-shirt, the weight set in the living room and the clank of iron they'd heard when they first approached the door, it was obvious that they'd interrupted him while he was lifting.

Jonah took the lead. "Terrance Andersen?"

A leery expression slipped over his rather plain features. "Yes?"

"We're—"

"Detectives," he broke in without even looking at the card Jonah held out. "I can tell. Is something wrong?"

Jonah didn't bother correcting him about their professions. For the moment, "detective" was close enough. "Yes. We're here about your wife."

He gripped the door frame. "Where is she? Why'd she leave me? Why didn't she ever call or come back for the rest of her stuff?"

"She *couldn't* come back," Francesca said. "She was murdered over a year ago."

His jaw dropped. "She…what?"

"Her body was found in Dead Mule Canyon last month," Jonah said. "It's taken us all that time to identify her remains."

Terrance shoved a hand in his hair, holding the long, curly locks back from his face. "No wonder I never heard from her. I thought it was all because of that last big argument. She walked out with a suitcase she'd packed right then and there, and I never saw her again. But…I never dreamed that…that she *couldn't* call me."

"When's the last time you saw her?" Jonah asked.

"It's been fourteen months. She never showed up for work after that, but…I thought it was because she'd left the area."

"You mentioned an argument," Francesca said. "What was it about?"

Drawing a deep breath, he allowed his hair to fall naturally. "She wanted us to quit our jobs and take off, see the world. We used to talk about it while we were dating, but…I thought it was a pipe dream, you know? I didn't see how we'd ever make enough money to travel like that. But she said we'd pick up odd jobs until we could save enough to move on to the next place. She said if we didn't leave now we'd become resigned to a life of drudgery like everyone else. She was scared to stay and I was scared to go. But I wish now that—" words failed him as tears gathered in his eyes "—that I'd had the guts to go for it the way she did. Maybe she'd still be alive."

To give him a modicum of privacy in which to deal with his emotions, Francesca studied the floor.

"Here I've been kicking myself for what I said that night," he went on. "Over and over, ever since. And praying she'd come back. I can't tell you how many times I've checked my answering machine, hoping to hear her voice. I thought she might contact me when she had her fill of adventure, if only to tell me how great it was. But I finally decided a little while ago that I had to let go of the past and move on, that she must've found someone else."

When Terrance dropped his head in his hands, Jonah motioned to the couch inside. "Maybe you should sit down for a few minutes."

Leaving the door open, Terrance crossed to the living room, where he fell onto the sofa and stared off into space.

Jonah nudged Francesca into the apartment. Other than the sofa, a chair and the weight set they'd been able to spot from the door, there wasn't much furniture, but large amateurish paintings covered the walls.

"She did all these," he said, following Francesca's gaze from a large sunflower with thick globs of yellow paint on each petal to a windmill towering over blowing grass to a portrait of Terrance himself. Although Bianca hadn't been a very good artist, each painting revealed a love of nature and an exuberance that made Francesca sad to think this life had been extinguished.

Jonah sat on the weight bench while she took the chair. "Are you going to be okay?" he asked Terrance.

"I don't know. Her being dead feels so…unreal." He pulled strands of his beard through his fingers. "I guess it helps to know she might've come back to me if she'd been capable of it, that she might've missed me as much as I've missed her. But to think she was hurt and I wasn't there…that, in a way, I caused her death because of that stupid fight…"

"You didn't cause it," Francesca insisted.

"She wouldn't have been out there alone if we hadn't argued." His eyes suddenly filled with anger. "Who did it? And why?"

"That's what we're trying to find out," Jonah said.

The hand fingering his beard grew idle. "You don't know?"

"No." Francesca's iPhone rang with a few strains of "I'll Stand by You." Adriana was trying to reach her. Unwilling to step outside, she silenced it instead of taking the call. "We're hoping you can help us find the person who's responsible."

He spread his hands. "How? Just tell me how."

"Have you ever heard the name Butch Vaughn?"

"Never."

"You're sure?"

"Positive. Butch isn't a very common name. It would've stood out."

Jonah described Butch, too, but this also drew a blank, so he moved on. "What about Dean Wheeler?"

Terrance started to shake his head, but doubt crept into his expression and he stopped. "Wait a second... that one sounds sort of familiar."

Francesca scooted forward. "Do you have any idea where you might've heard it before?"

"No, but...I suppose Dean could've been one of her patients."

"She was a doctor?"

"A nurse. At Laurel Oaks Behavioral Hospital on the other side of town. She was always coming home with stories about the crazies she met there. She didn't call them that, of course. She was pretty PC, defended them whenever I said anything about the nut house. She got to know some of the patients quite well. Felt sorry for most. Loved a few. Was afraid of others."

Had Dean ever been a patient at Laurel Oaks? If so, was he one of those Bianca had feared? "Maybe we've found the link," Francesca whispered to Jonah. It could be Dean and not Butch who'd committed the murders. But it couldn't have been Dean who'd cut her phone line, not unless she'd seen only what she'd expected to see when she looked out at the pool. Had her mind been playing tricks on her?

"It should be easy enough to check," Jonah said.

Terrance blinked several times. "What are you talking about?"

"There's a man with behavioral problems who's also been associated with another death," Jonah explained. "We need to find out if he was a patient at Laurel Oaks."

"After everything she tried to do for those people that would be ironic, wouldn't it?" Terrence muttered.

"What was she driving when she left?" Jonah asked.

"A gray Toyota Prius. Sort of charcoal-colored. She insisted on owning an electric car, wanted to go green and save the environment. I've never seen such a recycling buff. She was so…unusual. So…special," he added. "I've never gotten over her. Maybe I never will."

Francesca caught sight of a photograph sitting on the counter. A dark-haired, dark-eyed woman, slightly overweight and wearing a witch's costume, smiled out at the room. "Is that Bianca?"

Terrence nodded. "On our last Halloween together."

Jonah got up and strode over. "Did you ever recover her car?"

"No. Then I would've known something happened to her. She'd never abandon it."

"So where could it have gone?" Francesca asked, but even as the question passed her lips, she knew—the salvage yard.

16

The Dean Wheeler situation was an excuse to call Jonah. Adriana knew it. She could wait until Francesca called her back. She'd hear from her eventually. But she had something worth telling, something that could possibly affect Fran and Jonah and whatever case they were working on, and she couldn't resist calling Jonah with it.

In case Dean returned, she kept her boys where she could see them and used her cordless phone to dial Jonah's number. She'd memorized it and thrown away the paper on which she'd jotted it when he'd called her yesterday. She didn't want to risk having her husband come across that number. What if he thought it was a message for him and called Jonah?

That wouldn't be good. She hadn't even told Stan that Jonah was back.

"Hello?"

The sound of Jonah's voice caused the usual flip-flop in her stomach. She hated it. But, as much as she wished otherwise, she couldn't seem to manage a more acceptable response. "Hi, uh, Jonah? This is Adriana."

There was a slight pause. "What can I do for you, Adriana?"

"I've been trying to reach Francesca, but she's not

picking up. You wouldn't know where she is, would you?"

She hoped not. She wanted to use Dean's visit to strike up a conversation that might lead into the more personal questions she was dying to ask. But it wasn't to be.

"She's right here," he said. "Hang on a minute."

Cringing with disappointment—and a small amount of embarrassment—she held her breath as she waited, wondering what she'd expected to accomplish by talking to Jonah, anyway. Even if he suddenly decided that he regretted his choice ten years ago and wanted to be with her, they couldn't have a relationship. She had a family now, would never leave Stan. So why was she still so eager for his attention, still hoping he'd realize what she had to offer and want her the way she'd always wanted him?

"Adriana?"

At Francesca's voice, she released her breath and tried to act as normal as possible. "Hi. Where've you been? Why aren't you answering my calls?"

"Sorry. It's been a crazy day. What—what's going on?"

That little hitch worried her. Was Francesca's response cooler than usual? Maybe. Or was she imagining it? Sure she'd called Jonah, but she'd immediately requested Francesca. That should've made it okay.

However, she'd done similar things a decade ago whenever she could—and that made her self-conscious about it now. "I wanted to tell you that Dean Wheeler came by."

"What did you say?"

"Dean Wheeler. That guy you mentioned? The brother-in-law of the man you think might've murdered that woman?"

"I know who you're talking about. I just can't believe he showed up at your house."

"It was weird. He knocked at my door about—" she glanced at the clock "—an hour ago."

Fortunately, the information she had to impart directed all attention away from the fact that she'd called Jonah, just as she'd known it would. She felt both relieved and guilty about that. She hadn't talked to Jonah for more than a few seconds, but at least there shouldn't be a backlash for making the attempt.

"What did he want?" Francesca asked.

"He had your pictures, the ones you carry around in your purse."

"What was he doing with those?"

"He said he was trying to return them. That he'd already been to your place. I have them here now, but I don't know why he didn't leave them on your doorstep."

"Neither do I. Except…he seems very interested in my friends and neighbors."

"I have to admit his visit was kind of unsettling. Even after I promised to give you the pictures he didn't leave. He went around the house, into the backyard and peeked in the downstairs windows. He nearly scared Levi to death. The poor kid was just waking up from his nap when he saw a strange man staring at him from outside."

"Did Dean try to get in? Attempt to harm you or the boys in any way?"

"No. When he realized he'd frightened us, he ran away, and he hasn't been back since. I've kept a close eye on the yard, just in case."

"When's Stan getting home?"

Francesca's subdued response actually made Adriana feel more frightened than she'd been before calling. She'd already convinced herself that Dean was simply an un-usual but well-meaning person. "Any minute. Why?"

"I'll feel more comfortable if you're not alone. Keep the house locked up, and if Dean comes back, call the police."

Adriana watched Tyler wield the television remote, looking for a program he and his brother could agree on. "But you don't *really* think he's dangerous, do you?"

"He might be. Don't take any chances."

"I won't."

Someone spoke in the background, most likely Jonah. The voice was muffled, suggesting Francesca had cov-ered the mouthpiece. "How'd Dean get there?" she asked when she was back. "Did someone drive him?"

"Not that I could see. There was no car. He claims he took a bus."

"All the way from Prescott?"

"He acted as if no price was too high. Like he really wanted to do you this favor."

"He could've called me about it. Or mailed them to me."

"I think he wants contact. I'm telling you…it was as though he felt you two were in some sort of relationship. A close friendship, at least."

"That makes me shudder, Adriana."

"I can see why. Are you…are you going to be okay?" She wasn't really worried. Francesca was with Jonah, wasn't she? He'd look out for her. Adriana had always felt safe when she was in Jonah's company. She was sure he could handle himself in a fight if necessary, and he was street-smart, savvy in a way her soft, bookish husband was not.

"I'm fine. Worried. This case has me reeling. I've never been involved in anything like it."

"Do you think you'll be able to solve it?" she asked. But what she really wanted to know was whether Francesca and Jonah were getting back together. Francesca hadn't come home last night. Adriana knew because she'd driven by her place twice, had gone the long way to the video store just to see if she'd find Jonah's car out front. She would've asked Francesca about Jonah, except she'd lost all right to that information when she betrayed her ten years earlier.

"I hope so."

The phone beeped, signaling another call. She held it away from her for a second to check caller ID. "Stan's trying to reach me. I'd better go."

"Okay. Let me know if you hear from Dean again."

"I doubt he'll be back. Not tonight."

"He has your number, too. You should be aware of that."

"Got it. I'll talk to you later."

Thinking that had gone as well as could be expected, she breathed a sigh of relief as she hung up and answered her husband's call. "Hi, honey. You almost home?"

"I'm afraid not. One of my patients, a five-year-old girl, has just been admitted to the hospital with a serious infection."

"I'm sorry to hear that." Sometimes she didn't understand how he withstood all the stress of his job. Being a doctor paid well, enabled her to be a stay-at-home mom to their children. But she was concerned about him, knew the worry he felt for his patients weighed heavily on him. "Is she going to make it?"

"I hope so."

Gazing outside, she thought about her encounter with Dean. "How long do you think you'll be?"

"Who knows? Don't wait up, though. It might be late."

The shadows of the trees lengthened on the lawn as daylight faded to darkness. "Okay. No problem." This wasn't a night Adriana wanted to spend alone. She hadn't even had a chance to explain that she'd had an unwelcome visitor. But she didn't see any reason to tell Stan now. Why worry him? He couldn't be with her; he had to take care of that child.

Fifteen minutes later she didn't mind being alone quite so much. She was too busy digging through the old photographs she'd taken out of the garage and was actually grateful for the privacy.

"There it is," she murmured as she held up a picture of Jonah cradling their baby just before they had to relinquish her to the care of her new parents.

"Is everything okay?" Jonah asked as Francesca returned his phone.

She avoided his gaze in case he could see more in her expression than she wanted to reveal. She hated that Adriana had called him, even if it was to talk to her. She couldn't help suspecting her best friend of being a little too eager to hear his voice. Which was crazy. Adriana was married with two kids. She loved Stan. Francesca hadn't been a jealous person until ten years ago. After what had happened, she'd changed—and not for the better.

"I'm not sure," she said.

"What do you mean?"

She told him what Adriana had said, then added, "Dean could've left those pictures at my place but didn't. I'm afraid showing up at Adriana's was his way of making me aware of his familiarity with my friends."

"How'd he get there?" he asked, repeating the question he'd fed her when she was on the phone.

"By bus."

"So that's why we haven't seen him. He's not around." They were in the van Investigator Finch had arranged for them to use, parked on a dirt side road near the salvage yard. Through a pair of binoculars, they'd seen Paris come and go in the Impala, twice. Had watched Butch drive an old pickup around the property. Had even spotted Paris's parents driving off in a black Oldsmobile. But they hadn't spotted Dean. And now they knew why.

"He seems to get around pretty well for not having a car," she said.

Jonah tapped the steering wheel. "He's starting to make me nervous."

"How much longer until we hear from your guy about the meds?"

"He'll call when he has what we need."

What they needed was a profile on Dean's mental condition, a list of the medications he was taking and whether or not he'd ever been a patient at Laurel Oaks Behavioral Hospital. Jonah claimed Department 6 had people who could get that information—who could get just about any information. He said that'd be quicker than going through the sheriff's department here in Prescott. Since Hunsacker and Finch were out knocking on doors to see if they could find someone who might've seen April along the highway the night she was killed, Francesca had no problem with turning to an outside entity. Her father was trying to help, too, wasn't he? But it was getting late. She doubted they'd hear anything until tomorrow and wasn't looking forward to the wait.

"You really think we'll be able to search for Bianca's car?" she asked.

Jonah slouched in his seat. "Butch has got to go in eventually."

They'd been hoping for an opportunity to get close to the chain-link fence surrounding the salvage yard for hours. But there'd been too much activity. They didn't want to be seen snooping around, using binoculars, taking pictures. If he felt threatened, Butch could move or hide evidence. And if he *was* the person who'd cut her telephone line, Francesca didn't feel it was a good idea to keep jumping into his sights. She wanted to feel comfortable in her own house again. If that was even possible.

"This could take a while," she said when she saw Butch getting back in his truck. "He's still working."

She handed Jonah the binoculars to have a look for himself. "Surveillance too tedious for you?" he asked.

"I think it's the cramped conditions that are bothering me."

"Cramped conditions? We have the whole van to ourselves."

Therein lay the problem. It wasn't easy to be alone with Jonah during the day, let alone at night. Especially in such a private setting. They could do just about anything out here and no one would know about it. The potential for secrecy made Francesca feel free, daring, almost as if she could avoid responsibility for her own actions….

Catching her bottom lip between her teeth, she studied him for a moment, then drew a deep breath. "Tell me something."

He set the binoculars aside. "What's that?"

"What's it like?"

Her change in tone caused a certain wariness to come over him. *"It?"*

"Talking to Adriana after so long."

He didn't respond.

"What? You don't want to answer?"

"Are we really going to do this?" he asked, watching her from beneath half-lowered eyelids.

"You had a baby with her. Don't you ever think about her? The child? How things might've been different if you'd married?"

"Don't dredge this up."

"Why? You're the one who wanted to talk about it in the past. Well, now I'm ready."

He scowled. "You're not ready. You're looking for a pound of flesh. *My* flesh."

"And you don't think you owe it to me?"

"Fine." He shrugged as if he didn't care but she suspected he did. "I wish I'd married her, okay? Is that what you want to hear? God knows you won't believe anything else, so there you have it. I was an asshole with no heart, out to hurt anyone I could, and I tried to destroy your life and hers just for the hell of it. I used you both, like I use all women."

The muscle that jumped in his cheek warned her to back off, but the compulsion to hurt him as he'd hurt her goaded her to continue. "What if I'd gotten pregnant at the same time she did?"

He shook his head.

"It could've happened," she went on. "You were sleeping with both of us."

"I wasn't *sleeping* with both of you," he muttered with a scowl.

"She didn't get that baby by immaculate conception, Jonah."

It was only one night. At least, that was what Adriana had insisted all these years. Francesca wanted to hear

Jonah say it, too. But he didn't give her the satisfaction. He didn't even attempt to defend himself.

"You're right. She got it the old-fashioned way. And I enjoyed every minute of it, okay? Too bad she's married. Maybe we could go at it again, since a good lay is all that's ever mattered to me."

Francesca winced even though she knew he didn't mean it. *Couldn't* mean it. He was being purposely nasty. All the tension they'd felt since running into each other again was bubbling to the surface, slamming one jagged emotion into another. "What if Adriana and I had both gotten pregnant?" she asked again.

"Then I would've walked out on you the way I walked out on her," he said, his eyes glittering with reckless abandon. "Convinced you to give away my own flesh and blood. Never looked back. How can you expect anything more from a guy like me?"

"I don't know how I couldn't see it," she whispered.

She didn't need to spell it out. She could tell he knew she meant that he'd managed to deceive her, that she'd once thought so much more highly of him than he deserved.

"I guess you never looked close enough."

That muscle twitched in his cheek again, but she ignored it. Instead, she fought the tears clogging her throat. "At least I see you more clearly now."

"Good. Then you'll know to keep your distance. Dealing with me isn't for the emotionally fragile."

"Emotionally fragile?" She barked a laugh. "You couldn't hurt me if you tried. Not anymore."

"Oh, yeah? You think I can't sense the chemistry between us? It's not gone, Francesca. Whether you admit it or not, it's far from gone."

"What chemistry? You mean sexual attraction? So

what if it's still there? It's all physical. You think I can't enjoy a free ride and walk away when it's over just as easily as you can?"

He twisted in his seat to confront her more directly. "Is that what you want from me? A free ride? For old times' sake?"

It seemed that the color had drained from his face but in the failing light she couldn't be certain, and the edge to his voice challenged her to prove her words. "What's wrong with a cheap thrill? That's what you gave my best friend, isn't it? That's what you offer every girl you meet. Why should I be any different? Apparently, it was *my* mistake to expect more when we were together."

His gaze raked over her chest before moving lower and suddenly she wanted his hands every place his eyes touched. The tightly leashed aggression simmering inside him didn't frighten her. If they came together now, if they made love only to quench the desire clawing at her belly, she could have what she wanted without being forced to acknowledge that what she felt might be more than lust.

"Get in the back," he snapped.

To show him how much she resented him and the effect he had on her, she narrowed her eyes. "Make me."

His muscles contracted but he didn't reach for her. Dropping his head against the seat, he filled his lungs with the same air she was breathing—air that smelled of both of them, air they'd warmed with their angry words and the heat of their aroused bodies.

"What's the matter?" she asked when he made no move. "Don't tell me Casanova's lost his touch."

He swallowed but didn't open his eyes. "Sorry, I'm not interested."

Francesca wasn't sure why he'd changed his mind suddenly. Sexual tension radiated from him, proving the exact opposite of his words. So why was he holding back? What did *he* have to lose?

Afraid he really would deny her, she took his hand and placed it on her breast. "What's the matter? Sex no fun unless you're cheating on someone? Why not pretend you've got a wife at home? That should get you hot."

The fingers that had started to cup her breast stiffened, and deep furrows formed between his eyebrows. She'd stung him with that barb; she could tell. But she refused to regret it. She wanted him too badly—but she didn't want to love him.

"If you expect to be treated like a whore, you're going to have to find someone else," he said, and got out of the van.

Jonah strode down the dirt road, away from the salvage yard, as quickly as possible. He wasn't sure what had just happened but whatever it was, it'd felt as if Francesca had carved out his heart and served it up on a platter. He couldn't catch his breath, slow his racing pulse or feel anything except the overwhelming desire that had prompted him to make a difficult situation even worse.

What if Adriana and I had both gotten pregnant?

Did Francesca really believe he could've turned his back on her? He'd felt nothing more than mild friendship for Adriana, yet giving up their baby, giving up Summer, had been one of the hardest things he'd ever done. He thought of it, went through all the reasons it had to be the way it was, almost every day. But he could never have agreed to the adoption if that'd been his and Francesca's child.

But there was no point in trying to convince her otherwise. She would never understand that he'd honestly loved her. To her, his actions proved otherwise.

If only it could be that simple, that straightforward. But it wasn't. And because she didn't think he had feelings, she didn't mind stomping all over them every chance she got.

He deserved her revenge. But that didn't mean he'd let her prove he was the man she thought he was and not the man he'd fought to become. Regardless of the temptation she provided, he'd keep his hands to himself, make sure she was safe and then move on without affecting the world she'd built….

Finally coming to a stop, he rubbed his face. Where was he going? He had a job to do. But if he'd stayed in that van ten more seconds, he would've taken Francesca in the back and greedily accepted whatever she'd been willing to give him—even knowing she'd hate him that much more when it was over.

"That's pretty damned pathetic, Young."

Maybe he should take her home. He couldn't work with her around. The fight to overcome his feelings was too constant, too demanding, too tiring.

But he couldn't leave her unprotected, either. Whoever had cut her telephone line could come back. And maybe the bastard wouldn't just hang around the pool next time.

The image of April Bonner's rotting body arose in his mind. The fear that Francesca might be next kept him right where he didn't want to be—in limbo. He couldn't act on his feelings *or* escape them. He had to solve this case, make sure she survived it. Only then could he leave her and try, once again, to forget.

Heart still knocking against his ribs, he headed back to the van. They were here for a reason. He couldn't lose sight of that. But when he opened the door to climb in, she was gone.

17

What had come over her? Francesca didn't know. But she'd had to get out of the van in case Jonah returned before she could compose herself. Maybe Butch hadn't gone inside for the night yet, but at the moment, Jonah seemed like the bigger threat. Somehow, the warmth of his hand, which had settled so briefly on her breast, lingered, still felt hot enough to burn through her shirt. It didn't make sense. She'd been with other men, men she'd cared about at the time, but there'd been no one like Jonah. How could they continue to work together with such powerful undercurrents tugging at them constantly?

Maybe she'd be better off on her own. With Dean roaming around, showing up at odd places unexpectedly, Jonah would argue with her about that, but she couldn't expect him to protect her forever. Their relationship was too strained. It had to move in one direction or the other, and she knew what would happen if it went in the direction she wanted. They'd be right back where they'd been before he'd gotten her best friend pregnant.

But she wasn't the only one who had something at stake this time. What about the women who'd been murdered in Dead Mule Canyon? April? Their families, who were praying for justice?

And what about any future victims Butch or Dean might take?

Francesca had to put her personal life aside, keep herself together until they could solve this case.

At least she could avoid Jonah for the moment.

In this part of the desert, the flat ground hosted more cacti than trees. To compensate for the lack of cover, she moved as quietly as possible. Where had Butch gone? Before the whole drama with Jonah, she'd seen Butch driving his truck. Although that truck was no longer visible, she doubted he'd gone into the house. She guessed he was still around, perhaps in his office. A light glowed through the window. She thought he might be doing paperwork or making calls or whatever else he did in there.

Fortunately, the sinking sun created enough shadows to provide a degree of safety. Any later, and she wouldn't be able to see without a flashlight. So this wasn't a bad time to take a look around, especially since the dog, Demon, seemed to be inside the house or office. She couldn't go onto the property without compromising the admissibility of any evidence she might find, but there was no law against peeking over a fence.

As she took out her camera, hoping to get a couple of shots before the light grew too dim, she spotted Paris at the kitchen window. Butch's wife appeared to be doing dishes, but every once in a while she gazed out at the yard as if transfixed. Was she anxious for her husband to come in? Did she wonder where her brother was? Did anyone ever bother to check on Dean's whereabouts? Where had the old folks gone and when would they be back?

Keeping close to the fence, Francesca circled the yard, eyeing the cars that hadn't yet been completely stripped and smashed. Very few were Priuses. And, as night set in, it became harder and harder to determine each car's color. Terrance had said that Bianca drove a charcoal Prius. But surely, if Butch or Dean had brought her car here, they would've dismantled it immediately and hurried it through the destruction process. It'd been a year since Bianca had died. What were the chances that even a small remnant of her vehicle remained?

Suddenly a series of floodlights, spaced at regular intervals, snapped on in the yard. Unsure whether they were on a timer or Butch had seen her and thrown a switch, Francesca crept away from the fence and crouched behind some desert scrub, which was the best cover she could find.

"Butch?" The screen door slammed as Paris came outside. Francesca could see Mrs. Vaughn far more easily in the glaring light of those floods than when she'd been framed in that window with most of the light coming from behind her. She seemed upset. Why?

She wore a simple cotton shirt, baggy shorts and flip-flops, and her feet tapped the wooden steps of the porch as she descended into the yard. "Butch? Where are you?"

Butch poked his head out of his office. "Here."

Paris hurried over and went inside without closing the door. As it hung halfway open, the light from inside cast a distorted triangle on the ground.

Francesca crept as close as the fence would allow. Judging by the expression on Paris's face, something had changed. Francesca wanted to know what it was. Paris had started with, "I just got a call from…" but then she'd stepped inside and the volume of her voice had dropped too low for Francesca to hear.

The gate Francesca had used when she'd let herself onto the property the first time stood open only fifteen feet away. Wide enough for the flatbed trucks that transported clunker cars to the salvage yard, it provided easy access. If she slipped through it and sidled up to the building, she'd be able to hear everything….

But was it worth the risk of getting caught?

Considering the fact that Dean and his parents were both gone, and Demon wasn't in the yard, that risk didn't seem too high. Maybe Butch or Paris would say something that would give them a lead, some way to solve the terrible murders before another one occurred.

Hoping to see Jonah, to let him know what she was about to do, she glanced toward the van.

It was a mere speck on the horizon, and there was no sign of Jonah. But if she waited any longer, it would be too late. In order to hear what Paris was saying, she had to move, and she had to move now.

Seconds later, she stood inside the yard amid the car parts and scrap metal and the mannequin that'd caused such a fuss. When she rounded a heap of car frames, she could see the outline of that "body" beneath the tarp, but she chose to ignore it as well as the embarrassment her mistake had brought her. Instead of walking farther in that direction, she circled Butch's office, coming the other way.

No matter how slowly she walked, the rocky soil crunched beneath her feet, but she wasn't too concerned about drawing attention. Not right now. The closer she got to Butch's office, the more obvious it became that he and his wife were deeply immersed in an argument.

"I don't want her calling here anymore." That was Paris.

"You said whoever it was hung up," Butch responded.

"They did."

"Then how do you know it was her?" He sounded as if he was trying to come across as unconcerned, but Francesca wasn't buying it. She wondered if Paris was.

"Because she always hangs up when I answer."

"It doesn't make sense for Kelly to call the house, Paris. If she wanted to talk to me, she'd call my cell or the business line. And I'm telling you I haven't heard from her since I broke it off."

"She's not satisfied calling your cell. She wants to involve me. She's hoping it'll upset me, break us up. She thinks if we get divorced she'll have you all to herself."

"Come on. She knows we'll never split up. I told her that from the beginning."

"That doesn't mean she's willing to accept it!"

"She has a husband and children of her own."

"A husband she doesn't love. Matt's leaving her. You know that. She's only using her children to get as much financial support from him as possible. If it wasn't for the money, she'd walk out on them in a heartbeat, especially if she thought she could have you."

"You don't know what you're talking about."

"Are you *sure* you broke it off, Butch?"

"That's what I told you, isn't it?"

"Then where did *these* come from?"

That question resulted in the loudest silence Francesca had ever heard.

"Where'd you get those?" Butch asked at length.

"After that call, I went out and searched your truck. They were in the jockey box."

Francesca wished she could see Butch's face, his body language. In an attempt to do just that, she edged closer to the window but he and Paris were standing next to the desk, out of sight.

"That's bullshit," Butch snapped. "I'd never be stupid enough to put another woman's panties in such an obvious place."

"Then how did they get there?" she asked, her voice rising.

"I have no clue. But I didn't put them there."

"Do you recognize them?"

"No."

"You expect me to believe that? You collect them! You use them to relive your time with the women who owned them. You probably get off just touching them!"

He sidestepped the panties issue. "I haven't been with Kelly!"

"Then who?"

"No one!"

Paris came into view. Head down, the panties balled in her right fist, she looked completely dejected. "I can't take any more, Butch. After everything that's happened, after the nightmare we've been through, a nightmare that'll never end, you still can't be faithful?"

"I have a sex addiction, Paris. That isn't an easy thing to overcome."

"I've suggested counseling, but you won't agree to it."

"It won't do any good! Besides, I don't want anyone messing with my mind."

"So what do *you* suggest?"

"For what?"

"To stop this!" She held up the panties. "You have to quit cheating on me!"

"I have!" Butch insisted. "Come on. I'll take you over to the Martins' right now, have Kelly tell you herself that it's been over a month since we were together."

Paris's shoulders slumped. "If you're willing to do that, there's someone else. Yet again."

"No…"

She whipped around and disappeared from Francesca's view, but Francesca could hear her. "What about that woman who was found dead in Skull Valley? These didn't belong to her, did they?"

"No."

"That P.I. was here for a reason, Butch. And it wasn't to ask about Julia."

Who was Julia? Francesca wondered.

"That P.I. is chasing the wrong man. She's nothing but a stupid bitch."

At the mention of her, Francesca couldn't help taking a few steps back.

"Bitch?" Paris echoed. "Maybe. But stupid? I don't think so." She approached the door, which sent Francesca scrambling farther into a pathway between two piles of metal. But Paris didn't come out. Butch must've stopped her; he was still talking.

"Your brother probably stuck those panties in my truck. He knows we've been fighting, and he knows something like this could be the last straw. He's trying to get rid of me."

"That's laughable," she said. "Where would Dean get a pair of women's panties? With all the medication he's on, I doubt he can even get it up."

"Maybe he's not quite as sexually inactive as you think."

"Maybe *you* aren't, either."

The door hit the outside wall as Paris stormed out. But, once again, Butch stopped her.

"Come on, baby, don't leave like this. I have a problem. I've admitted that to you. But I'm working on it."

"You're working on it? You won't even get help."

"I have to do it my own way."

"And what is your way, Butch? You're still filling out profiles on dating sites, still meeting other women. That's your way?"

"It was a minor slipup. What I'm fighting has a strong hold on me. But I can break it."

"The last woman you slept with is *dead*. Tell me that was a coincidence."

"You know it was. Why would I kill anyone?"

"You have a temper. You don't need me to tell you that."

"Look, I had sex with her, okay? But it didn't mean anything. You're the only one who matters to me. I've already told you that."

Francesca peered around a stack of bumpers in time to see Paris shake her head. "You don't get it. You have no idea what's at stake here. What you've done," she said, and started off again.

"Francesca Moretti, the police, they have nothing on me," he called after her.

"That doesn't mean they'll stop trying to get something."

"They're wasting their time."

"Tell that to the people who are watching our house right now."

He jogged after her, but she kept going. "What are you talking about?"

Pivoting to face him, she said, "We're under surveillance, Butch. My parents called after I hung up with Kelly or whoever that was. They said the van I spotted when I was with them earlier is back, less than a quarter of a mile away."

He glanced around. "Where?"

"There." She pointed in the direction of the van, even though it was too dark to see. "It has two people inside, watching our place, waiting for you to make a mistake. And having them there is driving me crazy."

"That's it." Grabbing a piece of lead pipe from a pile of rubbish, Butch hurried through the gate.

"Butch? Wait! What are you going to do?"

He didn't answer.

Francesca would've hurried out right after him. Now that he knew about the van, he'd start looking for its missing occupants. Anyone would. She needed to get off the property. But Paris stood by the open gate, crying as she gazed after her husband.

As soon as he saw Butch coming out of the salvage yard, Jonah dropped to the ground. He preferred to avoid a confrontation, if possible. All he wanted to do was find Francesca and get the hell out of there, but that was much more difficult than he'd expected. Although he'd circled the property three times, he hadn't yet found her. And he was beginning to suspect the reason. If she wasn't on the outside of the fence, and she wasn't back at the van, she had to be *in* the salvage yard.

But where, exactly? And why? Didn't she realize she was risking the whole investigation by trespassing?

As Butch disappeared into the darkness, Jonah got to his feet. But then he noticed a car approaching the house and had to drop down again so he wouldn't be seen. Butch's in-laws were returning; he'd watched that same vehicle leave earlier with Butch's father-in-law at the wheel.

Shit. More anxious with every passing second, he waited for Butch's family to go inside. He couldn't do anything while they were out, couldn't even get into the yard. And they weren't the only ones in the way. The headlights of the old couple's car silhouetted a woman standing at the gate. Paris. Jonah knew it was Butch's wife because, once the engine died and the doors opened, she called out to her parents.

"Did you see anyone inside it?"

"Inside what?" her mother responded.

Three doors slammed. Jonah wasn't sure who the third person was, but someone had gotten out of the backseat.

"The van," Paris said. "The van you called me about a few minutes ago."

Her father came around the front of the car and was the first to start across the lawn. "Not a soul."

His wife followed him. So did the third person. The old folks blocked Jonah's view, but he figured it had to be Dean. They must've picked up their son at the bus stop. They'd been gone too long for such a short errand, but they could've had dinner or done any number of other things while they were out.

"How close did you go?" Paris asked.

"Close enough to see that it was empty. There were people in it earlier, though. I saw them when we left. I didn't think anything of it until the same van was there when we came back."

"Who?" The third person's voice confirmed his identity. It was Dean, all right. "What's going on?"

Paris answered him. "The cops. They're watching the place."

"Really? Are they hoping to prove Butch killed that woman?"

"Don't sound so excited, Dean," she snapped.

"I'm not excited. Just surprised. Seems they have a more realistic idea of Butch than you do."

Anger put an edge to Paris's voice. "Shut up! You wouldn't be saying that if he was standing here."

"True. But if he was as nonviolent as you claim, I could speak freely, correct?"

Hands curled into fists, she stepped up to him. "How dare you! You're lucky he provides a living for you. Where would you be without him? On the street? Lord knows you can't function like a normal human being."

He remained unflustered. "You think a killer is normal?"

Their mother finally came between them. "That's enough. Both of you. Don't let this throw us all into a panic. We know Butch would never hurt anyone."

Did she really believe that? Jonah wondered.

"You mean other than Kelly Martin?" Dean sounded as pleased as Paris had accused him of being. "Because he's smacked her around before. Remember? It was for driving by one too many times and making their affair too obvious."

"Dean!" her mother cried, but Paris tried to hit her brother and would've succeeded if not for the old lady, who did her best to protect him.

"You little prick!" she shouted. "You leave Kelly out of this. He never touched her."

Poking his head around his mother, Dean came right back at her. "Oh, yeah? An affair means he *did* touch her, dear sister. In some very intimate places."

"That's it! We're kicking you out. You can fend for yourself," Paris screamed.

"We still own this property," her mother said. "Don't forget that."

Paris appeared to have a ready response, but they all grew silent when Butch interrupted. Already on his way back from the van, he was carrying some object Jonah couldn't quite make out. "It's her," he called.

Jonah caught his breath.

"It's who?" Paris's father asked.

Distracted from their squabble, even Paris and Dean turned to face him, silently expectant.

"Francesca Moretti."

Smothering a groan, Jonah cursed to himself.

"How do you know?" Paris asked.

"Recognize this?" He held up what he carried and Dean began to laugh.

"That's her purse," he said. "Again."

"So where is *she?*" the old man muttered.

Butch threw Francesca's bag at their feet. Then he propped his hands on his hips and stared into the salvage yard. "She's got to be around here somewhere."

"She's got no right." Paris sounded worried. Was it because she secretly feared Butch might not be as innocent as she wanted to believe? There had to be some element of denial in her reaction. "She'll do anything to see you behind bars."

"What are you going to do now?" Dean asked.

Butch didn't react to the glee in his voice the way Paris had. He tossed a set of keys at Dean instead. "Lock up the yard."

18

Butch knew it was her. And he had her purse *again*. Francesca couldn't believe it. Her new phone was in that purse. She hadn't taken it with her when she left the van. She'd wanted to be light on her feet, hadn't wanted to carry anything, especially an object she could drop and break as easily as her iPhone if she had to move fast. That darn screen was expensive to replace. But she'd been thinking only as far as escaping Jonah. She hadn't planned for this. What now?

Careful not to make any noise, she hid behind a piece of heavy equipment as she waited for Butch and his family to go inside. She couldn't remember what the giant machine was called, but she knew what it was used for. Some kind of industrial-size lift, it stacked car frames. An excavator, which was even bigger, towered over the junk piles on her other side. Both pieces of equipment reminded her of a horror show she'd seen when she was a kid, where the cranes, bulldozers and lifts at a construction site came alive at night and killed the unsuspecting people who found themselves in proximity. To an adult the concept seemed corny, but those images had made a real impact on her when she was young. And, despite the impossibility of a machine killing on its own, it gave her the creeps to think about that movie now. Butch himself and all the garbage and the rats at the salvage yard made this the last place she wanted to spend the night.

When Butch, Paris and the others finally went into the house, the lights stayed on, but silence settled over the yard. Francesca had a chance to escape—if she could figure out how. She couldn't get out the way she'd gotten in. When Dean locked the gate, he'd used a heavy chain and padlock.

She studied her surroundings. The fence was too high. Even if she could climb it, she'd never get past the razor wire, not dressed in a pair of linen shorts.

Wondering where Jonah was, what he was thinking, she began searching for a weak spot in the bottom of the fence where the chain-link might already be bent or she could bend it enough to slide underneath. She wanted to get out of here on her own, would rather not put Jonah in the awkward position of having to come after her. But there was a chance she wouldn't be able to avoid it. She couldn't let Butch wake up tomorrow to find her here.

Deciding she might be able to create an opportunity along the back, far from most of the lights and myriad pathways that led through the cars, car parts and other salvaged items, she slipped deeper into the yard. But reaching the back fence was tricky. Butch obviously used this area to discard the stuff he wasn't all that interested in. She had to skirt past piles of sharp metal chunks and pieces, tramp over old toasters and other appliances and push some rusty bicycles out of the way.

When a sticky web clung to her legs, she almost screamed. Black widows spun sticky, stretchy webs like that, and they loved the desert. Tarantulas and scorpions lived here, too. So did the most poisonous of all spiders, the wolf spider...

No telling what she might encounter out here in the dark, but she brushed off the web and continued. She had to get out of here, couldn't let fear stop her for even a second.

The back fence wasn't in good repair like the fence toward the front. Even in the low light filtering to the ground from the closest pole, she could see that it had been patched in several places. But those patches seemed solid. And the chain-link didn't stop when it met the ground. Using the head of a shovel, which she found in a pile of rubbish behind her, she began to dig to see how far it extended and realized it was buried at least a foot.

Butch had this yard secured like Fort Knox. Why? Could he really be that frightened someone would steal scrap metal? She knew it had value. Some thieves went so far as to tear the copper plumbing out of new homes if they weren't properly protected. But what Butch had in the yard wasn't made of copper and it wasn't that easy to haul away.

Rocking back on her heels, she let her breath go in an exhausted sigh. That fence went down too far for her to get beneath it. Digging wasn't an option. It'd take all night to get that deep, especially in such hard, rocky soil.

She had to find a pair of bolt or wire cutters to cut the bolt on the gate. Thinking that was now her best option, she headed toward Butch's office and the sheds nearby, where she thought he probably stored his tools—and almost missed the panties lying on the ground. Even when she saw them, their significance didn't immediately register. She was several steps beyond them when she realized what they were and turned back.

Sure enough, the panties—presumably the same ones

Paris had been carrying earlier—were only a few feet from Butch's office. Paris must've dropped them, or thrown them at him while they were arguing.

Francesca curved her fingernails into her palms. Should she take them? She had to, didn't she? They wouldn't be admissible as evidence if Butch was brought to trial, but she couldn't risk leaving them behind in case they disappeared forever. What if they belonged to yet another victim from the Dead Mule Canyon site? If the police could establish that, they'd know Butch was their guy.

Repelled at what might've happened to the woman who'd once owned those panties, and careful not to destroy DNA evidence, she bent and very gingerly put them in her pocket. Butch was such a poseur, with all his talk about Paris and how she didn't care about his extramarital affairs. She cared, all right. Francesca had heard enough from Paris to be certain of that. She'd also noted his girlfriend's name—Kelly Martin—and planned to talk to her as soon as possible. Since he'd supposedly broken up with Kelly, and been violent with her on at least one occasion, maybe she wouldn't be quite as loyal as Paris. Maybe she possessed information that could assist the investigation and would be willing to talk.

Francesca pictured the insolent grin Butch had worn while shoveling all that bullshit her way in his office. "You're such a liar," she muttered, but then she heard a dog bark and felt every nerve go on high alert.

Unless that noise came from somewhere outside the fence, she had company.

Had Butch meant to lock Francesca in or out? Jonah couldn't say. He only knew that if she was inside the salvage yard, she didn't stand much chance of getting out

FREE Merchandise is 'in the Cards' for you!

Dear Reader,

We're giving away FREE MERCHANDISE!

Seriously, we'd like to reward you for reading this novel by giving you **FREE MERCHANDISE** worth over **$25**. And no purchase is necessary!

You see the Jack of Hearts sticker above? Paste that sticker in the box on the Free Merchandise Voucher inside. Return the Voucher promptly...and we'll send you valuable Free Merchandise!

Thanks again for reading one of our novels—and enjoy your Free Merchandise with our compliments!

Pam Powers

Pam Powers

P.S. Look inside to see what Free Merchandise is **"in the cards"** for you!

(FM-SUS-10)

We'd like to send you two free books to introduce you to the Suspense collection. These books are worth over $15, but they are yours to keep absolutely FREE! We'll even send you 2 wonderful surprise gifts. You can't lose!

REMEMBER: Your Free Merchandise, consisting of **2 Free Books** and **2 Free Gifts**, is worth over $25.00! No purchase is necessary, so please send for your Free Merchandise today.

YOUR FREE MERCHANDISE INCLUDES...

2 FREE Books from the Suspense collection

AND 2 FREE Mystery Gifts

FREE MERCHANDISE VOUCHER

2 FREE BOOKS
and
2 FREE GIFTS

Please send my Free Merchandise, consisting of
2 Free Books and **2 Free Mystery Gifts**.
I understand that I am under no obligation to buy
anything, as explained on the back of this card.

*About how many NEW paperback fiction books
have you purchased in the past 3 months?*

☐ 0-2   ☐ 3-6   ☐ 7 or more
E9M3   E9NF   E9NR

192/392 MDL

Please Print

FIRST NAME

LAST NAME

ADDRESS

APT.#   CITY

STATE/PROV.   ZIP/POSTAL CODE

NO PURCHASE NECESSARY!

▲ If offer card is missing write to: The Reader Service, P.O. Box 1867, Buffalo, NY 14240-1867 or visit www.ReaderService.com ▲

BUSINESS REPLY MAIL
FIRST-CLASS MAIL   PERMIT NO. 717   BUFFALO, NY

POSTAGE WILL BE PAID BY ADDRESSEE

THE READER SERVICE
PO BOX 1341
BUFFALO NY 14240-8571

NO POSTAGE
NECESSARY
IF MAILED
IN THE
UNITED STATES

on her own. He'd seen prison yards that would be easier to break out of. He planned to help her, but in order to do that he had to find her first—before Butch did.

Hoping that she'd come to the fence and stay put, he began walking the perimeter. He'd only gone a few steps, however, when he heard Butch and Paris on the porch with a dog and felt the hair stand up on the back of his neck. Jonah wouldn't have been half as worried, except the dog wasn't some friendly pooch. It was the mean Doberman that'd been chained up in the yard before.

"Shit," he muttered, and froze, waiting to see what Butch would do.

"You can't turn Demon out on her!" Paris trailed after her husband.

He sure as hell better not, Jonah told himself, but Butch seemed intent on doing just that.

"It's not my fault if she trespasses on my property and gets attacked by my dog when I'm in for the night."

"They'll *make* it your fault," Paris argued. "She's a police officer!"

Jonah's muscles tensed. *Damn it!*

"No, she's not," Butch said. "She's a private investigator who's not even from this area. She has no business here. And now she'll pay the price. I'm well within my rights. She's been warned before, and she already has a history of harassing me. I've got the scabs on my cheek to prove it."

Jonah grabbed hold of the chain-link fence. Surely Butch wouldn't really turn the dog loose, not in front of his wife, and with his whole family in the house—or would he?

Maybe he thought that would be the perfect cover.

Or he knew they'd stick by him, regardless.

Gazing up at the razor wire on top of the fence, Jonah

felt his heart knock against his chest. How would he save Francesca if Butch sicced that dog on her? A dog like that could kill her in minutes, long before he could scale the fence.

"Butch, please," Paris begged. "If Demon hurts her, they'll put him down. You don't want to risk his life. You love that dog. Just call the police. Hunsacker told you that if you mind your own business, this'll all blow over. I heard him."

Hunsacker had said that? Telling their number-one suspect to lie low wasn't exactly sabotaging the investigation, but Jonah didn't like the sound of it. It smacked too much of divided loyalties. Or did Hunsacker's words bother him because he feared they might lull Butch into thinking he had an ally, into believing he might be able to get away with something like this?

"She's the one who's in trouble now," Butch said. "Go inside. I'll be in when I've taken care of the problem."

"You're scaring me," Paris whined.

"*I'm* scaring you? What about *her?* She's probably busy planting evidence she can use to pin April Bonner's murder on me. I won't go to prison for a crime I didn't commit."

Paris's voice dropped so low Jonah had trouble hearing her. "None of this ever would've happened if you'd been faithful to me from the start," she said. But she was cowed. Jonah could see it in her body language, in the way her shoulders drooped as she went inside.

Butch waited for the door to close before walking to the edge of the porch and staring out over the piles of scrap metal and rubbish he sifted through on a daily basis.

"Come out, come out, wherever you are," he said in a soft, singsong voice.

"Don't do it!" Jonah yelled.

Butch looked over at the fence but he didn't respond. He acted as if he didn't hear a thing. Unhooking the leash from Demon's collar, he yelled, "Go get her, boy!"

And the dog took off like a shot.

Had she heard Jonah? Francesca thought she had. That gave her hope, until the dog began to bellow, drowning out everything else and making her legs go rubbery. She remembered the animal that'd growled at her with such ferocity when she came onto the property a few days ago.

Apparently, he was no longer in the house. And she didn't get the impression that he was being tied up.

Scanning the refuse and car hulks around her, she searched for something she could get inside or on top of, where the dog might not be able to reach her. But other than shutting herself inside Butch's office or one of the sheds, which might or might not be locked, she couldn't see any way to protect herself.

"Oh, God," she whispered as she heard Demon coming closer. It was only a matter of time before he found her and tried to rip out her throat. She could hear the purpose in his feverish barking. He meant business, and he was quickly closing in on her.

"Go get her, boy!" she heard Butch yell, but she could no longer hear Jonah.

Frantic, she ducked behind an old mustard-yellow Mercedes. It was the best shelter she could find, but she knew it wouldn't be enough. Set up on blocks, it had no windows and only two doors. The dog could easily scrabble over, under or through it.

I'm dead. Peering around the car, she strained to make

out the office. Stacked car frames blocked most of her view, but she could see the corner of its roof.

Could she make it that far? Get inside? What about one of the sheds?

They seemed miles away. Unless she wanted to get cut or twist an ankle, she had to stick to the valleys created by the junk all around her. The dog, on the other hand, knew the yard much better than she did. He could slip through a hole she didn't even know existed, or leap over a pile….

Where was Butch's family? They must be able to hear the intense baying, must wonder what had the dog so riled up. Were they turning a deaf ear? Or assuming he'd found a skunk or some other prey? It was even possible that Butch's in-laws were engrossed in a television program and weren't paying attention.

Regardless of the reason, help didn't seem to be on its way. She thought she'd heard Jonah, but she didn't know where he was, or how he'd get in to help her even if he was at the fence. She had seconds….

Mouth so dry she couldn't swallow, she decided to run for the office. It was her only hope. Her life depended on whether or not Butch had locked that door—

Wait! The blood thudding through her ears created a rushing sound as she hesitated. She should go around the other way. The house was almost as close as the office, and she doubted Butch would expect her to flee there. If she could reach it, she could charge in the back door and run straight through. Even if she encountered Dean or someone else, she'd have a better chance of survival than staying here.

You can do it. Drawing a deep breath, she inched around the car she'd been using for cover, trying to get a good look at the house. Although the dog seemed to be drawing close, she couldn't see it. The contents of the yard hid Butch and Demon from view. She was afraid the Doberman might go one way while Butch went the other. The last thing she needed was to run straight into his arms….

Refusing to imagine what would come next, she screamed at herself to go, and sprinted down the widest path. That particular route was too close to the dog for comfort, but with all its obstacles the yard was a maze. She couldn't risk getting lost. If the dog managed to corner her, she'd have no hope whatsoever.

As soon as he saw her, the pitch of the Doberman's bark rose an octave and he cut toward her.

He was ready to move in for the kill.

When his howling reverberated against the metal all around her, she knew Demon was only a leap away.

The house, still at least twenty feet from her, was too far. She'd taken a chance and lost.

No way could she make it.

19

Jonah had no idea what would happen when the van hit the fence, but busting through seemed like his only option. He couldn't risk going to the house in hopes of getting Butch's family to help. What if they wouldn't come to the door? Or stalled?

It was up to him to use whatever tools he had at his disposal to save Francesca. As long as he wasn't too late….

Pressing the accelerator to the floor, he clung to the steering wheel, trying to remain in his seat despite the jolting of the vehicle as it bounced across the rocky desert. One tire had already popped. He'd heard it go several seconds earlier, had to fight to keep the steering wheel from pulling too hard to the left as a result, and expected one or more of the other tires to follow suit. He was driving over cacti, broken bottles, who knew what else.

But he didn't care if all four wheels wound up rolling on their rims. He wouldn't stop. He'd seen Butch's dog shoot off that porch with single-minded intensity and was willing to bet he'd reached his goal by now. If Francesca wasn't dead, she would be soon, or she'd be severely hurt.

The fence loomed in front of him. In case the windshield shattered, he turned his face away but kept his foot on the gas. He'd decided to break through the gate, figured that would mean less of an impact than trying to mow down an entire section of the perimeter fence. There was also more empty space toward the front, so there'd be less to crash into *after* he went through.

Although he was braced for the worst, the impact rattled his teeth, especially when the air bag went off. It sounded like a shotgun as it punched him in the face. The resulting powder and gases burned his face and arms, but the bag had stopped him from cracking his skull on the windshield, which was what would've happened when the sudden deceleration threw him forward.

Dazed, he blinked several times, trying to clear his vision.

Steam rose from the van's engine. Something must've gone through the radiator. Jonah could hear the hiss. He just couldn't figure out where he was—until he heard the feverish growling of a dog.

Butch.

Demon.

Francesca.

The thought of Demon mauling Francesca brought him out of his stupor. He had to get to her. That was why he'd crashed the gate.

Grabbing the door handle, he jerked it up to release the latch, but it wouldn't open. He had to crank down the window and crawl through it instead.

Move! Now!

Scrambling faster than he was really capable of after such a blow, he fell as he cleared the window and banged his knee on a sharp object. It hurt like hell, but he ignored the pain and got to his feet.

"Hey!" Trying to attract the dog's attention, he flapped his arms as he ran. There was some action taking place about twenty feet away. He could hear the scuffle, see some figures, but thanks to the shadows cast by the pole lights and the black spots that danced in his vision from the crash, he couldn't be sure what was going on.

"Demon!" Butch called.

Was Butch urging the dog on or trying to call him off? Jonah couldn't tell. But if Butch was trying to stop Demon, the Doberman was too worked up to listen. He veered away from Francesca, but came bounding toward Jonah, teeth bared in a snarl, legs working in a fluid motion as he began to jump.

"Demon!" Butch cried again.

At this point, Jonah was fairly certain he was trying to call the dog off. But it was too late. Demon was already in the air, lunging for Jonah's throat…

With just a split second to react, Jonah had only one choice.

Drawing his gun from his shoulder harness, he fired.

The sound of the gunshot nearly deafened Francesca. Yet she managed to hear Butch's gut-wrenching reaction.

"You killed my dog!" he screamed as Demon fell to the earth.

Closing her eyes, Francesca held her injured arm against her body and murmured a silent prayer of thanks. She'd been bitten when she tried to protect her neck and face but, fortunately, Jonah had smashed into the salvage yard before Demon could make another attempt at her jugular. Two or three more minutes, and she'd be the one lying motionless on the ground.

"*You* k-killed your dog," she corrected, but she was shaking so badly she couldn't stay on her feet and sank to the ground.

Butch whirled on her as if he'd finish her off himself, and Jonah fired his gun again. Since he was aiming at the sky, the bullet went into the air above them, but the threat was clear enough to convince Butch that he'd better back off.

"You bitch! Why did you come back here?" he cried. "What's wrong with you? Why won't you leave me alone? What have I ever done to you? I've told you and told you, I didn't kill April Bonner! I've never killed anyone!"

Blinking fast to stop the tears that flowed of their own accord, Francesca gulped for the breath to speak. "You j-just t-tried to k-kill *me*."

"That's not true! The dog must've smelled you, because he took off on his own. I tried to stop him. It's not my fault if you won't obey the signs. There are Beware of Dog notices all over this place!"

Nauseous and weak, Francesca laid her head on her knees. "You sicced him on me, and you know it."

"Butch?"

Evidently, the blast of Jonah's gun had brought Paris to the porch. Hovering on the top step, she clutched one of the support posts as if she was afraid to come any closer. But afraid of what? Jonah's gun? Or her husband's reaction? "Butch, what's wrong?" she asked, her voice reed-thin. "What was that shot about?"

"They killed Demon," he called. "They shot him!"

"Get in the van," Jonah told Francesca, and jerked his head toward it.

Francesca wasn't sure the van was drivable. It looked pretty banged up. But she didn't argue. Wanting to get out of the salvage yard, she gathered her strength, got to her feet and limped past the inert body of the Doberman.

"You're in trouble, Butch," she heard Jonah say as she reached the passenger side and climbed in. "*Serious* trouble."

"She's the one who's in trouble," he insisted. "I'm going to get a restraining order against her. She has to stop harassing us. I was nice enough to return her purse when I found it, and this is the thanks I get?"

"Wow, he ran the gate." This came from someone else, someone who sounded emotionally removed.

Swiping at her wet eyes, Francesca ducked her head to see through Jonah's open window. Dean stood on the porch beside his sister, and from the tone of his voice, he thought this was good fun instead of upsetting and dangerous.

Paris was too worried about her husband to react to Dean. "Butch, come here. Don't say a word. We'll get a lawyer. They can't do this. They can't come onto our property, wreck our fence and kill our dog. We didn't do anything to them. They're going to pay for this."

Butch didn't seem reassured by his wife's solace. He was too focused on Demon. "You had no right," he told Jonah as he knelt and lifted the dog's body into his arms. "You had no right to even be here."

"Go get the video camera," Paris told Dean, and he hurried off.

Hugging herself to control the shaking, Francesca cringed at the thought of anyone recording the van sitting wrecked in the yard, Butch's dog dead, tears streaking down everyone's faces. She knew how it would look. The video wouldn't show Butch purposely locking her in and ordering his dog to attack her.

Something wet and sticky dripped onto her leg. Blood.

She hadn't realized she was bleeding but of course she would be. Demon had chomped down on her arm and refused to let go.

To staunch the flow, she wrapped the bottom of her shirt around her injured forearm. She shouldn't have come here. She'd wanted to stop a killer, but she'd only made the situation worse. Even Jonah was hurt. He favored his right leg as he backed cautiously away from Butch.

"Get me the purse you took," he said when he reached the front grille of the van. "And this time don't say you don't have it. I saw you bring it to your family."

Burying his face in his dog's fur, Butch ignored him.

"Now!" Jonah shouted. "Unless you and your entire family want to be arrested, you'll get the damn purse."

It was Paris who moved. She went inside and returned with Francesca's handbag. Dean followed closely behind her with the video, narrating as he filmed. "Demon is dead," he said. "And this is the man who shot him."

"I'm calling the cops," Paris yelled as she threw the purse at Jonah's feet.

"You do that." He gathered up the items that fell out before coming around to the driver's side of the van.

"I'm sorry. I— This was such a mistake," Francesca said as he got in.

He made no comment. "You okay?"

She wiped her wet cheeks again. "I think I might need a few stitches."

"How many times did he bite you?"

"J-just once." She couldn't seem to stop her teeth from chattering. "I don't know how bad it is. I c-can't see well enough in this light. B-but it hurts."

"Let's hope he's had all his shots." As he turned the

key in the ignition, the starter made a grinding sound but the engine didn't catch. Pumping the gas pedal, he tried again.

"What—what about you?" Worried, she watched him closely. "You're injured, t-too."

"It's nothing. I'm fine. Let's get out of here and find you some help." The van's engine finally revved, but it died and wouldn't start again, which meant they had to endure the red-hot glares of Butch and Paris, and more filming from Dean, as they waited for an ambulance.

"Dogs are more dangerous than cats. But some cats can surprise you," Dean said, as if anyone wanted to hear what he had to say.

Was that the meds talking? Francesca wondered as she struggled to recover from the shock and adrenaline rush of what she'd just been through. How could Dean be going on about cats in the aftermath of everything that'd taken place?

The paramedics and the police arrived at virtually the same time, and Francesca heard Butch's version while she received medical attention. He spun a fabricated story, but Paris and even Dean backed him up. His in-laws were in the yard by then, too, playing up their grief over the dog, although it wouldn't be dead if not for its owner, and venting their outrage at what had happened for the benefit of Dean's camera.

"I can't believe this," Francesca grumbled to Jonah. She felt like a rag doll, so spent she had no energy left to argue her case.

Jonah was refusing to let one of the paramedics look at his knee. "Ignore it," he said to her.

She wished she could. But Finch and Hunsacker

were glaring at her with such rancor that she knew this wouldn't end well.

Butch screamed that he planned to go on television and alert the public to the "abuses" he'd suffered and how the police and their "representatives" had infringed on his rights. No doubt the county investigators felt she'd jeopardized the reputation of the sheriff's office, as well as the integrity of the investigation.

Or had Hunsacker told Butch to slip that ace up his sleeve?

It was an insidious thought, but Francesca couldn't help recalling Finch's earlier words, when he'd expressed concern that Butch might sue the department. Had he and Hunsacker discussed it, too? She knew from what she'd overheard Paris say earlier that Hunsacker was doing a little coaching on the side. Maybe he was actively working against the investigation....

That idea was so disconcerting she hated to even consider it. This case was difficult enough to solve.

"You hanging in there?" Jonah touched her shoulder as the paramedics loaded her into the ambulance.

"Yeah."

"I'll have Finch drop me off at the hospital."

With a nod, she closed her eyes.

It wasn't until later, after she'd received a tetanus shot and twenty-four stitches and had been released from the emergency room, that she remembered the panties. Jonah was waiting for her in the lobby but, at that point, she wasn't sure she wanted to tell anyone she'd taken them from the yard. Her actions had caused enough problems for one night. So, hoping that what Paris had said about "Julia" might make a difference, she told him everything she'd overheard at the salvage yard but left out one small detail—that she might have possession of physical evidence. She didn't want to see how he'd react to learning she'd taken something that would now be inadmissible in court.

Seeing the Department 6 number on his call display, Jonah rolled out of bed and hit the answer button but carried his phone into the motel bathroom before saying hello. It was past eight, but he wanted to let Francesca sleep as long as possible. The emergency room had been so packed last night they hadn't gotten to bed until after two.

"What have you got for me?" he asked whoever was on the phone.

"Shit. It was right here. Where'd it go?" Nate Ferrentino. Although Nate wasn't generally on desk duty, Jonah recognized his friend's voice. They both preferred being in the field, doing undercover work or, at the very least, some good old-fashioned, beat-the-pavement investigating. But Nate's wife, Rachel, another operative at Department 6, was due to have their second son any day, and Nate wasn't about to risk missing the big event. Jonah hadn't seen him so excited since a little over a year ago, when they'd had their first child. He wouldn't go anywhere if he couldn't reach her within fifteen minutes.

Fortunately, the office was close to home. They were currently short-staffed in Los Angeles and needed some backup for the operatives who were on assignment. Milton Berger, the owner of the company, was opening an extension office in Tucson with Roderick Guerrero, Jonah's closest friend in the company, and was spending most of his time there.

"Here it is." Nate came back on the line. "I don't know how it wound up clear over there."

"You're not much of a secretary," Jonah said.

"I'm not a secretary at all, so kiss my ass," he responded.

Jonah chuckled. "How's Rach?"

"Uncomfortable and impatient. She's also eating me out of house and home. But that's to be expected at eight and a half months. It happened last pregnancy, too."

"Dylan ready for his new brother?"

"Hell, yeah. Now he'll have someone to pound on."

They hadn't planned on having children only sixteen months apart, but they didn't seem unhappy about it. "With the size of that kid, I feel sorry for the new arrival." Picturing Rachel as he'd last seen her, looking swollen and harried as she dragged Dylan through the office in search of his father, Jonah continued to smile. "You sure you're ready to do this all over again?"

"You kidding? There's nothing like it, man. Someday you'll understand."

Jonah's thoughts reverted to Summer, as they so often did. But this time it was as if he was standing in that hospital room ten years ago, smelling the sweet scent of a brand-new baby. *His* baby. Although it was something he never talked about, he already knew what having a child was like. But that moment, the one that was supposed to be so special, had turned into an ache that would never heal. Not only had he let Francesca down, and Adriana, too—he'd known she wanted far more from him than he'd been willing to give her—he hadn't been there for his own child. He'd opted to go the convenient route.

Little had he known how inconvenient giving her up would become for his conscience. "Someday maybe I will," he said. "What do you have on Dean Wheeler?"

"Quite a bit, actually. The man's spent the better part of his life navigating the mental health system."

Relieved by the change of subject, Jonah straightened his shoulders and tried, once again, to close the door on his past. "I'd guessed as much. But has he ever been treated at Laurel Oaks Behavioral Hospital?"

"He has."

Bingo. They had their connection. Jonah was grateful for that; he thought it might come in handy when he and Francesca met with the investigators later this morning. At least they'd have proof that a second murder victim had a link to someone at the salvage yard. Two links were better than one—and might help combat Finch and Hunsacker's upset over what'd happened last night.

"For a brief period, anyway," Nate was saying. "Looks like he was committed three different times, all for short stints. In 2006, he was in for a psychotic episode. Spent one week at the hospital. In January 2007, he was committed again, for violent behavior against his sister. I guess he pulled a knife on her—"

"He what?" Jonah broke in.

"Don't get too excited. It was only a butter knife, and the details were never clear as to whether he meant to harm her."

"How long did he stay that time?"

"Two weeks. Then his psychiatrist released him into the custody of his parents. He went back a month later for depression."

"So...he's what? Bipolar?"

"He has schizoaffective disorder with severe bipolar tendencies."

"That's a mouthful."

"Not a pleasant diagnosis."

"You mentioned a psychotic episode. He loses touch with reality?"

"According to his doctor, a Dr. Shishimu, he sometimes hears voices that tell him to act a certain way."

"Do they tell him to murder women?"

"Dr. Shishimu said he'd be very surprised if Dean ever harmed anyone. The voices tell him what clothes to wear, what bus to take, even if that particular bus doesn't go where he originally wanted to, what to eat and so on. You get the picture."

Unable to pace or do much of anything else in the bathroom's confined space, Jonah sat on the edge of the tub. "What a way to live."

"That's not all. A nurse at Laurel Oaks told me she remembered him having a persecution complex. When he was there last, he insisted there was someone out to kill him, and the voices were telling him he had to get home in order to protect his mother."

"He thought it was someone in the hospital?"

"He wouldn't say."

"Interesting." The man Jonah had met didn't seem that far gone. Apparently, his meds were working well enough to make him appear somewhat functional. "What medication do they have him on?"

"Geodon."

"Never heard of it." But then, he wasn't very familiar with mental illness or its treatments.

"Neither had I, so I searched the Internet for info. It's considered one of the 'newer generation' anti-psychotics."

"Which means…"

"I'm not sure exactly. It's more recently developed, I guess. It inhibits the absorption of dopamine in the brain, but I think they all do that. Anyway, he's also on Depakote, a mood stabilizer, to treat the bipolar."

"I see. Anything else?"

"That's it."

"Thanks, man. I appreciate the legwork."

"No problem. I'll send you an e-mail with all the names and dates."

Jonah had just hit the end button when another call came in, this one from his ex-wife. Apparently, Lori was tired of sending him text messages without getting a response. Since even his mother's involvement hadn't brought results, she was breaking away from their usual mode of communication.

"What's it going to take to get some breathing room?" he muttered, then answered so he could finally get her off his back.

20

The pain in Francesca's arm half woke her. Then something else disturbed her sleep. Someone talking in a low voice in another room. Problem was…she lived alone.

Butch! A jolt of panic shot through her—until she opened her eyes and recognized where she was. Jonah's motel room. She'd been so drugged up from the pain medication, she'd stayed over.

Raising her arm to shield against the harsh light slicing through the blinds, she squinted to see if any blood had seeped through the bandages, but it didn't seem to have.

Relieved, she slumped onto her pillows, listened to the air-conditioning chug and contemplated what she had to look forward to this morning. Finch and Hunsacker had called to check on her while she was getting her stitches last night and set up a meeting for 10:00 a.m. But she could tell from Finch's peevish voice how that meeting was likely to go.

She'd have some difficult questions to answer—like why she'd made the decision to go back onto Butch's property. She'd explain that she'd been hoping to come up with some evidence that might save lives, which was the truth. But she doubted they'd be sympathetic, especially

Hunsacker. As a private investigator, she often bent rules she couldn't or wouldn't have bent as a police officer. Knowing which rules could be flexible, and when to test them, was what made a good P.I.

Rolling over, she kicked off the blankets and sat up. She needed to use the bathroom, but Jonah was in there.

Should she knock or wait until he'd finished his conversation? She didn't think he was using the facilities. She was pretty sure he was just doing his best to be quiet since she'd been sleeping. So she padded barefoot to the door and lifted her hand to knock. But when she heard him mention a woman's name, she hesitated.

"Look, Lori, I'm fine with it. I'll write the letter when I get home. I hope you get the baby. But I don't appreciate you calling my mother. Although this should go without saying, leave her out of whatever happens between us."

Who was Lori? His most recent girlfriend? Someone he was still dating but didn't classify as a girlfriend? And what was this about a baby? Had he fathered another child?

The answers to those questions were none of Francesca's business. Lowering her hand, she scurried back to the bed and tried to ignore the conversation. But now that she was aware of it, she couldn't avoid hearing the rest, particularly when he raised his voice.

"It's not up to you to decide that," he said. "I've kept your little secret all these years, the least you can do is have some courtesy when you want something from me…. What's the rush? Anything I have to say probably won't matter, anyway. It's been too long since we were married."

Francesca sank onto the edge of the bed. He'd been married and divorced since they were together? Somehow she hadn't expected that. She was quick to remind herself that once she'd turned him loose, he had every right to do what he pleased. It just came as a surprise—and added fuel to her determination to keep some emotional distance between them. He was racking up quite a number of failed relationships....

Not that her romance record was much better. She hadn't been married or had any children, but she'd drifted from one man to the next. Even Roland, someone she'd dated steadily for over a year, hadn't meant enough to her to continue the relationship once he started pressing for a permanent commitment. Her feelings never passed "lukewarm" for anybody.

Except Jonah. From the beginning he'd been unique.

"I'll send it to you when I get home," he said again. "Until then, I'm tied up with an important case.... No, I can't meet you.... That's not true.... I have to go. I'll be in touch," he said, and the silence told her he'd disconnected.

Trying to feign sleep so he wouldn't realize that she'd picked up on so much of his conversation, Francesca crawled toward the pillows, but he came out of the bathroom immediately, catching her before she could settle in. At that point, she thought he might comment on his phone call, since he had to know she'd overheard it, but he didn't.

"Want to shower?" he asked. "I'd like to grab breakfast before our meeting today."

She deliberated whether or not to ignore what she'd heard, but couldn't quite convince herself to do so. "Who's Lori?"

Wearing nothing but a pair of jeans with the fly half-buttoned, he rummaged through the closet for a shirt. "No one important."

"You don't consider an ex-wife important?"

He selected a clean T-shirt. "Not anymore."

"How long ago were you married?"

"Long enough that I'd rather forget all about it."

As unreasonable as it was, jealousy lanced through her. "You have a child with this woman?"

He threw her a scowl. "What, were you taking notes?"

"I couldn't help overhearing." That was true—sort of.

"We don't have a child together. Thank God."

But he'd definitely referred to a baby…. "Why all the secrecy, Jonah?"

"It's not secrecy. There's just no reason to go into it. These days you and I have a professional relationship, remember?" he said with a facetious wink.

"Fine. Be that way." Getting up, she went into the bathroom, but by the time she'd stepped out of the shower and brushed her teeth, curiosity had gotten the better of her again.

"I'll trade you," she offered, poking her head into the room.

He stood at the desk, shoving his wallet and change into his pockets, but at this he turned. "What are you talking about?"

"You answer one question of mine, and I'll answer one question of yours."

Evidently less interested than she'd expected him to be, he powered down his laptop. "What makes you think I have any questions?"

She should've dressed in the bathroom, but she'd been so preoccupied she hadn't thought to bring any clothes in with her, so she pulled the towel she'd wrapped around her higher. "You cared for me so little that you're not curious about anything that's gone on in my life since we were together?"

Scowling, he glanced up; he'd been about to slide his computer into its case. "Do you really believe I didn't care, Francesca?"

She smiled to hide the fact that she didn't know *what* to believe. "That's a question, isn't it?"

Kneading his forehead, he blew out a sigh. "I know I shouldn't get involved in this, but…it won't be the first time I've done something I regret."

"Then we have a deal?"

His obvious suspicion created a marked hesitancy. "What do you want to know?"

"How long were you married?"

"One year."

"Only one year?"

"Thirteen months, to be exact."

"How long ago?"

"Uh-uh-uh." He wagged a finger at her. "That's two questions. It's my turn."

Concealing her frustration with a shrug, she said, "Fine. Shoot."

"Who's the man standing with you in front of the Lincoln Memorial in that picture on your bar?"

"His name's Roland Perenski."

"I don't care about his name," he said with a grimace. "I want to know his significance to you."

She arched her eyebrows. "Then you should've asked, because a second question is breaking the rules, as you've already pointed out."

He came around the bed. "You cheated me on that answer."

"No, I didn't. I answered honestly." But it wasn't the answer he'd been after, and she knew it.

"Okay, one more question," he said.

"Each?"

"Each."

"No problem."

"Roland is…"

She pretended to adjust the bandage covering her stitches, which was now a little damp, thanks to her shower. "One of my ex-boyfriends."

"How long ago were you together?"

"Sorry. My turn." She bestowed the sweetest smile she could muster on him. "When were you married?"

"Before I ever met you."

This came as a total shock. "But we were only twenty-three when we met! How could you have already been married? And why didn't you ever tell me?"

He cocked his head to one side. "Wait a second—are we trading *more* questions?"

She pursed her lips as she considered whether or not to continue.

"Well?" he prompted. But before she could answer, he went back to the desk. "Never mind. This is pointless."

She followed him as far as the aisle between the two beds. "That was a quick reversal. What's the matter? Got a few secrets to hide? Like the fact that you were married when we were dating?"

He rolled his eyes. "I wasn't married when we were dating. That one's for free. But Twenty Questions is now officially over." Pivoting, he stalked toward her. "Unless…"

As he advanced, she backed up until her spine touched the wall, but the subtle lift in his tone had caught her like a baited hook. "Unless what?"

"Unless you're willing to trade something else."

She couldn't believe he'd been married and never told her. She had a million questions. But what would he demand in exchange? "Like what?"

His gaze fell to her lips. "A kiss."

Again wishing she'd gotten her clothes and dressed before starting this conversation, she hugged the towel to her body. "No," she said with a shake of her head.

Lowering his voice to a seductive whisper, he leaned in until his lips were only a fraction of an inch from hers. "Is this the same woman who was willing to get into the back of the van with me last night for a hit-and-run? The same woman who said making love wouldn't mean anything?"

Her throat was suddenly so dry she had difficulty swallowing. They were treading on dangerous ground again. "I said it doesn't *have* to mean anything."

"Neither does a kiss."

She couldn't argue with his logic. But the butterflies rioting in her stomach made her feel too vulnerable to take that kind of intimacy in stride. "Maybe not. But…" But what? She already knew she wouldn't refuse. His proximity jammed all the frequencies in her brain. "If I agree, you have to satisfy my curiosity about your marriage. Even if that means three or four questions."

She noticed a brooding quality in his expression, which surprised her. He'd asked for this and yet he didn't act as if he was getting what he wanted—he acted as if she was leading him to the hangman's noose.

"Lori isn't a subject I like talking about," he said. "One kiss per question. Take it or leave it."

21

He was a fool to whet his own appetite. No question about it. For some reason, he'd rather torture himself with what used to be—what could've been—than steer clear of physical contact. Kissing Francesca would be a poignant, perhaps painful, reminder of all he'd lost. But Jonah couldn't persuade his worthless heart to accept the no-touch policy he'd tried so hard to follow.

He'd always had to learn his lessons the hard way. Apparently, this one would be no different....

"Who's going first?" she breathed, her amber eyes filled with an unsettling mixture of doubt and desire.

"I am." Maybe he'd pay for this later, but God, what a way to go. It'd been so long....

Propping his hands against the wall on either side of her, he bent his head and brushed his mouth across hers. He didn't want to come on too strong. All he needed was one taste, he told himself. But when her palms cupped his chin and her lips softened, he couldn't have pulled away even if the motel was on fire.

Jonah had enough sense left to realize that he was sliding down a very slippery slope, but the kiss had started out so perfect—gentle, slow, controlled. He was determined to finish it just as perfectly, to give her a moment of tenderness to remember him by, a bittersweet farewell to the relationship they'd once shared.

Or maybe that wasn't his real goal. Maybe, if he was completely honest, he'd admit this was his way of showing her that he could exercise some restraint, that he wasn't out to use her or any other woman. But then her lips parted, welcoming his tongue, and he wasn't sure he'd be able to hang on to his restraint....

She groaned. He hadn't expected it, hadn't thought she'd let him know she was enjoying this, but that encouragement sent an onslaught of testosterone into his bloodstream. Chest rising and falling, he explored the warmth of her mouth in a leisurely manner, hoping to drive the pleasure higher, to make her want him with a desperation that rivaled his own....

And then her body arched into his and she moaned again.

He almost moved his hand, almost went for her towel. But his cell phone rang, and the personalized ring identified the caller as Finch or Hunsacker. The detectives were probably confirming that they'd be at the meeting.

Pulling away, he turned so she wouldn't be able to see that he was shaking. He'd missed the call and didn't plan to return it until they were in the car, but the interruption had brought him to his senses, reminded him of his responsibilities—and his limitations where she was concerned.

"It's your turn," he said as he strode to the bed to put on his shoes. "What did you want to ask me?"

If he'd been interested in sharing any details about Lori, he would've mentioned his ex ten years ago. But a deal was a deal. He'd gotten even more than he'd wanted. The least he could do was reciprocate.

Francesca didn't answer right away. When she did try

to talk, she had to clear her throat first. "Why—why did the two of you break up?"

He recognized the doubt in her voice. She wondered if he'd cheated on Lori, too. After what he'd done, there was no way to reclaim her trust, no way to rectify his mistake. Knowing the past would always stand between them made him crazy for kissing her. He couldn't have what he'd once had; he'd already destroyed it. "Not what you're thinking."

"So what was it?"

Did she believe him? Probably not. Why would she?

"Jonah?" she persisted.

He managed a sardonic smile as he looked back at her. "I wasn't her type."

Hunsacker rested his hands on his bulging stomach as he sat next to Jonah and across from Francesca in the conference room they'd used before. He hadn't spoken yet, merely nodded when they filed into the sheriff's station. But something was up. Francesca could feel it. Instead of being angry, as she'd assumed, he seemed pleased with himself. Far *too* pleased.

"What's going on?" she asked.

"You'll see when Finch gets here," he replied.

Clasping his hands loosely in his lap, Jonah leaned back and studied Hunsacker from beneath half-closed eyelids.

"What's with you?" Hunsacker asked, bristling beneath Jonah's unyielding scrutiny.

"What's with *you?*" Jonah replied.

Hunsacker stretched his collar as if Jonah made him nervous. Jonah would make anyone nervous with the hard-ass expression he was wearing. He could tell something was up, too.

The door opened, and Finch walked in, carrying a file. He dropped it on the conference table, but didn't sit down. "How's the arm?" he asked, nodding toward the big white bandage covering her stitches.

Knowing he wasn't truly concerned, only trying for a decent start to what would likely be a less than pleasant meeting, she shrugged. "It'll heal."

"Could've been a lot worse. You're aware of that, right?"

She braced for his full reaction. "Nice segue."

"Dog like that could've torn out your jugular," he went on. "Then where would you be?"

"With a severed jugular, I'm quite certain I'd be dead." Careful not to put pressure on her stitches, she leaned on the table. "That means we should be able to charge Mr. Vaughn with attempted murder."

"You think so? When you were warned, by us and by the Beware of Dog signs, to keep your distance yet returned to his property, anyway?" He folded his arms. "Tell me. If you're so scared of Mr. Vaughn, why did you go back?"

"Because I'm determined to stop him before he kills anyone else. And I want to be able to quit looking over my shoulder."

"You think what you did last night will help?"

"Whether or not I should've been there, what he did was illegal. You can't order your dog to tear someone apart just because that person's on your property."

He rested the bulk of his upper body on his knuckles. "The 'order' part is where I'm having trouble, Ms. Moretti. From my perspective, it looks as if you ignored our directive to stay beyond the fence and went snooping around, even though there was a watchdog in the yard."

"Typical P.I. bullshit," Hunsacker muttered.

Finch threw his partner an irritated glance, and ignored the interruption. "At that stage, you were accidentally locked in when they closed for the night."

Jonah uncrossed his ankles. He'd been sitting silently, letting Francesca take her lumps. They'd both known what was coming, but he seemed to have reached the end of his patience with how they were proceeding. "I told you what happened last night. It was no accident. So if you want to berate her, at least stick to the facts."

"And I wasn't snooping," Francesca argued. "I was trying to hear a conversation between Butch and his wife."

"Eavesdropping is just as bad!" Hunsacker snapped.

That was enough to make Jonah jump in again. "Come on. What she did took guts. If she'd come away with some piece of information that nailed Butch you'd be calling her a hero. You can't have it both ways."

Unwilling to let Jonah draw their fire—what had happened certainly wasn't his fault—she spoke before the investigators could respond. "I got the name of his mistress. That opens up a lot of possibilities."

"Does it?" Hunsacker said. "*What* possibilities? Because I've already visited Kelly Martin's place. She has nothing but wonderful things to say·about Butch."

"It's nice that the two of you have so much in common," Francesca said.

"You can go to hell!" he retorted.

Sitting taller, Jonah directed his comments to Hunsacker. "That doesn't mean Kelly won't change her mind."

Francesca spoke up again. "What about the other

woman Paris brought up? Julia. Did you check the missing persons list? It would certainly be suspicious if she's on there."

Hunsacker clicked his tongue. "I hate to break this to you, but there is no Julia."

This took Francesca aback. She knew that name had *some* significance. Paris had seemed relieved that the police hadn't come knocking, looking for information about Julia. That meant someone *should* be asking, didn't it? "What Paris said means something. I know it does. You won't find Bianca on any missing persons list, either. Yet she's dead."

"You're stretching." Hunsacker again.

"No, I'm not. This Julia could be from out of town, and in that case she wouldn't be reported as missing in *this* area." She tucked her hair behind her ears as she puzzled through it. "Or…maybe she was a runaway. Or she could've been a homeless woman. Or even a prostitute. There're a lot of reasons she might not be on the list. But that name is significant."

Hunsacker's whole body jiggled as he laughed. "You've got quite an imagination, you know that?"

She glared at him. "Stop patronizing me."

"What else do you want me to do?"

"Charge Butch for what he did to me last night!"

"You might want to listen to her about Butch," Jonah said. "He knew she was in the yard when he told Dean to close the gate. You don't seem to be listening—I told you this last night—but I witnessed the whole thing. I watched him bring the dog outside, even heard his wife pleading with him not to turn the animal loose."

Hunsacker rolled his eyes. "Or you're trying to protect her. You come to her rescue every time she gets herself in trouble."

"Kiss my ass," Jonah snapped. "*You* weren't there."

"Exactly! I wasn't there," he responded. "But I know Butch puts that dog out every night."

"It wasn't like that. It wasn't a routine act," Jonah insisted.

Finch straightened his tie. "How would we prove that he knowingly locked her in?"

The investigators' stubborn resistance made Francesca feel hopeless. "What are you talking about? You have two witnesses. We told you what happened."

"Like you told us he had a dead body in the yard?" Hunsacker said.

With a bitter laugh, she got up. "Under the circumstances, anyone would've thought that mannequin was a body, Hunsacker. Or do you have your head so far up Butch's ass that you would've turned a blind eye, regardless?"

Hunsacker's face turned scarlet. "Are you questioning my ethics?"

"I'm wondering if your relationship with Butch is making it impossible for you to view him objectively."

Spittle shot from Hunsacker's mouth as he clambered to his feet. "Because I'm demanding proof?"

"Because you're ignoring the obvious!"

"Whoa, calm down." Finch held up a hand to each of them but spoke to her. "The problem here is that what *you're* saying not only contradicts Butch's side of the story, it contradicts what his wife, his brother-in-law, his mother-in-law and his father-in-law are saying. So how do you expect the D.A. to take your word against that of all four people who live in the house, when you already have a history of overstepping your bounds?"

"A history of overstepping my bounds?" she echoed. "Give me a break! The first time I went there, it was just to speak with him. I was searching for a missing woman—and *he* was the last person to have seen her alive."

"That doesn't make him guilty," Hunsacker said. "Whether he and April Bonner had an affair or not doesn't matter. That's not proof of murder."

"He nearly attacked me with a baseball bat. Which, I might add, is how seven other victims have been killed in this area!"

Sweat began to bead on Hunsacker's forehead. "But he *didn't* beat you. *You* assaulted *him!*"

Francesca narrowed her eyes. "That's probably what saved my life."

"It's cost you your credibility. That's what it's done."

Jonah was the only one still seated. "Butch Vaughn is trouble," he said. "Believe it or you'll be sorry later."

Hunsacker turned to Jonah. "Oh, so if you say it, we should take it as gospel, is that right? Why? Because you're Mr. Big Shot from California? What have you been able to accomplish since you got here, huh?"

"Hunsacker, stop," Finch said. "You know these investigations take time. We've hardly begun."

"I didn't want his help from the beginning. He's no better than we are!"

Finch slanted Hunsacker a dark look. "I don't want to get into that."

"Whether you're happy with what I did last night or not won't change the truth," Francesca said. "Butch had his mentally ill brother-in-law lock me in, and then he sicced his dog on me. All you have to do is get Dean to talk."

Hunsacker smacked his forehead. "Oh, why didn't I think of that? That should be easy to do. We just need to get him to turn on Butch, to bite the hand that feeds him. And if we could convince him, his testimony would be completely reliable, wouldn't it? Considering he's psychotic and hears and sees things that don't exist!"

Finch spoke before Francesca could retort. "You say Butch locked you in and set the dog on you."

Ignoring Hunsacker, she focused on him. "Yes."

"I personally believe that. I have no reason not to. But did he also kidnap you from the van, where you were supposed to be, and carry you off to the salvage yard?"

Refusing to respond to a question he already knew the answer to, Francesca frowned at him.

"That's what I thought," he said. "So, in other words, the incident last night could easily have been avoided if you'd stayed beyond the fence where you belonged, correct?"

"If you're saying that makes it my fault—"

"It does make what happened your fault!" he told her. "How do you expect me to charge Butch with attempted murder when all the evidence supports his story instead of yours?"

"I told you. *Dean* is the key. He knows what happened, and he wants to talk. I bet his doctor would testify that as long as he takes his meds he's coherent enough to know fact from fiction."

Skepticism created grooves in Hunsacker's jowls. "And you know you can get Dean to turn on Butch because the two of you are such great friends?"

Jonah tossed his pen on the table. "Not as close as you and Butch, apparently."

"Why are you protecting her?" Hunsacker cried. "What is it with you? Are you hoping to get in her pants?"

Unfolding his lean body, Jonah towered over the short,

round Hunsacker. "Do you have some kind of death wish?"

"Don't you threaten me!"

Feeling guilty for dragging Jonah into this with her, Francesca hurried to interrupt him. "Stop it. You all heard what Dean said when I was wearing that wire."

Hunsacker refused to look at her, wouldn't take his eyes off Jonah. "I also heard him recant it."

"So?" She glanced from one investigator to the other. "I'm telling you he wants to help us. He contacted me via my friend yesterday. He's definitely reaching out. Why would he befriend the 'enemy' if he's defensive of Butch?"

"Maybe he wants to get in your pants, too," Hunsacker said.

She pinned him with a glare. "You're an asshole."

Hunsacker chuckled. "Just calling it the way I see it, honey."

She appealed to Finch instead. "The answers and proof we need won't simply fall into our laps. We'll have to work for it. I hope *you* don't have a problem with that."

"No. But I have a problem with this." Retrieving the remote control from the eraser tray on the chalkboard behind him, Finch turned on the TV in the corner. A recording of the news came on. He fast-forwarded through the first few segments until he found what he wanted, then pushed Play.

Butch stood in his salvage yard next to an attractive female reporter. He was telling her all about this private investigator from Chandler who showed up one day and went snooping through his property, then ran to the police claiming he had a dead body in the salvage yard.

The camera panned to the mannequin as he pulled

back the tarp. "This is what she was talking about," he said.

"Nice effect, don't you think?" Hunsacker piped up.

Too absorbed in what she was seeing to respond, Francesca watched Butch talk about how she'd said he attacked her but how she'd really attacked him. Then, of course, he showed the scratches on his face. Paris and his son stood by him, making him look like the consummate family man.

"This is ridiculous," she said. "What about his sex addiction and his cheating?"

"What about it?" Hunsacker said. *"That's not murder!"*

"The card from the bar he frequents was found at the grave site!" she hollered back.

Hunsacker grimaced. "That's a popular bar. A lot of people frequent that place, including me."

"Be quiet. You don't want to miss this next part," Finch said.

That was when Butch, wearing a lugubrious expression, started crying on-screen. He said a consultant hired by the Yavapai County Sheriff's Office had killed Demon, only he didn't use the dog's name. "Demon" didn't exactly make the animal sound friendly. He went on to add that the bullet could've struck *him,* that it was dark and he was running around, trying to figure out what had set his dog off. He said he didn't even know Francesca had "broken into" the yard and, of course, added "again."

The whole thing made Francesca sick. "It's all lies. He's the biggest liar I've ever met."

Apparently satisfied that he'd shown her the worst of it, Finch paused the television. "I don't have to tell you the backlash has been huge. Every TV station in Prescott has called, asking why we think we can infringe on the rights of innocent citizens."

"You're pretty skilled at letting the public know only what you want them to, so you should be able to dance your way around that, don't you think?" she said. "I mean, seven women have been murdered but the public doesn't even know there's a serial killer on the loose. Instead, they're getting this martyr crap—" she waved at the frozen image of Butch crying over his dog on screen "—and thinking *I'm* the bad guy."

"You might not be the 'bad guy,'" Finch said, "but you're no asset to this investigation. I called you in here to inform you that you've been ordered to stay a mile away from Butch, his property and every member of his family."

Francesca felt her jaw drop. "That's crazy. Laughable."

"Maybe it is to you."

"You're getting too carried away with damage control," Jonah warned. "Butch isn't the nice guy he seems to Hunsacker. I don't care if he gives the poor every dime he's got. Don't forget that someone cut Ms. Moretti's phone line the night after she had that little scuffle with Butch. It'd be pretty damn coincidental if it was anyone else."

"And we're keeping an eye on him," Finch said. "Which is what *you* were supposed to be doing last night, watching from a distance. It's not as if we're ruling him out. We're just...taking a less aggressive stance until this blows over."

"So public safety becomes less of a concern than saving face?" Jonah said.

"Look, I don't give a shit what you think!" Finch jabbed a finger in Francesca's direction. "I'm stuck with the mess she created and this is the best way to clean it up." Turning back to Francesca, he lowered his voice, suggesting he felt at least a little bad about what he was doing. "Just so we're clear, this is a court order. If you break it, you'll be jailed. I suggest you return to Chandler, keep your mouth shut about any proprietary information you have on the investigation so far and leave us the hell alone to do our jobs. Otherwise, you'll be charged with interfering in a police investigation."

"This doesn't end here," Jonah said.

"It won't do any good to talk to the sheriff." Hunsacker smiled. "You have nothing more to do with this case, either."

Jonah's nostrils flared. "What did you say?"

Finch slid the file he'd brought in across the table. "It's true," he said with a sigh. "You've been terminated."

"You think you two can solve a case this size all by yourself?" Jonah demanded. "You've never even worked a serial murder before."

"We won't be by ourselves. We're forming a task force. Prescott P.D. is loaning us some manpower. So is the state patrol. It'll be announced today, when we go public with the news of what was found in Dead Mule Canyon." Finch drew a deep breath. "And now, I have to get back to my office."

Circumventing Hunsacker, Jonah caught Finch's arm before he could leave. "So I'm the scapegoat? Firing me is how the department plans to repair its image?"

"You're an independent contractor. That makes you expendable," he said.

22

Although Jonah had never been fired before, there was a small part of him that was actually relieved. He'd been struggling with this assignment ever since Francesca became involved in it, but he would never have allowed himself to bail. That would've smacked of running from the challenge—not the challenge of the case but of dealing in any sort of normal manner with a woman he was afraid he still loved. Finch's actions alleviated that problem, removed personal choice from the matter. All he had to do was take Francesca back to Chandler, where he'd left his rental car. Then he could book a flight to L.A., return the car when he hit the airport and say goodbye to Arizona. The next time he was invited to accept an assignment in this state, he'd think twice.

"I can't believe that just happened." Francesca had been so worked up she'd insisted on driving, but Jonah didn't mind. Somehow, becoming a passenger further relegated him to the "along for the ride" category. He was no longer responsible for anything, he realized as he sat with his seat partially reclined, gazing out at the passing scenery.

"It's politics," he said with a shrug. "You've got other clients, right?"

She lowered the volume of the radio. "I wasn't getting paid, anyway."

"What do you mean? I thought you were hired by April's sister."

"Jill just lost her only sibling. I can't charge her fees on top of that."

He studied her for a second. "Isn't that what private investigators do? You've got a mortgage like everyone else, don't you?"

"My mortgage isn't the point. This isn't about making money. I've got plenty of work. It's about putting away the guy who murdered all those women. I think we've got the leads to do that. I mean, what about the card from that bar that showed up at the burial site? That Julia person Paris mentioned? The fact that Dean was a patient at the mental hospital where Bianca Andersen worked?"

"No longer our problem. None of it. You heard Finch. They're creating a task force. Hopefully, they'll put those pieces of the puzzle in the proper order."

"How? By asking Butch whether or not he did it and then thanking him for his time when he says no?"

Jonah didn't want to think about it. He'd never left a case unfinished before. It was hard to let go of an investigation before he'd given it his all, especially one this critical. But if the Yavapai County Sheriff's Office wanted him to bow out, he'd leave them to their own devices.

"There might be some folks on the task force who are willing to dig as deep as they need to," he said, and knew that could be true. Someone else could solve this. He had to disregard his own compulsive nature, which told him he had to be the one. "Considering what's happened between you and Butch, it's probably better that you won't be involved. Dropping out of the picture might be what keeps you safe."

She slowed for a traffic light. "You think he'll forget about me?"

Jonah *wanted* to believe it—that was the only positive he could find. "Why not? He made us both look bad. Hopefully, he feels we're even."

"We killed his dog, Jonah. I doubt he's going to let that go."

"*He* caused it."

"He won't see it that way. People like Butch never do. He might come after me again."

Trying to persuade himself that she wasn't in danger, he began to list the reasons she could be wrong. "You live two hours away, which makes you an inconvenient victim. And now that he's succeeded in getting us off his back, he'd be stupid to do anything that might risk involving us again. He should consider himself lucky to have won the last round, sit back and enjoy his schadenfreude."

"His schadenfreude?"

"Pleasure over another's misfortune."

"If he's a serial killer, he won't settle for that."

Francesca's words reminded him of Winona Green, the profiler he'd contacted. He'd faxed her the details they had on the Dead Mule Canyon killings but hadn't heard back. What with recent discoveries—the identity of one of the bodies and details about Dean—he could provide a bit more information. But what was the point? The task force would call in a profiler of their own, if they had any confidence in that sort of thing.

Still, he should contact her, let her know not to worry about finishing up....

He'd take care of it in the morning, when he was back

home and away from the gravitational pull of this case with its many unanswered questions.

"Maybe it's not Butch. Maybe it's Dean," he said.

"What if it is Dean? That doesn't mean the killings will stop," she responded.

Old-town Prescott was replaced by newer buildings set farther and farther apart.

"So what do you suggest we do?" he asked. "Ignore what we were told? Act like we weren't kicked off the case?"

Scowling, she stared out at the desert landscape. "I don't know. I can't just drop this. Partly because it doesn't feel as if Hunsacker and Finch are paying enough attention to Butch and Dean."

Jonah understood. He felt the same way. But there were advantages to what had occurred this morning, which he'd been busy trying to tell himself.

"Don't you care about how Finch and Hunsacker treated you?" Francesca asked.

"If you want the truth, I was tempted to break Hunsacker's jaw. If he wasn't so fat and incapable of defending himself, maybe I would have. But I held on to my temper. And now I'm proud of myself for that. I'm thinking we both might benefit from taking this opportunity to…"

She finished his sentence before he could unearth the words he was searching for. "Put some distance between us?"

"To work on something a little less sexually frustrating," he muttered.

She turned to look at him. "If it wasn't for me, you'd fight for this case, wouldn't you?"

Propping his chin up with his fist, he gazed out the window. "Maybe." Definitely. But leaving meant he wouldn't be forced to endure her company anymore or the confusing emotions she evoked. Once he got to California, if all went as planned, those feelings would dull in intensity, at least enough that he could function without thinking of her constantly. He'd managed it before.

Of course, it'd taken him ten years to reach that point, but he didn't want to concentrate on *that* detail. It was too damn depressing.

"In any event, we'd be crazy to give them a reason to charge us with interfering. Because they'll do it if we provoke them."

"What if you talked to the sheriff?" she said. "Maybe you can get him to change his mind."

"He's the one who signed the notice of dismissal, remember?" He pulled the file from between the seat and the console and waved it at her.

"So that's it? You're leaving because of me."

He shrugged. "More or less."

She didn't seem to like the sound of that. "What will you do when you get home?"

"Same thing you should. Take on a different case. Try to forget this one."

"Are you worried that your boss might be upset by how it went down in Prescott?"

"No."

"Why not?"

He stretched his seat belt. "Because I've already proven myself. I'll tell him what happened and that will be that."

"You're sure?"

"Positive. Contracts get canceled now and then. With the task force they're forming, this isn't all that unusual. Besides, I haven't done anything wrong. I couldn't let

Demon kill you. As far as I'm concerned, there's nothing bad they can say about my work."

"What secret have you kept for Lori?"

The sudden change of subject took him by surprise. "What?"

"You told your ex-wife you've kept her secret all these years. What did that mean?"

He felt his mood shift, grow darker, despite all the effort he'd put into shoring it up. "Nothing."

"You're *still* going to keep it."

"Why not? Running my mouth won't improve the situation."

Francesca obviously wasn't satisfied with that answer. But she didn't press him. A Chevron station came up at the very edge of town, and she pulled into it. "We'd better fill up."

"I'll get it," he said.

He pumped the gas, then went into the Mini Mart to pick up a couple of cold drinks. He wanted some iced tea. But as he stood in line at the checkout, his gaze landed on a rack of condoms.

"Will that be all?" the clerk asked as he set the two bottles near the register.

"Yeah." He had no need for condoms. He wasn't even dating anyone. But after he put down a twenty, he threw a box on the counter, anyway.

"Wait, you want those, too?" the clerk asked.

Jonah glanced through the front window of the store, where he could see Francesca waiting for him in the car. "Those, too," he said. "And give me a sack."

During the rest of the ride to Chandler, the thought of the panties she'd taken from Butch's house—and still had in the pocket of the pants she'd worn last night—burned in Francesca's mind. If she told Jonah about them, would he stay in Arizona? Did she want him to? She didn't *need* him in order to continue the investigation.

But if she didn't push ahead with what she believed to be true regarding Butch, what would she do about them? She couldn't discard evidence or hang on to it indefinitely.

She should've mentioned those panties to Finch and Hunsacker. But she was so angry about the investigators' reaction to last night, she'd shied away from admitting what she'd done. She wasn't convinced they'd see it as helpful. They'd just use her actions as more proof of "typical P.I. behavior."

Considering Hunsacker's friendship with Butch, she wasn't even sure the investigators would have those panties analyzed, not unless and until they had other evidence, irrefutable evidence, that he was their man. She could easily imagine Hunsacker saying, "Why spend the state's money on such a long shot?" She'd told them what Paris had said about that Julia person, hadn't she? And they'd blown it off. She doubted they'd do any more to find Julia than they'd already done by checking their list of missing persons.

On the other hand, what if no other evidence surfaced? What if those panties were indeed a conclusive piece of the puzzle? Then Finch and Hunsacker had to know about them.

"April is dead, and Kelly's alive," she said to Jonah. "If Butch is guilty, why would he kill one and not the other?"

"There could be a lot of reasons," he said. "Maybe the women who give him what he wants live, and the others die. Murder to cover for rape would be nothing new in the criminal world."

In the case of April Bonner, Francesca could picture that exact scenario….

"Or it could come down to the specific personalities involved," he said. "Do you remember hearing about that guy who was kidnapping women from shopping malls as he traveled across America?"

Francesca shook her head. Although she paid attention to most major crimes, this one didn't sound familiar.

"He brutally tortured and raped each one for days before killing her," Jonah explained. "But his last victim he treated differently. Somehow she managed to develop a relationship with him. He stopped torturing her and let her live. And just before he was caught, when he knew the end was imminent, he gave her money and set her free."

"There are so many variables," she muttered. "Nothing's absolute."

"That's what makes serial murder so difficult."

The beginnings of a headache made Francesca wish she'd let Jonah drive. Her arm hurt, too, but at least it wasn't broken. The doctor in the emergency room had told her she was lucky Demon hadn't chomped right through the bone.

"You okay?" he asked when she rubbed her eyes.

She sighed. "Just getting sleepy."

"Want me to drive?"

"No, that's okay." She was too upset with him and the situation to let him ease the load.

They listened to a song on the radio before he spoke again. "What are you thinking about?"

"Nothing in particular."

He raised one eyebrow. "Your expression is certainly intense for not thinking about anything 'in particular.'"

She adjusted the air-conditioning vent closest to her so the air wouldn't hit her so directly. Should she tell him she had the panties? Why not? Maybe he could help her decide how to proceed. "I have something," she said.

"Something?" he repeated.

"A pair of panties."

His lips slanted into a crooked grin. "Are you talking dirty to me?"

She tried not to smile at his joke. She felt bad for getting him fired, which was beginning to neutralize some of the resentment she'd been harboring toward him. He'd saved her life last night and bruised his knee in the process. She figured she owed him some credit for that, too. Regardless of what he might or might not have done in the past, she couldn't stop liking him. It was that simple.

"Nothing that exciting. I'm referring to the investigation we're no longer part of."

He tapped the dash. "And?"

"I have the panties Paris found in Butch's jockey box last night."

She wasn't sure if it was concern or anger that sharpened his voice. "How'd you get those?"

"They were on the ground. I just...picked them up."

"I don't remember you telling Finch and Hunsacker about any panties."

"Because I didn't."

He adjusted his own air-conditioning vent. "Why not?"

"You were there. You know why."

The beard growth on his chin rasped as he rubbed it. "Yeah, I guess I do."

"So now what? We're off the case. Do I forget about

them? Mail them anonymously to the sheriff's office? What?"

Twisting in his seat, he leaned against the door. "Give them to me."

"What will you do with them?"

"There's a lab we use at Department 6. I'll have them tested. If the tech finds sufficient DNA, I'll have him create a profile."

"At whose expense?"

"If my company won't cover it, I will."

She changed her grip on the steering wheel. "Why would you do that?"

He stared at her. "You have to ask? Why wouldn't I if it might stop a murderer?"

"You make it very difficult not to like you," she said grudgingly.

That crooked smile reappeared. "Too bad you're still fighting it."

23

The panties were gone. Butch searched his office, retraced Paris's steps to the house, even went through his jockey box, where she claimed to have found them. But they weren't there, didn't seem to be on the premises.

Where had she put them? He had no idea, but he hoped it was someplace safe.

"Daddy? What are you doing?"

Spotting his son playing in the planter by the front door as he came around the house from the carport, Butch conjured up a smile he didn't feel. It hadn't been an easy morning. First they'd had to put on that circus act for local television. Then they'd had to bury Demon. That had just about killed him. He'd cared more about that dog than ninety-five percent of the people in his life. "Looking for something I've lost, buddy."

"Demon?"

"No, Demon died, remember?" Champ didn't understand; he seemed to think Demon was sleeping, and his next words proved it.

"When's he going to wake up?"

"He won't be waking up. But we'll get another dog, okay?" Butch couldn't believe another dog could really replace Demon, but he hoped Champ would.

"Okay." He continued to drive his miniature cars around the dirt roads he'd created between the plants. He even had a watering can beside him, so he could refill his "lake."

Butch brushed past him, then stopped. Champ ran around the property all day, picking up one item or another for his pretend worlds. He couldn't go into the salvage yard during working hours, when it was open to the public, or when Butch was using the big machinery, but it was a wonderland for him after hours. Was there any chance…

When Butch didn't go inside, Champ angled his face up, squinting to avoid the glare of the sun. "Do you like my racetrack, Daddy?"

Butch moved over to provide him with some shade. "I do. Listen, bud. Mommy's lost a pair of panties. Have you seen them?"

He wrinkled his nose. *"Panties?"*

"Yes. Underwear. The kind women wear. She dropped them after…after she finished the laundry, and I'm trying to find them for her. You haven't seen them, have you?"

"Nope." Champ made the sound of a motor as he pushed his cast-iron truck to the top of a small hill he'd created.

"You're sure?" Butch asked.

His first question already forgotten, Champ looked up again. "What, Daddy?"

"Never mind." What would Champ want with a pair of women's panties? At that age, Butch's fetish had already taken strong root. He could remember stealing his mother's panties and bringing them to his room to fondle while hiding under the bed. But Champ hadn't encountered what Butch had encountered. He was normal. Butch was eternally grateful for that. It offered him hope that he could create something positive from his life.

Tousling his son's hair, he went inside, letting the screen door slam behind him. "Paris?"

"What?" She came out of the kitchen but didn't give him a chance to tell her why he'd called out for her. "Have you seen Champ?" she asked. "Is he still out front?"

"Yeah, he's playing in the planter."

She tucked her hair behind her ears. "I wish I could put him in the dog run."

"We just buried Demon and you're already taking over his cage?"

"That dog was mean. He only liked you. And I'm thinking about Champ's safety."

"The run is filled with dog shit."

"It wouldn't be if you cleaned it."

"Can't your brother do anything?" Slipping past her, he went into the kitchen and poured himself some coffee.

She followed him. "You know how Mom and Dad protect him. They'll think we're being abusive if we give him such a nasty job."

"Then clean it out yourself," he grumbled, adding cream to his cup.

"I can't. No time. So don't blame me if Champ wanders off."

Champ was as well-balanced as Butch could've hoped to be, and Butch wanted to be sure his son never met up with anyone or anything to change that. "You'd better watch him."

"I try to. But if you want the house clean and the laundry done and the meals prepared, someone's got to do it. And that someone is always me."

"Bring him in when you're in the house. And quit acting like you have it so damn rough."

She muttered under her breath. He couldn't tell exactly what she'd said, but he noticed that she was careful not to let her irritation go too far. Somehow, she still loved him. That realization brought a flood of relief because he had to ask her a difficult question.

Lowering his voice so no one else in the household would hear him, he spoke over the rim of his coffee cup. "Where'd you put those panties you found in my jockey box?"

She checked the mudroom behind her as if she feared Dean might be hiding there. Her brother seemed to overhear everything, to be right where they didn't want him to be all the time. If it wasn't for the old folks and the fact that this was their place, Butch would've kicked him out long ago. Dean didn't have an outside job, so he didn't contribute financially. He didn't do much around the house, either. Occasionally, he volunteered to watch Champ, but Butch wouldn't allow him to babysit without supervision. He understood better than most the damage a twisted adult could wreak on a young mind. Except for a few hours a day spent answering phones, filing, filling out invoices or accepting deliveries in the yard, Dean was a total waste of space. Mostly, he rambled aimlessly around town, bothering people who'd rather be left alone.

"I don't know where they are," she said. "Unlike you, I'm not attracted to other women's underwear."

When he ignored that, she backed off a bit, grew less combative. "Why?" she asked, now sulky.

"I can't find them," he admitted.

Her eyes narrowed. "Why do you *want* to find them? So you can jerk off while you remember?"

"Because we can't afford to have them floating around, that's why!"

The color drained from her face. "So they *do* belong to the Bonner woman."

"No." April had worn the ugliest old-lady panties he'd ever seen, probably because she'd never planned on getting naked with him. Her underwear had been as practical and unattractive as he'd found her, once they met. Like so many others, she'd posted a far more flattering picture of herself on the Internet. Maybe Butch occasionally lied about his name and his exact location, but he was truthful about everything else. He wished the women he met were that honest.

"Then why are you worried?" Paris wanted to know.

Because the sexy leopard-print panties Paris had brought into the yard last night connected him to someone else entirely. Someone he'd promised Paris he'd never mention again. "I'm afraid that Moretti woman got hold of them. That she'll try to make more of them than she should."

"How could she do that?"

He preferred not to go into detail. Paris was already a nervous wreck. And that hang-up call last night certainly hadn't helped. "She's convinced I'm guilty. She might even try to say they belonged to April."

"That can be proven one way or another. If they were ever worn, there's DNA on those panties, like in the movies, right?"

"That's why I've got to get them back." He'd said more than he wanted to, so he concentrated on stirring his coffee.

"What if she has them? She was inside the yard while

we were arguing. She could've heard about the panties, decided to steal them."

If she'd heard about the panties, she could also have heard Julia's name…. "You would've had to drop them for that to happen. Did you?"

She blinked rapidly as she struggled to remember. "I don't know. I was so upset. I—I wasn't worried that someone might find them. I—"

"When's the last time you saw them?" He broke in to keep her focused so she wouldn't fall apart.

"In your office."

"I checked there."

Nonplussed, she shook her head. "Then they have to be in the yard."

"Son of a bitch." Setting his cup aside, Butch grabbed his truck keys off the hook.

"Where are you going?" she asked.

"I need to take care of some business."

She grabbed him by the arm. "What kind of business?"

"Let me go."

"You're not going to confront that Francesca woman…"

"I have to. Don't you understand? I need to get those panties back before she hands them off to someone else. It might be too late already." He dropped a kiss on her forehead. "Don't worry. I'll be home as soon as I can. If your parents ask, tell them Dean's watching the yard. He should be able to handle it for a couple of hours."

"Butch?"

He turned.

"If only you'd quit like you promised."

He wished he had, wished he could. What compelled him to do what he did? He'd asked himself that since he was a boy, but he was just…different, and there didn't seem to be anything he could do to make himself normal. "I'm sorry."

"Be careful," she said. Then she closed her eyes and her lips moved in what looked like a silent prayer, but Butch knew prayers wouldn't save them. He'd never been acquainted with any god, couldn't believe one existed. Even if there was some deity that took a benevolent interest in humankind, he wouldn't protect Butch's family. Not with the life Butch had lived. Not with the things he'd done. Butch had to take care of his own.

With a wave, he headed for the door.

"When will we be able to put it all behind us?" she whispered from the entrance to the kitchen.

He paused to look back at her, and gave her the same empty promise he'd given ever since she'd first caught him cheating. "Soon. Real soon."

"It won't end, Butch. It'll never end, will it."

"Sure it will." Flinching at the tears in her eyes, evidence of pain *he'd* caused, he stepped out on the porch, where he stood gazing down at his son.

"Look, Daddy!" A grin spread across Champ's face as he held up his Corvette. "This car goes fast."

"That's a cool car," Butch agreed. He knew in that instant that he wouldn't hesitate to do whatever he had to, but another voice interrupted him before he could leave the porch.

"Going somewhere?"

Butch jerked his head around to see Dean standing in the shade of the overhang near the empty dog run. "What are you doing out here?" he asked. "You're supposed to be in the yard."

"Don't worry. I'm keeping an eye on things."

"Not the things you're supposed to."

His smile grew faintly mocking. "For now, I'm keeping an eye on you."

"Be careful with that," Butch warned.

Straightening his frail, slim body, Dean pulled a woman's thong from behind his back and twirled it around his finger. "Don't worry. Your secrets are safe with me."

Francesca watched Jonah from her driveway as he moved his luggage into his rental car. "I guess this is goodbye," she said.

Jonah wondered how quickly he could arrange a flight. If he didn't do it fast, he might change his mind. "I guess so."

"I never dreamed I'd see you again. Let alone kiss you," she added.

"Yeah, well, that kiss could've turned into a lot more," he teased. "My mistake."

"Actually, you did the right thing."

"Why's that?"

"It taught me something about you."

"Like…"

"You're not *all* bad."

"Is that meant to be a compliment?" he said with a laugh.

"Yes. I appreciate all you've done." She held up her injured arm. "Thanks for looking out for me."

"You're welcome." He bent his head in farewell as he took his keys from his pocket, but she surprised him by closing the distance between them and putting her arms around him.

"It was good to see you again," she murmured.

He wanted to apologize to her, to finally let her know how guilty he felt about what he'd done when they were together. She seemed more open now. He thought she might allow him that opportunity, might actually *believe* him this time. But a blue van pulled up at that moment, and Adriana got out.

"Hi." She fidgeted with her keys while glancing from Francesca to him. She looked a lot different than when he'd seen her before. With her hair curled and her makeup on, she'd obviously gone to some trouble to clean up. Jonah wished he didn't get the impression she'd done it for him, but that old feeling came over him, the one he remembered from ten years ago, and it had the same suffocating effect.

Francesca's smile tightened as she released him and moved away. "Hi. What's up?"

"I just came by to make sure you two are okay. I've been so worried, what with the case you're working on. That Dean guy really gave me a bad feeling."

"I've got to go." Eager to extricate himself from the conversation, Jonah walked toward his car. "Nice seeing you both."

It appeared as if Francesca had more to add to their earlier exchange, but now that Adriana was here, he knew she wouldn't say it. She nodded instead. "Thanks again."

"No problem."

He waved at Adriana, who smiled a little too broadly in return, and got in his car. That moment when Francesca had softened, when she'd looked up at him with a hint of the old trust, had rattled him—and given him hope. But he was foolish to reach for it. What they'd had was long gone. They'd be crazy to try and resurrect it.

"Just get the hell out of here," he told himself. "Do the safe thing for once in your life."

And he did. He almost couldn't believe it, but less than an hour later, he was waiting to board a plane to L.A.

* * *

Butch waited until Champ went inside, like he'd told him to do, before addressing Dean. "Where'd you get those?"

Filled with the adrenaline of being more daring than he'd ever thought he could be, Dean considered the scrap of fabric he'd taken from the metal box buried beneath the train car. "Where you keep all the others," he said. "I found your little stash. You recognize them, don't you? Or have you collected so many you can't tell them apart anymore?"

Butch didn't yell, didn't holler at him to get the hell out of the way or to crawl back under whatever rock he'd crawled out from, like he normally did when they crossed paths. His brother-in-law approached this situation with some caution, maybe even a touch of respect. "How did you find my box?" he asked, dropping his voice so they couldn't be heard inside the house.

"I didn't *find* it, exactly. It was more a matter of… stumbling across it," he said, although he'd been searching for it or something like it ever since Butch and Paris had married. Even with his extensive knowledge of the yard—and the abundance of time he spent in it—it'd taken years to unearth Butch's precious trophies. He could hardly believe he'd done it. "Imagine my shock when I opened it," he went on. "There have to be…what? Fifty pairs of panties in there?" He whistled. "I'm impressed, Butch. How many women have you slept with?"

"That's none of your business." His initial flash of surprise now over, Butch wasn't messing around any longer. His hands curled into fists and the veins stood out in his neck. He wanted to kill Dean as brutally as he'd killed Julia. That wasn't hard to tell.

Fortunately, Butch wouldn't go that far. He cared too

much about Paris and Champ, was already close to losing them. And he had his home and job to consider; all of it came through Paris.

"Paris might consider it *her* business," he mused.

Butch spat at the ground. "You think she doesn't know?"

"If she does, she has no clue about the magnitude. Or what you do to the women after you get their panties."

"Shut up!" His voice turned into more of a rasp as he struggled to control his temper. "You don't know what you're talking about. Have you taken your meds today?"

"Forget my meds." Finally feeling safe enough to reveal the irritation and anger that welled up inside him so often, Dean grimaced. "My medication is *my* affair. And I'm tired of you and everyone else around here getting involved in it."

"You need those pills. You act crazy when you're not on them. Because of that, I'm going to forget this little… incident."

Butch was discounting him again. Refusing to let that happen, Dean stepped forward. "Collecting proof of your conquests may not be *crazy,* but I'm pretty sure everyone would agree that murder is a serious problem."

After shooting a wary glance at the front door, Butch moved closer to him.

Fear tempted Dean to back away. He'd witnessed how drastically his brother-in-law's moods could shift. Today, he'd given Butch a reason to be upset. But he stood his ground. That stash of women's underwear supplied him with leverage he'd never had before. That was why he'd wanted to find it so badly.

"I haven't murdered *anyone,* Dean." Butch towered

over him like a giant redwood. "Francesca Moretti is wrong. *You're* wrong."

Pursing his lips, Dean studied his treasure as a way to avoid the malevolence in Butch's eyes. "Good to hear. So…you can probably explain why Julia's body is in the old freezer?" He finally looked up. "Had to get there somehow."

The dark stubble on Butch's chin contrasted sharply with the sudden white of his face. Putting his brother-in-law in such a compromising position made Dean feel powerful. He was glad he'd found those panties. Butch would never dare mistreat him again.

"Are these hers?" Dean asked. "Julia's?" Bringing the panties to his nose, he sniffed. "Nope. Couldn't be. They still have the distinctive scent of the wearer, which means they came into your possession too recently. Could it be that they're April Bonner's?"

Butch's Adam's apple bobbed as he swallowed. "You're the one who put that other pair of panties in my jockey box."

Widening his eyes, Dean played dumb. "I don't know what you're talking about."

"The underwear your sister came across. That's what you hoped would happen. Are you the one who called her, too? The hang-up she thought was Kelly?"

"That must've been someone else," he lied, but his chuckle gave him away, as he intended.

"What did you hope to accomplish, Dean? Did you think she'd leave me? That it would get me out of your life once and for all?"

Dean would've liked nothing more. He'd hated Butch since the day they'd met. Butch was every bully he'd ever known. But he had to be careful. At the moment, Butch was the only one capable of taking care of them all, and

Dean would never do anything to harm his family, especially his mother.

"You're jumping to some terrible conclusions, Butch."

"Where are those panties? Did you pick them up after Paris dropped them? Are you hiding them somewhere, trying to scare me?"

"No." This time Dean wasn't lying. He had no idea where those panties had gone; neither had he realized, until now, that they were missing.

"Tell me the truth!" Butch lunged forward, and Dean screamed.

"Mom! Help! He's going to hit me!"

Butch grabbed him as if he'd strike, but then the door opened and his mother came out.

Dean wondered if Paris had summoned her. His sister would've been much more likely to hear his cries, and although Paris generally sided with Butch, she understood how easily her husband's temper could upset the delicate equilibrium that kept them all sheltered, fed and safe.

"What's going on here? What's the matter with you two?" Elaine asked.

Butch let him go. "Your son hasn't taken his medication today, that's all. He's coming up with all kinds of ridiculous accusations against me."

Elaine scratched under the wig she'd taken to wearing ever since her hair became thin enough to show her scalp. "Like what?"

"He claims I murdered Julia and put her in a freezer."

Dean couldn't believe Butch had just blurted it out. He'd thought he was the only one privy to that terrible secret. But his mother's response surprised him even more. She grabbed his arm so fiercely it hurt, then jerked him toward her so she could put her mouth next to his ear. "What are you doing, Dean? Do you want to ruin the whole family?"

Ruin the *family?* This had nothing to do with the family. Dean was trying to help them by curbing Butch's power. "I can prove it," he cried. "We—we thought she ran away, but she didn't. I can show you where she is right now. She's in back, in the freezer. I cut off the padlock, but I put on another one just like it, and I've got the key."

"Where?"

"Here." He retrieved it from his pocket.

"Give it to me. And don't ever open it again. Forget what you've seen," Mother hissed.

"But…I'm telling you." He pointed at Butch. "He murdered Julia! He's dangerous!"

She shook her head. "Butch didn't kill Julia."

Dean felt his mouth drop open. "Then…who did?"

"As far as you're concerned, no one." She checked the key he'd given her, seemed satisfied with it. "Forget whatever you saw, like I said, and stay away from that freezer. Do you hear? *Never breathe a word of this again!*"

Searching for some sense in what he heard, Dean sifted through his fractured thoughts. *"You know what happened to her?"*

"Of course I know. I helped hide her body. You don't want me to go to prison, do you?"

"No! Of course not." But how could she go along with this? She'd always liked Julia, tried to give her a chance in life….

"Then we have to keep it in the family. If what happened to Julia gets out, we'll all be in trouble."

He couldn't imagine losing his mother to prison or anything else. She was the only person in the world who understood him, who truly loved him. Paris had always viewed him as a cross to bear, and his father tolerated him for his mother's sake. "But…" Was it because he hadn't taken his medication that this all seemed surreal? Butch appeared to be fine with it, almost…smug. "What about the panties? What about the women they belonged to?"

"Forget them, too." Snatching the underwear from his hands, she threw them at Butch. "Get rid of those once and for all."

24

"This is Butch?"

Francesca turned from hanging up the clothes she hadn't worn, left from what Heather had packed in her overnight case, to find Adriana going through the file she'd created on Butch.

"Yep, that's him."

Adriana, who'd been lounging on the bed, sat up to examine the personal information he'd submitted to the dating service. "Is he really six foot six?"

"And two hundred and fifty pounds."

"Wow."

"He works outside, and it shows. You definitely wouldn't want to meet him in a dark alley."

Adriana continued to stare at his picture. "He looks like he'd be hell in a boxing ring, but he doesn't look like a murderer."

Even though she'd already memorized every aspect of the photograph, including the laughter in Butch's eyes, Francesca crossed the floor to get another glimpse of it. She'd never seen him that happy in real life. But their dealings hadn't been positive. "They rarely look the part. Anyway, it's not his physical strength that scares me." She bit her lip, trying to identify what made her so uneasy about Butch—other than her suspicion of what he'd done. "He has no humanity." Aside from lending Hunsacker the money he needed to save his house, anyway. But Francesca didn't mention that incident to Adriana. She couldn't reconcile such generosity with the man she believed Butch Vaughn to be, so she preferred to classify it as an anomaly. For all she knew, it was Paris who'd asked him to help the Hunsackers, and he'd acquiesced to keep peace in the family.

"What's his wife like?" Adriana asked.

Francesca didn't know nearly enough about Paris. Or anyone else close to Butch. But filling in the blanks was no longer her job. She had to leave it in the hands of the task force the Yavapai County Sheriff's Office was in the process of creating. "Her name's Paris."

"What does she look like?"

Her overnight case empty, Francesca slid it under the bed. "She's thin, almost bony, with long, stringy blond hair. Not outrageously attractive, but not bad, either." Francesca shrugged. "She's just a young mother living on a junkyard at the edge of Prescott."

"How'd she get involved with Butch?" Adriana asked.

Francesca removed her earrings and dropped them in her jewelry box before climbing onto the bed. "No idea. But she married young, probably too young to know any better. She has a five-year-old child but she can't be more than twenty-three or twenty-four."

Shoving a pillow behind her back, Adriana leaned against the headboard. "How old is Butch?"

Francesca motioned toward the file. "Isn't it in there?"

"Let's see…" She perused the document. "Thirty-one? That's correct?"

"That's got to be about right. Except for the bogus name he used when he created 'Harry Statham,' it seems he was mostly honest about himself."

Adriana looked skeptical as she scanned his profile. "If you were a serial killer, wouldn't you be more…clandestine than to post a profile?"

"It's the appearance of innocence that makes it effective."

"So he's trolling for women on the Internet."

"Right. He has to overcome the limitations of being married and living in a remote area, and a computer gives him far more possibilities than he'd have without it. Not only that, it enables him to remain anonymous."

"Wow, when you put it like that, dating sites are ideal. So, from his perspective, where'd he go wrong?"

"He should've met April somewhere farther away, where he was less likely to be recognized. Instead, he had her come to a bar he frequents, and the bartender saw her getting into his truck. Otherwise, I never would've been able to trace Harry to Butch."

"Besides providing an abundant supply of women, these dating services allow for some serious foreplay," Adriana mused.

Francesca winked. "Now you're thinking like a sociopath. That might be part of his ritual, part of the fun."

"So he's kind of like a fisherman who gets a bite, then plays with his catch as he slowly reels it in."

"That seems accurate."

"It's disturbing!"

"The reality *is* disturbing," Francesca said.

Adriana tapped the page as she continued to read. "Where do you think he got the name Harry Statham?"

"I don't know. But I'd like to find out."

Adriana dropped the sheet into the space between them. "I thought you were off the case."

"I am."

"You're not going to accept that?"

If she pursued the investigation, she could be charged with a crime. Finch had made that clear. But if she walked away, she'd feel she was letting Jillian and Vince—and April—down. "Maybe."

"This Butch guy is scary, Fran," Adriana said. "So's his weird brother-in-law. I say you leave it alone. And what about your other cases? Don't you have enough to keep you busy?"

"I have plenty to do. I haven't made it through my voice mail in days." She hadn't been running or doing anything else she normally did, either. "But—"

"But nothing," Adriana broke in. "Play it safe." She held up Butch's picture. "Why provoke him? He's already shown up here once."

Reminded of Butch's last visit, Francesca rolled over to check the phone. Still dead. But she had her iPhone; she wasn't cut off, like before. "He could come after me again."

Jonah had considered it unlikely, and Francesca wanted to believe him. But she knew the animosity Butch felt toward her might not disappear so quickly. What if making her look bad with that interview on TV didn't satisfy his desire for revenge? What if it had only whetted his appetite for more? He'd tried to hurt her, if not kill her, last night when he turned Demon loose....

Adriana sat up and hugged her knees to her chest. "Do you want me to stay with you tonight?"

Francesca thought about the panties she'd passed on to Jonah. Would Butch realize they were gone? Would he suspect that she'd taken them? If so, what would he do about it? If he responded violently, she didn't want Adriana to be at risk, too. "You can't stay with me. You have a family. Stan leaves at, what…six-thirty every morning? Who'll be there with the boys after he goes?"

"He can go in late."

"He wouldn't like it. He uses that time to go over his patients' files."

"One morning won't set him too far behind."

"One night might not make any difference, either, so there's no need to put him out."

"Then…what will you do? I don't want you to be here alone. Or…is Jonah coming back?" She started reassembling Butch's file as if she'd never performed such an interesting task.

Francesca wasn't sure what it was, exactly, that gave Adriana away. She'd waited long enough before mentioning Jonah, and she'd kept the reference casual. Over the years, they'd had similar discussions about any number of men. *Are you going to see him again…? Don't tell me he's spending the night…! So, how was it…? Is it serious?*

And yet this conversation felt different. If Francesca hadn't been able to read Adriana quite so well, maybe she could go on pretending Adriana was no more interested in Jonah than in all the other men Francesca had dated over the years. But Francesca had been through this with Adriana once before. She couldn't be fooled a second time.

Suddenly doubting everything she'd ever believed about what had happened between Adriana and Jonah, other than the fact that a baby had been created, she clasped her hands in her lap. "You're in love with your husband, aren't you, Adriana?"

Adriana shifted uncomfortably. "Of course. You know Stan and I are happy. Why do you ask?"

Why? Because there was love, and then there was *love*. Regardless of Adriana's denials and protests, did she still care for Jonah?

Although Francesca had been reluctant to discuss him with Adriana for fear the truth would ruin their friendship, she felt compelled to finally broach the subject. She wanted to hear what Adriana had to say about Jonah *and* Stan, needed to know why what'd happened ten years ago had happened—probably because it no longer seemed fair to place so much of the blame on Jonah. She supposed she'd originally done it because his betrayal hurt more. And doing so made it possible for her to save at least one of the two relationships that meant so much to her. But the time she'd spent with him this week had convinced her that he couldn't be defined by that incident alone.

In order to be fair—to Jonah, to Adriana and to herself—Francesca felt she needed to look at the past a little more objectively.

Realizing the answers to the questions she had to ask wouldn't be easy to hear, she took Adriana's hand as if physical contact might thwart an emotional separation. "What happened that night?"

Adriana's fingers remained limp in her grasp but she didn't pull away. "I—I told you. We've gone over this."

"You told me you made a mistake. That because of the alcohol you'd both consumed, things got out of control. You said you were sorry and never meant for it to happen."

"That's true."

"*How* did things get out of control? *Why?* What part did *you* play in sleeping with my boyfriend? Did you two care about each other? Was I keeping you apart? Did you give him up for my sake? *What?*"

Adriana stared at their joined hands but didn't speak.

"Are you going to tell me?" Francesca prodded.

When Adriana lifted her eyes again, they were filled with misery. "He never cared about me. You were everything to him—"

Francesca let go of her hand. "Don't you dare do this again!"

"What?"

"Say he loved me just because it's what you think I want to hear!"

"I wish that's what I was doing, but…you're giving me too much credit."

Because her best friend had always been such a Goody Two-shoes, Francesca had assumed Jonah must have been the aggressor, but… "What are you saying?"

"I'm saying it's true. He loved *you*."

She struggled to accept that. *"Then why'd he do it?"*

"Who knows? He never responded to me before."

Francesca caught her breath. "What do you mean by 'before'?"

Adriana's shoulders rose in a weak shrug.

"Addy?"

Tears rolled unheeded down Adriana's cheeks. "I don't have all the answers. What he was going through. Whether or not he was as drunk as he seemed. I believed what I wanted to believe, okay?"

"Which was…"

She jumped off the bed. "Do I have to spell it out? There's only *one* thing that could make me betray you, Fran."

The truth hit with surprising clarity. "You were in love with him. It wasn't an 'accident.' It was an opportunity."

She managed a pitiful smile. "In a way, I'm still in love with him."

All the excuses she'd received—the apologies, too—passed through Francesca's mind. None of it was sincere? And now Adriana claimed she still had feelings for him? "You're married! You have kids!"

Adriana closed her eyes. "Have you ever read *The Bridges of Madison County?*"

Francesca hadn't read it, but she'd heard enough about it from her mother to know that the story revolved around a woman, married to a good man, who unexpectedly met a photographer traveling through the area while her family was away. The photographer was far more exciting than her plodding, dependable husband, and she fell in love with him. They had a torrid affair, but knowing her husband would soon be back, the woman chose to tell the photographer goodbye and stay with her family. Her brief relationship with this man was a secret she kept hidden until she died and the truth came out via a journal and some clippings found by her children.

Adriana identified with this character? She saw Jonah as the photographer and herself as the tragic figure who chose to sacrifice her true love to stay with her family?

Dropping her head in her hands, Francesca laughed bitterly. "Get out," she said, and thankfully, when she looked up, Adriana was gone.

25

Due to the fallout from his confrontation with Dean, Butch had changed his plans. Instead of driving to Chandler, he'd spent the better part of the afternoon and early evening at the Pour House. He'd had a shitload of soda water and only two beers, which wasn't enough, but he didn't dare drink more. As distasteful as it was, he had a job to do.

Sitting in his truck, he let the engine idle while searching, one more time, for a viable alternative. But he couldn't see one. If Francesca took those panties, she hadn't given them to the sheriff's office or Hunsacker would've mentioned it when he called earlier. Instead, the investigator had said that Francesca Moretti had been kicked off the case and Jonah Young had been fired at the same time. That was good, overall. Butch was damn sick of them and their constant scrutiny. But it didn't mean he could relax. What if Francesca went ahead and did some more digging? Found out who Julia was and that she'd gone missing? It wouldn't be hard. She'd lived with them for several months. Been seen. And what if Francesca had those panties analyzed? If the lab managed to get a DNA sample and the police were able to match it, via relatives or whatever, to Julia, they'd have grounds to get a search warrant. Then they'd come into the salvage yard and discover her body in the freezer....

No matter how many ways he looked at the problem, he always came up with the same solution.

"Quit wasting time, you dumb bastard," he grumbled to himself. Then he shifted into Reverse, backed out of the parking space and headed for the highway.

Francesca sat in her living room, staring at the TV. She'd just watched the news, which showed footage from the grave site at Dead Mule Canyon while a voice-over stated that seven bodies had been found "in this remote location near the ranching community of Skull Valley." Next, a correspondent interviewed Dr. Price, "the forensic anthropologist who's working day and night at a makeshift lab in the community center to gather as much information from the remains as possible." The same reporter then spoke with Investigator Finch, who was on hand with a smarmy smile to assure the public that the Yavapai County Sheriff's Office was forming a task force to look into these murders and would do everything they could to keep the community safe.

"I feel better already." Rolling her eyes, she turned off the TV and shut Investigator Finch out of her house. She needed to get some rest, but there was no way she could sleep. She kept wondering if she should've listened to Jonah when he tried to apologize all those years ago, if, with enough forgiveness, they could've made their relationship work in spite of his betrayal.

What was *his* side of the story? What was the *real* reason behind what he'd done? He hadn't blamed Adriana for his infidelity. She knew that much. He'd taken full responsibility. But maybe Francesca's own lack of trust—of men, of love, of the happiness she felt whenever she was with Jonah—had tainted her willingness to understand, as well as her ability to overcome.

Both Adriana and Jonah were to blame. It took two to make love. And yet…certain nuances affected her understanding of the situation, the full impact of which she hadn't realized until now. All the time they were growing up, Adriana had been such a good person, so kind and supportive, that Francesca had been far more willing to give her rather than Jonah the benefit of the doubt.

Or was she more generous with Adriana because she'd always felt guilty about the way her best friend was so often overlooked or pushed into the background when it came to men? Adriana had seemed content to let Francesca have the spotlight. It wasn't as if Francesca had ever *tried* to upstage her. The response they got was the response they got. But what if Adriana secretly resented her? What if, deep inside, she'd wanted Jonah for herself all along?

She'd just admitted she'd been in love with him….

And what about Jonah? Had he been dealing with issues she should've been aware of but wasn't? He'd never mentioned having been married or divorced. Had it been such a painful experience he didn't want to look back? Was it an embarrassment to him? What had gone wrong? He didn't love lightly, so she couldn't imagine he'd jump into that kind of commitment without real depth of feeling. She also found it a little curious that Jonah had started acting up—drinking, becoming less reliable and picking fights for no reason—only after their relationship grew serious.

When he'd cheated, she'd assumed he was shallow and disloyal. She'd made herself believe it so she'd never get sucker-punched like that again. But maybe there was more to it….

*I wish I'd married her, okay? Is that what you want
to hear? God knows you won't believe anything else, so
there you have it. I was an asshole with no heart, out to
hurt anyone I could, and I tried to destroy your life and
hers just for the hell of it. I used you both, like I use all
women.*

He didn't use women. She had to be honest enough
to admit that. And it wasn't as if he'd go to bed with just
anyone. She'd seen him gently deflect unwanted female
attention plenty of times. Heck, she'd even given him the
chance to "use" her the other night, and he hadn't taken
it, although she could tell he wanted to. Why?

She glanced at her cell phone, lying on the couch
beside her. A direct flight to California took less than
two hours. Jonah would be home by now. Should she
call him? If she did, would he believe she was calling
to talk about what she'd just seen on TV? Finch hadn't
divulged any new information. As usual, the police had
kept what they released purposely sketchy....

Why did she even need a reason? So what if he realized she wanted to talk to him? What was so bad about
that? Did she really have to insulate her heart to such a
degree? Or was it her pride she was protecting?

Probably both. But at this point, she had nothing to
lose.

Except everything she'd guarded so fiercely for the
past ten years...

She remembered their kiss at the motel and how
quickly it had brought back all the desire she'd ever felt
for him. "You scare me," she said, but she picked up her
phone, anyway, and punched in his number.

Jonah was just drifting off to sleep when his phone
rang. He almost let it go to voice mail. He wasn't feeling

quite as sanguine about getting fired as he'd tried to convince himself before leaving Phoenix. The more he thought about that meeting in the conference room, the angrier he became that Hunsacker and Finch hadn't stood by him or Francesca.

But in case the call was important, he checked to see who was trying to reach him. And when he recognized the number, he answered. It was Francesca. Had Butch tried to contact her again? Was she frightened? Hurt?

"Are you okay?" he asked without so much as a hello.

"I'm fine. Sort of."

She didn't sound fine. *Something* was wrong. "What's the 'sort of' all about? You haven't heard from Butch, have you?"

"No."

"But you have your pepper spray ready?"

"It's on my nightstand."

"Where are you?"

"In the living room."

Just seeing her number had spooked him, made him realize he wasn't as sure as he wanted to be that she'd be safe without him. Denial could hit anyone, especially someone so eager to get back on stable ground, and it had hit him.

He already regretted letting that happen. What had seemed reasonable in the light of day no longer seemed that way in the dark of night. "Go get it. Right away. Then you can tell me what's wrong."

She seemed to be moving when she spoke again. "When Adriana came by earlier, she had a few things to say about you that were a little different than anything she's told me before."

If he never heard Adriana's name again it would be too soon.

Rolling over, he gazed at his daughter's picture in the moonlight coming through the windows overlooking the cityscape. What could've changed? And did he even want to know? He'd hurt so many people…. "What'd she say?" he finally said.

"You seem reluctant to ask."

He *was* reluctant. But he was also resigned. "You're entitled to your pound of flesh, remember?"

She didn't laugh. She was too serious for jokes tonight. "Adriana told me she was in love with you when she slept with you ten years ago."

He said nothing, didn't know what to say. Hearing that made him feel even worse, because, for the most part, she'd been both nameless and faceless to him. He'd only been reacting to the desperate panic he experienced whenever he realized how much he loved Francesca. It made him feel too out of control, too vulnerable—placed him right where he'd been when he was married, and he couldn't deal with that.

"This doesn't come as a surprise?" she asked.

"I guess I sort of knew she felt…something. Or thought she did." He wasn't sure her emotions had ever been stronger than a crush. Until that night, he hadn't so much as flirted with her.

He would've explained that to Francesca, except he feared it would look as though he was minimizing his mistake or trying to excuse his own actions, and he refused to do either. Francesca had made the right decision when she cut him out of her life. She deserved better.

"Did you guess before you were, um, together?" she asked.

He pulled his eyes from Summer's smiling face and sat up. "Are you holding your pepper spray?"

"I am now. Yes."

"Good."

"Can we get back to the discussion?"

Massaging his left temple, he slumped onto his pillows. "Do we have to?"

"You'd rather not?"

He sighed. "I could sense some…interest. Why?"

"I don't know what to think about it. It's not every day you hear something like that from your best friend."

Adriana had hurt Francesca all over again. Remembering how Francesca had thrown up during the drive to Prescott, he decided it was time to quit being so damned selfish and put a stop to her pain, if he could. "Listen, that night was entirely my fault, okay? Every bit of it. If I've ever claimed otherwise, I was just…passing the buck. I knew she had a thing for me, and I took advantage of it. Hate me, not her."

There was a slight pause. He thought he heard the sniffle of tears. "What if I can't hate you?"

His chest suddenly tightened so much he couldn't have taken a deep breath if he'd wanted to. "You should. It would make everything easier for you," he said gently. Then he hung up and turned off his phone so he wouldn't be tempted to call her back. If he accepted all the blame for what he and Adriana had done ten years ago, the two women would patch up their friendship and move on, just as they had before. In another few months, Francesca would probably have new pictures sitting on her wet bar and mantel, pictures of her with another man similar to Roland Perenski.

She'd be happy, smiling, maybe even thinking about getting married….

* * *

When the phone rang, Francesca couldn't help hoping it was Jonah. She wasn't sure what was left to say, but somehow it didn't feel as if their conversation was over.

As she grabbed her phone, however, she saw her father's name on caller ID.

Trying to rein in her disappointment, she made an effort to put some life into her voice. "Hi, Dad."

"Francesca? I didn't wake you, did I?"

She glanced at the alarm clock on her nightstand. "It's not quite eleven, Dad. What's going on? Are you and Mom okay?"

"We're fine."

"Good. What's up?"

"I've been doing those background checks for you."

With everything else that'd been going on, Francesca had almost forgotten she'd asked him to do some research. Now that he was calling to report, she didn't have the heart to tell him she'd been kicked off the case. It wouldn't hurt to hear him out. If what he had to say seemed significant, she'd pass it along to the task force—anyone other than Finch or Hunsacker—just like she planned to do with the DNA results on the panties. If Walt's contribution didn't seem significant, at least she could thank him and make him feel she appreciated the time he'd spent. "Right. On Butch Vaughn," she said.

"And that other fellow, Dean Wheeler."

She pulled back the covers on her bed so she could wriggle beneath them. "What have you found?"

She heard the shuffle of papers on his end of the line.

"Butch Vaughn was born and raised in Queen Creek, first by his mother, and then by a friend's family."

"What happened to his parents?"

"His real father took off before he was born, never paid any child support, and Butch didn't get along with his stepfather—or his younger half siblings, for that matter. When his stepfather was laid off, Butch's mother had to go to work, and the situation became untenable. According to one of Butch's school counselors, who agreed to chat with me off the record, he had severe behavioral problems, anger-management issues and he was failing most of his classes. He improved once he went to live with the Stathams."

Francesca immediately noted the name. "Was the father Harry?"

"No, but Butch's friend was. Why?"

"He's used 'Harry Statham' as an alias. Now I know where he got it."

"His half sister, a Marcie Reed, told me he never forgave their mother for turning him out, for choosing her husband over him. He still has no contact with his siblings. His brother refused to talk to me, said as far as he was concerned Butch died the day his mother did."

She whistled. "That's harsh. How did the mother die?"

"Drowned in the bathtub."

"Any evidence of foul play?"

"There was an investigation, but it was an open-and-shut case. Her blood-alcohol level was sky-high, suggesting she passed out. Her death was ruled an accident."

Francesca rearranged her pillows to make herself more comfortable. "How old was she?"

"Thirty-six."

Could the police who'd performed the investigation be wrong? Was that when Butch first began his killing spree? "Did Butch attend the funeral?"

"No. Once he went to live with the Stathams, he never contacted his real family again and they never contacted him. He played football in high school, then went to ASU on an athletic scholarship, which lasted for a year—until he blew out his knee."

Francesca pictured Butch striding to his office. "These days, he doesn't even walk with a limp."

"Maybe the doctors managed to fix him up. I'm guessing he's had several operations. In any case, the injury was bad enough to end his football career."

"Is that where he met Paris? At ASU?"

"No. Without the scholarship, he didn't have the money to continue his education. By this time he was estranged from his adoptive family, too. I hung up with the father, John Statham, a few minutes ago. He said they did everything they could to help Butch, but Butch got into a fight with their son Harry and broke his jaw, and that was the end of their patience. Butch had just graduated from high school and would be eighteen within a few weeks. They felt they'd done all they could for him. He was too volatile for them. So they asked him to move out."

Francesca knew that conversation couldn't have been an easy one, not with someone known to be violent. "Did he go peacefully?"

"Apparently he did. He packed up and left without a word, and they haven't heard from him since."

"Not keeping up with previous relationships seems to be a pattern."

"Fortunately, no one in this other family has died."

The air-conditioning came on so she burrowed deeper under the covers while toying with the pepper spray Jonah had insisted she keep close at hand. "How did he meet the Wheelers?"

"According to the guy who owns the property adjacent to the salvage yard—"

"Whoa, whoa, wait. There're no other houses close to the salvage yard."

"I said 'property.' It's raw farmland, but the owner works it himself, so he's out there regularly, growing alfalfa—I found him through county records. Anyway, he said Butch answered an ad the Wheelers placed in the paper. They were looking to retire and wanted someone to run the salvage yard for them. Butch was looking for a job. I'm guessing he met Paris once they hired him."

That made sense. Paris seemed young and rather naive, as if she'd never had the chance to experience life beyond the salvage yard, where she'd been raised. "What brought him to Prescott?"

"I can't say. I get the feeling he was rambling around a bit, looking for the right situation. I also spoke to an old girlfriend who still lives in Phoenix," her father went on.

Francesca smiled at his diligence. "I'm impressed. How'd you find her?"

"His football coach is still at ASU. He told me about her, said she lives down the street from him now and gave her my number. She was nice enough to call."

"Wow. That was lucky. Was she any help?"

"Definitely. She said he has the worst temper she's ever seen. That he's egocentric and insensitive. She also told me he had an insatiable sexual appetite."

Francesca had overheard Paris mention Butch's sex addiction, but she hadn't passed that detail along to her father. "Did she *volunteer* the sexual appetite information?"

"You think I asked about it?"

She laughed. "No. It's just…not what I would've expected a woman to blurt out."

"Shows you how marked that behavior really was."

"Did she say whether he ever grew violent or tried to force her to have sex with him?"

"She said it never went that far. But he used his desire for sex as an excuse to chase other women, so she broke up with him."

Considering his track record with Paris, Butch's cheating didn't surprise Francesca. "Were you able to find any connection between him and Bianca Andersen?"

"Not yet. I'm still working on that. But Dean is where it gets interesting."

Francesca had thought it was interesting from the start. "How so?"

"He has a morbid fascination with death and violence."

"Who told you this?"

"Several of his classmates. They said he was drawing grotesque pictures of cadavers and devils with knives and things like that from the third grade on."

Definitely a red flag. Francesca had read enough about profiling to know that. "Did he have any friends?"

"None. He was a loner. The other kids considered him weird, maybe even dangerous. He once asked a girl at school to come over for his birthday party, said he 'needed' to show her to his mother. He promised to pay her if she'd agree."

"And?"

"He made her too uncomfortable. She refused. When she returned to her locker after the next period, she found blood all over her books. Then she heard that Dean had been sent to the hospital after slitting his wrists."

Francesca tried to fit that into her impression of Dean. "How'd he get her locker combination?"

"He was so obsessed with her he'd stand in the hall and wait for her between classes. Sometimes, he'd seem lucid. Other times, he'd rock and mumble to himself. But he watched her so closely he probably learned the combination."

The conflict Francesca felt over whether or not to continue this investigation suddenly grew by leaps and bounds. The culprit was somehow connected to that salvage yard. She felt it in her bones. "Maybe you were getting to this, but Dean has schizoaffective disorder."

"I've got his entire medical history. You still want it?"

Despite everything, she had to feel sorry for Butch's brother-in-law. It wouldn't be easy to deal with his problems. Neither would it be easy—especially since he was already suffering a mental handicap—to live with Butch. Had it twisted Dean? Made a killer out of him? She'd heard similar backgrounds attached to a number of serial killers. Dahmer, for instance, murdered to stop people from abandoning him and had been trying to figure out a way to preserve their bodies; he'd thought eating their flesh might satisfy that desire. "Of course I'd like it. Would you mind faxing it to the office?"

"I'll send it along with the other stuff I've noted as soon as we hang up."

"Great. Thanks, Dad. I really appreciate your help." She wasn't sure what to do with the information he'd uncovered, whether or not to use it herself or turn it over to the as-yet-unformed task force, but she was genuinely grateful for his research.

"One more thing," he said.

She could tell by his voice that whatever he was about to reveal was important. "What's that?"

"It's about Dean."

"Yes?"

"He worked at the post office for a brief period of time five years ago. As far as I can tell, it's the only real job he's ever held. I guess his parents know the postmaster or someone else who put in a good word for him, so he was given a shot at being gainfully employed."

"I take it this arrangement didn't work out?"

"No. While he was there, he got involved with a fellow employee, an older woman—older by fifteen years—named Sherrilyn Gators."

"When you say involved…"

"They were lovers."

"So it was serious."

"It seemed to be leaning that way. They weren't together all that long, only a few months, and yet Dean wanted to marry her. But Sherrilyn had three children, one of whom, a boy named Neal, was only a few years younger than Dean was. Neal didn't like the idea of his mother as a cougar and began poking around and asking questions about his potential stepfather. Once he discovered that Dean had severe mental problems, he went to his mother and convinced her to end the relationship."

"How did Dean react?"

"As you might expect. He was heartbroken, wouldn't let it go. For months afterward, he peeped in their windows, left gifts at the door or in her car, called her constantly, followed her home from work."

"He stalked her."

"Basically. That behavior cost him his job."

"Wasn't he taking his meds?"

"Who knows? He was supposed to be on them."

"Did she ever get a restraining order?"

"She did, but he went over to her place even after that, the last time with wine and flowers. Sherrilyn was too afraid to let him in, but—"

"Why do I have the feeling this doesn't end well?"

"Because it doesn't. When she refused, he threatened to kill her. Said he'd come back one night and kill the whole family, that he could get into the house anytime he wanted."

Francesca slowly rose to her feet. *"He threatened her life?"*

"Yes."

"Oh, God. Tell me she's still breathing."

"No one knows. She's been missing for four years."

26

Dean stood in the side yard of Francesca's house, hopping from foot to foot while he waited for her to go to bed. Constant movement helped him cope with the anxiety that was making him itch all over. Maybe he should've taken his medication this morning. It'd been too long since his last dose. He was heading into withdrawal. But if he'd taken his meds, he wouldn't be able to do what needed to be done. That was the reason he sometimes pretended to take them but threw them away. They made him feel as if he was living inside a bubble, looking out at life instead of experiencing it. When he was drugged, he didn't care deeply about anything, and he *had* to care about this, had to be able to fix his mistake. Like his mother said, he should never have put those panties in the jockey box of Butch's truck. If not for that, they wouldn't have fallen into the wrong hands, and he wouldn't be here, so far from the places that were comfortable and familiar to him, so far from his family.

Too bad Francesca had capitalized on his mistake. He'd returned her purse. He'd returned her pictures, too, even though he'd desperately wanted to add them to his growing pile of treasures and pretend to be part of her life. Why couldn't she have left well enough alone? Was it because she *wanted* to cause him problems?

Maybe not. But she didn't care if she did. Francesca was like every other woman he'd found attractive. None of them liked him. Look at the way her friend had treated him. Adriana wouldn't even give him a drink of water.

He didn't have to feel bad about what he was going to do because Francesca had earned it....

"It's for Mom," he mumbled to himself. He'd been saying the same thing ever since he'd left Prescott, and that was hours ago—so many he'd lost track in the fog of panic and preoccupation. He'd been so upset he'd gotten confused, taken the wrong bus and wound up in Casa Grande. He'd had to backtrack an hour and a half.

But he was here now. And he knew what he had to do.

Thank God it was dark. Hiding calmed him. He'd always enjoyed standing in the background, watching....

Finally, the light gleaming around the edges of Francesca's blinds disappeared. Taking his lock picks, mini-flashlight and flathead screwdriver from his backpack, he imagined himself as invisible, a moving shadow, and slipped silently through the gate and around to the back door.

Fortunately, Francesca had a pin-and-tumbler-style lock, just as he'd expected. Most residences had these, so he'd encountered them before, numerous times.

All he had to do was rake all the pins, then pick any that remained. Getting in would take him two minutes, tops.

"What are you doing?"

Butch froze at the sound of his wife's voice, coming

from behind him. Hoping she was asleep and hadn't heard his truck, he'd entered the salvage yard through the gate instead of the house. A gruesome task awaited him. He didn't want her involved in it.

"Don't worry about it." Determined to see his decision through, he marched toward the back corner.

It was warm enough that Paris didn't need a robe, but she was wearing one. Eyes wide, skin chalk-white, she looked small and frightened as she caught up to him. "What's the matter? Didn't you get the panties?"

Feeling like a failure for dragging his family into his addiction, he allowed her to stop him. "No."

"Francesca Moretti didn't have them?"

"I didn't go to Chandler."

"Why not?" she gasped.

"What would be the point?"

Obviously smelling the alcohol on his breath, she sniffed. "You've been drinking."

"Two beers. I'm sober. Listen to me."

"I don't understand why you didn't go to Chandler!"

"Because even if Francesca took those panties, who knows whether she still has them? Maybe she gave them to someone other than Finch or Hunsacker, someone like that consultant. It's been more than twenty-four hours. She could've shipped them to a lab herself. And if she does have them, it's not as if she'd hand them over to me. I'd have to force her. Then she'd really think I'm a killer and the cops would believe it."

Paris hugged the collar of her robe to her chin. "But… we can't let those panties be tested. Not if they belonged to who I think they did."

She knew. Butch could tell. "How'd you figure it out?"

"The way you've been acting."

After that little confrontation with Dean, he'd explained the situation to Elaine. He shouldn't have. Paris's mother must've told her.

Placing his hands on her shoulders, Butch tried to reassure her with a squeeze. She had to put up with so much because of him. He felt bad about that. If only he'd curbed his appetites when he had the chance. If only he hadn't been so careless! "Paris—"

"We should've gone to the police," she whispered. "Right when it happened."

He lowered his voice. "And tell them what? That you *accidentally* killed a girl I was having an affair with?"

"Yes! Why not? It *was* an accident!"

"You were upset when you pushed her. That's manslaughter. A felony."

Tears filled her eyes. "I didn't expect her to fall. I just wanted her to leave you alone. We shouldn't have let her live here in the first place!"

"I know that, and you know that, but no one is going to understand. The police won't care. The D.A. will paint what happened in the worst possible light. Are you willing to go to prison for a crime you didn't mean to commit?"

She shrank even deeper into that fluffy robe. She'd lost weight in the past twelve months, was thin as a rail. The burden of their secret weighed too heavily on her. "Of course not. But living in panic and fear…all the time. I'm not sure that's any better."

"I won't lose you," he said hoarsely. "I won't let Champ lose you, either."

She wrung her thin fingers. "But if they find her body they'll take me away no matter what."

"They won't find anything. I'm getting rid of it right now. That's our only alternative."

Her eyes flew wide. "No! You know what my mom said. It's best to leave the body here, to keep it under our control. We can't risk someone else stumbling across it."

"The situation has changed, Paris. We *have* to get it off the premises. Thanks to those missing panties, and the evidence they probably contain, the cops could show up with a search warrant. If they do, how long do you think it would take them to find Julia?"

She covered her face as if she couldn't bear what he was telling her.

"Paris?"

"Not long," she admitted.

"Exactly. Now go inside. This is my fault, and I'll handle it. Forget it, like I told you before."

"I *can't* forget it!" she whispered. "I haven't been able to forget since the day it happened. She *haunts* me. She—she's trying to make me as crazy as Dean!"

"Julia Cummings is dead and gone, Paris. There's no such thing as ghosts. Go on in. You don't want to see this."

She broke into sobs, but he didn't have time to comfort her. "Didn't you hear me? Go!"

Her hands dropped to her mouth, but she talked through them. "Where will you dump her?"

"Somewhere no one'll ever find her, okay? We'll be fine. We'll *all* be fine if you leave this to me."

"Right. You'll take care of me," she muttered, but he couldn't imagine she really believed it. If he hadn't cheated on her, they wouldn't be in this mess. But when it came to other women, he couldn't stop himself. He'd tried. The best he could do was damage control. And Julia had been so accessible, so easy and eager to please….

"If I wanted anyone else I would've let you go to

prison," he said. "Instead, I'm here for you like you've been here for me, ever since the day we got married."

When she looked up at him, her expression was so miserable, so pitiful, he almost couldn't stand it.

"We may not be perfect, but we love each other, Paris," he whispered. "Just remember that."

This elicited only a feeble smile and a nod, but he didn't have time to try for more. It was getting late, and he had a lot of driving to do.

"I'll join you as soon as I can." Waiting until she left, he singled out the key to the padlock from the ring in his office.

Even after she turned out the lights, Francesca couldn't sleep. What she'd learned about Dean Wheeler had her spooked, made her fear she'd wasted the few short days she'd spent on April's case by focusing on the wrong person. She'd never ruled out Butch's brother-in-law, but neither had she expected to hear that his one and only girlfriend had gone missing just weeks after he'd threatened to kill her. She almost couldn't believe it. As odd as Dean was, Butch seemed the more dangerous of the two. Sure, Dean might have known Bianca via the hospital, but no better than Butch had known April. If Francesca had been placing a bet, she definitely would've put her money on Butch....

But, armed with a bat or a shovel, anyone could batter a defenseless person to death. So maybe it *was* Dean who'd dumped all those bodies in Dead Mule Canyon. Maybe his ex-girlfriend was one of them.

Francesca wished she could discuss what her father had learned with Jonah. She'd tried to call him, but her calls kept transferring to voice mail.

Should she contact Finch? He seemed to be her only remaining option….

Chances were he was in bed right now. But if she waited, she'd lie there, going over and over her questions. Had anyone followed up on Sherrilyn Gators's disappearance? If so, what had they found?

Maybe, as was true of so many investigations, the police had suspicions but no real proof. If Sherrilyn's body hadn't turned up, perhaps they couldn't even establish, for sure, that a murder had taken place. Unless they had enough physical evidence to compensate for that, a lot of D.A.s refused to go to court without a body. What with double-jeopardy laws, Francesca couldn't blame them. But why hadn't Finch or Hunsacker mentioned that Dean had been a prime suspect in another case? That could've propelled the investigation in a much more promising direction….

Could it be that Sherrilyn's disappearance had been assigned to a different investigator, or maybe the Prescott P.D., and Finch and Hunsacker hadn't yet realized that this old case might have some relevance to the bodies in Dead Mule Canyon?

There was a great deal of work to be done on these murders and only so many hours in a day. Whether the Yavapai County Sheriff's Office formed a task force or not, she couldn't sit back and hope they'd eventually come up with this information on their own. Lives could be at risk. She had to call and share what she knew as soon as possible.

Telling herself she didn't care how she was received, she slid over to her nightstand, where she'd left her cell phone, and used her electronic address book to call Finch.

He sounded groggy when he answered, which made

her nervous about interrupting him—and jealous that he could sleep.

"It's me," she said.

"I know." The flatness of his tone indicated that he wasn't thrilled to hear her voice, but she hadn't expected him to be. "I'm wondering why you're calling," he went on. "Don't tell me you're inside Butch's salvage yard."

She ignored his sarcasm. "Did you know Dean threatened to kill a love interest five years ago?"

"You had to wake me up with that little tidbit, Francesca? Something Dean said five years ago couldn't have waited till morning?"

"I—"

"Is there anything else you'd like to pass along at midnight?" he interrupted. "You know Butch is the killer because it's been revealed to you by your secret decoder ring?"

Francesca felt her muscles tense. "You're an asshole, you know that?"

"I have a right to be. You woke me up. And I distinctly remember telling you to butt out of this investigation."

"Maybe I will and maybe I won't."

"I'll throw your ass in jail if you don't."

She stared into the darkness that seemed to press in on all sides. "If I save just one life it'll be worth it."

"You might think so now, but—"

"If you'd like to go back to sleep, shut up and listen for a second," she broke in. "I want to make sure you're aware that Dean Wheeler threatened to kill a woman who went missing three weeks later. In case you plan on doing any police work at all, her name's Sherrilyn Gators."

Silence descended. When Finch spoke again, he sounded slightly humbled. "Not my case. That was

Prescott P.D. But she's on our list. She worked for the post office, didn't she?"

"That's right."

"How do you know Dean knew her?"

"I used my secret decoder ring," she said, and disconnected. She'd given him the tip. He could dig for the details himself.

It took Dean much longer to pick the lock on the back door than he'd thought it would. But Francesca still wasn't asleep when he entered the house. She was in the bathroom. From where he stood in the hall, he could hear the toilet flush. Then the sink taps went on. She kept muttering to herself, too. She wasn't happy with someone named Finch. She called him a jerk, said that she was sticking with the investigation whether he liked it or not.

Dean seemed to recall that Finch was one of the investigators. Fortunately, the various people working on the "good" side didn't get along. He figured they'd be a lot more effective if they did. He was surprised no one had ever come to the salvage yard asking about Julia. She'd been estranged from her family in California— they probably didn't even know she was dead—but she'd lived and worked at the yard for nearly six months. Any number of people had seen her and would most likely remember her. Why had no one raised the alarm when she'd simply disappeared from the face of the earth?

Because of that appalling lack of interest, Dean had created some missing persons flyers on his computer and had often considered printing them and posting them at the grocery store and post office. Julia deserved that much of a tribute, didn't she? A small shred of proof that *someone* had cared about her? She hadn't been a bad girl.

She'd been kinder to him than his own family, acted like the sister Paris never had.

Besides, he enjoyed the thought that seeing Julia's image in public would give Butch a good scare. At times, he'd even been tempted to locate Julia's family and divulge the whereabouts of her body. He wasn't sure they'd care. She'd told some pretty awful stories about them. But revealing what he knew would get rid of Butch. This past year, Dean had been able to tolerate his brother-in-law mostly because he felt he *could* get rid of him if he really needed to.

But now that he realized his mother was also at risk, he was glad he'd kept his mouth shut. He doubted she had any direct involvement in the murder. His mother had always liked Julia. She was the one who'd taken pity on her and given her a job and a place to live. It was far more likely that she was covering for Butch. She wouldn't want Paris and Champ to lose their husband and father just because she'd taken in a poor runaway.

Expecting Francesca to come out of the bathroom any minute, he wrapped the ends of the rope he'd brought in his backpack tightly around his hands and pressed himself against the wall. He hated that it had come to this, wished there was some other way. But he had no choice.

Think of Mom. He'd do anything for Elaine, wouldn't he? Of course. Despite his many shortcomings, he'd always been a loyal son.

But the door to Francesca's bathroom didn't open. The tub went on instead. She was taking a bath.

Grateful he'd have a little more time to acclimate and do what he liked best—look around and imagine being romantically involved with a woman of Francesca's beauty—he moved into her bedroom and searched through her drawers. If he could find Julia's panties, all would be well. Then he could slip out as quietly as he'd slipped in, and Francesca would never have to know he'd been in her house.

But life was never that easy. Especially *his* life. He turned her entire room upside down but found nothing. And by then he didn't dare look anywhere else. Francesca had just pulled the plug on the tub.

He could hear the water drain.

She was getting out.

The sleeping pill Francesca had swallowed before climbing in the bathwater was beginning to take effect. She could feel her body relax, her thoughts slow. Afraid she might slide under the water—which had reportedly happened to Butch's mother—she'd cut her bath short.

Secret decoder ring. Finch had upset her. But that was nothing new. And why did his opinion matter? There wasn't any point in dwelling on him or Hunsacker. She'd do everything she felt was necessary on the Bonner case, do what her conscience dictated, regardless of what they had to say about it. If the sheriff's department felt strongly enough to act on their threats and tried to prosecute her, she'd get a lawyer, a damn good one. She wasn't without resources.

As for Jonah... She didn't know what to think about Jonah. Her resistance to acknowledging her feelings about him seemed to be ebbing away with her tension. Every time she closed her eyes he was there, taking her in his arms and making love to her like he used to. It was crazy, but she wanted him now more than ever.

Then there was Adriana, and all the issues of trust and distrust, love and loyalty, their last conversation had dredged up...

Refusing to go over that again, she toweled off. If she allowed herself to dwell on Adriana, the sleeping pill wouldn't work.

After blow-drying her hair, she pulled on her night-gown and walked into her bedroom. She was so eager to fall into bed, it didn't occur to her that the lights shouldn't be off. She was halfway across the room before she realized. Then she stopped.

She'd spoken to Finch in the dark, but she'd turned on the lights after she disconnected so she could grab fresh underwear to put on following her bath. How was it that they were off?

Had she hit the switch as she passed into the hall? That was what she wanted to believe. But she was almost positive she hadn't. And, as her eyes adjusted to the darkness, she spotted something that made her blood run cold. Someone had pulled out her dresser drawers. Clothes spilled onto the floor. Her room had been ransacked.

Adrenaline overcame the sedative as Francesca squinted to see if she could locate her iPhone on the nightstand. Should she tiptoe over and get it? Search the blankets for the pepper spray she'd taken to bed with her? Or run out of the house without wasting another second?

She decided to lock her door, reclaim her pepper spray and her phone and hide under the bed to place a distress call. But a quick movement caught her eye, and it dawned on her that whoever had broken in wasn't just in her house.

He was in her bedroom.

27

Francesca didn't bother trying to run. She had nowhere to go. Dean had already closed the door and locked it. Because it locked on the inside, she could undo it if she had the opportunity, but that would take a second or two more than dashing through an open doorway.

And she had a feeling every second was going to count.

"What are you doing here, Dean?" she breathed.

He looked frustrated. Unhappy. "I didn't want to come. I had to."

She wondered if she could get out through the slider, which was on the opposite side of the room, but thanks to the scare she'd been given by her last visitor, she'd secured it with a broom handle so it couldn't be lifted off its track. By the time she removed the handle, unfastened the latch and slid the door open, it'd be too late. "No one made you come here."

"You don't understand. It was my fault."

Envisioning poor, frightened, mother-of-three Sherrilyn, who might've been down this road before her, Francesca backed slowly toward the bed. She'd left her pepper spray under the blankets and needed to find it. But it was only a two-ounce can, not large enough to see easily. Would she be able to lay her hands on it—and spray Dean before he overtook her?

There was a small chance she could. If she moved fast and the can wasn't tangled in the bedding...

"What was your fault?" she asked.

"The panties. I'm the one who hid them in Butch's truck."

Trying to put the bed between them, she veered to the left as she stepped away from him. "What panties?"

If he knew she was stalling, he didn't let on. "You know the ones. You took them. I need them back. If you cooperate, this night will end a lot better than if you don't."

She managed to clear the bed while there was still ten feet or so between them. "What if I don't have the panties?"

"You *have* to have them. They're not at the salvage yard."

"What if I do have them? Why would you care about some underwear I picked up in the yard, Dean?"

He had an object in his hands—not a bat, not that large. She couldn't make out any details in the dark, but she was almost positive it was a piece of rope.

"Don't play stupid," he said. "It insults my intelligence."

She might be battling the effects of a sleeping pill, but he sounded chillingly lucid. Struggling with the dull-witted feeling the medication gave her, she changed tactics. "So you're the one?"

"The one who what?"

"Who's been beating women to death."

He grimaced. "No. Of course not. It's Butch. You know that."

She was no longer so sure. Dean could've followed

him the night he met April at the Pour House, could have murdered her in an attempt to set up his brother-in-law. If Dean was indeed a sociopath, the sociopath who'd murdered seven women over a span of five years, what was one more? And there was certainly no love lost between the two men. Seeing that Butch went to prison would be a decisive way to remove him from the salvage yard without a body and without being blamed by Paris or their parents. It might even have been Dean who placed that business card from the bar near the bodies in Dead Mule Canyon.

The only problem with this reasoning was the fact that Dean had admitted to putting the panties in Butch's jockey box. If he wanted them to be found, why was he here, hoping to retrieve them? Had he changed his mind? Had he realized that his plan could backfire and bring *him* under police scrutiny? "How do *you* know it's Butch?" she asked.

"Who else could it be? Besides, there are certain signs."

"Like…"

He started coming around the bed, so she jumped on top of it, planning to hop off the other side if he ever abandoned that spot between her and the door.

But he stopped, choosing to guard against the possibility that she could dart past him and beat him out of the house. "His eyes," he said. "His eyes are empty. And his heart is cold."

Attempting to locate her pepper spray with her feet, Francesca inched to one side. How had she been positioned while holding it? Had she been on the right or the left? And where might it have gone during her conversation with Investigator Finch, when the desire for a sleeping pill and a hot bath had superseded her fear?

She'd been too preoccupied, couldn't remember letting it go. Or was her fuzzy memory because of the sedative? "Paris doesn't seem to think he's so bad."

"Paris loves him. She's blind to his faults. Besides, she hasn't witnessed his handiwork. I have."

"Handiwork" likely meant the kind of brutal murder suffered by April Bonner—and the others, as well. His words raised the hair on the back of Francesca's neck. But she wasn't convinced he was telling the truth, not after learning about Sherrilyn. Was Dean projecting his own actions on to someone else? Someone who seemed capable of killing? Someone he'd hoped to frame?

"You've *seen* him kill?"

"I've seen the body."

"What body, Dean? Sherrilyn's? Or Julia's?"

Dean jerked as if she'd shot him. Had he taken one more step, Francesca would've had no choice but to dive for the pepper spray, even though she hadn't located it yet in the bedding.

"How do you know about them?" he asked.

"I've been doing my research. They're dead, right? You killed them."

"No." Seeming stricken, he shook his head. "Sherrilyn's not dead. She's just…missing. I've been looking for her for years. Almost every night. All over. I'll find her eventually."

His voice sounded so childlike. Had he slipped into a psychotic episode? And, if so, would that help or hurt her chances of getting out of this alive? "What about the others?"

"Don't confuse me. This—this isn't about anyone else."

"Who's Julia, Dean? Where did she come from?"

"Why should I tell you? I can't trust you. You're not

my friend. I tried to be nice. But you—you weren't interested." He moved forward again. "I need to think of my mother. What did you do with the panties?"

What did this have to do with Elaine Wheeler?

Francesca came up against the headboard. She still hadn't found the pepper spray, but making a run for it seemed just as big a gamble as a search. "They're on their way to a police lab. So this is pointless, Dean. You might as well go home and not get yourself into any more trouble. If there's DNA on those panties, the police will build a case against you, and they'll put you in prison."

"Why me? I haven't killed anyone! And I'm not going to kill you. Whether you die is up to Butch. *He's* the murderer."

She wanted to believe him, but Butch wasn't the one standing in her bedroom. And she couldn't see why Dean would be holding a rope if he meant her no harm. "Then why are you helping him? Why are you doing this?"

"I told you. I have no choice."

"You always have a choice."

"Not this time." When he lunged forward, she dropped onto the bed and shoved her hands under the blankets. Terrified that she wouldn't come up with her pepper spray, she almost couldn't believe it when her hand closed around the canister and she withdrew it so easily from the sheets.

Dean was already on her, forcing her onto her back, using his body weight to subdue her. But he didn't realize she had a weapon.

Knowing that some of the spray would fall on her, Francesca squeezed her eyes shut and turned her face away as she aimed and pressed the button.

It hadn't been a direct shot. They'd been moving, fighting. But her action had taken him by surprise, and he gulped in some of the spray when he gasped. Coughing and screaming, he seemed to forget that he had the rope in his hands. He dropped it and swung at her wildly, hitting her in the head, the jaw.

Francesca lost her grasp on the can as she coughed, too. The pepper spray burned her eyes, temporarily blinding her, but she knew her bedroom better than Dean did. Ignoring the flash of pain in her forearm from the recent dog bite and using every ounce of strength she possessed, she slammed him into the headboard.

A second later, she broke free.

He cursed at her, telling her she was dead, as he flailed around, trying to find her. And then he started to cry for his mother.

Stumbling toward the hall, guiding herself with her hands, she managed to make her way out of the house. But by the time Josephine let her in to call the police, and a patrol car arrived, Dean was gone.

Pounding on the door woke Jonah from a restless sleep. He'd been dreaming. Of Summer, who'd been drowning in a crystal-clear lake; try as he might, he couldn't grab her. Of Adriana, who'd refused to help him, then screamed when she saw their daughter floating facedown, just out of reach. Of Francesca, who kept weaving in and out of the other sequences, while trying to escape an ax murderer. Beyond the woman-in-jeopardy theme, the dream made little sense. Except to magnify his fears. And fill him with a sense of foreboding.

Hearing someone at his door before dawn only intensified that feeling.

"Coming!" After scrambling to get out of bed, he pulled on a pair of basketball shorts and jogged over to check the peephole. Then he threw the door open.

Nate Ferrentino stood in the hallway, wearing sweats that didn't match and a pair of slippers. He'd obviously just rolled out of bed, still had the imprint of a blanket on one cheek.

"What's the matter? Is it Rachel? Is she having the baby?" Jonah had never been part of their birth plan before. But perhaps Nate's mother was unavailable and they needed someone to watch Dylan….

"Where the hell's your cell phone?" Nate demanded.

"I turned it off so I could get some sleep. Why?"

"You need to get a home line."

"I'm not here enough. What's up?"

He scratched his head, which did nothing to improve the state of his uncombed hair. "The answering service called me. They said someone from Arizona needs to get hold of you. That it's an emergency."

Fear swept through Jonah with the force of a raging river. "Did they say what's wrong?"

"No." Nate shoved a piece of paper at him. "Call this number," he said, and shuffled off.

Jonah recognized the number. He'd called it earlier, just after he'd spoken to Dr. Price to let her know he was off the case and while he waited to board his plane. He hadn't felt one hundred percent comfortable leaving Francesca behind, so he'd purchased a little insurance.

As he closed the door, he turned to glance at the clock. Four.

Nothing good ever happened so early in the morning.

Powering up his cell, he stood at the window, gazing out at the headlights snaking along the streets of L.A. far below.

A male voice answered on the second ring. "Ray Leedy."

"Ray, it's Jonah. What's going on?"

"Where have you been, man? I've been trying to reach you since midnight."

Jonah hadn't really expected trouble. He'd hoped Finch and Hunsacker would keep a close eye on Butch, as promised. This security guard was basically an afterthought, a backup system, a way to put his mind at ease. "Forget it. You've got my attention now. What's happening?"

"Your man was busy last night, bro."

Jonah's stomach muscles contracted. "What do you mean by that?"

"He's been up most the night. Wasn't easy to tell what he was doing. I couldn't see a whole hell of a lot, especially when he came home from wherever and went into the junkyard. Then I spotted him carrying something in a heavy-duty garbage bag to his truck."

No... "What'd he do with it?"

"He loaded it in the back and took off."

Jonah sucked air between his teeth. "What time was this?"

"Around midnight. That's when I first tried to call you, to see what you wanted me to do."

"I hope you followed him." Jonah wished he'd given Ray more detailed instructions, but he hadn't expected him to have to do anything more than sit outside and watch. Besides protecting Francesca, Jonah had thought it might be handy to be able to confirm Butch's whereabouts should another murder take place. He hadn't anticipated *this*....

"I followed him, all right. You said I wasn't to let him

out of my sight. But he didn't go to Chandler, like you were worried about."

"Where'd he go?"

"The mountains."

Jonah gripped the phone tighter. "Which mountains?"

"The Juniper Mountains, to the west."

"What for? What was he doing?"

"I'm not completely sure. I couldn't get too close. What with all the trees and having to stay back far enough that he wouldn't see me…"

"You lost him."

"Yeah. I'm sorry."

At least this guy was willing to accept responsibility. "Can you take me to the general area?"

"Sure."

"That should help."

"What do you think he was doing?" There was a note of insecurity in that question, because Ray already had an inkling or he wouldn't have asked.

"Who knows, but a suspected killer toting a black garbage bag into the mountains in the middle of the night always makes me uncomfortable."

"Since I'm sitting about twenty yards from his front door, that shit makes me uncomfortable, too," he said with a nervous laugh.

Jonah pressed his palm to his forehead. "Where is he now?"

"He got home not long ago. All the lights are off. I assume he went to bed."

"Did he see you?"

"No. I kept my distance. That's why I don't know what he did with that black bag. I only know it's gone. I checked the truck."

He'd tossed it out or buried it along the way. Jonah had no idea if they'd ever be able to recover it, but he planned to try. "Have you noticed anyone else who might be watching the place?"

"You mean I'm not the only one?"

That answered his question, and made Jonah damn glad he'd decided to spend a few extra bucks to keep Francesca safe. A fifteen-dollar-an-hour rent-a-cop had never been more worth the money. "I guess you are. What about Dean?"

"Who?"

"The slight man I told you about."

"Haven't seen him."

"What time did you get to the salvage yard?"

"'Round ten, like you asked."

"Perfect. Thanks."

"You want me to stay until dawn?"

"I'd like you to stay until I get there, if you can. I'll be on the first plane. Consider it time and a half."

"You got it, man."

They disconnected, but before Jonah could get showered for the day, his phone rang. "Hello?"

"Jonah?" It was Francesca. He was about to tell her what he'd learned but she didn't give him the chance.

"It's not Butch. It's Dean," she blurted out. "He broke into my house last night and tried to kill me. If—if not for that pepper spray…"

"What?" His free hand curled into a fist. "Are you injured?"

"No. Since the effects of the pepper spray have worn off, I'm just…rattled."

Now that he knew she wasn't hurt, he realized what she'd told him didn't make sense. If Dean was their killer, why had Butch been driving that garbage bag into the woods? If the two brothers-in-law were partners in crime, they were the most unlikely duo ever, so unlikely that Jonah couldn't bring himself to believe it.

Something else was at play. But what that "something" was, Jonah couldn't begin to guess.

"Where are you now?" he asked Francesca.

"On the road to Prescott."

"Finch and Hunsacker know you're coming?"

"I called them right away. They're trying to get a search warrant."

He considered telling her about the black bag Butch had transported, but decided to wait. If Dean was a threat to Francesca, he wanted him caught, first and foremost. No need to throw the investigation off-kilter before that could happen, especially when they were about to search the salvage yard. Let the investigators take the evidence technicians in there; he'd go to the Juniper Mountains himself.

"I'm heading to the airport right now," he said. "I'll call you as soon as I land."

28

Francesca told Finch and Hunsacker about the panties. Those panties were the reason Dean had come after her, which made them as significant as she'd suspected they might be. She couldn't in all conscience keep that information to herself any longer. So she'd braved their tirade and breathed a sigh of relief when the search warrant came through and they left with a couple of forensic science technicians. They were finally going to look beyond the mannequin they'd found before, and maybe they'd discover some piece of evidence that could bring this case to a satisfactory close.

But she was as uneasy as she was excited. No one knew where Dean had gone. Although Finch had sent a deputy to arrest him the moment he returned to the salvage yard, he'd never shown up. And Paris, Butch and the Wheelers claimed he'd left his phone at home so they had no way of contacting him, no idea where to find him. Unless that had changed and she hadn't been notified—which was entirely possible with Finch and Hunsacker—he was still missing.

Where could he be? And what was he doing? Francesca was more than a little afraid to find out. Not only was he mentally ill and emotionally unstable, he had the names and addresses of all her family and friends. And he'd shown an inclination to contact them....

Expecting Jonah to arrive at any moment, she slumped over the table in the small interrogation room, where she'd been sleeping since the investigators left, and told herself everything would be fine. The investigation was on the downhill slide; it had to be. Surely Finch or Hunsacker or a tech on the team would discover some trace evidence—fibers, a piece of jewelry, hair—*something* to connect Dean with one or more of the victims, even if it was only a spot of blood he'd tracked in on his shoe.

She'd wanted to go with the investigators but, after what she'd been through and the effects of that sleeping pill, she'd been too exhausted to stay on her feet. Besides, Finch hadn't wanted her with them. Because of her encounter with Dean last night, her antagonistic relationship with Butch and the bad press her involvement in this case had already brought the department, he claimed that her presence would actually make it more difficult to achieve their goal.

"The testimony of the people closest to him will be important. I need to talk to Dean's family, get them to trust me enough to open up. I can't believe that will happen with you there," Finch had said. "Not considering how they feel about you..."

"Just have Hunsacker do the interviews," Francesca had responded with a heavy dose of sarcasm. "He and Butch are like family."

The fact that Finch had shaken his head instead of speaking up to defend his partner told her that his anger over the panties and everything else was spent. He acted as if he felt bad for being such a jerk. Hunsacker, on the other hand, showed no remorse. He'd simply muttered, "Told you it wasn't Butch," as he passed her on his way out.

Her cell phone rang. Lifting her head, she pressed the answer button. "Hello?"

"Jonah there yet?"

Finch. "No. But he should be coming soon."

"You stuck on palling around with him? Or do you want to make yourself useful?"

Covering a yawn, she got up to stretch her sore muscles. As tired as she was, she thought she could've slept anywhere, even standing, but that chair hadn't been remotely comfortable. "I'm ready to help. What's going on?"

"Not much. We haven't found anything incriminating yet."

Disappointment weighed as heavily as her fatigue. "I'd settle for suspicious."

"These things take time."

She switched the phone to her other ear. "So why are you calling me?"

"The interviews aren't going much better than the search."

"No one's talking, even though *I'm* not there?" she said, taking a jab at his refusal to include her.

He didn't rise to the bait. "Not the old folks. Not Butch's wife. And certainly not Butch."

"I told you to let Hunsacker do the interviews."

Irritation sharpened his voice. "Enough with the bad blood between you and Hunsacker. If you two want to go at each other, leave me out of it."

He had a point. Letting her dislike of Hunsacker get in the way wouldn't help. She was just so…sleep-deprived. And worried.

Resting her forehead against the wall, she stared down

at the commercial-grade carpet. "Maybe Dean's family doesn't know anything. He was able to stalk Sherrilyn, which means he has a great deal of freedom. This might sound a bit harsh, but Butch and the others are probably glad when he takes off on his little walkabouts, because then they don't have to deal with him."

"Maybe they are glad when he's gone. But they know more than they're saying about Julia. I can feel it."

She toed a spot where the carpet was coming loose from the wall. "I thought you didn't put much store in instinct."

"I don't put much store in *your* instinct. *My* instinct's like a compass." The chuckle that followed indicated he was joking.

"You can be funny?" she said dryly. "I didn't know that about you."

"There's a lot you don't know about me."

And she wasn't really interested in learning more. "You think they're protecting him?" she asked, getting back to what mattered most.

"Hell, no. Butch and Paris would love to make someone else responsible for Dean. Even a prison warden."

Francesca still wasn't sure where Finch was going with all this, why he'd reached out to her. "You haven't told me what you want from me."

"I need you to find Julia."

What? She lifted her head. "The Julia Paris mentioned to Butch?"

"That's the one. We kept Butch, Paris and the Wheelers separated so they couldn't hear each other's testimony. Standard procedure. But every time I asked about her—if Dean had any friends by the name of Julia or if they've ever known a Julia—they mumbled something vague, like, 'Not that I remember,' or, 'Not in recent

years,' and that was it. I couldn't get another damn detail
out of them."

*That P.I. was here for a reason, Butch. And it wasn't
to ask about Julia.* Those words had meant so much to
Francesca when she'd first heard them. She'd assumed
Paris knew of another woman who'd gone missing, that
she suspected why and was keeping mum about it to
protect her husband. But after Dean broke in and came
after her with his trusty choke rope, Francesca had decided those words could have another meaning entirely.
"Maybe I was wrong," she said. "Maybe this Julia hasn't
been victimized. She could just be another woman,
alive and well, with whom Butch has been romantically
involved."

"That's what I told myself when you first reported
what you'd heard. I didn't find the comment particularly
damning. Not on its own. But if this Julia is alive, and
Butch and the Wheelers have nothing to hide, why won't
anyone provide me with a name and an address so I can
talk to her?"

Francesca tried to reason that out, but he went on
before she could arrive at an answer.

"And there's something else that's curious," he said.

Stifling a groan because she still felt as if she'd been
hit by a truck, she sank back into her chair. "What's
that?"

"I found a whole box of love letters in Dean's
room."

"To Sherrilyn?"

"To Julia."

This woke her up. "Do you know how long ago they
were written?"

"The most recent is dated last week."

"Which would suggest she's alive," she said, smoothing the tape on the fresh bandage she'd put over her stitches.

"Except that they were never addressed, let alone sent. There has to be a reason."

"Maybe he doesn't know where she is."

"I thought of that, too. But in them he talks about how much he wishes he could've protected her from Butch. It seems to be a recurring theme."

Protect her from Butch? It was Dean who was dangerous. They'd just established that, hadn't they?

Too tense to sit still, Francesca got to her feet again. "What does Butch say when you ask him about those letters?"

"Nothing."

"Try asking Paris."

"I can't. They all invoked their right to have a lawyer present. As soon as I mentioned her name."

So the interviews were over almost before they'd begun. That wasn't good. "You think I can track down Julia without their help?"

"You're supposed to be a crack P.I., right?"

"Not according to you and your rotund partner," she grumbled.

"Listen, forget all that. We've got work to do."

Now he was willing to collaborate. Because he needed her.

"Hunsacker and I have our hands full here," he went on. "I'd be tempted to believe this Julia is merely a figment of Dean's imagination. He's psychotic, so that has to be considered a possibility. But—"

"Paris talked about her to Butch, which proves they know her—or know of her—too."

"Ah, the crack in the 'he's making up imaginary friends' hypothesis."

Just because Julia was real didn't mean Dean's perception of her situation was. He wrote about Butch being a threat. But it was possible that Dean had hurt her himself and blamed Butch for making him angry enough to do it, or used some other convoluted justification for his actions.

"A first name isn't a lot to go on," she said.

"But it's all we got. Can you do it? Can you find her?"

She couldn't offer any guarantees. No woman named Julia had been reported missing from this area in the past twenty years. They didn't have a body—at least, not one they'd positively identified. And her name hadn't come up in any other context—just the letters Finch had found and what Francesca had overheard Paris say.

"I'll do my best," she replied. "But I need you to do me a favor."

"What's that?"

"Give me the date of the very first letter."

Paper crinkled on the other end. "Assuming they're all here, and it certainly looks that way since they were all shoved in the same box under his bed, he wrote the first one on—" a few seconds of silence ticked by "—May 15, 2008."

Two years ago… "Okay. I'm coming to get them," she said. "Maybe there's a reference or a name in one that could start a chain for me to follow."

"Daylight's wasting," he said. Then he was gone.

Francesca's call came in when Jonah was about thirty minutes from Prescott. He sped up as he answered, even though he was already at risk for a ticket. *What if I can't hate you?* He'd been hearing her voice in his head ever since he'd hung up with her earlier, when he was still in

California, had been telling himself not to invest that question with more meaning than he should. Not hating him was a far cry from loving him, or being willing to give him a second chance.

"Almost there," he told her. "What's going on?"

"I wanted to let you know that you can go straight to the salvage yard, if you like."

"Don't tell me you're heading back to Chandler." He didn't like the sound of that, didn't want her to be alone.

"No, I'm not sure where I'll be. I'm hoping to find Julia."

He couldn't recall who she meant. "Julia?"

"The woman Paris mentioned when I was in the salvage yard. Finch feels she's important to the investigation."

"What's changed? He didn't seem too interested before."

"He found a box of love letters written to a Julia under Dean's bed. Now he's convinced that whatever role she played might be significant."

"I'd say that's more likely than not," he mused and turned down the radio. "Any sign of Dean?"

"No. None."

Knowing how much he'd worry about Francesca if Dean remained at large for any length of time, how impossible it would be to leave the state and go home, he cursed. "Not the answer I wanted to hear."

"Not the answer I wanted to give you," she responded.

He slowed for a light, thought again of their earlier conversation in which she'd hinted that she still cared for him—and purposely avoided asking if it was true. "Where do you plan to start your search for Julia?"

"If Butch, Paris and Dean all know her, chances are

she's either related to one of them or she's local. And since Butch is completely estranged from his family, even the family who took him in, and has been for a number of years, I figure the Wheelers' relatives are much more likely to possess information that might help us."

"Seems reasonable to me. Has Finch come up with anything besides those letters?"

"Not yet. But it's a big property. They have a lot of looking to do."

The light turned green, and he gave the Jeep Grand Cherokee he'd rented at the airport some gas. "What about Butch and Paris? Anyone talking?"

"No one. All the principal parties are planning to get an attorney."

Because of what he'd learned about that black garbage bag, he'd expected as much. "They definitely have something to hide. But what? What could've happened to bring them all into collusion? I have a hard time believing they'd stick together to protect a serial killer, even one who's part of the family. That would make them as culpable as Dean."

"I agree. Maybe one person might let loyalty interfere with doing the right thing, but *four?* The question isn't just *what* they're hiding but *why.*"

"It would have to be a compelling reason…."

"Maybe they're all benefiting from these deaths in some way or another."

"How? Unless it's petty robbery. And I can't imagine that'd be nearly enough incentive."

"Me, neither. But there's a common thread in this. We just have to find it."

Maybe he'd do that when he and the security guard traveled into the Juniper Mountains. Although he'd originally planned on taking Francesca along, keeping her by his side every second, he felt she'd be safe for a few hours, since Dean wouldn't have any idea where she might be. But, considering what Ray Leedy had seen the night before, he wanted her to know that Butch might be a threat, too; there could be *anything* in that black bag, including the body of the woman she was hoping to find.

"You're kidding me," she said when he finished explaining.

"No. So…this thing is far from over. Keep your eyes open, okay?"

"I will."

He knew she was about to hang up but, for some reason, felt compelled to stop her before she could. "Francesca?"

"What?"

Don't ask. Let her meet someone who hasn't hurt her the way you have. "Never mind," he said. "I'll catch you later."

What was it Jonah had wanted?

Tempted to call him back to see if she could get him to tell her, Francesca stared down at her phone as she left the sheriff's station. She was fairly certain he hadn't been about to make another comment on the case. The energy of those last few seconds had seemed far too personal, as if the world had suddenly shrunk into an intimate bubble that included only the two of them. But if he'd been about to admit that he cared for her, what would she say in return? What did she want from their renewed association?

That was a difficult question to answer because as much as she still loved him, she wasn't sure it would be wise to hope for a future together. Too many obstacles

stood between them. For one, it'd been a decade since
their earlier relationship. Those years had changed them
both. For another, they lived in different states. Then
there was Adriana. Was there room in her life for *both* of
them? Or would it become painful and awkward, eventually making her resent one or the other? She also had to
think of her family. If she and Jonah decided to marry
at some point, could she really expect her parents and
her brother to embrace him?

Her phone flashed to the main menu as if trying to
tell her that the past was too big a hurdle to clear. The
last thing she wanted was to reunite with Jonah only to
go through another breakup. It'd been hard enough the
first time….

Dropping her phone in her purse, she told herself she
was better off leaving the relationship as it stood. Sure,
she'd missed him. But if she'd learned to build a life
without him once, she could do it again. She'd be wiser
to make that decision now, before she formed as many
new memories of him as she had past ones. At least
after the last few days she'd be able to remember him in
a more positive light. Sometimes one had to be grateful
for small things.

Pushing the button on her key that would unlock her
car, she took a deep breath. Maybe she wouldn't have
the sense of completion or happiness that felt so tanta-
lizingly close whenever Jonah was around, but that happiness could be just an illusion.

From the moment she got out of her car, Francesca
could feel Butch's glare. It cut through the summer heat
like the searing blue flame of a welding torch as he
watched her approach from where he sat in a cheap plastic lawn chair, while his son played on a tire swing that

hung from the same kind of rope Dean had brought to her house. She made that connection right away, planned to ask the police to take a sample, since Dean had left that short length of rope behind.

The Impala was gone. She guessed Butch had suggested his wife leave, possibly to avoid the painful process of having half a dozen police officers crawl over the house and yard, searching through everything and anything, including her underwear, tampons and birth control products. It wasn't like she had to stay. Search warrants were very specific, and since Dean didn't drive, the judge hadn't allowed Finch to include the vehicles.

It didn't look as if the old folks were home, either, which made Francesca wonder whether Finch was having them tailed. If Dean's parents felt any sympathy for their boy's situation, they could be meeting up with him right now, passing him money or giving him a lift to someplace they deemed safe, someplace out of reach of the law—like Mexico, which was only a four-and-a-half-hour drive away.

Planning to ask Finch if he'd considered that possibility, she started to skirt around Butch when he came to his feet and stepped in front of her. "Well, look who it is," he said, raising the can of beer in his hand.

She wished she had more energy, but last night had taken its toll. "I have nothing to say to you," she told him. "Please get out of my way."

He didn't. Wearing a baseball hat with his typical sleeveless shirt and jeans, he took a swig of beer. "I hear Dean gave you a scare."

The taunt in his voice said he wasn't displeased by his brother-in-law's actions, and that surprised her. After learning about his activity with that black garbage bag, she would've expected him to be upset that Dean had brought the police down on them.

"That's right," she said. "And I gave *him* a shot of pepper spray. Considering he's wanted by the police and will probably spend the rest of his life in prison, I'd say he got the worst of it, wouldn't you?"

Muscles bulging, he folded his arms across his massive chest. "Too bad that boy ain't more of a man."

"And what would a man have done, Butch?" She wanted to taunt him in return, let him know he'd been observed last night, but she wouldn't risk compromising their case. First they had to get him on record saying he hadn't left the house.

His gaze dropped to the slight cleavage above her V-neck shirt. "A real man would've had you on your back in ten seconds flat."

A tingle of fear went through her. Dean had shown up at her house with a rope, yet this man frightened her even more. "Are we talking about rape, Butch? Are you suggesting a real man, a man like you, would've raped me?"

He gave her an evil smile that made her feel shockingly vulnerable. "Rape you? Heck, no. That's illegal."

"Not to mention immoral."

"That, too." He took another drink of his beer. "I'm just sayin' a real man would've been able to pin you so you couldn't spray him, that's all," he said with a wink as he stepped aside.

When she came even with him, she paused. "You think you're helping your case by making comments like that, Butch? Isn't your family in enough trouble?"

He made a show of appraising her calves, the only part of her legs visible beneath her knee-length skirt. "I'm not in any trouble. They won't find anything here, except maybe a few trophies from the women I've—" his smile widened "—*pinned*."

"You'd better hope all those women are still breathing, or you'll have a much bigger problem than just putting up with a mess," she said as she gestured at the chaos surrounding them.

He reached out to grab her arm before she could walk away, but the front door opened and a forensic tech came out at the same time. Laughing, Butch shoved his hand through his hair as if he'd intended that action all along. "Let's hope *you're* still breathing when all this is over, huh?"

Francesca couldn't believe his nerve. She was so appalled she didn't realize the forensic tech had spoken to her until he repeated himself. "I said, are you Francesca Moretti?"

Pulling her gaze from Butch, she focused on the man who'd been trying to hail her. "Yes. Yes, I am."

His eyes cut between her and Butch. Obviously, he sensed the tension but didn't understand the reason behind it. "Finch asked me to keep a lookout for you. He's in back."

"Right. In back," she said, and began to follow him. Then she caught the tech's arm, so he couldn't go in without her, and faced Butch. "I'm going to find Julia, or find out what happened to her. Then we'll see who's safe and who's not."

The unconcerned mask he'd worn since she arrived disintegrated. "You don't know when to quit, do you?"

"When whoever's been murdering women and dumping their bodies in the desert or on the street, like so much trash, has been put behind bars, I'll quit," she said, and walked off.

29

After taking the letters Finch had given her to the car, Francesca sat in the driver's seat reading. She thought she might have some questions for the investigators or run across a detail she'd need to check out while she had access to the property. But she felt so sleepy she was hardly in top form. And Butch was making her uncomfortable with the way he kept watching her.

When glaring didn't seem to intimidate her, he got up and fetched the bat he'd come at her with the first day they met. Whenever she glanced up, he'd grin wickedly and take a big swing, as if he was happily knocking her head off. In return, she'd smile and give him a nod of acknowledgment, then hold up the letter she'd just read, as if it contained so much damning evidence he didn't have a prayer of staying out of jail.

He didn't like that. After three such exchanges, he cursed and threw the bat aside, then slumped in his chair. The next time she looked up, she noticed that his expression had darkened to a glower. She smiled, anyway, but soon started her car and drove half a mile down the road, where she could still be close but read without the anxiety.

Dean had dedicated the first page of almost every

letter to effusive compliments and pledges of undying love. But in this one there was also a poem using every letter in Julia's name, one he'd obviously written himself.

> J—Jazzy, joyous, jinxed, jewellike eyes of green
> U—Unique, unpredictable, unbelievable, under eighteen
> L—Lovely, ladylike, laughing, long dark hair
> I—Important, inquisitive, interesting, isolated as a bear
> A—Angelic, alluring, abandoned, all I ever dream about

"Isolated as a *bear?*" she read. That line stuck out because it didn't make a lot of sense, until she realized that the last item on the list for each letter created a separate poem.

> Jewellike eyes of green,
> Under eighteen,
> Long dark hair,
> Isolated as a bear,
> All I ever dream about.

He'd wanted to rhyme.

Francesca doubted Dean would ever win any awards for his poetry, but at least he'd provided a physical description for the girl she needed to find. Maybe it was rudimentary, but it was still more than she'd known a moment earlier. Julia was under eighteen—but since Dean had written this last May, maybe not anymore. She had green eyes and dark hair. Francesca wondered if Dean had included the physical details as a way to remember her. That seemed plausible, especially since his writing had grown less specific and more flowery as time went on, implying that he hadn't seen her in quite a while, or that he was writing to someone fondly remembered. This poem might even be his idea of a memorial.

Going through each line again, she studied the other adjectives. According to Dean, Julia was also *jinxed, isolated* and *abandoned*. Those three words caught Francesca's attention because they were the only negative ones in the poem, and they didn't reflect directly on Julia but on her circumstances.

Had this girl run into bad luck? Why was she jinxed, abandoned and isolated?

Dropping the letter in her lap, Francesca rested her head on the back of her seat and gazed off into the distance. The salvage yard was fairly isolated. Could Dean have been speaking about his own reality, projecting again? He was also jinxed and, to some extent, abandoned. Those adjectives would actually be quite appropriate for someone in his situation.

A truck chugged along the dirt road to her right. Watching the dust churned up by its tires, she tried to figure out why the letters she'd read gave her the feeling that Dean knew this girl well, that the whole family did. In the earlier letters, he made several references to Butch, and "the way he looks at you." There was even "Don't mind Paris. She's just jealous." And "Mom knows it wasn't you."

If those passages could be believed, they'd all spent time together, maybe a lot of it. But Francesca couldn't imagine Butch and Paris going out anywhere with Dean, not if they could avoid it. Which meant the only way they could all associate as closely as these letters intimated was if—

Francesca's heart began to beat faster. The girl lived around here!

Her eyes riveted on the truck she'd been watching earlier and she recalled her father's words about the man who owned the farmland adjacent to the salvage yard. *The owner works it himself, so he's out there regularly, growing alfalfa....*

This had to be that farmer, didn't it? Or someone he'd hired...

Francesca had left her car idling because she'd needed the air-conditioning. Pushing the gearshift into drive, she punched the gas pedal, swung around the corner and barreled down the road. The truck, a dented old Ford, clearly a work vehicle, was pretty far ahead of her, but she managed to get the driver's attention by laying on her horn and flashing her lights.

He stopped, allowing her to draw even with him.

Hoping this might be the break she needed, she hopped out and hurried over to greet him. "I'm really sorry to bother you. You must think I'm crazy racing after you like that, but I had to catch you."

The driver, an older man with a craggy face and iron-gray hair, wore bib overalls and a T-shirt dampened with sweat. A wad of tobacco filled one cheek. "What can I help you with?"

She dug through her purse and handed him her card. "I'm looking for someone."

He spat through his open window. "You're a P.I."

"I am."

"Who are you looking for?"

"It's a teenage girl, about eighteen. Green eyes. Dark hair. Most likely Caucasian."

He gawked at the dust coating her high heels. "The closest house is that way half a mile or so, at the salvage yard. You could check there."

The engine revved as if he was about to drive off so she put her hands on the window ledge. "I know where the salvage yard is. Please, if you could just…think for a moment. I'm guessing this girl hasn't been around for a while. I'm not sure how long. But I believe she lived in the area at one time. Her name was Julia."

His bushy eyebrows resembled two caterpillars inching toward each other. "Well, why didn't you say so? I remember Julia. She's been gone…oh, couple years. Maybe two."

"Where did she live?"

"The house I pointed out to you." He jerked his head in the direction from which she'd come.

"The salvage yard."

"That's right."

Relief, hope, even disbelief, surged through Francesca, giving her a respite from the dragging fatigue. "She lived with Butch?"

"For a while. She was some sort of runaway they took in. Nice of 'em."

"How well do you know Butch and the Wheelers?"

He adjusted his ball cap, which was even more stained with sweat than his shirt. "I know Elaine and Bill better'n the kids. Bought this land from 'em twenty years ago, but they've retired since then. Butch is runnin' the place nowadays." He peered at her more closely. "You okay?"

She felt as if she'd won the lottery. "I'm fine. It's just… hot." She swiped at a drop of sweat rolling down from her temple. "Can you tell me anything about Julia?"

"Not much. There was only one time that we actually spoke. The needle on my gas gauge was sticking." He tapped the glass below the dusty dash. "I thought I had plenty in the tank but turns out I didn't. I ran out right in front of their place, had to knock at the door and ask if I could buy a couple gallons off 'em."

"What did they say?"

"Julia came to the door. She was real sweet. Ran and got me a gas can and invited me in for a glass of iced tea."

"Did you see Butch or any of the Wheelers when you were there?"

"Paris was in the kitchen. Dean, too. They were just finishing lunch. They said hello, told me Julia was from California, that her parents didn't treat her right so they'd taken her in. Dean mentioned that she helped out in the yard. Didn't see Butch, Elaine or Bill."

"Did that incident occur in the summer?"

"Had to be. Damn hot that day. That's why the iced tea tasted so good."

"And this was two years ago?"

"Yup."

Francesca used the back of her wrist to dab at the sweat beading on her upper lip. "I see. And then Julia was gone shortly afterward?"

"Oh, I saw her out front once or twice after that, and we waved. But when I stopped by a few months later to see if Butch had a carburetor for a '57 Chevy, she wasn't around no more."

"How do you know?"

"I asked about her. He said she'd run off. Said it was the damnedest thing, kind of ungrateful 'cause of everything they'd tried to do for her."

If she was gone three months after this man had initially spoken to her in the height of summer, she'd disappeared in September or October, maybe even November

2008. "Has Butch or Dean or anyone else who lives at the salvage yard ever done anything you'd consider… unusual?"

Deep grooves formed in the farmer's weathered face. "Unusual in what way?"

"Are they up late at night? Moving objects in and out of the house? Have you heard any fighting?"

"I only work here. I don't live here. So I can't say what goes on after hours. They've always seemed okay to me. They mind their own business." He chewed on his tobacco. "What's with all the questions? What's going on over there? I saw the police cars when I arrived. And you're the second person this week to ask me about them. Guy from Montana, another P.I. or some such, called a few days ago, wantin' information. Somethin' wrong?"

She lifted her hands from the window ledge. "One or more of them might be in trouble."

"With the law?"

"Let's just say we need to find Julia, make sure she disappeared by choice."

"You don't think Butch *killed* her." When the farmer spat again, he nearly hit the frame of the window.

Francesca slid to one side for fear his aim would falter even more. She liked the shoes she was wearing. "I hope not. But it's a possibility."

Shifting his tobacco to the other cheek, he shook his head. "No. If someone's actin' out, it's gotta be Dean."

She was putting another twelve inches or so between them, but at this, she paused. "Why do you say that?"

"Dean's always been weird."

"That's it?"

"If you knew *how* weird, you'd know his type of weird is enough."

Francesca understood why he'd say that. It was Dean

who'd threatened his ex-girlfriend right before she went missing, Dean who'd broken into her house.

And yet…it was Butch who frightened her.

"Are we getting close?" Jonah asked.

Ray Leedy, the young security guard who'd followed Butch into the mountains the night before, sat in the passenger seat of the rented SUV, leaning into the harness of his seat belt as he concentrated on every bend in the road and every tree and rock that came into sight. "It feels like we're close," he said. "But…a lot of this area looks the same, you know? And it was dark."

Jonah was losing hope. He'd been driving back and forth, going around the same bends, going down this turnoff and then that one for hours, searching for where Butch had gone, all to no avail. Ray insisted he'd seen a cabin near the place where Butch had disappeared into the trees, but numerous cabins dotted these mountains.

"This one had a big *S* above the front door," he explained. "The initial of the family who owns it, I guess. It was right there in the beam of my headlights."

Ray had shared this detail before, several times, but they hadn't come across a cabin fitting that description.

"Do you think it could be up a little farther?" Jonah asked.

"Maybe. When I headed back, I clocked the distance on my odometer, but not right from the start. I didn't think of it immediately."

Jonah rubbed his face. They *had* to find where Butch had gone, had to recover that black garbage bag.

Spotting a cabin they'd passed twice already, he pulled into the drive.

"What are you doing?" Ray asked.

"Checking to see if anyone's around."

"Looks empty."

"Maybe we'll get lucky." Jonah jogged to the front door and knocked, but there was no answer. Primarily vacation getaways, these cabins were used mostly on holidays and weekends.

Ray rolled down his window as Jonah returned. "Nothing?"

"Nothing," Jonah said, but he wasn't ready to give up. He visited the next cabin they saw, and the next and the next one after that. It wasn't until he'd approached six different cabins that he finally found someone at home. And then she wouldn't open the door.

"Go away. Or I'll call the cops," a female voice called out.

Jonah didn't blame her for being scared. For all she knew, he could be someone like Dean.

"Will you just answer one question for me?" he called back.

After a long pause, she responded. "What do you want to know?"

"I'm looking for a cabin with an *S* on it. Can you tell me if it's in this area?"

"Who are you?"

"I'm slipping my card under the door." He leaned down to do that. "Name's Jonah Young," he said as he straightened. "You can call the Yavapai County Sheriff's Office and someone will vouch for me."

"You're a deputy?"

"Not quite. I work for the private sector—Department 6, as it says on my card. I'm consulting with the sheriff's office on a very important case."

"And what do you want with the Schultzes' cabin?"

Now they were getting somewhere. She knew of it,

which meant she probably also knew where it was. "I have reason to believe some evidence was placed or buried nearby."

"What kind of evidence?"

"That's what I need to find out."

"What's the number for the Yavapai County Sheriff's Office?"

Was this a test? He pulled up the directory on his phone so he could read it to her. "Ask for Investigator Hunsacker or Investigator Finch," he said.

Although she didn't open the door, she must've been satisfied because she didn't actually make the call. "The cabin you want is owned by Doug Schultz. Go back to the highway, turn left and drive another mile and a half. Take a right at Liberty Bell Road. Cabin's on the corner."

They hadn't gone quite far enough. "Thanks," he said, and hurried over to the SUV.

Ray watched him as he settled behind the wheel. "Any luck?"

"It's another mile and a half down the highway."

"Really? I could've sworn we'd gone too far already."

Jonah checked the clock on the dash as he popped the car into reverse. It was past five. He'd hoped to be back in Prescott by now but, with the way things were going, he wouldn't get to Francesca's until seven or eight.

As long as he made it by dark…

Shortly after ten, Butch sat at the kitchen table with a bottle of Jack Daniel's and a half-filled glass. Every one else in the house had gone to sleep, but he was looking to finish what he'd set in motion. It was almost over. All he had to do now was wait.

Sliding back in his chair, he stared up at the ceiling

and wished he felt bad about what he was doing. He knew
he should. But Dean had caused this mess. If the dumb
bastard hadn't put those panties in his jockey box, none
of it would've happened. Butch wouldn't have had to send
him to Francesca's, the police wouldn't have shown up
with that damn search warrant and Hunsacker and Finch
wouldn't have found the freezer.

It was Hunsacker who'd come to tell him about the
blood. The detective had gazed at the ground as he explained that Luminol reacts to the iron in hemoglobin.
There were traces of blood in the freezer. He'd quickly
added that it could be from an animal. But Butch knew
the drill. All they had to do was test it.

Holding his glass up to the light, he swirled the amber
liquid around the sides. Finch had walked up right after
to say he'd received a call from Francesca. She already
knew what Julia looked like, that she'd lived with them,
the time of year she'd gone missing and that she was from
California. With such a start, she'd be able to gather more
information, and if he let that play out, the investigation
might not take the direction he'd like.

So…since he couldn't get the panties back and Dean
had failed to subdue Francesca, he'd told them Dean was
the last person to see Julia alive. That she'd disappeared
soon after, but he'd trusted Dean when he said she'd run
away because he'd had no reason not to. She wasn't all
that stable an individual.

Finishing his drink, he smiled at how smoothly it had
all come together. The investigators had bought every
word, just as Butch had known they would, because it
matched the scenario they'd created in their minds. It
was so easy to lie to someone who was already prepared
to believe….

Turning the bottle of Jack Daniel's, Butch peeled the

corner of the label. Elaine had given him hell when she learned that he'd set Dean up to take the fall for Julia's death, but as he'd explained to her, if they wanted to save their normal daughter, they had to sacrifice their mentally ill son. Dean wasn't living in the real world half the time, anyway. He *should* be institutionalized.

Shoving his glass closer to the bottle, he poured himself another splash and used it to toast his brother-in-law. "Excellent job," he said. "Very convincing."

Once the investigators connected the panties to the blood in the freezer and the missing Julia Cummings, they'd have an airtight case. Even Dean's corny love letters would work against him. He'd go to prison for the rest of his life, the police would stop their surveillance on the salvage yard and life could go on as before. *Better* than before because Dean wouldn't be part of it anymore.

Somehow everything was working out perfectly. And, ironically, it was Dean who'd made it all possible.

Butch's cell phone rang. Peering at caller ID, he breathed a sigh of relief. It was a number he didn't recognize, most likely a payphone. Dean had left his cell at home, just as Butch had directed. This was what he'd been waiting for.

"Dean? What happened?" he said, feigning concern.

"I tried, Butch. I tried to do what you told me. But she…she sprayed me with some…stuff. Right in the eyes! I couldn't see. I couldn't breathe. It burned so bad! And—and then she ran. I had to get out of there. That was all I could do."

He was crying, gasping for breath like a child. It sickened Butch to hear it. A man should never cry like that. But Dean hadn't taken his medication.

"It'll be okay," Butch said.

"Tell Mom I—I tried to tie her up so I could call you, but…you should've come with me. She's stronger than she looks."

"I understand."

At that, there was a slight pause, a gap in the hysteria during which he sounded quite calm. "You're not mad at me?"

"Of course not. You did your best, didn't you?"

"I did. I did everything I could."

"So where are you now?"

"Phoenix? Glendale? I don't know. I've been riding the buses, riding and riding, all over, everywhere. I don't know what else to do. You said I couldn't come home unless I tied up Francesca, and that didn't go so good."

"Calm down, Dean. I'm going to help you."

He sniffed. "You are? Does that mean I can come home? I want to see Mom."

"Soon. But for now, it's too dangerous. The police are watching the yard."

"The *police?* Oh, God! What should I do?" His voice crescendoed in a wail.

"You'll go to the Schultzes' cabin."

"I will?"

"Yes. Right away. You remember it, don't you?"

"Yeah, sure. That place we rented last Christmas? Where we taught Champ to shoot a pellet gun?"

"That's the one."

"That was so fun," he said. "But won't the cabin be locked?"

"Since when is any lock a problem for you?" Butch asked.

"It's not. But I thought… I mean, you want me to *break in?*"

"If that's the only way."

"Then what, Butch? How long do I stay?"

Standing, Butch set his glass in the sink and put the Jack Daniel's back in the cupboard. "Once you get there, sit tight, Dean. Someone will be coming for you shortly," he said. Then he hung up and called Hunsacker. "It's me."

"Butch? What's up?"

Judging by the thickness of Hunsacker's voice, he'd been sleeping. Butch gave him time to collect his wits before continuing. "I know where you'll be able to find Dean."

"You do?"

"Yes. He just called here, looking for our help."

Hunsacker's next words sounded much more alert. "You were smart to contact me. Turning him in is for the best, Butch. The only way."

He was right about that. "Do you have a pen and paper?"

"I— Yeah, sure. Go ahead," Hunsacker said, and Butch gave him directions.

30

"I can't believe we haven't been able to get hold of Finch," Francesca complained. "It's been *hours* since we heard from him."

Jonah hovered over her fax machine. After his unproductive attempt to find whatever Butch had left at or near the Schultzes' cabin, he'd spoken to Winona Green, the profiler who was studying the Dead Mule Canyon case for him. She'd indicated that she was finished with her research and would e-mail her notes in the morning, once she'd had a chance to type them up. Unwilling to wait, and knowing he'd be going to Chandler—he refused to let Francesca spend another night alone—he'd asked Winona to fax her handwritten version to Francesca's office. But there was nothing in the bin when they arrived, and they'd already been there twenty minutes. "Let's hope it's because he's had a major break in the case."

"I'm dying to know what that might be. What else did he discover at the salvage yard?" She'd spent the early evening at the sheriff's station, trying to determine Julia's last name, but he and Hunsacker hadn't returned.

"They must've found something interesting, or we

would've heard from them, if only to ask whether or not you'd obtained more information on Julia."

"I'm frustrated that I haven't been able to come up with a name," she said.

He was aware of that. They'd spent the two-hour drive to Chandler on the phone together. They'd started out discussing the garbage bag Butch had removed from the salvage yard, the farmer who'd helped Francesca figure out that Julia had once lived with Butch and the many police departments in California she'd called looking for a runaway who matched Julia's first name and description. But it hadn't been long before they'd ventured on to other subjects—her parents, his parents, Department 6, his condo in L.A. The comfortable companionship that had developed over the course of that call made him feel closer to her than was probably wise. He'd be a fool to allow himself to fall back in love with her. But it seemed to be happening, anyway….

"Did she say she'd send the fax right away?" Francesca asked.

"She certainly gave me the impression it'd be tonight," he replied. "But…maybe she dozed off." He was about to do the same. It wasn't very late—only eleven o'clock—but it'd been weeks since he'd had a decent night's sleep.

Francesca didn't appear to be any fresher. She sagged onto the edge of her assistant's desk, tired but prettier than ever. He wished he didn't find her so damn attractive, but every time he looked at her he felt a strong reaction. The years they'd been separated hadn't changed anything.

"This isn't a bad place to work," he said, glancing around. He'd complimented her on it before, when she first showed him through, but small talk distracted him from the condoms in his suitcase, which seemed to be screaming his name from the trunk of his car.

She put back the picture she held of her assistant, Heather, and Heather's little boy. "I like it."

A renovated old house fronting Chandler Boulevard, it contained a reception room, a small kitchen, two bathrooms, a storage area and Francesca's private office. Decorated in burgundy and blue, the place had expensive-looking black shutters, hardwood floors covered with traditional area rugs and mahogany bookcases. He couldn't resist feeling a sense of pride at what she'd accomplished. It wasn't easy for an independent P.I. to make a living, but she'd created a situation that was very different from the "barely making ends meet" stereotype so often portrayed in the media. Francesca had done very well for herself.

"You've built your business working missing persons?"

"Background checks are still our bread and butter and probably always will be—that and helping one spouse prove the other's cheating. But missing persons is the challenge that keeps me interested."

Outside, the wind picked up, and he wondered if they were about to experience an early monsoon. The weather in Arizona didn't usually change much this time of year, vacillating between hot, dry and sunny, and hotter, drier, sunnier. Until August. Then a series of giant dust storms swept through the area, breaking up the monotony of "perfect" weather by bringing visibility to zero, uprooting trees or breaking off limbs and dumping leaves, twigs and dirt into the swimming pools in the valley. Occasionally, these storms also brought thunder, lightning and rain.

"How long is your lease?" he asked.

"I don't have a lease," she replied. "I own it."

He nodded, impressed. "Nice. Good investment."

Silence fell. He consulted his watch. If the fax didn't come in the next ten minutes, he'd call Winona again.

He scrambled to come up with more small talk, something he could say that was safe and far from what was really on his mind. But before he could utter a word, he caught Francesca watching him—and the expression on her face made the blood rush straight to his groin. "I love it when you're this tired," he said.

Clearing her throat, she sat up straighter. "Why?"

"Because then your guard is down."

"And when my guard goes down…"

He drew a deep breath. "I can tell you want me as badly as I want you."

Caution quickly masked the longing so apparent a moment earlier. "Why would that excite you? You turned me down last time, remember?"

Closing the gap between them, he lifted her fully onto Heather's desk, shoved up her skirt and stepped between her spread knees without making physical contact. "You weren't offering me a deal I could accept."

Her fingers lightly traced the swelling in his jeans. "And you think something's different now?"

Removing her hand, he brought their lower bodies together. "I hope so."

Her eyes slid closed as he clasped her bottom and pressed into her. "I already offered you sex," she said. "What more do you want?"

Bending his head, he kissed her neck, her jawbone, her cheek. He craved what he'd been craving since they broke up. The word for it sat on the tip of his tongue, but he didn't dare speak it because he knew he had no right to ask.

"Jonah?" Her legs went around his hips, holding him in place.

The idea of having her right here, right now, became a possibility. That meant he *had* to say it. He couldn't go any further without making his needs plain. It wouldn't be fair to either of them. Maybe he didn't deserve a second chance, but as much as he wanted her body, he wanted her heart more, and he couldn't settle for less.

Cradling her face between his hands, he summoned his courage. "Forgiveness," he murmured. "I'm sorry, Francesca. I can't even tell you how sorry I am."

She released him. He'd made a mistake, asked for too much, just as he'd known he would before the words even left his mouth.

"It's okay. I understand why you can't forgive me," he said before she could respond. His voice sounded harsh to his own ears, but he couldn't control the raw emotion pouring through it. He felt as if he'd dropped his weapon and begged for mercy, and she'd thrust a knife in his chest. It was a wound she had every right to inflict, but that didn't ease the pain.

Eager to hide what he could of his reaction, so she wouldn't have to take any of the blame for what was essentially his fault, he tried to go back to the fax machine, but she caught hold of his arm.

"Hey, look at me."

Prepared for the worst, for some explanation telling him she'd never be able to believe in him again, he set his jaw. But when their eyes met, she smiled. "I forgive you."

Jonah almost couldn't believe his ears. He'd carried the burden of his mistake for ten long years, had regretted his actions every minute of every day. Even now he hated what the past said about his character. But if *she* could forgive him, maybe someday he could forgive himself....

"Do you mean it?" he asked.

"I mean it," she said. "I promise."

Tears welled up in Jonah's eyes, tears he seemed powerless to stop. He hoped she wouldn't notice. Revealing his sensitive side terrified him. But she didn't exploit his vulnerability. Tears streamed down her own cheeks as she kissed him—again and again and again.

And then their clothes came off.

The fax machine hummed. The profile they'd been waiting for was finally coming in, but Francesca wasn't sure she cared. And Jonah didn't seem to be aware of it. He'd taken a minute to run out to his car, said he had some condoms in his bag, but since his return he was too eager for her to pay attention to anything else.

"That's it. Let's get rid of these," he breathed when she began to wiggle out of her panties.

The lights were on, which meant she was completely exposed to him, but Francesca didn't mind. She liked watching the intensity on his face, felt exultant when he closed his eyes and gasped as she took him in her hand. This was it. She was making love with Jonah again, just like she'd always dreamed. There were times, lots of them, when she'd thought the prospect—if it ever came to pass—might frighten her. He was the only man who could really hurt her. And he had. But his hands on her body didn't scare her now. He was bringing her home.

They were *both* coming home.

"Your body's changed," he murmured. "It's even more beautiful."

She smiled up at him. His had changed, too. He felt thicker, stronger. He was just sliding his leg between hers when she caught sight of a tattoo on his thigh. He hadn't had any ink when they were together before. And, as far as she could tell, he didn't have any now, other than this.

Holding him back long enough to get a better look, she raised curious eyes to his. "That's the Chinese symbol for 'forever in my heart,' the one I was planning to have tattooed on *my* hip," she said. "But then we broke up and…" And she'd never returned to the parlor they'd visited the day she'd selected it. "You went back?"

He rested his forehead against hers. "It was all I had left of you," he whispered. Then he kissed her tenderly and what had started out as a frenetic, driving need ended with a powerful reverence she'd never experienced before, even with him.

"You love me," she said in awe as he threaded his fingers through hers and pinned them above her head.

They were on the floor, spent, exhausted, but happy, as they listened to the storm rage. Slowly rolling to one side, he propped his head up with his fist and lifted a sweaty tendril of hair from her cheek. "I always have."

Jonah got the fax while Francesca finished dressing.

"That looks like a lot of pages," she said, coming up behind him. "What's she sending? An entire encyclopedia on criminal behavior?"

Heedless of the papers he was crushing, Jonah pulled her close. "Winona likes to back up her opinions with case histories and various theories on human behavior developed by psychologists, criminologists—even other forensics specialists, if they're reliable. Since profiling includes a lot of guesswork and stereotyping, she provides as much research as possible to bolster her conclusions."

Just looking at Jonah made Francesca smile. "She seems very thorough."

"Oh, yes."

The desire to head home and get into bed, with Jonah curled securely around her, made it difficult to concentrate. But they had a job to do, a responsibility to the people they were trying to help, so she tried to shake off her fatigue. "What does she have to say?"

He released her so he could flip through the pages. "Not surprisingly, she says the killer is filled with rage."

Francesca leaned against him. "What killer isn't? Anything else?"

He began to read aloud. "'As you know, rape is about anger, not lust. And beating someone to death is intensely personal. I believe the man you're looking for has reason to hate his victims and feels justified in violence. That's why he left April Bonner on the street. Maybe she caused him extra trouble or threatened him in some way. He responded by humiliating her, not necessarily to show off his deeds but to make a statement that those who cross him will get what they deserve. I draw this conclusion from the pictures you sent, in which the victim is nude and posed with her legs splayed and her arms akimbo. It's almost as if he's calling her a whore.'"

"That's so unfair," Francesca interjected. "April wasn't even close to being a whore."

"A killer's perception is hardly ever the reality," Jonah responded.

"So do you think it's Butch, with his threats and cutting my telephone line and hiding a black garbage bag in the middle of the night? He could be punishing the women who threaten his marriage, even though he's really the one who's to blame. Or is it Dean, acting out because he hates the women who reject him?"

"Nothing I've seen so far rules out one *or* the other," he said. "If you haven't worked with forensic profiles before, I should warn you that they're pretty general. If profilers get too ambitious, too specific, and they're wrong, they can throw off an investigation, and I know Winona's very careful not to do that."

"I didn't expect her to *name* the killer, but it would've been nice if she'd been able to recognize some detail or signature that would point to one rather than the other. Even if Finch and Hunsacker managed to dig up a body at the salvage yard, our two main suspects live in the same house. How will we know which one put it there?"

Jonah shifted so he could slip his arm around her again. "Trace evidence, I hope—a hair or a footprint. But…there's something else troubling me about this case."

"What's that?"

"I don't get the feeling any of the victims were simply in the wrong place at the wrong time, you know? I think Winona is right about the perpetrator seeking vengeance against specific individuals."

"But for what? What could these women have done?"

"You mean, what could Butch or Dean have *perceived* them as doing? Anything."

Francesca frowned. Maybe that was true, but it wasn't very helpful. "Does Winona have anything else to say?"

"Just what I already know. That killers who pose their victims are almost always white and generally older." He paused. "Here's something you might like. She also feels the person we're looking for is small in stature."

"*Small* in stature?" Francesca echoed.

"There's your differentiation between Butch and Dean, huh?"

Except that, even after her skirmish with Dean last night, in her heart she believed it was Butch and not his brother-in-law. "What makes her think so?"

"The killer used a weapon to bludgeon these women to death. She claims that a man who's already raped a woman and who's confident in his own strength would most likely resort to strangulation. It's quieter, it's not as messy and it takes about the same amount of time."

"But the reason for the weapon could tie back to the rage she's mentioned. Bludgeoning is far more violent."

"True."

The ring of Jonah's cell phone interrupted them. "Finch," he muttered. "Finally." Setting the profile aside, he turned on the speaker phone and leaned against the desk, still keeping her close. "Hello?"

"We've got him," Finch announced.

Suddenly all business, Jonah came to his feet. "What did you say?"

"We have him."

"Who?"

"Dean. Who else? He's in custody."

Francesca and Jonah exchanged an uncertain look. "They've been busy, all right," she murmured.

"So it's over?" Jonah asked. "You're *sure* he's the one?"

"He's the one."

Francesca joined the conversation. "What physical evidence do you have?"

"The rope he left at your house, for starters. You need more than that?"

"Pardon the pun, but we want to know exactly what ties him to the murders," Jonah persisted.

"How about an old freezer with traces of blood? And just an hour ago, we came up with human remains."

Jonah shoved a hand through his hair. "Can you identify them?"

"No, the victim died a year or more ago. What's left of her is on its way to the morgue. We should know more tomorrow, once the coroner's had a chance to take a look. But what do you want to bet it's Julia?"

"How'd you find Dean?" Francesca asked.

"He called home, and Butch got in touch with Hunsacker."

Jonah massaged his left temple. "Butch is the one who turned him in?"

"After we found that blood, he realized what his brother-in-law was and became very cooperative."

"I…see," Jonah said.

"You don't sound too excited," Finch complained.

"I'm not convinced he's the killer we're looking for."

"What?" Irritation suffused the investigator's voice.

"None of the evidence conclusively rules out Butch."

"Because we're still processing it all. Give us time."

"Does that mean you'll keep an eye on him in the interim?"

"Come on! We have a lot less on him than Dean!"

Hands in his pockets, Jonah began to pace. "A freezer showing traces of blood was found on his property."

"Because of Dean."

"You sure about that? If Dean's the one killing women, how's he getting their bodies to Dead Mule Canyon? And how did he dig up and move April Bonner's body without a vehicle? I doubt he took her corpse on the bus."

"Stranger things have happened," Finch replied. "For all we know, he stole Butch's truck."

"Without Butch being aware of it?"

"He could find a way."

"That might be true," Francesca conceded, "but... Dean doesn't seem that resourceful."

Finch heard her. "He doesn't? He can pick any lock in existence. If that's not resourceful, I don't know what is. Anyway, it's been a long day, I'm exhausted, and now I'm sorry I took the time to notify you. I thought we'd finally be on the same page, but... Never mind. I have to go. I've got a lot still to do."

"Wait a second." Jonah stopped him before he could hang up. "You said there was blood in the freezer."

"That's right."

"So where did you find the remains?"

"Same place we found Dean. At a cabin in the Juniper Mountains."

Jonah's eyes met Francesca's. *"The Schultz cabin?"*

A shocked silence followed, then Finch asked, "How do you know about the Schultz cabin?"

"I hired a security guard to watch the salvage yard last night. He saw Butch put a black garbage bag filled with something in the back of his truck. He drove it up to that cabin. When he came home, the bag was gone. I was there all day, looking for it."

"Why is this the first time I'm hearing about it?" Finch demanded.

"Because you haven't been returning our calls, for one!"

Finch cursed. "I don't know why I'm getting upset. It doesn't matter. That business about Butch driving to the cabin doesn't necessarily mean anything."

"Are you kidding?" Jonah said. "Why would Butch drive a black garbage bag into the Juniper Mountains in the middle of the night?"

"Because he was looking for Dean."

"And the black bag?"

"Could've been garbage. That's what black bags are generally used for. Wait until you see some of the other stuff we uncovered on the property. Most of it can be attributed to Dean, like a notebook full of macabre drawings of skeletons and cadavers. Dean's fascinated with death."

News of the drawings, which fit so closely with what her father had relayed, made Francesca question whether they were just being obstinate in thinking it had to be Butch.

"Tell me about the remains," Jonah said. "What were they in? Where were they found?"

"They were in the cellar, in a black bag, but that doesn't mean it's the same bag your guy saw in Butch's truck," he was quick to explain.

"You have to admit it's a major coincidence," Jonah insisted.

"I'll give you that much. But black bags are so common that one coincidence isn't enough to override all the other evidence."

"The drawings?"

"And the letters. And Butch's testimony about his brother-in-law spending a lot of time where we found the freezer. And Francesca's testimony about him breaking into her house. We also have his computer. Once we go through his files, who knows what we'll find?"

"I hope you're right."

"You don't sound like you hope anything of the sort. You already have your mind made up about Butch. Even though we found the remains in the cellar."

"So?"

"Did you check the cabin? Was it locked?"

"Yes."

"If it was Butch who put that bag there, how could he have gotten in? Dean's the one who can pick any lock in existence. He even had a set of lock picks on him. That, if anything, should put your mind at ease. If Butch was the one who took those remains up there, he would've found the cabin locked up, just like you did."

"Unless he's the one who locked it in the first place," Francesca said.

"Oh, come on," Finch snapped. "That cabin's a vacation rental. How would Butch have a key? Dean's got to be our man."

"Possibly." Jonah sounded unconvinced, and Francesca felt equally torn.

"Hang on a sec," Finch said. "Hunsacker's trying to talk to me."

They heard voices but couldn't make out any words until Finch came back on the line. "Dean just confessed."

"To what, *exactly?*" Francesca asked.

"To killing Julia," Finch replied. "He admits it was her remains in that freezer."

"Did he also confess to the other murders?" Jonah wanted to know.

Finch checked with Hunsacker again. "Not yet. But we'll get him on those, too. We have plenty of time. I'll talk to you tomorrow," he said, and hung up.

Francesca watched Jonah hit the end button and toss

his phone on the desk. "They have letters, a bloody freezer, human remains. They even have a confession."

"Then it must be Dean."

He nodded. "Has to be."

So why couldn't she accept that? Why did she feel so apprehensive?

Because she was a skeptic. And she'd always had a hard time admitting she was wrong. "So we can relax, let Finch and Hunsacker finish up."

Jonah framed her face with his hands. "Why not? Last I heard we were kicked off the case. And I have the only woman I've ever really loved right here."

She smiled at his statement but, just in case they were doing Jill and Vince a disservice, she had to voice her concerns. "He could've figured out a way to move April's body. He might be mentally ill, but that doesn't mean he can't overcome obstacles."

Tilting up her chin, he kissed her lightly on the lips. "I can't argue with you there."

"It's interesting that Butch is the one who turned him in, though."

Another kiss, this one deeper, told her he preferred to be distracted. "According to Finch, he didn't believe his brother-in-law was guilty until they found the blood."

That made sense, but… She put her hands on his chest to stop him so she could think clearly. "What about that line, the one that was repeated so often in Dean's letters?"

Jonah hadn't read the letters, but she'd told him about them while they were on the phone. "'I wish I could've protected you from Butch'?"

She could feel the beat of his heart through his shirt and relished the freedom to touch him again. Although she and Jonah hadn't discussed the future, she knew he'd be part of hers, that what had happened here would change their lives. The details would be difficult to share with Adriana. But she didn't want to think about the moment when she'd have to come face-to-face with the reason they'd been apart. She had Jonah with her now. That was all that mattered. "You remember it word for word, which means you think it's significant, too."

"We talked about this, remember?" Removing her hands, he bent forward to kiss her again. "You said yourself that he might blame Butch for inciting him."

When Jonah cupped her breasts, she wanted to experience everything he could make her feel, but her doubts made her resist. Why did Butch drive to the Schultzes' cabin? Knowing what she did of him, Francesca couldn't believe he'd done it to help Dean, or even to assist the police in capturing him. What Jonah's security guard had seen was a loose thread....

She opened her mouth to say this, but Jonah held a finger to her lips. "They have a confession, Fran."

Her arousal made her feel tipsy. "Maybe Dean's confused and Butch is taking advantage of that."

"Stop," he whispered, and his lips moved across her cheek to her ear and then her neck. "We have better things to do than poke holes in Finch's case. Let's go home."

The way Jonah touched her was the perfect balance between familiarity and exploration, and she loved how he kissed. Why not let go, as he suggested, and simply enjoy the physical expression of what they felt? Perhaps the investigators would reveal more damning evidence in the morning, evidence that would support Dean's confession and eliminate their doubts.

With that hope in mind, she allowed Jonah to lead her out to their cars. But as she got behind the wheel and he followed her home, she considered what Dean had said when he was standing in her bedroom last night. He'd talked about his mother. Elaine's connection to anything that had happened still wasn't clear. And he'd pointed a finger at his brother-in-law. *I'm not going to kill you. Whether you die is up to Butch.* He's *the murderer.*

Had he been passing the buck—or telling the truth?

31

The second time they made love was far less reverent and far more passionate than the first. It was almost as if they were trying to make up for every fear, every hurt, every longing. The past faded, and so did the details of the case. Only Jonah existed in this new universe, yet Francesca felt that everything was finally as it should be.

"I missed you," he murmured, pulling her close as they were about to fall asleep. "God, how I missed you."

She touched his face, traced his lips with her finger. "Then I take it you're the one who put every picture I have of Roland Perenski facedown?"

He chuckled. "You saw that?"

"We weren't home ten minutes before those pictures disappeared."

"I can't stand the guy."

"You don't even know him," she said, laughing.

"I hate that I let him take my place, that I wasn't the one to travel with you to Washington, D.C., and everywhere else you went."

She played with his hair, letting the locks fall through her fingers. "I never loved him," she admitted. "As hard as I tried, I *couldn't* love him. That's why we broke up."

He rolled over and rested his head on her chest. "Why do you think you couldn't love him?"

She stopped touching him and simply stared at what she could see of his face in the dark. "Because I never stopped loving you." That was a frightening confession, one she'd been loath to make, even to herself, but it was true.

Slumping onto the pillows, he grew silent and Francesca sensed that his mood had become slightly morose.

"That makes you unhappy?" she said.

"No." He took her hand, kissed her fingers. "It makes me want to explain what life was like for me when we first met, but…I'm hesitant to bring it up."

She noticed that the storm outside had quieted. "Tell me."

"You asked, at the motel, about the secret I keep for my ex-wife."

"Lori."

"Yes."

She sat up. "And now you're going to tell me?"

He leaned against the headboard. "I'm thinking about it."

Francesca wanted him to trust her enough, to be able to say *anything,* but she also feared how she might react, considering the problems they'd had in the past. Had he been in love with Lori when he claimed to be in love with her? Was he still carrying a torch for his ex? He'd never even hinted at such a thing—the exact opposite, in fact—but her fears suggested the worst. And he was obviously uncomfortable about what he had to reveal. "She broke your heart?"

"It was more that she shattered my confidence."

"By…"

"She left me for someone else, someone she'd been seeing all along."

Francesca could understand why he might be reluctant to delve into this, given his own indiscretion with Adriana, and became even uneasier about hearing it. She'd just forgiven him. They were trying to start over. Why dredge up all the negative feelings?

On the other hand, maybe it was time for him to talk—and for her to listen, with her heart open instead of closed, as it had been for the past ten years. "So... you decided to pass along the hurt by doing the same thing?"

"No. I panicked."

"You told me you loved me."

"I did. That was the problem."

"I don't understand."

Judging by the pause that followed, he was collecting his thoughts.

"Lori left me for a woman, Fran," he said at length. "She's a lesbian, was then, too, and somehow that made the end of our marriage so much more...complicated."

Francesca blinked in surprise. This was the last thing she'd expected, probably because she was so attracted to Jonah she couldn't imagine a woman choosing another man over him, let alone another woman. But she kept her mouth shut.

"I told myself it shouldn't matter whether it was a man or a woman. Someone else was someone else," he continued. "But...I was young and immature, and not only was I hurt, I was humiliated and embarrassed. I couldn't even tell my closest friends. She'd asked me not to for fear word would get back to her family. They still don't know the woman she's living with is anything more than a roommate from college."

At this point, Francesca *had* to interrupt. "How could they miss it?"

"I'm sure denial plays a role. And they have her marriage to me to prove otherwise."

"Why would you be duty-bound to keep her secret? After what she did to you, you certainly didn't owe her that."

"I told myself to take the high road. Or maybe I was just protecting my ego. Who knows? It was hard enough that my marriage had failed, especially after such a short time. What guy wants to admit losing his wife to another woman?" The muscles in his arms and chest flexed as he adjusted his position. "Anyway, I preferred to forget her, my marriage, the whole thing, as quickly as possible. And I thought I'd done that. I'd moved from Mesa to Phoenix, had met you, was no longer remotely in love with her. But...I couldn't seem to get over the rejection I'd experienced. I think now that I sabotaged our relationship so I wouldn't have to face how much I cared."

"I'm glad you explained." Smiling, Francesca reached for him, but he held her off.

"There's more," he said. "And this will probably be harder to hear."

"Do we have to go into it now?" she asked. "Can't it wait until...until we're stronger?"

"No. It wouldn't be fair to put this off. You need to know because—" he shoved a hand through his hair "—because it'll be big, especially for you, and it won't change."

Drawing her knees up to her chest, Francesca nibbled on her bottom lip. "Okay...then I guess I'm as ready as I'll ever be."

"The daughter I had with Adriana..."

Instinctively tightening her clasp on her knees, Francesca drew a nervous breath. "What about her?"

"I don't exactly have a relationship with her. Not yet. Her adoptive parents don't allow me much, just a few pictures here and there. But, financially, at least, she's part of my life. She'll always be part of my life. And when she turns eighteen and is able to choose for herself, I'm hoping she'll want to know me."

Francesca wasn't sure how to respond. She felt proud of Jonah for caring about his child, for hanging on when it would've been so much easier to walk away. She also felt selfishly angry. She shouldn't have to deal with this. She hadn't caused the problem, and yet, if she stayed with Jonah, it would affect her life, too. His daughter was nine years old. Eighteen wasn't that far away.

He lowered his voice. "I can't turn my back on her, Fran," he said. "Not even for you. Because it would be denying who I am. *I'm* the reason she's here in this world. I should take responsibility for her, give her all I can."

Francesca waved for him to stop talking. "You don't have to explain. I get what you're saying, but…"

"You can't live with it?" He sounded afraid her answer might be yes.

"I don't know," she admitted. "I honestly don't know."

The old-fashioned alarm clock her father had given her as a child ticked loudly in the silence. She'd had that clock for so long. It reminded her of the steadiness of her family, the fear they'd feel for her if they learned she was getting involved with Jonah again.

"Right," he said at length. "I won't push you. Just… tell me what you decide, okay?"

She rested her chin on her knees. "Do you think love

is enough?" she asked. "Do you think it can conquer even this?"

"That's what I'm waiting to find out. Come here." He coaxed her to him but didn't attempt to kiss her or touch her intimately. Spooning her as they settled down to sleep, he whispered one more time that he was sorry, and she believed him. It wasn't his contrition she doubted. It was her ability to handle what the future might hold. Could she live with a constant reminder of Jonah's betrayal, one that came in the form of another completely innocent person she didn't even have the right to resent? Someone who deserved as much of his love and support as she did?

She told herself to let the dilemma go, for the moment, that she'd figure it out in the morning. But sleep wouldn't come. One minute slipped into the next and still she worried about how she'd deal with a situation that included not only Adriana but Adriana and Jonah's child. Would there be a day when she'd blame Jonah for the fact that she couldn't handle it? Or was her heart big enough to accept a daughter whose conception had caused her more pain than she'd ever experienced before?

"It's your father."

Groggy from lack of sleep, Francesca struggled to reclaim her faculties. Jonah had gotten up earlier. When he left her bed, she'd almost stopped him. She'd wanted to continue to snuggle against his warmth, to sleep in his arms, but with so much undecided between them, she'd refrained. She didn't know where he'd gone—to make calls, read the paper, go on the computer—but he was back, freshly showered and handsome as ever, standing over her with her cell phone.

When she belatedly grasped what he'd said, she

scrambled into a sitting position and whipped out her hand. "You didn't answer it, did you?"

Jonah scowled. Obviously, he realized that she didn't want her father to know they were seeing each other. "I didn't need to. His name's on your screen."

Francesca would've explained that they had to deal with her family carefully, that it might take time for the Morettis to forgive him as she had. But what was the point of explaining, or speaking to her parents about him, until she was sure they had a chance of making it? There was no time for explanations, anyway. She didn't want to miss her father's call. He'd given her a lot of valuable information before. She hoped he'd have more this time around, something that would convince her Finch had put the right man behind bars.

Pushing her sleep-tangled hair out of her face, she ignored Jonah's "thanks for treating me like your dirty little secret" reaction and hit the answer-call button. "Hello?"

"There you are," her father said. "After that many rings, I expected voice mail."

"No, I'm here. Sorry for the delay. I got in late last night and—and overslept this morning."

"What's going on?"

"They arrested Dean Wheeler." He didn't know Dean had come after her, that the police had searched the salvage yard, that they'd found blood. But he knew Dean's old girlfriend had gone missing.

"A few days ago, I would've applauded that move," he said.

"And now?"

"Now that I've done more research, I feel it was unlikely Bianca Andersen ever knew Dean."

Because of Jonah's gaze on her breasts, she became

conscious of her nudity and pulled up the blankets. She wanted him as much as ever, but…she was trying not to let that be the deciding factor in her future. "How do you explain that she worked at the mental hospital where he was committed on three different occasions?" she asked her father.

"She didn't start at that hospital until almost a month after he was released the second time. And she was on vacation when he was admitted the third."

"The *entire* two weeks?"

"The entire two weeks. She always arranged her vacation schedule to be off in December."

"There could be some other way their paths crossed."

"I've been in touch with her husband. The Andersens never lived anywhere close to the salvage yard, haven't ever been over there. She didn't frequent that bar you told me about, the Pour House. Her husband wasn't even familiar with the name. If she and Dean met, it had to be a chance encounter. We might be able to prove that *if* we managed to run across someone who saw them together. But there's no foolproof method of establishing it otherwise, which is why I call it unlikely."

He was always so precise. "'Unlikely' is a step in the right direction, I guess," she said. That wasn't as definitive as she'd hoped it would be, but it was worth mentioning to Finch, worth double-checking to see if they could find some other connection.

"Butch, on the other hand…" her father went on.

Unsure whether she'd heard correctly, Francesca gripped the blanket tighter. "Did you say Butch?"

"I did."

Jonah sat on the bed beside her, and she leaned over to share the phone. "But you told me last time that you *weren't* able to establish a link between Butch and Bianca."

"I told you I was still working on it. And what I came across is definitely curious."

"What is it?"

"They lived at the same rent-by-the-week motel for almost three months."

Francesca's pulse quickened. "Where was her husband?"

"She hadn't met him yet. She was dating Butch."

Dating Butch? That was more than a chance encounter. "I can't believe it. How did you find out?"

"I realized it was unlikely that Butch had learned about the job at the salvage yard while living in Phoenix, which meant he'd probably moved to Prescott before interviewing there. And if that was the case, he would've had to stay somewhere. It wasn't as if he had family or any history in the area. He was drifting. So I called all the hotels and motels in Prescott. Given his size, he's distinctive. The manager of the Desert Oasis remembered him. He also remembered Bianca, because she was such a free spirit, as he put it. He said he used to catch her skinny-dipping in the pool."

Francesca adjusted the blankets to keep them from slipping. "Was Butch already in contact with the Wheelers? Is there any way he could've introduced Bianca to Dean?"

"No. I called and asked a librarian in Prescott to check the microfiche for me. He found the ad. Going by the date of the paper, it wasn't placed when Butch first came to town, so I'm guessing he was doing odd jobs for cash. According to the motel manager, he moved into the salvage yard after the Wheelers hired him, into a little apartment off the office."

"The manager knew this?"

"Butch bragged about the compensation package, which included room and board."

That apartment off Butch's office was most likely where Julia had lived when they'd taken her in. Francesca had seen it. "And Bianca never went out there to visit him?"

"They'd broken up by then. Apparently, the day they split was memorable, too. The manager said he'd never seen such a terrible fight. He almost called the cops. They were both out of control, screaming and throwing things. It took him and three other tenants to break it up. At that point, Butch got in his car and drove off. A few days later, he landed the job at the salvage yard and moved out."

"Don't tell me. That fight was over another woman," Francesca said.

"You got it. The manager heard Bianca yelling about some lingerie Butch had purchased for the young lady next door. She'd found the receipt in one of his pockets."

Francesca let Jonah hold the phone for them. "But why, after several years, would he kill her?"

"Maybe he tried to rekindle the romance and she rebuffed him. Or they had an affair and she threatened to tell his wife. Who can say? I only know she had a lot of very personal contact with Butch, but I can't prove she even knew Dean."

"You're amazing, Dad. I can't tell you how much I appreciate this."

"I like doing it. Keeps me fresh."

Jonah was so close. It would've been easy to melt into him, but Francesca resisted. "And it gives you a good excuse to skip out on antique hunting with Mom."

He chuckled. "That, too."

"Any chance you'd like to see what you can find out about a seventeen-year-old runaway from California named Julia? I'm having trouble digging up a last name. She went to work for the Wheelers, lived with them for a bit—"

"—and now she's missing and likely dead."

"That's right."

"I'll get on it," he said, and hung up before she could thank him again.

Jonah hadn't heard the first part of the conversation. "What'd I miss?" he asked.

"I'll explain in the car. We've got to talk to Dean."

He climbed off the bed without touching her. "You shower and dress. I'll make breakfast."

Finch and Hunsacker refused to let them see Dean. Jonah managed to arrange it only by going over their heads to the sheriff, who ultimately agreed to the interview because of how bad the department would look if they prosecuted the wrong guy. Although Jonah prevailed in the end, Finch had insisted on being present. He made his displeasure obvious as he sat in the corner, glowering, while Jonah and Francesca took chairs across a small table from a bewildered and sleep-deprived Dean.

They'd also asked if Dean would like an attorney to join them. He hadn't been at the yard when his family invoked that right. But his mother was still trying to select one she felt would be good, and he didn't want to wait. According to Finch, all he could talk about was going home. He wouldn't insist on anything he felt might delay that.

"Wh-what's going on?" Dean asked. "What are you guys doing here?"

Jonah deferred to Francesca. Knowing Dean's relationship with his mother was a close one, he felt Dean might be more responsive to a female.

"We'd like to visit with you, Dean," she said. "You don't mind, do you?"

Dean sat on his hands. "I wasn't going to hurt you, Francesca. I—I was only doing what I was told. I had to get the panties back."

Jonah wasn't so sure he wouldn't have hurt her, but neither was he convinced that Dean was the Dead Mule Canyon killer.

"Who told you to come to my house?" she asked.

Clamping his mouth shut, he ducked his head and began to rock back and forth like a fidgety little boy, making Jonah fear he might lapse into a psychotic episode.

"Dean?" she pressed. "Will you answer me?"

"I can't."

She bent to see his face. "Why not?"

"I—I can't tell you that, either," he mumbled.

"We're trying to help you. You understand that, don't you?" Jonah said.

"No." His sulky response was also childlike.

"It's true," Francesca said. "If you don't talk, I'm afraid you'll go to prison. You don't want to go to prison, do you?"

"No." His voice broke, and tears ran down his face.

"Then you need to explain exactly what happened the day you came to my place. Who sent you there?"

"I can't tell you."

"Why not?"

He dashed a hand across his cheek. "I don't want my mother dragged into this."

"Unless your mother's hurt someone, she'll be

fine," Francesca said. "She hasn't hurt anyone, has she, Dean?"

He finally met her eyes. "No. My mother would never hurt anyone."

Francesca smiled. "That's what I thought, too."

Obviously relieved by her friendliness, he sniffed. "So...you believe me?" Dean glanced in Jonah's direction as if to confirm it. "I can go home?"

"I'm afraid not," Jonah said. "Not yet. Someone's killed at least nine women. Julia is one of them, but there are others."

"How many others?" he asked.

If he'd done it, he'd already have that information, and Jonah didn't get the impression he was faking. "That's one of the things we're hoping to find out."

"I don't know about anyone else, except...except that woman Butch had dinner with. The one *she* was looking for when she first came to the yard," he said with a jerk of his head to indicate Francesca.

"April?" Francesca clarified.

"Yeah, her."

Jonah had to admit he seemed sincere. "You told Investigator Hunsacker—"

Puzzled, Dean broke in. "Who?"

Jonah pointed to Finch. "You see that man right there? You told his partner, Investigator Hunsacker, that you killed Julia."

"No." Dean shook his head. "They...they wouldn't leave me alone until I signed their papers. But I told them it wasn't me."

Finch jumped to his feet as if to argue, but Jonah motioned for him to sit down and, fortunately, he acquiesced. "So you didn't confess?"

"I told them I went to Francesca's house and...and I

picked her locks. I'm good at that. I can get in anywhere."
He seemed reluctant to look at her. "I know it's not nice,
but…I'm good at it," he repeated. "I also told them Julia
was the one in the freezer. But I don't know how she got
to the cabin. I didn't take her there."

"Maybe someone else did," Francesca suggested.

"Yes!" His eyes focused, grew more lucid. "It had to
be Butch. He copied the key when we rented the cabin
last Christmas so we could go up there whenever we
wanted. And he told me to wait there. He must've done
it. He killed her, 'cause he knew she couldn't stay in the
yard if you still had her panties."

Francesca scooted forward. "Did you see him kill
her?"

"No. You asked me that before." He acted as if he
suspected a trick.

"Then you saw him put her body in the freezer?"
Jonah asked.

"I didn't see that, either. I used to keep my books and
drawings there, but I found them in the trash pile so I
went to see what happened to the freezer. It was running,
although it wasn't before. And my key wouldn't unlock
the padlock. It was easier to cut it off than try to pick it,
so I did. But when I opened the lid, I found a garbage bag
with Julia inside it." He shivered in revulsion. "I barfed
the first time I opened that bag. I should've protected
her. She was so pretty. And…and nice. Julia was nicer
than Paris. Paris never liked me."

Jonah crossed his ankles. "Who did you feel you
needed to protect Julia from?"

"Quit leading him," Finch interjected from his corner,
but Dean didn't allow him to interrupt. He didn't even
seem to hear it. He was too eager to answer.

"From Butch! He's a monster."

"What about Sherrilyn?" Francesca asked. "Can you tell us what happened to her?"

"I don't know. She was fine until she came to the yard to—to wish me happy birthday. We'd been fighting. But…she was sorry. She said she was sorry."

Francesca picked up her purse from the floor and placed it on the table. "You saw her there? Spoke to her?"

"Yes."

"Could you be wrong about that?"

His eyebrows knitted. "No. Paris saw her, too. So did Butch and my mother. Sherry said I'm the only man who's ever really loved her and it wasn't fair of Neal to break us up. We were miserable without each other. We were going to get back together."

"Where did she go after that?"

"Home, I guess. How would I know?"

Jonah changed up the interview with an easy question. "Neal's her son?"

"That's right. He's not very nice. He—he doesn't want his mother to love me. He wants her all to himself."

Had Sherrilyn really shown up at the salvage yard? She had a restraining order against Dean, and she'd just been through that terrible experience caused by his stalking and death threats. But she wouldn't be the first to go back to someone she knew might hurt her. "Was this after you went to her house and threatened to kill her?" Jonah asked.

"I didn't say I was going to kill her! I said I'd rather we were both dead than apart. I loved her!"

Francesca jumped back in. "What about Bianca Andersen? Did you love her, too?"

The name distracted him. "Who?"

"Bianca Andersen. She was a nurse at Laurel Oaks. You recognize Laurel Oaks, don't you?"

"Of course. I've been there. Three times."

At least he was capable of remembering correctly. Jonah thought that lent him *some* credibility. "But you don't recall a Bianca?"

"No." He splayed his hands. "I've never heard of her before."

Francesca took a pack of gum from her purse and offered Dean a piece. "Why do you draw what you do, Dean?" she asked.

He studied the gum as if it might bite him, but when she held it closer, he accepted. "I don't know. Because they're…interesting, I guess."

"Have you ever acted out any of those drawings?"

"No!" He responded almost before she could get the words out.

Jonah cleared his throat. "Tell us why you feel you had to protect your mother, Dean."

Although he'd unwrapped the gum, he was too worked up to put it in his mouth. "She told me I *couldn't* tell. She said I had to forget what was in that freezer or it would get her in trouble. Then Butch said I could fix my mistake if I got the panties back."

Francesca set her purse back on the floor. "Butch sent you to my house?"

He crammed the chewing gum in his mouth and spoke around it. "Yes. Because you took the panties." He frowned. "I wish you'd never done that. I wish you were my friend. None of this would've happened."

"This isn't about our friendship," she said. "This is about April and Julia and Sherrilyn and Bianca—"

"I don't know Bianca. I've never even met her. You don't believe me?"

She didn't answer that question. "Why did you put those panties in Butch's truck in the first place?"

"Because I wanted him to get caught. He thinks he can sleep with women, and hurt them, and hurt my sister, and have my parents put up with it, and have me put up with it, and…and get away with anything."

Jonah had to agree with Dean's assessment. Butch was pretty arrogant. "He's the one who told the police you must've killed Julia."

"What?" Dean's tortured eyes shifted to his. "I didn't kill her. I swear it!" Fresh tears pooled along his lower lashes. "Can I talk to my mother? Please? I can't protect her if I don't know how."

"You can't talk to her just yet," Jonah replied. "But we'll speak to her for you, okay?"

He wiped his runny nose with the back of his hand. "Tell her Butch is trying to hurt me. She—she'll stop him. She always does."

32

"What are you two doing here?" Paris stood in the doorway. Defensive from the moment she'd first seen them, she gripped the door as though she might slam it at any second.

Jonah gave Francesca a slight nod, one she interpreted as permission to take the lead on this as she had with Dean's interview. "I have a message from Dean. For your mother," she said.

Paris's eyes cut between them. "She doesn't want to talk to you. Either of you. We…we're getting an attorney. We already told the police that."

Before she could close the door, Jonah stuck his foot in its path. "Why do you need an attorney? I was under the impression that you were now cooperating with the police. I know Butch is."

She smirked. "Don't think you can fool me. I'm not letting you in. Butch isn't even home."

Francesca noticed that Champ wasn't in the yard, either. "Champ go with him?"

"That's none of your business," she snapped. "And don't say my boy's name as if you know him."

"No matter what you think of me, I'm only searching for the truth," Francesca said.

"You don't care about the truth. You've been out to get us from the start."

Francesca shook her head. "No."

Hatred flashed in her eyes. "You're charging my brother with a crime he didn't commit!"

Jonah spoke up. "We believe you about that."

"What?" She gaped at them.

"I said we believe you. So why not tell your mother we're here?"

Confused, she said, "I don't want to, that's why. Now go away. You've caused us nothing but grief. Our dog's dead because of you. Don't think I'll forget that."

Francesca hitched her purse higher on her shoulder. "What about all the women who've been killed, Paris? You care more about a dog than you do about them?"

"Maybe Dean *did* kill them. I don't know. He's a whack job. I'm not responsible for what he does."

"I'm touched by your empathy," Jonah muttered.

She tried to shut the door again. "And I'm calling the cops if you don't get your foot out of the way and leave me alone!"

Francesca scrambled to stop her. "Julia must've been close to your age, Paris. Were you two friends?"

Paris's fingers whitened as she clutched the door, but she lowered her voice. "She was a worker here, that's all. Someone my mom hired. That doesn't mean we had to be close."

"And April Bonner? Did you know her, too?"

"You think I want to talk about all the women my husband slept with? Get out of here, like I said!"

She kicked at Jonah's foot, giving him no choice but to remove it. Anything less could be construed as forcible entry; Finch and Hunsacker hadn't been pleased to learn they were coming out here in the first place.

Paris slammed the door and they started back to the car, but before they could get in, Francesca heard her name.

"Ms. Moretti?"

Elaine Wheeler had come to the door. Francesca turned back. "Yes?"

"You…you have a message for me? From my boy?" Dressed in a flowery summer shirt and what Francesca's mother would call culottes—longish shorts that looked more like a skirt—she could've been taken for a sweet grandma except for the obvious signs of distress. Gone was the wig she normally wore, revealing a few wisps of gray hair pinned tightly to a pink scalp. And red-rimmed eyes peered through cat-eye glasses with bifocal lenses.

"He's scared, Mrs. Wheeler," Francesca said. "He wants you. He wants to come home."

"Are they…are they treating him okay? He needs to be segregated, you know. A man like Dean wouldn't be safe circulating with other inmates. He's…too eager for friends, tries too hard to fit in."

"I'm sure the police will do all they can to protect him, but…until he's convicted and sent to prison, they have limited housing options."

"I realize that." And, apparently, it weighed heavily on her. Her lips quivered, then pursed as Paris's voice rose behind her.

"Come on in, Mom. There's nothing you can do for Dean. Maybe he'll finally get the care he needs."

With a sniff, Elaine raised her chin. "It's *my* care he needs. I'm the one who's always been there for him. I'm the only one he trusts."

Jonah beckoned her outside. "Come and take a ride

with us, Mrs. Wheeler. Maybe we can arrange for you to see your son."

"Don't do it!" Paris cried. "You know Butch told us not to talk to anyone, especially them. He'll handle it."

"Butch doesn't give a damn about Dean, and sometimes I don't think you do, either," her mother said. "Tell your father where I went," she added, and walked to the Jeep Cherokee without bothering to get her purse.

Jonah parked in the shade of a cypress tree at Willow Lake Park. RVs in orderly rows extended to their right, but only a few stalwart golfers walked the adjacent course. It was too hot to be outside for long, even with the sun in rapid descent, but this gave them a quiet place to talk.

"Do you believe your son murdered Julia?" he asked Elaine as he turned off the engine and shifted in his seat to face her.

She stared into the distance.

"Elaine?" Francesca prompted from the backseat.

Lifting her glasses, she dabbed at her eyes. "I know he didn't."

Elaine wanted to talk. She was dying to rescue her son. She'd already spent most of his lifetime doing it. All they had to do was give her the opportunity to speak.

"So…are you willing to let him take the rap for it?" Jonah asked when she didn't say anything.

"That's what Butch thinks we should do."

When she lifted her glasses again, he delved into the jockey box for the napkins he'd stuck there after grabbing some fast food on his way from the airport. "Here you go."

She didn't thank him. She was too immersed in her own worries for that, but she accepted the napkins.

He rolled down the windows. "What do *you* think you should do?"

"Some of what Butch says makes sense. But…I'm not sure I can keep silent. It shouldn't have come to this. It was just a—a terrible accident."

April Bonner's death, and the deaths of those women in Dead Mule Canyon, was no accident, but Jonah held back, hoping she'd feel comfortable enough to reveal what she knew. "If it was an accident we can work it out."

She seemed to forget that Francesca was even in the car. "Can I depend on that?" she asked as if it was just the two of them. "Will the police believe me if I tell the truth?"

"They'll do what they can. No one's out to get anyone here."

Seeming to take solace in his response, she blew her nose. "You already know that Butch likes the ladies."

"That's become apparent, yes."

"When I took Julia in, I had no idea he would…get involved with her. This was before we found out what a womanizer he is. I'm guessing Paris knew, or suspected, but she never came to us with her concerns. She was probably embarrassed or trying to protect him. She loves him. And he is the father of her child. But…"

"But?" Jonah repeated when her words drifted off.

"If she'd confided in me, maybe I wouldn't have been foolish enough to try to help Julia."

Jonah could feel Francesca's interest but was careful not to respond to it. He didn't want to destroy the sense of intimacy that made Elaine feel safe enough to talk. "You can't blame yourself for attempting to do a good deed."

Once again she had to raise her glasses to wipe away

tears. "I felt awful for her," she said. "Julia wasn't a bad person. She was just a kid. Too eager to have her own way, perhaps, like most teenagers. But she didn't mean any harm."

"So they became…intimate?"

"I guess so. Although I didn't sense anything wrong, not until the argument."

Jonah used the electric controls to slide his seat farther back. "What argument?"

"It was late at night. Butch and Paris had been drinking. I could hear it in their voices. Their shouts woke us up, but I tried to ignore the noise. It's not my place to get involved in their marriage. Living in the same house, I have to be very careful to allow them their privacy. But then I heard screaming and knew something was terribly wrong. By the time I could get out of bed and up the stairs, Julia was lying on the cement outside the back door, bleeding from the head."

"Was it Butch?"

"No." She laughed bitterly. "I wouldn't risk Dean for Butch's sake. It was Paris. She'd seen Butch pat Julia's bottom and was certain they were having an affair. She confronted Julia and demanded she move out, but Julia had nowhere to go. She tried to reason with Paris, claimed she hadn't been sleeping with Butch, but Paris couldn't or wouldn't believe it. The argument escalated, and Paris shoved her off the stoop. She landed on a piece of wood with a long nail protruding from it. I think it killed her instantly. She was dead when I reached her."

This "accident" didn't explain what had happened to April Bonner or the other victims, so there had to be more to the story, but Jonah played along. "And you didn't call the police?"

"No. Paris was frantic they'd put her in prison, and I

was afraid of that, too. She'd had a reason to hate Julia, and she'd pushed her." She sniffed, folded her hands in her lap and looked straight ahead as she spoke. "I know how it sounds, but there was a little boy sleeping in the house, my grandson, who needs his mother. I—I couldn't bring myself to turn her over to the authorities. I didn't see any point in her going to prison for a death she didn't mean to cause. I knew how much it would change her, how much it would change all our lives, especially Champ's. And the accident was because of Butch as much as Paris, although he wouldn't be the one punished for it. He shouldn't have been cheating on her." She shook her head. "That girl has been through so much."

"Putting her body in the freezer was better?"

She settled her glasses more firmly on her nose. "We knew that Julia's family weren't likely to come looking for her. Even if they did, we knew they'd believe us if we said she left without telling us where she was going."

"And your husband went along with this?"

"Of course. He agreed with me, even helped. He's her father. He didn't want to see her go to prison any more than I did."

"Why didn't you bury her?"

"We wanted to have easy access in case we ever lost the salvage yard to the bank—there've been some pretty lean years—and we had to move. We couldn't leave that behind for someone else to discover."

"Where was Dean when this occurred?" Francesca asked.

"Out. Like he usually is. Rambling. He didn't know anything about it until he came across the body. And I'm guessing that just happened recently or I would've heard about it before. He thought Butch had killed her, so he put Julia's panties, which he must've taken from her body at some point, in Butch's truck for Paris to find. I think he was hoping to get rid of Butch. Butch has never been very nice to him."

Francesca broke in for the first time. "Will Butch and Paris back up this story—about the accident?"

Elaine Wheeler's voice cooled. "I have no idea. They'll be angry that I put Paris at risk for Dean's sake. For all Butch's cheating, he loves Paris. But like I said, my husband was there that night. He'll tell you what he saw."

"What about Sherrilyn Gators, Mrs. Wheeler?" Jonah asked.

Sweat glistened on her scalp. Jonah was getting hot, too. He needed to start the car, but he didn't want to interrupt the conversation.

"The police already asked about her," she said. "Years ago. And I'll tell you what I told them. The night Dean went to her house and got so upset? That wasn't the last time they saw each other. A few days later, Sherrilyn showed up at the salvage yard in tears and told Dean she hadn't been happy since they split up. She wanted to get back together, said they could work around his problems." Her chest rose as she drew a deep breath. "She only wanted to be loved. Her son had no right to deny her that. Dean was absolutely devoted to her."

Francesca angled her head to see around the seat. "So where did Sherrilyn go?"

Mrs. Wheeler didn't act as though she wanted to talk to Francesca, although she answered. "She had some car trouble, but eventually went home. That's all I know. Dean didn't kill her. He might have his challenges, but he doesn't have a violent bone in his body. That's why I can't sit back and let this happen. It's not right."

Mrs. Wheeler had confirmed what Dean had told them

about Sherrilyn. "His drawings might suggest he at least fantasizes about violence," Jonah said.

"Those drawings don't mean anything. They're a way to vent the anger he feels, a safe way to vent it."

"Is there any chance Sherrilyn knew Butch?" Francesca asked.

"Not well. The day she came to the yard, her car wouldn't start, so he gave her a ride to town and bought her a new battery. But that's it. We were nothing but nice to that woman."

"And Bianca Andersen?"

"I don't know who that is."

"What about April Bonner?"

"I don't know her, either. Look, I've told you everything I know. I've endangered one of my children to save the other, but I'm hoping...I'm hoping there'll be some understanding of what happened and why. Paris didn't mean to kill Julia. I was there. I know. Now...can I please see my son?"

If the coroner backed up Elaine's testimony by establishing that a nail puncture to the head was the cause of death, the police wouldn't have enough evidence to hold Dean. Elaine had just explained why there'd been a body in that old freezer and how it'd gotten there. Jonah guessed the forensics would support what she'd said, exonerating Dean. And the police didn't have any hard evidence tying him to the other murders, either.

"Sure," he said, and started the car.

By four o'clock that afternoon, Dean had been released. Butch remained free. And Paris had been charged with involuntary manslaughter. Her parents were working hard to get her out on bail, and Hunsacker was, of course, doing his best to help them. But because she'd hidden the "accident" for so long, and would've hidden it even longer had events not conspired against her, Francesca believed she'd get the maximum sentence once the case went to trial. Six years in a federal penitentiary wasn't a stiff penalty in this instance, but it was a big chunk of time when you were raising a child. Champ would be close to twelve when she got out. Butch's wife was distraught to think she'd be away from her family for *any* length of time.

After dinner, and before leaving Prescott, Francesca and Jonah had visited Camp Verde Detention Center to see if Paris had anything to say about the other women who'd been murdered. They thought she might be more forthcoming now that she didn't have her own secret to guard anymore. But their attempt hadn't succeeded. Paris had alternately railed at them for being the reason she'd been arrested and pleaded with them for their help, but she'd revealed nothing new or hopeful.

Francesca felt sorry for her but was frustrated at the same time. Paris insisted Butch wouldn't have killed a single person, that it had to be Dean if it was anyone at the salvage yard. But she could offer no firsthand account or other proof, and Francesca felt she had to know *something,* had to wonder about a particular night or a particular woman. Paris hadn't even given them a list of the women she believed her husband had slept with so Francesca could check on their whereabouts, although Paris had obviously known about several of them.

Bottom line, other than solving one murder out of a possible ten, Paris's incarceration did little to advance the overall investigation. What about April and the other victims who had some connection, if only a circumstantial one, to Butch? They hadn't died accidentally, like Julia.

"We'll figure it out," Jonah said, covering her hand with his own as he drove them back to Chandler.

Francesca felt a measure of relief. She knew she should probably resist the comfort he offered, at least until she could sort out the questions that stood between them, but it was too easy to succumb. She enjoyed his company, enjoyed his touch. Somehow, she told herself, they'd make it work.

"I hope so," she said, and wove her fingers through his.

Then she leaned against the door and drifted off to sleep, only to be awakened by Jonah saying, "We've got company."

33

Adriana was sitting on the patio, waiting for Francesca to come home. Her eyes flicked over Jonah as he got out of the car. Francesca couldn't miss that, even in the dark, because she'd been watching for it, and it upset her. She didn't want to be suspicious, didn't want to constantly expect the worst, especially when it came to her best friend.

"You haven't been answering my calls," Adriana said, getting up as they approached.

Grateful for any distraction, Francesca opened her purse and began to search for her house keys. She could feel Jonah's warmth directly behind her, felt him place his hand at the small of her back. It was a gesture of support. Or he was trying to tell Adriana he was taken. But as far as Francesca was concerned, he should've delivered that message loud and clear ten years ago. "I've been busy."

"That's all?"

"And maybe I didn't want to talk to you," she admitted, her head still bent over her purse.

Adriana's voice grew tight. "That's what you want? You're choosing him over me?"

Francesca's statement had clearly provoked Adriana,

but Francesca didn't care. She *wanted* to provoke her. She was just so…angry again. "You chose him over me first, remember? That night you took advantage of the opportunity you'd been waiting for all along? He was my boyfriend, Adriana. My. Boyfriend!"

"Francesca, take it easy." His voice soft, Jonah caught her elbow. He was making an effort to calm her before she said or did something she'd regret, but she couldn't seem to quell the desire to lash out.

"Whatever you do, *don't* stick up for her," she snapped.

He lifted his hand. "I'm not sticking up for her. I love you. I have always loved you. But I don't want to cost you your best friend. That would just hurt you again, and I've already done enough."

She rounded on him. "So…what does that mean? If we stay together, I'll have to associate with her *and* the child you two created?"

He blanched as if she'd slapped him. It was only last night that he'd begged her forgiveness and she'd granted it. She'd been sincere in that moment, hadn't she? She'd told him so with her body, when they'd made love right afterward. So what was she doing now? Taking it all back?

God, it was too much. The stress of the investigation. The fear that loving Jonah would only result in more pain. The doubt that they'd be able to overcome the past. Especially now that she knew Adriana's betrayal had been far more purposeful than she'd ever indicated before…

Finally locating her keys, Francesca opened the door and stepped inside, blocking them both out. "I need to be alone."

She could feel Jonah's confusion. It matched her own.

But she didn't want to be responsible for how he felt, didn't want to be the one in the wrong.

Tears streaked Adriana's face. "Francesca, I—"

Francesca refused to look at her. "Please, don't apologize. I'm tired of *sorry*. I just want to be able to forget."

A muscle twitched in Jonah's cheek. "Will that ever be possible?"

Fighting tears of her own, Francesca closed her eyes. "I guess not. Maybe it's better if I don't have any more to do with either one of you," she said, and shut the door.

Jonah dropped his head. This was exactly what he'd been afraid of, what he'd tried to avoid by going back to California. Instead of staying there, however, and letting the police take care of business here, he'd returned to Arizona and to Francesca. He'd allowed his hopes to rise, recommitted himself to the relationship and...and now *this*.

"She's still in love with you," Adriana said.

Jonah had all but forgotten she was standing next to him. He'd been too busy recalling Francesca's unhappy expression as she closed the door in his face to notice or care about anything else. "Love isn't the problem. It never was." The problem was fear. Fear had caused the first breakup and would likely cause the second.

Adriana wiped her eyes. "Maybe love's not the problem, but it's the solution, right?"

He looked over at her. "Is it? She asked me last night if love was enough. I wanted to believe it was. Now I'm beginning to wonder."

"If you give up this easily, you don't love her as much as you think you do," she said, then started walking away.

"What are you going to do about…you and her?" he asked.

She turned to face him. "I'm going back to my family to do what I should've done a long time ago. I'm going to face the fact that you've never cared about me, forgive myself for loving you even though I shouldn't have and be grateful for the people who do care about me. I don't deserve Francesca's friendship, but if she ever gets to the point where she can handle having both of us in her life…and if you do, too…you know where to find me."

Was she really walking away? If so, maybe he and Francesca had a chance. Suddenly, he had more respect and admiration for Adriana than ever before. "Adriana?"

She stopped. "Yeah?"

"Thanks."

Wearing a sad smile, she nodded. "Make it worth it to me and…be happy together."

Jonah stood at Francesca's door long after Adriana was gone. He wanted to knock, to tell her he *did* believe love was enough. They could make sure of it if they were equally committed. But he hesitated to push her too far, too fast. Now that Adriana had stepped aside, he felt they might have a shot, a true second chance, and he decided to give Francesca the time and space she needed to work through her own doubts.

In other words, he was going to have the faith he should've had in her from the very beginning.

Hunsacker was calling. Did he have to answer?

Butch stared at the investigator's number displayed on the base of his cordless phone, which also provided the time. It was still early, only eight in the morning and, while he was usually at work by seven, the past twenty-four hours had been hell on him and everyone else in the family. With Elaine turning Paris in to rescue Dean, there had been and would continue to be so much tension in the house Butch didn't see how they could go on living together. But he'd figure out what to do about that later, once he'd had a chance to rebound from the shock and the upset. He was just glad he'd taken Champ to a friend's house yesterday. It helped to know his son had no clue what was going on and was probably playing happily at Joey's. It also helped that Paris was home and sleeping next to him. Because he had Hunsacker to thank for getting her out of jail so quickly, he forced himself to take the phone out of the room so he wouldn't wake her and hit the answer button.

"What's up, Hugh?" He kept his voice low as he made his way down the hall to the kitchen.

"Sorry to bother you so early, Butch. I know you can't be happy to hear from me. But thanks to the forensic anthropologist we've had working around the clock, we've been able to identify some of the remains found in Dead Mule Canyon."

Butch breathed a sigh of relief as he put on some coffee. All his secrets had been laid bare. He had nothing more to hide, so he didn't really care what they learned about those victims. He had his own problems to worry about, like who he was going to hire to represent Paris and how he'd pay a good attorney if they were still at odds with her folks. "What do you need from me?"

"I'd like to run the names past you to see if you've ever heard of these women. Maybe Dean associated with one or more of them at some point."

Butch sank into a chair to wait for his caffeine fix. The way Dean traveled around at night, Butch thought he might've killed those women. It wasn't as if anyone had been watching over him. Dean certainly gravitated toward female companions when he had the chance, craving their attention and their love. Unlike Butch, his preoccupation didn't seem to be sexual in nature, but he was definitely looking for someone who'd be as good to him as his mother. And knowing Paris would likely go to prison because of Elaine made Butch more than willing to cooperate. "I'll do what I can."

"Great. Thanks." Papers rustled on the other end of the line. "One woman, a twenty-eight-year-old white waitress from Prescott Valley, was named Venice O'Cleary. You ever heard of her?"

Butch knew Venice. He'd slept with her. They'd had a brief fling after he'd met her while having breakfast at the Golden Griddle. He'd even given her a hundred bucks to help her pay the rent one month. After that she'd never answered his calls, but he hadn't been all that interested in her, hadn't tried to reach her more than three or four times.

"Butch?"

Feigning preoccupation, Butch cleared his throat. "Sorry about that. I got…distracted. What was the name again?"

"Venice O'Cleary." Hunsacker repeated the information about her age and where she'd worked, too.

"Never heard of her."

"What about Wanda Erickson?"

"No," Butch said, but he'd had to stifle a gasp.

"She was a bit older, almost thirty-five," Hunsacker was saying. "She came from Nevada, where she worked in a brothel for a few years. She called herself a masseuse once she hit Arizona, but she might've been selling sexual favors along with her back rubs. Do you know if

Dean ever frequented massage parlors, ever talked about one or mentioned a woman named Wanda?"

Was this some sort of nightmare? Butch knew Wanda, too! Three or four years ago, he'd spotted her massage sign hanging outside the quaint little house she'd rented near old town and stopped in for whatever he could get—and always came away very happy. She was clean and she worked cheap. She also knew how to be professional. He'd made her place a regular stop whenever he had a few bucks in his pocket and the excuse of errands to run. The last time he'd tried to visit, however, he'd bumped into the owner of the house, who'd told him she'd cleared out. He'd assumed she headed back to Nevada to be with her sick mother. He'd never dreamed she'd gone missing or…been *killed*. What had happened to her things? Her family must have come for them. The landlord hadn't mentioned anything being left behind.

"No," he hurried to say, before Hunsacker could prod him again. "I've never heard Dean mention a Wanda."

"Besides Bianca Andersen, there's one more. We're still working on the last three. Her name was Jane Pew, from Phoenix."

Hunsacker explained a bit about her, too, as he had the others, but Butch wasn't listening. Like April, he'd met Jane via an online dating service. The fact that he'd known, even slept with, every woman who'd been killed was no longer a coincidence.

He'd also known Sherrilyn, he realized. But he hadn't slept with her. If she was dead, she didn't fit the same pattern.

Still…what was going on? Who was murdering these women? Was it that little faggot Dean? Had Dean been following him around, killing any woman he touched?

Why would he care that much? He and Paris had never been close....

"Sorry." It was difficult to talk when he could scarcely breathe, but he had to deny knowing these women, and he had to be convincing. Otherwise, the police would return, and this time they'd take *him* to jail. Anyone would think he was the killer. These women came from different places and different walks of life. Who else could've known them all?

Dean? He couldn't have followed Butch's every move. Sometimes when Butch left the house, Dean was already gone.

Then it occurred to him. *Paris.* Remembering her rage when she caught him grabbing Julia's ass, he stood so fast he knocked over the chair. Maybe what she'd done that night *hadn't* been an accident. Maybe she'd gotten violent because she was used to getting violent...

Drained of strength, he let the phone dangle in his hand. When would she have had the time and opportunity to attack his lovers? How would she have arranged it?

Hoping and praying he was wrong, he tried to calm down, but he couldn't. She must've gone through his phone, his office, his pockets. Checked up on him at every opportunity. Eavesdropped on his conversations. And those P.I.s he thought Kelly's husband had hired? Maybe one or more of them had worked for his own wife. Paris must've met each woman while Champ was in preschool, he decided. Butch couldn't come up with another occasion when she'd be away from the house for any length of time without his knowledge. Except when he was out himself, of course. He was pretty sure she'd picked up April on the highway where he'd left her or someone else would've seen her before she disappeared.

"Butch? You there?"

Hunsacker was still on the phone. What should he do? If he talked, Paris would be taken away from him and Champ for life.

He had to prevent that. It was *his* fault she'd done those terrible things. And he could make her stop. He just had to quit cheating and spend more time with her. Keep an eye on her for a change.

If only you'd quit like you promised….

Who knew how literally she'd meant that?

The image of April's body, described by Hunsacker and Finch, came into his mind. April had been propped out there for all to see. Only someone who hated her, on a very personal level, would do that. The police had said as much. And who would hate her more than Paris?

"Butch?"

"I'm right here." He managed to squeeze each word past the lump in his throat. "I—I wish I could help you, but I haven't heard of any of those women."

"No problem. I knew it was a long shot. Just thought I'd ask. I might bring some pictures by later, if that's okay."

"Of course. Good luck with it." He hung up, then sat staring at nothing. Why hadn't Paris killed Kelly? She'd known about them for weeks.

Maybe she'd tried….

With a surge of purpose, he dialed his ex-girlfriend's cell phone.

"This had better not be who I think it is," she whispered.

"Kelly, listen to me—"

"No, you listen to me," she interrupted. "How dare you

call me again! You said it was over. You said I couldn't contact you, that Paris was on to us, that she meant more to you than I could ever dream of meaning. And now you're crawling back?"

He hadn't been especially kind when he'd broken things off. He'd needed her to realize he was serious about stopping all contact. "I was—" he still couldn't wrap his mind around what he suddenly believed "—just wondering if you've heard from Paris, if she's ever tried to call you."

"Of course she's tried. But I won't pick up. Do you think I'm stupid? What would I say to her? 'Sorry I've been sleeping with your husband'?"

He pressed the phone tighter to his ear. "Has she ever come by your place?"

"She's sat out there, watching the house a time or two. Once she even came to the door. She wanted me to go for a ride with her. Said we needed to talk. But Matt came home right then, and she left."

"Don't go anywhere with her," he said.

"Why not?"

He didn't answer. He'd just thought of something else. There were other women he'd slept with that Paris hadn't killed. Was it because she didn't know about them? Or because, like Kelly, they'd been too careful to let her get that close?

And what about Sherrilyn Gators? She'd gone missing even though he'd never slept with her.

But the day Sherrilyn had come to the house he'd been the one to help her when her car wouldn't start. He'd thought she was attractive enough for a quick fling, but she'd barely spoken to him. She cared about Dean and only Dean. Had Paris taken the fact that he'd replaced her car battery as more than simply the favor it'd turned out to be?

The smell of coffee was making him sick. He had to shut it off. No way could he eat or drink right now.

"What's wrong with you?" Kelly complained. "You're acting like you're…on drugs, spacing out."

She'd been talking to him and he hadn't responded. "Just don't go anywhere with her," he said, and disconnected. He expected Hunsacker to call him back any moment to say they'd identified Sherrilyn's remains. Butch had no doubt she was out there. Somewhere, if not in Dead Mule Canyon. Rotting like the others. All because Paris believed they'd had a sexual encounter.

Why couldn't Paris understand that those women meant nothing to him? They were good for a cheap thrill, nothing more than that.

Actually, now they did mean more. They were dead because of him. And unless he could get Paris to stop, Kelly, or any woman he looked at, smiled at or passed on the street, could be next.

Blotting the sweat on his forehead with a paper towel, he returned to the bedroom. He had to confront his wife, had to hear the details so he could help her. Concealing what she'd done was the only way to save her, the only way to keep his family together. Maybe he'd have to take her and Champ to Mexico. Killing as many people as she had, she'd probably get the death sentence….

He chuckled bitterly. Elaine had no idea what she was doing when she revealed Paris's complicity in Julia's death. Would she have done it if she'd realized? Probably. She wouldn't protect Paris from the consequences of murder. Even Elaine had her limits. But Butch didn't. Someone finally loved him; he would never let anyone take that away.

The door squeaked as it swung open. He stepped inside, then locked it behind him. With the blinds down, it was difficult to see, so he concentrated on the lump in the bedding. "Paris?"

No response.

He sat on the edge of the bed. "Hey, you need to wake up. We have to talk." He didn't want to hear her answers to the questions he had to ask, didn't want her to confirm the worst. But if she denied what she'd done, he knew he wouldn't believe it. He finally understood how deeply angry he'd made her and the lengths to which she'd go to appease that anger. He also knew what she'd done with her time while Champ was in preschool. It wasn't the shopping she'd claimed.

"Paris?" He reached out to nudge her shoulder but the bedding gave way beneath his hand. He'd touched a pillow. She wasn't in bed.

Standing, he whirled around and noticed that her purse, which she'd left on the dresser when he brought her home last night, was gone. Her cell phone was missing, too.

Heart pounding, he rushed to the window and raised the blind. So was the Impala.

34

Francesca didn't usually drink, at least not more than a glass of wine at dinner. Inhibiting her ability to think clearly or move without stumbling seemed counterproductive. She didn't enjoy the blinding headache and cottonmouth of the morning after, either. But she'd gotten drunk last night. That old bottle of tequila Roland had left behind had provided a way to dull the pain of sending both Jonah and Adriana away. A few drinks beat calling her parents, didn't it? She was getting a little old to turn to them whenever she got hurt.

"Maybe calling my parents would've been better," she grumbled as she squinted against the light filtering around the edges of her blinds. It was morning, time to get up and face the day. But the prospect was hardly tantalizing.

Considering how much she hated the taste of tequila, she should've gone to the store for something else. But she hadn't wanted to leave the house at midnight any more than she wanted to leave now.

She was thinking about staying in bed all day when her cell phone rang. Afraid it might be Jonah—she definitely wasn't ready to talk to him, not in this condition—

she supported her pounding head with one hand while reaching for her phone.

She didn't recognize the number.

Curious, she answered, and tried not to sound as under the weather as she felt. "Hello?"

"Francesca? This is Paris."

Stifling a groan, Francesca managed to prop herself up. She couldn't imagine why Paris would be calling her, but she wanted to find out. "What can I do for you?"

"Dean isn't as innocent as he'd like you to believe," she announced.

Had Elaine's choice upset Paris enough that she was now willing to share details about her brother? Something that might break the case?

Regretting her alcohol binge even more, Francesca pressed two fingers to her temple. "Why do you say that?"

"He killed all those women in Dead Mule Canyon. I know he did."

Fortunately, Francesca's high level of interest helped override her physical distress. "How do you know?"

"I have proof."

At this, Francesca scrambled off the bed. But she'd moved too quickly and her vision dimmed to black; she had to double over to avoid passing out. "What kind of proof?"

"I'll show you. Can you meet me?"

"Where?"

"Halfway?"

"You mean somewhere along Interstate 10?"

"No. Dean might be coming to look for me."

Taking a deep breath, she slowly stood. "In what car?"

"He takes my parents' sometimes."

"But what are the chances he'd find you on such a busy thoroughfare?"

"I don't want to risk it. Now that I've got what I got, I'm scared of him. I'd rather he didn't know we've talked. He'll tell my parents, and they may not like it. They've protected him his whole life."

What had she discovered? Physical evidence? "Where, then?"

"I was thinking Wickenburg."

Francesca had never been to Wickenburg, but she'd lived in Arizona long enough to know it was an old mining town. They wouldn't have much trouble meeting each other in such a small place. "Fine. Is there a Starbucks?"

"I'm not sure. I'll call you once I arrive. Then we can pick a more specific location. Are you bringing that guy with you? What's his name?"

"Jonah? No. Do you want me to?"

"I'd rather you didn't. This isn't easy for me. Dean's my brother, after all. It's not like I want a big audience."

"I understand."

"See you soon."

"I'll be there." Tossing her phone aside, Francesca dragged herself to the kitchen, where she downed a couple of painkillers before heading to the bathroom. Once she was out of the shower and dressed, she considered calling Jonah or Finch to let them know about this latest development. But after the way she'd behaved last night she was reluctant to speak to Jonah. It was probably her turn to apologize. And she was afraid calling Finch would blow her rendezvous with Paris. He might mention it to Hunsacker, who'd could pass the information on to Butch, who could act to squash the idea. There was no way he'd want to help *her*.

She decided to call Finch when she had Paris's "proof" in her hands, which would also give her time to figure out how to approach Jonah.

In a further attempt to ease the jackhammer in her head, she put on her sunglasses. Then she found her keys and hurried out the door.

The little Jonah had slept had been in the Jeep Cherokee he'd rented, which he'd parked a mile or so away from the salvage yard after driving back from Chandler last night. He'd spent most of his time watching the house and drafting Lori's character reference on his laptop. He'd finally realized he didn't have the right to hope Francesca would ever forgive him if he couldn't forgive Lori, so he'd just e-mailed it—

He sat up. Something was wrong...

Grabbing his binoculars, he took a closer look at Butch's house. With Dean being released from jail and Paris charged with manslaughter and subsequently posting bail, he hadn't expected Butch or Dean to be active. They'd gotten in late. But he hadn't been willing to bet Francesca's life on that, either. Regardless of how she felt about him, he still loved her, and if he couldn't stay with her to keep her safe, he'd protect her some other way, even if it meant watching Butch and Dean until he could determine, for sure, that they weren't a threat to her anymore.

Now he was glad he'd made that commitment....

Although the results of his surveillance had been unremarkable until several minutes ago, when he'd seen Paris drive off, that no longer held true. There weren't a lot of people moving around, but the way Butch came in and out of the house, making several trips to his truck and pacing the front yard, reminded Jonah of an anthill after a stick had been jammed into it. Butch seemed to be reacting to a recent and rather upsetting change. But what?

The binoculars revealed him unshowered and unshaven, an intense expression on his face and his cell phone jammed against his ear. He hung up, dialed again, hung up and threw his phone. Then he raked his fingers through his hair, recovered his phone and had to replace the battery that'd gone flying when it hit the ground. A second later he got into his truck and drove away.

Debating whether to follow him or take advantage of his absence by talking to Dean or Elaine, Jonah decided to try the house.

Once Butch was out of sight, he drove closer and went to the door.

Dean answered. Judging by the hair sticking up on one side, he'd just rolled out of bed. "Hey there! What's going on?" he asked as if they were now good friends.

Jonah glanced in the direction Butch had gone, toward town. "That's what I want to know."

"Excuse me?"

"What's up with Butch this morning?"

Dean didn't seem to realize Jonah had been watching the house. Apparently, he assumed Jonah had tried to speak with Butch and been rebuffed. "Who knows?" he said with a shrug. "But don't let it bother you. He can get like that sometimes."

"He didn't say anything before he left?"

A wry smile curved Dean's lips. "Does 'fuck' or 'damn' count?"

Jonah couldn't help chuckling. "As long as you can give me a reason he might be using those words."

"It has to do with Paris. He doesn't know where she went."

"That's it?"

"Plus, he's afraid she might confront his girlfriend. I heard him call Kelly and tell her Paris could be on her way over. He said that she wasn't to open her door and to contact him immediately if she tries to get in."

Jonah arched his eyebrows. "Tries to get in? You think she might be that aggressive?"

Dean yawned but spoke through it. "She's pretty tired of him cheating."

"Does she know about *all* the women he's been with?"

"A lot of them. I once saw a list in her purse." Now that they were "friends," Dean seemed eager to confide whatever he knew.

"How do you know it was a list of the women he's cheated with?"

"I'm not positive because I just saw the top of it before she shoved it back in. But Kelly was on there. So was Wanda Erickson, who used to be a masseuse in town. I stopped by once in a while, but Butch went there every chance he got. I saw his truck in her driveway all the time. No way my sister would've missed it."

Jonah's heart skipped a beat. "You're sure? It was Wanda Erickson?"

"Yeah, but her name had a line through it, probably because she moved back to Nevada."

Wanda hadn't moved back to Nevada. Dr. Price had called Jonah late last night to say they'd managed to identify more of the remains. Wanda Erickson was one of the victims. "Any chance you can give me Butch's cell phone number. I'd like to see if I can help," Jonah said.

"Sure, no problem," he replied and rattled it off.

Dean shut the door as Jonah walked slowly back to

his car. *She's pretty tired of him cheating.... I once saw a list in her purse.... Her name had a line through it....*

Bits of the forensic profile also came to mind: *Beating someone to death is intensely personal. I believe the man you're looking for has reason to hate his victims and feels justified in violence.*

The *man* they were looking for? What if they weren't looking for a man at all? What if it was a woman? A woman who thought her victims deserved the worst possible treatment? A woman who used a bat to make up for what she lacked in size and strength? A woman who'd already attacked one rival in a jealous rage? Maybe if Julia hadn't been killed accidentally, in front of Butch, she would've been killed on purpose, behind his back. Like the others...

"Shit!" The killer was associated with the salvage yard. They'd been right about that. But they'd been looking past the real culprit. And, if Jonah had his guess, Butch had figured it out, too, or he wouldn't have called to warn Kelly....

Taking his phone from his pocket, Jonah dialed Finch's number. They had to find Paris—before she attacked anyone else.

Paris slowed to make a U-turn. This had been a good choice; Wickenburg was the perfect place. She'd been scouting towns since she left home early that morning. Now all she had to do was travel back toward Prescott until she found a desolate spot....

After twenty minutes, she felt she'd gone far enough. She was in the middle of nowhere, precisely what she wanted. Only a handful of cars passed by. Since it was noon, most people were inside, working a day job, not driving from one small town to another in the middle of the Sonoran Desert.

Spotting an alcove where she'd have the cover of some scrub brush and palo verde trees, she turned around so she'd be facing in the right direction, and pulled to the side of the road. Then she got out and went to the trunk, taking out the hammer and nail she'd put there.

Would the nail be long enough? Frowning, she held it up. If not, she'd have to find something else. She hadn't had much time to prepare for her encounter with Francesca. But she wasn't particularly worried. It wasn't that difficult to pop a tire.

Wincing against the blistering heat, she circled the Impala while deciding which tire to flatten. Francesca would be more prone to believe her "crippled car" predicament if she could see the problem immediately, wouldn't she?

That made sense, so—when there was no one else on the road—Paris crouched beside the front right tire.

She'd just finished hammering the nail through the rubber, could hear the hiss of escaping air, when her cell phone rang. It was her husband. Again. He'd called more than a dozen times. She hoped he'd been in touch with Champ's friend's mother, made arrangements to pick him up, because she couldn't answer the phone and remind him. He'd be upset with her for leaving and would try to talk her into going home.

She'd call him when it was all over, she told herself, after Francesca got what was coming to her.

But what if Francesca proved to be more of a challenge than the others? Dean hadn't been able to overpower her, had he? No. She needed to make her plans accordingly. Fortunately, she wasn't as stupid as Dean. And she'd done this before. Only Sherrilyn had given her any real problem, but she'd managed to overpower her. They'd find her remains in Dead Mule Canyon with the rest, if they hadn't done so already. She knew they were still looking and had two more to find.

Returning to the trunk, she gathered up the rest of her tools, including the one that would cause the most pain. Maybe Francesca hadn't slept with Butch, but she was a whore all the same and deserved the treatment Paris saved for the women she hated most.

Finding a nice spot in the shade, she sat down and went over every aspect of her plan while awaiting Francesca's call.

By the time she reached Wickenburg, Francesca had her headache under control. She was grateful for the cessation of pain; her nerves were difficult enough to deal with. Paris claimed to possess evidence that would blow the Dead Mule Canyon case wide-open. As far as Francesca was concerned, that couldn't happen soon enough. But she was still reluctant to believe it was Dean who'd been murdering people. Despite those macabre drawings, he didn't seem to have the killer instinct.

Fortunately, Paris said she had proof. If that was true, they'd no longer have to rely on intuition or profiling or anything else.

As she passed an old schoolhouse painted bright red, obviously a historic building, she called Paris's number. "I'm here."

"I've been trying to get hold of you." Paris sounded discouraged.

"You have? Nothing's come through."

"Coverage is spotty out here."

"Out where?"

"I'm stranded along the highway. And, God, is it hot. I wish I'd brought some water."

Already at the end of town, Francesca pulled to the side of the road. "What's wrong?"

"I was almost to Wickenburg when I picked up a nail. My tire's flat."

"You don't have a spare?"

"I do, but...I don't know how to change it. I've been trying to flag someone down to help me since it happened."

Francesca turned the air conditioner to low so she could hear over the fan. "No luck?"

"It's too hot for anyone to feel like stopping. There aren't many people out, anyway. But I called Butch. He's coming to get me."

Butch hated Francesca. He'd only ruin this opportunity, which meant she had to get to Paris before her husband did. "Maybe I can help you change it. Where are you?"

"On the side of the road about twenty minutes east of town. In the Impala."

Checking for traffic, she eased back onto the road. "I'll be there as soon as I can."

"Could you bring me some water?" Paris asked.

"Of course," Francesca agreed, and stopped at the first convenience store she came across.

When Paris saw Francesca's BMW coming toward her, she waved. She had the stun gun Butch had purchased for her personal safety—along with the handcuffs she planned to put on while Francesca was incapacitated—in her baglike purse, which was slung over one shoulder. The bat lying in the backseat as, supposedly, "evidence" of Dean's guilt would serve a dual purpose.

She'd use one end to make it appear as if Francesca had been raped, the other to finish her off. The only thing Paris didn't have handy was the garbage bag hidden in her trunk. But she wouldn't need that until Francesca was dead. She'd stuff her body in that bag, placing it in the trunk of her own car, and drive the BMW as far into the desert as she could safely walk during the return trip, and the sun would do the rest. Francesca's body would liquefy in a day, two or three at most, and it would probably take weeks, maybe even months, for someone to find her. There wasn't much reason for people to be out walking in the desert this time of year. As a matter of fact, it was downright dangerous in these temperatures. Paris was glad she'd remembered to ask Francesca for water. She was going to need it.

The tires of Francesca's car crunched on the gravel-like dirt as she swung around and parked behind the Impala.

Paris pasted a smile on her face and approached. "Thanks for coming all the way out here," she said as soon as Francesca opened her door. "Can you believe this? Look at that tire."

"It's flat, all right." Francesca didn't immediately get out. She glanced around as if checking to be sure they were alone. She was a little leery, but Paris wasn't worried. She knew how harmless she appeared. Although Francesca wasn't a big woman, she had Paris beaten by several inches and probably twenty pounds. That wouldn't make any difference once Paris zapped her, of course, but it meant Francesca would feel more confident that she could defend herself, if need be, than if their sizes were reversed.

That confidence would be her undoing.

"Did you remember the water?" Paris asked. "I'm dying out here."

She barely refrained from laughing at her own joke, but her preoccupation with water seemed to put Francesca at ease. After digging into a paper sack on her passenger seat, she handed Paris a bottle.

Paris took the time to open it and drink. "Thanks a lot. This is great."

"No problem." Francesca pushed her sunglasses higher on the bridge of her nose. "What did you have to show me? Once I take a look, I'll help you get that tire fixed. Maybe Butch won't have to come all this way."

"That would be nice," Paris said, and took another drink. The less hurried she acted, the more Francesca would trust that she was what she seemed to be—an innocent wife and mother who'd come across the sad proof of her brother's complicity in murder. "It's in the backseat."

When Francesca got out, the BMW dinged to let her know she'd left her keys in the ignition.

Paris made a note of it. In a few minutes, she'd need to be able to drive that car.

"What kind of evidence is it?" Francesca asked.

"A wooden bat," Paris explained. "But not just any bat. I could be wrong, but it looks as if there's blood in the crevices. And a couple of long strands of hair are stuck to the end." That much was true. It just hadn't been Dean who'd raped and killed with that bat....

"You're kidding." Now Francesca didn't seem frightened at all. She was too eager to become the big shot who solved the Dead Mule Canyon slayings. "Where'd you find it?"

Paris followed her to the Impala. She had to come up with some explanation for why it hadn't been discovered when the cops did their search, but she'd already decided how to deal with that. "Champ's coach called to tell me he left his baseball bat at practice a few days ago. I didn't think that could be true, because I'd seen Champ with his bat since then, but when I drove over to pick it up this morning, I realized he had Dean's bat."

"How do you know it was Dean's?"

"Because we only have two. And Dean etched his name on the handle when he was a little boy. It's still there."

As Paris opened the back door, Francesca leaned in to get a closer look. "There's hair, all right. And I'm positive that's blood."

"I told you," Paris replied, and reached into her purse.

35

Where was Francesca?

When he couldn't contact her, Jonah had driven hell-bent for Chandler, but she hadn't answered the door. Fearing she was hurt, he'd broken a window to get in. But she wasn't there. And if someone had dragged her out of the house, it wasn't apparent. Her bed was rumpled and unmade, which wasn't like her, but if she'd been in a hurry, maybe she hadn't bothered making it.

The only odd thing was the bottle of tequila in the living room. Tequila wasn't something she'd ever liked. He couldn't imagine *her* drinking it, especially alone. But there was only one glass....

His cell vibrated. Hoping she was returning one of his many calls, he answered without even glancing at the screen. "Jonah Young."

"It's Finch. We've got Butch here. We picked him up twenty minutes ago, not far from Kelly's house. He won't say why he was sitting there, watching her place. Won't say much of anything at all, which has me worried. I just spoke with Wanda's former neighbor. She said Butch's truck was parked at Wanda's house on several occasions, and yet he told Hunsacker he'd never heard of her. Are you *sure* it's Paris we want?"

"I'm sure," Jonah said. "Ask Butch if he thinks his wife might've gone after Francesca."

Jonah heard Finch repeat the question but he couldn't make out Butch's response.

"He says you can go to hell," Finch said.

Pivoting, Jonah headed back across Francesca's living room. "What do you think? Paris wouldn't go after Francesca, would she?" he said. "She hasn't slept with Butch." But she'd been a threat to Paris and her family. If not for Francesca's appearance at the salvage yard, and her dogged pursuit of Butch as the probable killer, the spotlight of this investigation might never have turned their way.

"Your guess is as good as mine," Finch said.

"Tell Butch he'd better start talking. Because if Paris kills Francesca, or anyone else, I'll do everything I can—hire investigators or consulting attorneys, whatever is necessary—to make sure she gets the death penalty. And he'll go to prison as an accomplice. Then who'll take care of Champ?"

"We tried that—"

"Tell him again!" Jonah shouted. "Tell him I'll make it my life's mission to destroy him and everyone he loves if he doesn't do what he can to help me now!"

"You've really pissed him off," he heard Finch say to Butch. "You'd better consider what's best for your son and help us stop your psycho wife. There's no way to save her now, Butch. It's time to think of Champ. Hunsacker's right here, backing me up. And you know he wouldn't lie to you. You might as well do all you can for your son."

"But I don't *know* anything!" Butch screamed. There was no need for Finch to repeat it. Jonah had heard every word—and every word made him sicker. "I have no idea where she is," he went on. "If I knew, I wouldn't have been sitting out on the street, hoping to spot her!"

"What about the Wheelers?" Jonah asked Finch. "Maybe they—"

"I've talked to them. They don't know any more than Butch does."

Jonah had to find her. But how? "She's got a cell phone," he said. "Use triangulation. Now!"

"But we're not even sure Francesca's in danger."

"Paris is missing. So is Francesca. That means chances are good she *is* in danger. Just figure out where the hell she is, and do it as fast as possible," he snapped. Then he hung up and did the only thing he could—he dialed Francesca's cell yet again.

When her cell phone rang, Francesca moved to answer it. Jonah had been trying to reach her all morning. She'd purposely ignored his calls because she hadn't been willing to talk to him, hadn't wanted to explain what was going through her head last night. But now that she'd seen this bat, she couldn't wait to tell him they had physical evidence. She wasn't sure if they could actually prove Dean had killed someone with it—Butch or someone else could've been responsible for the blood—but that could be established later. This might be their first link to one of the other victims, someone besides Julia, which meant she hadn't been so wrong in believing these killings were tied in some way to the salvage yard.

But she didn't get the chance to tell him anything. Just as her hand moved, Paris hit her with what felt like a two-by-four.

She went blind for a second as every muscle in her body locked. Falling onto the seat, she struggled just to breathe. But it didn't take long to figure out what had happened. Paris hadn't hit her with a board. She'd used a Taser. Francesca knew because it wasn't her first time being shocked. She'd experienced a similar jolt while in the police academy—routine training for all cops—and remembered the immediate soreness of her body, the disorientation. Had she not reached back when she did, and unknowingly knocked the device, she probably would've sustained an even longer charge.

The reason for this attack was more difficult to figure out. "Why" required logic. And that part of her brain was slower in recovering. Paris was trying to force her hands into a pair of handcuffs before Francesca put the obvious together—that Paris had incapacitated her for a very deadly reason—and she only realized that because Paris was swearing at her.

"You stupid bitch! You're dead now. You think you can take me away from my family? You think you can sic the police on my husband? I'll show you what happens to people who mess with us!"

Francesca wished she'd opened the door on the other side of the car, facing the highway. There wasn't much traffic on the road, but an occasional car or truck rumbled by. She heard the motor of one now, wished the driver would be able to see more than a woman standing on the desert side of an Impala with a flat tire—but she knew that was unlikely.

Afraid Paris would shock her again if she didn't seem to be in sufficient pain, she jerked and writhed as if she couldn't gain control of her body. Depending on size and muscle mass, as well as the length of the jolt, reactions to Tasers varied widely. She used that knowledge to her advantage as she rolled her eyes and flopped around.

"You didn't like that, did you?" Paris said, laughing. "Hold still and let me cuff you or I'll shock you again."

Francesca couldn't allow Paris to cuff her hands. If she did, she'd have no chance of defending herself. But she was headfirst in the backseat of a car, on her stomach. She had nothing to fight with, not even her fists.

A second later, she heard the sickening catch of the cuffs snapping into place. Then Paris dragged her out of the car and, threatening her with the Taser, told her to walk toward her BMW. And when Paris paused to get the bat out of the backseat, Francesca knew what was coming.

"You don't feel bad?" she asked as she stumbled across the uneven ground. "About all the women you've killed?"

"Why should I feel bad?" Paris held her by her handcuffs. "They tried to hurt me first."

"Butch is just as much to blame. April didn't even know he was married. He lied to her, lied until he could get what he wanted."

"Shut up! That's not true."

"You're going to prison," Francesca muttered. "And this is only going to make it worse."

Pain shot up Francesca's arms as Paris yanked on her cuffs. "We'll see about that."

Paris was so used to being overlooked, to not being viewed as a suspect at all, she didn't even seem scared. She really thought she could pull it off. And Francesca was worried that might be true. She and Jonah had been too busy suspecting Butch or Dean to consider Paris. They'd been looking for a rapist, which made her wonder what she had coming along those lines, too…

They'd nearly reached the BMW when Francesca heard a car down the road. Hope flickered briefly inside her but didn't last. Paris swung her around to hide the cuffs, and the Toyota Avalon drove right past.

That didn't really surprise Francesca. Although the driver had glanced over at them, there was no reason to suspect serious problems. With two cars on the side of the road, one of them as new as her BMW, it would be natural to assume the person with the flat was already receiving the help she needed.

After the Toyota was gone, Paris opened the door to the backseat of the BMW, shoved Francesca in and jogged around to get behind the wheel.

Francesca couldn't tell where Paris was taking her, but she knew her chances of survival diminished with each passing second. Paris would need privacy in order to kill her, so they were probably heading to a motel room or some other place she felt safe. She'd obviously picked this location because it was remote. Maybe they weren't going anywhere—except farther into the desert.

After checking in both directions to make sure she wouldn't be seen, Paris eased around the Impala, then abruptly turned off the road, as Francesca had expected. Cactus needles scratched the sides of the car as they bounced along. They wouldn't get far driving on such rough terrain with low-profile radials, but they didn't need to go far. Only a mile or two, just out of sight of the road. That was where her life would end.

Desperate to jump out while she might still be able to flag down another driver, Francesca twisted around so she could reach the door latch with her cuffed hands.

Paris cursed when she realized what Francesca was doing and fumbled in the front seat, no doubt searching for her Taser.

Francesca didn't give her the opportunity. Maybe the fall would kill her, but it would be better than being raped and beaten to death by a woman with a bat. Either way, jumping was her only chance.

Somehow she managed to release the latch and push the door open with her feet. Then she closed her eyes and flung herself out.

Paris had slammed on the brakes, but the jolt of hitting the ground still knocked the wind out of Francesca. She could taste tequila at the back of her throat, could smell car exhaust and dust. It felt as if the sun-baked earth would swallow her whole, suffocate her. Was she really handcuffed and lying in the desert in the middle of a scorching afternoon? Or was this some kind of nightmare?

Dimly she heard Paris turn the car around, knew she was racing toward her in the Beemer and understood that it wasn't a nightmare. It was as real as real could get; Paris didn't plan on stopping.

Get up! Now! Francesca's mind screamed and, somehow, she got to her feet and began to run. All she could think about was putting a barrier between her and the BMW.

With mostly flat terrain and no large rocks anywhere close, the Impala seemed to be her only option. At this point, it was barely six feet away, but she didn't believe she'd reach it.

She thought of Jonah and regretted that she hadn't really forgiven him as she'd promised. Holding a grudge suddenly seemed so contrary to her own happiness, so pointless. What good was it? No good, because it kept them apart. She wished she could tell him she was finally ready to start over and make it work, to forgive Adriana, as well. But it was too late. The BMW was bearing down on her. At most, she had a second before it struck—a second she used to dive beneath the Impala.

As Francesca landed she heard an earsplitting crash.

* * *

A man's voice registered. Francesca wished it was Jonah's, but knew instantly it wasn't. Struggling to raise her eyelids, she moaned his name, hoping he'd somehow hear her, come for her. Instead, the person who'd spoken a moment earlier touched her shoulder.

"It's okay, ma'am. You're going to be okay."

It was an EMT. She recognized his uniform through her eyelashes; she couldn't open her eyes any wider. The sun shone too brightly, seemed to be slanting directly into her face. "Where am I?"

"The desert outside Wickenburg."

Right. She remembered now. "Wh-what's wrong with me?"

"You've sustained some injuries."

She knew that much. If she could've laughed, she would have. Every bone in her body seemed to be broken. "I'm…I'm on fire."

"That's the pain. We're taking care of it."

A needle pricked her arm. Painkiller. This would dull the pain but would also make it impossible to think clearly. And she wanted to be able to talk, to explain what Paris had done, and to understand what she heard in reply.

Swallowing, her throat gritty with dust, she forced her mouth to form more words. "Wh-what happened… to *her?*"

"The woman who tried to run you down?"

"Yes."

"There's only the two of you out here?"

She licked dry lips. "Yes."

"She sustained a head injury but she's in better shape than you are."

"She…she tried to kill me. She…should be…arrested."

Francesca sucked air into her lungs as they lifted her onto a gurney.

"Don't worry," the EMT assured her. "The motorist who called in the incident was an off-duty cop. He kept a good eye on her until the cavalry arrived. She'll go to the hospital, be checked out and then released to the police. Everything's under control."

About half of what he said went right over her head, but she grasped that Paris was where she needed to be, at last. She let her eyelids slide closed but couldn't rest. She wanted Jonah. "Will—will you...find Jonah Young for me? Please?"

"Careful. Watch that edge." The EMT was speaking to someone else Francesca hadn't even realized was there, a partner. Obviously preoccupied, he was trying to get her into the ambulance. But she didn't want to go to the hospital or anywhere without telling Jonah how she felt about him. Just in case...

The painkiller was already making her thoughts fuzzy, her tongue thick, but she managed to grab hold of the EMT's sleeve. "Jonah..."

"Ma'am, you need to relax."

Tears rolled into Francesca's hair. Jonah wasn't around. She couldn't tell him, had to go through this alone. She was just trying to come to terms with that when a police officer approached the back of the ambulance. "She able to talk?"

"Not really," the EMT responded. "Why?"

"I've got a Jonah Young on the phone. He wants to speak to her."

The EMT shut one door of the ambulance and was about to shut the other. "He'll have to do it later. She's got a few broken bones and might have suffered some internal injuries. We need to get her to the hospital."

"Wait!" Francesca tried to sit up and fell back. From then on, it became even harder to drag words to her mouth. "Let me...talk...to...him."

She knew she'd said it, but didn't know how her words were received. She seemed to be fading in and out of consciousness. It was the pain, the drugs, the shock. And then, seemingly out of nowhere, she felt a phone pressed to her ear and heard a voice she immediately recognized.

"Francesca?"

"Jonah...I—I'm...sorry. I...want...to be...with you... forever," she said, and then she slipped into a black void. When she came out of it again, it seemed as if hours, maybe days, had passed. But Jonah was there.

"Hey, how do you feel?" he asked, hovering over her hospital bed.

She managed a half smile. "Better now." Her voice was hoarse from disuse. "Am I...am I going to live?"

"You're going to be as good as new," he promised, and leaned down to kiss her forehead.

Epilogue

"What about these flowers? Aren't you going to take them?"

Leaning on the crutches that made her mobile despite a broken leg, Francesca hesitated near the hospital bed where she'd spent the past few days and glanced at her mother. Every other bouquet she'd received was waiting in the back of Jonah's Jeep Cherokee—the small teddy bear and single rose from Heather, the tiger lilies from her parents, the wheelbarrow plant from Hunsacker and Finch, the vase of wildflowers from Jill and Vince, and several dozen red roses from Jonah. But these flowers were from Adriana, who'd sent them instead of calling or stopping by.

"I've got a free arm, I can grab them," her mother said and started to reach for the vase, but Francesca stopped her.

"No, leave them."

Her mother turned to her in surprise. "You don't want them?"

"Not now."

Her mother peered more closely at her. "You're not making sense, honey. It's not like you can get them later. They'll be dead and gone."

Maybe the flowers would be dead and gone, but

Adriana would be living her own life, taking care of her family, just as she should be. And, for the time being, Francesca needed to know Adriana was giving her the chance to love Jonah without thinking about their friendship. This alone proved she was the type of friend Francesca had always thought. "What they represent won't be gone."

"What do you mean?"

"I mean that love *is* enough—when the time is right," she added with a smile.

Her mother probably would've asked her to elaborate, except that her father wheeled himself into the room. "Hey, how's my girl?"

Francesca hobbled over to give him a hug. "Fine, Dad. We were just on our way."

"Jonah's got the car downstairs by the lobby doors."

Jonah had been by her side night and day since she was injured and yet she couldn't wait to see him. "I'm coming."

Her father let her go out ahead of him, but then caught her wrist. "About Jonah...you sure you want to risk your heart again?" he asked softly.

"I'm positive."

He chuckled. "Well, if he can make you smile like that, I'll have to trust you, won't I?"

She bent to let him rub his knuckles against her cheek. "Thanks."

His thick, callused fingers curled through hers. "Francesca?"

"What?"

"I'm proud of you," he said.

* * * * *

USA TODAY BESTSELLING AUTHOR

TARA TAYLOR QUINN

Continue to follow psychologist Kelly Chapman
in *The Chapman Files* series.

THE SECOND LIE

Kelly's friend, Deputy Samantha Jones, finds herself facing
the case of her career—a case that appears to implicate the
man she loves. (October 2010)

THE THIRD SECRET

This time, a professional acquaintance of Kelly's comes to her
for advice. Erin Morgan is about to defend Rick Thomas on a
murder charge. Rick's apparently been framed. He's also not
exactly who he says he is.… (November 2010)

THE FOURTH VICTIM

Kelly herself is at the center of this next case—she's been
kidnapped. And it's up to FBI agent Clay Thatcher to find
her. Which means he has to figure out who did it…and why.
(December 2010)

Available wherever books are sold!

The more you run, the less you can hide in the brand-new *Secrets of Shadow Falls* trilogy from *New York Times* and *USA TODAY* bestselling author

MAGGIE SHAYNE

Available wherever
books are sold!

REQUEST YOUR
FREE BOOKS!

2 FREE NOVELS
FROM THE SUSPENSE COLLECTION
PLUS 2 FREE GIFTS!

YES! Please send me 2 FREE novels from the Suspense Collection and my 2 FREE gifts (gifts are worth about $10). After receiving them, if I don't wish to receive any more books, I can return the shipping statement marked "cancel." If I don't cancel, I will receive 3 brand-new novels every month and be billed just $5.74 per book in the U.S. or $6.24 per book in Canada. That's a saving of at least 28% off the cover price. It's quite a bargain! Shipping and handling is just 50¢ per book.* I understand that accepting the 2 free books and gifts places me under no obligation to buy anything. I can always return a shipment and cancel at any time. Even if I never buy another book, the two free books and gifts are mine to keep forever.

192/392 MDN E7PD

Name _____ (PLEASE PRINT) _____

Address _____ Apt. # _____

City _____ State/Prov. _____ Zip/Postal Code _____

Signature (if under 18, a parent or guardian must sign)

Mail to **The Reader Service:**
IN U.S.A.: P.O. Box 1867, Buffalo, NY 14240-1867
IN CANADA: P.O. Box 609, Fort Erie, Ontario L2A 5X3

Not valid for current subscribers to the Suspense Collection
or the Romance/Suspense Collection.

**Want to try two free books from another line?
Call 1-800-873-8635 or visit www.morefreebooks.com.**

* Terms and prices subject to change without notice. Prices do not include applicable taxes. N.Y. residents add applicable sales tax. Canadian residents will be charged applicable provincial taxes and GST. Offer not valid in Quebec. This offer is limited to one order per household. All orders subject to approval. Credit or debit balances in a customer's account(s) may be offset by any other outstanding balance owed by or to the customer. Please allow 4 to 6 weeks for delivery. Offer available while quantities last.

Your Privacy: Harlequin Books is committed to protecting your privacy. Our Privacy Policy is available online at www.eHarlequin.com or upon request from the Reader Service. From time to time we make our lists of customers available to reputable third parties who may have a product or service of interest to you. If you would prefer we not share your name and address, please check here. ☐

Help us get it right—We strive for accurate, respectful and relevant communications. To clarify or modify your communication preferences, visit us at www.ReaderService.com/consumerchoice.

BRENDA NOVAK

32667	THE PERFECT COUPLE	___ $7.99 U.S.	___ $8.99 CAN.
32725	THE PERFECT MURDER	___ $7.99 U.S.	___ $8.99 CAN.
32724	THE PERFECT LIAR	___ $7.99 U.S.	___ $8.99 CAN.
32885	DEAD SILENCE	___ $7.99 U.S.	___ $9.99 CAN.
32886	DEAD GIVEAWAY	___ $7.99 U.S.	___ $9.99 CAN.
32902	DEAD RIGHT	___ $7.99 U.S.	___ $9.99 CAN.
32903	TRUST ME	___ $7.99 U.S.	___ $9.99 CAN.
32904	WATCH ME	___ $7.99 U.S.	___ $9.99 CAN.
32905	STOP ME	___ $7.99 U.S.	___ $9.99 CAN.

(limited quantities available)

TOTAL AMOUNT	$ _____
POSTAGE & HANDLING	$ _____
($1.00 for 1 book, 50¢ for each additional)	
APPLICABLE TAXES*	$ _____
TOTAL PAYABLE	$ _____

(check or money order—please do not send cash)

To order, complete this form and send it, along with a check or money order for the total above, payable to MIRA Books, to: **In the U.S.:** 3010 Walden Avenue, P.O. Box 9077, Buffalo, NY 14269-9077; **In Canada:** P.O. Box 636, Fort Erie, Ontario, L2A 5X3.

Name: _____

Address: _____ City: _____

State/Prov.: _____ Zip/Postal Code: _____

Account Number (if applicable): _____

075 CSAS

*New York residents remit applicable sales taxes.
*Canadian residents remit applicable GST and provincial taxes.

MIRA®

www.MIRABooks.com

MBN0810BL